CAGE OF STARLIGHT

Also by Jules Arbeaux

Lord of the Empty Isles

CAGE OF STARLIGHT

JULES ARBEAUX

First published in Great Britain in 2025 by Hodderscape
An imprint of Hodder & Stoughton Limited
An Hachette UK company

The authorised representative in the EEA is Hachette Ireland, 8 Castlecourt Centre, Dublin 15, D15 XTP3, Ireland (email: info@hbgi.ie)

1

Copyright © Jules Arbeaux 2025

The right of Jules Arbeaux to be identified as the Author of the Work has been asserted by them in accordance with the Copyright, Designs and Patents Act 1988.

All rights reserved. No part of this publication may be reproduced, stored in a retrieval system, or transmitted, in any form or by any means without the prior written permission of the publisher, nor be otherwise circulated in any form of binding or cover other than that in which it is published and without a similar condition being imposed on the subsequent purchaser.

All characters in this publication are fictitious and any resemblance to real persons, living or dead, is purely coincidental.

A CIP catalogue record for this title is available from the British Library

Hardback ISBN 978 1 399 72514 9
Trade Paperback ISBN 978 1 399 72515 6
ebook ISBN 978 1 399 72516 3

Typeset in Baskerville by Manipal Technologies Limited

Printed and bound in Great Britain by Clays Ltd, Elcograf S.p.A.

Hodder & Stoughton policy is to use papers that are natural, renewable and recyclable products and made from wood grown in sustainable forests. The logging and manufacturing processes are expected to conform to the environmental regulations of the country of origin.

Hodder & Stoughton Limited
Carmelite House
50 Victoria Embankment
London EC4Y 0DZ

www.hodderscape.co.uk

To everyone who's done surviving and is ready to live

Break ye the walls—
break them down to dust.
To iron, rust
and flake away
For only through destruction, yea
shall all become new.

— Arlunian Proverb

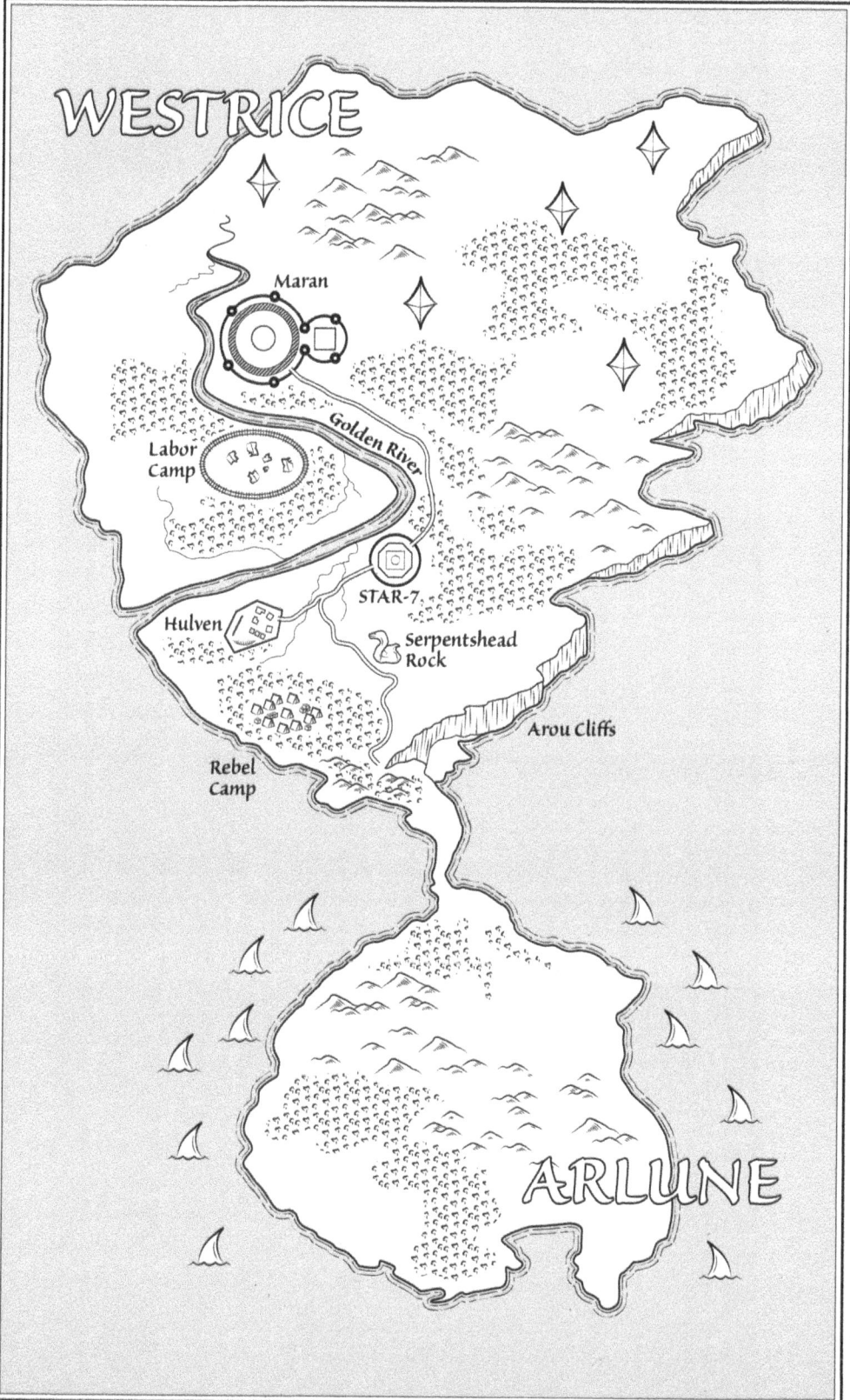

PART ONE:

Flight

CHAPTER ONE

TORY ARKNETT IS no stranger to the dead and dying, so when the bell on Thatcher's repair shop tinkles to admit a group of blood-soaked miners, he greets them with no more than the usual amount of dread.

Captured in the streaked glass of the display case Tory's dusting, the miners make a ghastly picture as they huddle on the wide circle of Thatcher's beloved (and exceptionally ugly) floral rug—placed just inside the shop's door for situations like today's. One man even stuffs his dripping hands into his pockets to spare the rug. Thoughtful, but unnecessary: someday soon, when Thatcher's not looking, Tory's going to bury the appalling thing in the woods.

"Tory, a moment?" The tall man at the head of the group wrings his hands. "This one's urgent."

Like he couldn't tell. "What is it this time?"

"Kelly got it bad in a cave-in. You got his wages for a week if you can save him."

There's always something like that. A week's wages. An armful or three of obscenely large gourds. Some token payment so they can pretend they're not gently coercing Tory to do this and he can pretend they don't ever-so-politely have him by the throat.

Tory sets his dust rag down. "Where is he?"

"With Fedri." His wife. "You gotta help him—they ain't assigned a Healer here."

Only because Hulven hasn't requested one. A government-licensed Healer's fees for life-threatening injuries are the sorts of debts parents pass to their children. The bastard Grand General needs all the Healers he can find for his war machine. He won't surrender any to a small town unless they can pay generously for the honor.

Tory looks to Thatcher, hoping the cheery old man will intervene on his behalf.

Thatcher only smiles. "It's your choice. Do whatever you think is best."

"I hate to say this"—he doesn't, actually—"but I'll be useless for days if I heal him."

"That's fine! There's always Doc if we need anything."

Easy for them to say.

Tory breathes in. *Don't make waves.* Then out. *Keep your head down. Don't be difficult.* The scriptures of survival his mother left him with have kept him alive this long, so he calms himself and speaks only when sharp words don't crowd up his throat. "Lead the way, then."

The miners surround him like a wall on the way to Kelly, head and shoulders above Tory even though he'll turn twenty this winter. Outside this wall of blood and bone, there's the wall around Hulven, then another, and another—one for every city along the way. Tory wouldn't be surprised if this rotten country had a wall at every border: cages as far as the eye can see.

Years before he was born, before the first rumblings of war shook the ground, Westrice was a country without walls ruled by the Four Families, each with an equal seat. The Rost family specialized in law, Eastrin in commerce, Chimre—the public face of the four families—in the art of saying nothing of substance very charismatically, and Vantaras in military might. When the war started, Vantaras stepped in to take the reins.

First, he stuck his fingers in commerce. No more trade with the enemy, he advised. Westrice was years behind Arlune in harnessing stellite's capacity to store and amplify energy. Every shred of stone in Arlunian hands was a weapon. Vantaras pulled the brightest minds from every corner of the country and set them to work. If Westrice could not beat its enemy at magic, it would beat them at everything else. And they have. The war, in fits and starts, has been going on for almost as long as Tory has been alive, and Westrice's never-tiring inventors have masterminded weapons that spit bullets and durable, pourable building materials that harden like stone.

Then in the legal system: better if the caps on prison sentences were removed, Vantaras whispered. War demands weaponry, he coaxed, when the Rost family resisted. What a shame it would be for Rost's own daughters to have to make rifles. If criminals refused to serve their country when free, they would serve it indefinitely in captivity. So, they built manufacturing facilities inside the prisons, and Vantaras didn't care that some of the hands that assembled his guns were the hands of children.

After he'd stabilized the country and enlisted his own people to build and man impregnable walls around the most populous cities, Vantaras showed his face in front of the once-frightened citizens. With a politician's smile, he convinced them his walls made them safe, made them *free*. Quick-minded Chimre knew himself beaten and surrendered his throne. Vantaras, once a mere general, became the Grand General—the Vanguard, builder of walls and orchestrator of armies.

He placated the much-weakened three families, promising they'd be back in power as soon as things stabilized. Until then, he'd protect them. Never would they smell a whiff of blood or smoke from a battlefield.

Fools, every one of them. No wall has ever made anyone free.

Tory has spent every moment since he was eight trying to stay outside them, living on the fringes or in forgotten places like Hulven, where the crumbling wall is barely taller than he is and the only place Vantaras' awful soldiers bother to patrol is the stellite mine. In Hulven, brightly painted mudbrick houses flourish between the hardy grasses, and the residents hang glinting charms from the trees to call for wind to drive off the fuel stench from the mining machinery.

There's no wind today.

Fuel fog coils over the ground toward them as they walk. A crash reverberates through the trees, and Tory jerks back, nearly colliding with the miners behind him. He's closer to the mine than he'd like. There's something indefinable about it, a terrible charge to the air that raises the hair on the back of his neck and makes him ache to flee. The vines that choke the woods outside the wall have flooded over it here. They snake along the ground and twine around trees, hanging strings of bell-shaped blossoms that tickle Tory's shoulders as he passes.

He sees the mine in snatches between the trees, the way the setting sun casts eerie bars of light through its wrought-iron fence and silhouettes the patrolling soldiers in their crisp, double-breasted navy uniforms. Tory's known those uniforms since he was big enough to know anything. Soldiers like these guarded the camp he was born in. If they see him—if they discover he's healing without a license, that he escaped the camp without pardon—they could drag him back.

He picks up the pace, thankful for the first time in his life that he's small, invisible at the center of this group.

But they don't lead him away from the mines and toward the cramped mudbrick home Fedri shares with her husband. The men guide him, instead, closer to the wrought-iron gates.

A chill creeps outward from Tory's stomach. "You *said* he was with Fedri."

The tall miner at the lead looks steadily ahead, expression guilty. "She came out to be with him when we told her what happened."

They planned this, then. Oh, he's going to hurt them. He'll let wild animals into their homes to gnaw their feet while they sleep.

"No. Let me out. I won't do this." It's his *only* rule. No work near the mines.

"Tory—"

"Tory nothing! I won't do it."

They continue walking, slow but steady, with Tory trapped at the center.

He turns to the tower of a man behind him. What's his name? Eli. Eli with the six young daughters and a harried son left to corral the girls while their father is at work.

"Eli. Let me out."

Someone to his left whispers, "Make a fuss and they'll find us. You want that?"

"I want *out*!" His heart roars in his ears, a whoosh that drowns even the earth-deep clank of man's hunger meeting steadfast stone in the mines. To his left, too close in his peripheral vision, one of Vantaras' navy-clad soldiers paces in front of the fence, a thick rifle resting on his shoulder.

Tory's hands ache with remembered pain. It would be nice if he could be angry, but the tar-slick churning in his belly and the way his blood retreats from his numb lips is fear, plain and simple. He thought he left it behind twelve years ago. "I told you—you *know*—"

Behind him is Eli of the many daughters. To his right is Carn, who lives in a small home with his elderly mother and whips up an excellent mushroom stew. When Tory healed old Mrs. Carn's broken hip, he and Thatcher feasted on that stew all winter. The stocky woman with her nose pointed at the ground works the mines while her partner watches their young twins. He knows them all.

He hates them.

One rule. He had one rule.

"We tried, Tory!" It's the hand-wringing miner at the front, a transfer from one of the many dried-up towns down south. "If we move him any farther, we'll kill him. You'll understand when you see him. Please. We got him out the employee entrance and a little ways into the woods. The trees should keep anyone from seeing. Please, he'll die if you can't help. Kelly's a good man."

It stings because it's true.

Tory wants to bite his tongue all the way off and spit it at them. He wants to leap over Hulven's walls and keep running until his feet fail him, because if he learned nothing else from cleaning up after clients in one of the pleasure houses as a boy, he learned this: people who knowingly violate your boundaries once will do it again.

Instead, he forces a tired smile and says, "All right."

More fool him for believing the bargain he struck meant he'd be safe here. He let this place weaken him, let himself forget the laws he lived by. *Only fools grow roots,* his mom used to say. *Getting comfortable is how you get caught.* It was how she got caught. He'll learn. Next time, he'll get it right.

"Just get me to him fast," he grits out, and he hates the way their shoulders slacken and their breaths come easy, hates how one of the men—Carn, probably, the big softy—sniffs back tears. Most of all, he hates that he wants to relax into the hand squeezing his arm.

"Stop crying," he grumbles. "I already said I'd do it."

This will be the last time.

*

Fedri kneels in a slurry of filth beside Kelly's stretcher, stroking her husband's face.

It's easy to see why they didn't move him farther. The canvas stretcher is a swamp of blood, its wooden handholds dripping. Kelly breathes in labored, erratic bursts, his belly a ruined mess. It's a miracle he's not dead.

The eerie feeling from the mines is just as bad here as it was closer to the gate. It's an anticipatory feeling—an indrawn breath before a scream.

Tory hunches over Kelly and tries to ignore the towering iron fence. He'll be fine, probably. The one blessing of the vines that make an impenetrable canopy of the trees and anything else they can crawl along is that no one can chop them down fast enough to keep the fence clear. The guards won't see Tory unless they're looking.

"Keep watch," Tory tells the miners, and they scramble away.

When they're gone, he examines Kelly's wounds. They're the worst he's ever been called on to heal. He'll be lucky if he can stand when this is over. Slanting a glance at Fedri, Tory says, "Catch me if I'm about to fall into your husband's intestines," and rolls up his sleeves.

Too far.

Fear lances through him. *Hide the tattoos*, his mother begged him.

The sharp blue edge of the mark that identifies him as the child of a convicted prisoner peeks from the sleeve on his left arm. Without the complex marking indicating that Tory's freedom has been bought and paid for, the tattoo is a problem. As far as Westrice is concerned, it still owns him. Tory's never found an artist willing or able to reproduce the hue of the pardoning mark, so the best he can do is keep it out of sight. He tugs the sleeve down before pressing his hands to the wet mess of Kelly's abdomen.

The telltale tingling starts in his fingers—a strange sensation, like a shudder in reverse—as he seeks out the glow of Kelly's natural healing energies and puts them to use—restoring damaged organs and ruined blood vessels, sealing torn skin. Kelly's body remembers wholeness like all bodies do. The challenge is making it do the work. But a wound this bad will need far more energy than Kelly's weakened body has to spare. Tory pushes the last wisp of the miner's strength toward healing, then shifts gears. His ears ring, veins sizzling as he lends his own body's reserves to the effort.

"Is he okay?"

Tory clenches his teeth, vision dimming. "He will be."

"It's taking so long. How much longer?"

". . . N-not much."

They always tease him like this, like Tory's the slowest Healer in Westrice. *My old Auntie Ghaile says Maran's Healers can close a wound in a snap!* they'll say. *You need more practice.*

The way Tory sees it, if they want the capital's Healers, they can damn well pay for one.

Sweat stings his eyes. He's *close*. He can't heal it all at once, but he can seal the worst of it. With numb fingers, he shoves Kelly's shirt aside. Thin, pink flesh arches across what was once an open wound, flecks of dirt and gravel slipping down Kelly's side from where his body pushed them out. There's only a little section still bleeding. He can close it. Just a bit more.

But his vision writhes, mouth dry and body burning. He's never gone farther than this.

The unwritten law is that he does what they ask, and they keep his secret. It's been like that since his powers manifested at fifteen after he fought with an *exceptionally* irritating girl and knocked them both down an incline. Tory arrived scuffed and wide-eyed at the bottom. The girl landed, screaming, with one leg twisted in an unspeakable direction. Panicked, he gripped her leg, apologizing and urging her to *shush* (because she was no less annoying screaming in pain than she was raging about how *of course anyone sent to the labor camps deserved it*, and by the time Hasra and the villagers arrived, the girl's broken leg was halfway healed, and the hungry-eyed townspeople had an offer for him: their silence for his service.

So he keeps going.

One last time. One final kept promise. Their unspoken agreement kept him out of Vantaras' greedy hands and off the front lines of the Grand General's war for years. He's grateful for that, at least. Better this mundane, familiar pain than whatever Vantaras' soldiers could deal out if they ever caught wind of his skills.

It's been nice here. Thatcher and his kind smiles. The room upstairs with its feather blanket. Tory has stopped running for so long, he's not sure his legs remember how to do it anymore.

He'll relearn fast. He always has.

He just has to finish up and recover from wherever the work leaves him, and he'll slip out of their lives the way he slipped in. But even though he pushes the sputtering dregs of his healing energy into Kelly, the last wound won't close. The world drifts sideways, trees on their sides and the snatches of gray sky far away, drifting farther. His arms unlock and nearly drop him, and it's only by virtue of Fedri's strong arms that he doesn't fall face-first into the slurry of blood and dirt. His mouth tastes like metal and his vision swirls, but he's nearly done. Eyes shut, he grasps for any energy he can take and use.

Something bright and light and warm leaps into his hands, and the rest of Kelly's wounds close in a snap. Tory doesn't even need his vision to know they're healed. He feels it.

Normally he'd stop here. Kelly would be in a coma for a few days and would have recovery left to do after he woke, but this energy is like nothing Tory's ever known. He'll have Kelly on his feet again in an instant, awake and laughing, ready to work.

"Tory." It's Fedri's voice, awful and afraid. "Tory, stop."

"M'almost done," he slurs. "S'fine."

The next voice to speak is the stocky miner. "Whatever you're doing, I need you to stop it right now." The men who scattered into the woods to stand guard must be here, too, by the crunch of urgent footsteps all around. "Shit. *Shit.* They'll find us. Stop it, Tory!"

He opens his eyes to *light*.

Not overhead, through the trees, but from the other side of the fence, where men who push carts of stellite from the mine have dropped their carts to stare—where tiny flecks of the precious crystal have mixed with the earth, invisible until they started to glow bright blue. The light glares through the thick vines on the fence, making skeletons of the bell-shaped blossoms.

The light fades the moment Tory tears his hands from Kelly's torso, but it's too late.

A soldier races into the fray, half-obscured by the vines, demanding answers no one can give. Tory freezes, begging him not to turn around.

Naturally, that's the moment Kelly gasps dramatically awake.

The soldier spins and wrenches the vines aside, squinting into the dim woods. "Is someone out there?"

No. Not now. Not like this.

Tory's on his unsteady feet, fleeing through the woods, before the hand-wringing miner has the presence of mind to shout *run*.

CHAPTER TWO

THE TREES BLUR PAST.

Everything blurs. Tory's feet tangle, consciousness barely tethered to his body. He's lucky to be walking after a healing like that. He won't be walking for much longer. He needs someplace safe. Thatcher's. He needs to get home—get *back*—to Thatcher's, but his vision is a haze of light and smoke and the dark blots of tree trunks. There's no chance he'll find his way to the old man's shop. Someplace dark, then. Small. A place he can hide.

Before he can stop to get his bearings, he runs straight into a solid torso. A strong grip closes just above his elbow, over the tattoo. His hands might as well be feathers for all the strength they have to free him.

"Tory! Whoa there, it's just me," a laughing voice says.

His brain is slow to identify it, but his nose serves up the comforting smell of turned earth and the spice of pipesmoke.

"Hasra?" He blinks her into focus. Lit gold by the lamps hanging from the eaves of Hulven's pleasure house and painted with a kaleidoscope of color from its faceted glass windcharms, Hasra offers him a smug smile, hazed in curls of smoke from her long pipe.

His fool brain says *safe, safe, safe,* but he swats the thought away.

"Who else would it be?" Hasra blows smoke at the sky. "Knew I'd be seeing you as soon as I felt the collapse. Why the hurry?"

He blinks and light pours sideways across his vision. "It's—Kelly was . . ." His knees nearly buckle but he catches himself. He can't fall here. "Soldiers saw me. *Hasra*—"

Her grip on his arm goes tight, expression flattening. "Okay." She taps her pipe out on the windowsill.

"Okay," she says again, and drags him behind the House to the barrel they use to catch rainwater. Dipping a basin out, she presses him to his knees. "Wash your hands. Wash them *now*, get the blood off."

It takes a moment for the words to register, and by then she's kneeling to help.

He splashes Kelly's blood off his fingers and scrubs ineffectually beneath his nails. Too soon, he hears running footsteps, and Hasra pulls the bowl away, slinging the bloody water down the hill. Tory clenches his fists and hopes they're clean enough as a soldier rounds the corner.

"We're looking for some men," the soldier says when he sees them. "Tall, moving fast. There was blood at the scene. One of them might have been injured."

"Haven't seen anyone." Hasra winds a protective arm around Tory and gestures away with her chin. "Heard rustling over that way, though."

The soldier pauses. Delicately, he says, "*He's* injured."

Shit. He didn't get it all off. A blot of watery red dribbles down between his fingers.

Hasra stiffens. "A client of mine."

"A client," the soldier repeats, dubious.

They're an odd match-up, for sure. Hasra is old enough to be Tory's mother, even though she's nothing like his mom, who was pale and mild-mannered and slender like a waif. Hasra is taller, all lean muscle beneath brown skin.

"Ma'am, I'll have to ask you—"

"A *client*," Hasra says again. She turns Tory's hand to show the soldier his fingers and palms, marked with thin white lines and thicker, rounded scar tissue he earned assembling weapons as a child.

The horror that unfurls in Tory at the soldier's widening eyes is instinctual, instilled in him since he was young. Will the soldier recognize the marks? Has he seen hands like Tory's before?

"What can I say?" Hasra continues blithely. "This one likes a whip."

Tory's panic morphs all the sound in the world to the bright ring of a bell, so he barely hears her when she says, "If you'd like a sample of what I can offer, you only have to ask."

The soldier sputters a response, but by the time Tory's hearing fades back in, they're alone, and Hasra is stroking his hair back like he's a child. She only smiles when he flicks her hand away.

"Let's get you home. Can you stand?"

He knows without trying that he can't, but that's not important. "Hasra, I need . . ."

It's harder to say now that his heart is slowing, Hasra's wide hand warm against his back, but that's why he needs to say it now. Once he sleeps, the situation will feel even less urgent, and he'll promise himself he'll do it *next week*, then *next month*, and then *after the winter, perhaps*. Plenty of time for these foolish roots to grow so deep he'll never be able to leave.

For years, he's told himself he stayed here for practicality, because his mother told him to lay low and his deal with the people of Hulven was no worse than any other he'd struck in exchange for food or shelter. He told himself—and Hasra, when she bothered him about it—that Arlune might not be better. It could just be a different sort of bad.

What a good liar he's become.

"What do you need?" Hasra coaxes when the silence stretches long.

"Need . . . some help getting up," he finishes, pathetically.

He'll say it. He will. He just needs a second.

Hasra hefts him to his feet. "And?"

The soldier bought Hasra's story. Healing Kelly didn't kill Tory. With the sunset and the vines, there's no way that soldier saw any of them clearly, or Hasra's little bit wouldn't have worked. Hulven is the closest active mine to Arlune's border, but none of the infiltrators have made it far enough inside the country to bother anyone here yet. The strange blood tests Vantaras supposedly uses to single out people like Tory and draft them into government service are only set up at the gates to much larger cities. He could keep his secret here a while longer. Hulven is a good place, maybe the best he'll ever find.

Tory's eyes burn. He forces a laugh. "Got any openings at the House?"

It's a bald delaying tactic. He and Hasra sometimes joke about Tory signing a contract here. Sex, while he has no particular interest in it, is no more burdensome to him than selling his body as a Healer, and he'd certainly make better money—and have a better chance of being able to stand up afterward, too. But they've long since established that he abhors the idea of serving Vantaras again, even indirectly, and a portion of every licensed House's profit goes into the Grand General's war fund.

"*Tory,*" Hasra says, more patient than he deserves.

He could stay. He could *stay here*. He's so damn tired of running. His work here hurts, but it could be so much worse. Hulven has familiar people, familiar pain. He knows what to expect here. But those are the sorts of thoughts that will get him killed, so he makes himself say, "I need to leave."

"I've heard *that* one before. Watched you fall flat on your face trying to make it home on your own too many times to believe you."

"Not that kind of leave. Is your offer still open?"

His chest aches as the silence spreads. At last, Hasra draws a deep breath. The white blur that spreads in front of his eyes is probably a smile, but Hasra sounds sad. "Oh? Will you really take me up on it? I can contact Belmin's man tonight, have you halfway to Arlune by dawn."

Belmin earned his fame as a merchant of artisanal blown glass and an enterprising trader of Arlunian wares, but in Hasra's circles, he's better known as a merchant of men and trader of information. She's one of his trusted informants. He takes people like Tory and, for a fee, will shuttle them across the border to Arlune where they can't be conscripted into Vantaras' war. That's the story, anyway.

"Not tonight," he whispers, heavy eyelids closing. "Need a few days to recover."

"Okay. Three days, Tory. I'll arrange it." She loops an arm behind him. "I'm gonna carry you. If you've got any complaints, start walking." She gives him a few seconds to move, but he doesn't because he can't, and he knows better by now than to try.

She lifts him with a clucked *far too light, need to eat more,* and booms a warning: "I'm out for the evening!"

"Yes, Hasra!" a soft voice calls back.

Clarity filters in: most of Hasra's regulars are working men. They'll come after dark. Unlike the illegal House his mother was arrested for working in, this one's government certified, but payment still works the same. If she leaves, she's losing the night's earnings.

"Wait, you can't—"

"Hush. Unlike you, I have the sense to look after myself."

He hushes, but not everyone is so considerate. A pale, crinkled raisin of a woman stomps out the front door. Stellite earrings glint at her ears, worth more than Hasra and all her employees make in a month.

"Leaving, Hasra? What of your appointments?"

"They'll understand."

"You can't do this," the woman snaps.

"I think you'll find I can, Madam, if you examine my contract."

Hasra walks away while the Madam of the House gapes.

Tory's eyes slip closed, but he forces them open. "Your contract?"

Hasra's laughter rumbles through her chest and into his. "If she checks it, I'm in trouble. But did you see her *face*?"

"Mm, was it good?"

"The best." Hasra whistles a slow tune as she walks. "Where to?"

He should say *get me out of here*. He should leave Hulven tonight. Instead, so low Hasra shouldn't be able to hear, he says, "Take me home."

Maybe she hears it or maybe she knows he's weak, and a fool to boot, because she does. By the time they reach Thatcher's shop, Tory can't stop shaking.

Thatcher darts to his feet when the door's bell, made from twisted pieces of shrapnel, clatters their arrival. "Oh! I was wondering . . . he was late. I was about to go and look."

Tory's long wondered if they have some sort of alliance, an unspoken pact to make sure he doesn't pass out in a gutter somewhere.

"Thatcher, love, it's been too long! Still letting wily customers barter your work down to a fraction of its worth?"

Thatcher chokes on a noise that means *yes*, because of course he is. He's far too susceptible to sad stories. He took Tory in, after all.

Hasra chuckles. "I'd better put the kid to bed."

"Ah, of course!"

She carries him up and tucks him under the covers, and Thatcher flutters around him, tapping a sweating pitcher. "Drink a little before you sleep, all right?"

Hasra waves him away. "Don't worry, Alvorn. I've got it from here."

Thatcher takes this as his cue to leave, but not before his fidgeting hands tuck the blanket tighter around Tory. For all that he earns his living mending broken things, he's helpless with the human body, for which the best fix is often *just wait*.

When the door creaks closed, Hasra lifts the pitcher, deadpan. "Little sips. No whining."

He takes three. They don't sit easy, but she's right. Dehydration is kindling on this fire.

"You gonna be all right?"

He'll sleep for a day, at least. That'll leave two days before he has to go. Arlune, a country with no walls and no tattooed children in prisons, with sea-salt air flooding over fields fragrant with impossible harvests and stellite lanterns swinging from the eaves of dusky sand-glass buildings.

Arlune, with unfamiliar faces and an unfamiliar language. One more place to run to in a list as long as a lifetime.

Tory's mouth sours. Running and running and running. Do people like him ever get to *fight*?

The thought settles in his chest and blooms there. Exhaustion drags him down, but he makes himself speak: "What if I don't want to go?"

"No take-backs. Three days, Tory."

"What about the rebels?"

Hasra sighs, but she's the one who shared the story with him in the first place. *They live in the woods off the fruit of the land,* she told him when he was fifteen and angry and in need of a dream. *They freed a whole unit of captured Seeds, once. They turned over a truck of supplies and picked it clean before Vantaras' goons even noticed. People will say they don't exist, but sometimes Belmin gets a call for help, and when he gets there, someone has already helped them.*

They're ridiculous stories. A child's stories. For all he knows, Hasra made them up.

But if they're out there, maybe he doesn't have to run anymore. Maybe even someone like Tory can be allowed to fight for something.

"Sorry, they've been kinda quiet lately," is all she says, and Tory's stomach sinks. Cool fingers drift over his temple before vanishing. His door creaks as it opens. "Get some sleep."

The next day passes in a haze—heat and darkness and a gentle arm behind his neck and Thatcher saying, *one more sip.* Thatcher makes beauty even of brutality. When he was a young man near the border, he gathered the shrapnel that washed up on shore. He used it to make the shop's bell. It's his fault, probably, that Tory started to believe Hulven was a place he could be happy.

The following morning, wobbling on his feet, Tory sets to convincing Thatcher to let him do the shopping. "Gotta earn my keep somehow."

Earn his keep. That's all this ever was. All he can allow it to be.

Something throbs in Tory's chest. One more day.

He'll give Thatcher's shop the deepest deep clean it's ever seen. He'll scale that thorny evergreen by the ridge and pick a whole basket of the berries Thatcher uses for his mother's heirloom tea. Maybe steal the Madam's earrings for Hasra. She'd get a laugh out of that. It won't be enough to pay them back for what they've given him, but it might be a start.

Thatcher flaps a tired hand. "You take too long and I'll come looking, you hear?"

Tory blinks the sting from his eyes and laughs. "You worry too much!"

*

Tory, it turns out, doesn't worry nearly enough.

Hulven's small market lines the central road leading to the mine. The rutted road is a mess in any rain, deadly slick with mud and worsened by the wide-wheeled, matte-black armored carriages that come through to pick up stellite. For now, the sun beams down to melt the morning's frost, and a brisk wind clears the air of fuel fog. Marketgoers scurry from stall to stall, loosening shawls and pulling hats from their heads to let the light brush them. Everyone pretends the budding storm to the west will pass them by.

Fedri, whose booth boasts trays stacked with buttered herb twists, waves Tory over when she sees him and rolls two fragrant loaves and a large twist in paper, shoving them under his arm before he can protest the generosity. She tuts over how he staggers and slurs.

You need rest after what you did for my Kelly. Go home, she says, like home isn't a word with sharp edges.

It's fine. Tomorrow, he'll be gone.

Tory receives two pity gourds from the farmer whose bad elbow he soothed last winter and a painted rock from a six-year-old who was stoic when he set and sealed her broken wrist in spring.

His legs are reedy and disobedient when he's done, and the vendors laugh at how he staggers. He's frozen to his core, shirt damp with cold sweat. The grumpier he looks, the more free things they give him, and the harder it all is to carry.

Thatcher will be delighted.

Tory's legs fail him, as things do, at the worst possible moment. He goes to his knees in the middle of the street (a gentler fall than he expected) and wheezes with Thatcher's groceries scattered around him.

He registers the quiet, first—the hushed gasps and murmurs. The sudden emptiness of the crowded road, marketgoers receding like the tide.

Then the noise. Wails rattle his eardrums, backed by a cacophony he can't translate. Clacks and cracks and rattles. The clop of—hooves.

When he sees the matte-black carriage barreling toward him, it's already too late.

Sharp nails scrabble against his arms, and the wailing makes sense. Of course his fate couldn't be so simple as his own imminent death. He fell on someone. Tory blinks to clear grainy blackness from his eyes and locates her: mud-streaked, tiny, and furious. Baby tooth missing in the front. He hooks his hands under her arms, but she won't move. She probably doesn't know the soldiers won't risk their precious cargo by stopping. Probably her knees hurt, and she wants her mother.

The carriage hurtles on. Maddened beasts whinny, spittle flying, eyes white as the whips crack down again.

"Go on!" He pushes her.

Not far enough. There's no time. It'll take them both out, he has to move—

Right before it hits them, the carriage stops.

Instant, *impossible* stillness, like all its speed and momentum were snatched away by some great hand. There's no squeal of ungreased wheels on rickety axles or cries of "Halt, halt!" from the man who whips the beasts. The stop is sudden—so sudden and so quiet it seems absurd the thing was ever moving. If not for the wild-eyed horses stamping and frothing a half-length away, flanks rippling with shivers, he might believe the carriage had been sitting there all along.

It should tremble and moan with arrested motion. There should be deep ruts in the earth from the sharp deceleration. The horse should have whinnied its distress, at the very least. But the carriage just *sits there*, when moments ago it was on a deadly collision course. It doesn't make sense.

There must be a trick to it, one of Vantaras' newfangled mechanisms, some impossible thing that can stop a rampaging carriage in its tracks. Tory searches the crowd for a culprit but instead finds every eye fixed on him, every person waiting in breathless silence.

The soldier with the reins gasps and stares down—down at him—with dawning realization.

Pain shivers up through Tory's marrow, followed by a bolt of sick horror: Tory *recognizes* this pain. It's *exactly* like when he performs a healing.

The carriage, the horse, their impossible, immediate stop—somehow, Tory caused it.

The townspeople will hide a Healer. They benefit from a Healer. They won't hide this, whatever it is.

He forces strength into his limbs. While the onlookers catch their breath, he ducks between the blacksmith's and the butcher's and sprints past colorful vendors' tents toward home. There's no time. He has to run again, find another place to hide. He'll settle in and smile and make nice, like his mother told him before he escaped the labor camps at the cost of her life.

Her wisdom lasted him ten years. Funny that something so ridiculous, so unforeseeable, should ruin it all.

Tory runs, breath sawing from tired lungs, and wishes he could turn back time.

CHAPTER THREE

THREE DAYS, Tory said. He's so stupid. He should have left years ago.

Stormclouds sap color from the world as he hurries toward Thatcher's shop. He owes him a few words—enough to keep him safe when Vantaras' soldiers come with their questions. The shrapnel bells clang his arrival, jolting Thatcher from his vigil by the door.

Tory falls to his knees. The first words from his lips are, "I'm sorry."

"Tory!" Thatcher grabs his forearm to help him stand. "Oh, dear, did you take on another healing? Here. Stand up, we'll get you someplace comfortable."

Tory can count on one hand the times he's cried since he left the camp. His eyes burn now, because when he looks up, there's Thatcher, face lined with worry and gray-brown hair unbrushed. Two steaming cups of tea sit together on the table—one for each of them, because Thatcher's grumpy old mom always touted the restorative effects of her special herbal blend.

Tory forces himself up. "I have to go."

If Vantaras' soldiers catch him, they'll lay the red tattoo over the blue cuff already etched into his skin. Red for a criminal, blue for children born to them in the camps, and the bruise-purple of the two for Tory, who couldn't run far enough away.

"Not another job! You know I try not to interfere in your work, but—"

"No, I have to *go*. I won't see you again." Tory shoves out a hand when Thatcher opens his mouth to interrupt. "If they ask, you took me in out of pity. You don't know about the healing, okay? You don't know anything."

"Tory—"

"No!" Damn it, he really did let himself grow roots here. Thatcher has always been patient and foolishly kind, the sort of man who takes in angry boys and asks for nothing but offers a home. He's the type death snatches young, the stupid and selfless type who meets the world with wisdom and wonderment and infinite patience.

And tea. That ridiculous herbal tea, sweet with mountainside medicinal flowers and treeberries. Tory won't drink it again.

Tory bites the inside of his lip to keep his voice from shaking. "I need to get my things. There were witnesses. There's no way the soldiers haven't called for backup."

"Soldiers? Tory, please—" Thatcher's warm hands wrap around his upper arms. He casts Tory in his shadow, a head and change taller and twice as wide. In the shop, he'll carry brick-mix bags two to each arm like sacks of feathers. His face with its wide eyes etched with smile lines and the thick hands that hold his mother's floral teapot so delicately say *father*. His body says *fighter*. "Tell me. I can help. You don't have to go."

Maybe he doesn't.

But one man's strength means nothing. If Tory stays, Thatcher will become an accessory to the crime of unlicensed healing and whatever happened with the carriage. If he stays, Tory will make a million more excuses, and one of them will land him in his grave.

The stairs up to Tory's room go on for days. He clutches the rail. "Tory!"

Thatcher's heavy cloak hangs over the window. Tory slept until almost midday because of it, slept through Thatcher chopping firewood and cleaning the shop—Tory's chores.

He pulls the cloak away, and light floods in. In the back-slung canvas sack Thatcher made for him, he shoves some money, matches, and a small knife. Thatcher's standing in the doorway when he turns to go. He tries to edge past, but a hand lands on his shoulder.

"I knew pretty quick what I was getting into when I took you in."

"Doesn't matter." Tory trains his eyes on the well-loved wood beneath his feet. "Thanks. I really . . ."

Thatcher tries a nod, like he understands, but this must feel like betrayal. Another son running off and leaving him behind.

"The cloak." Thatcher snatches it from the bed and presses it into Tory's hands. It's warm and smooth, heavy like an embrace. Thick thread along the bottom draws a rudimentary outline of the flowering vines that spill over Hulven's walls, of buds like bells, painstakingly sewn. "The hide's been treated so it's waterproof. You might need it in this weather. It'll cover you and three more people besides. Find some folks to share it with, won't you?"

Thatcher's hand on his shoulder burns like a brand.

Tory leaves him at the top of the staircase without an answer, bell tinkling against the door when he leaves. He shouldn't look back, but he can't help it.

Thatcher waits halfway down the stairs, mouth open as if to call out. When he sees Tory, he stops and looks away.

Tory runs.

On the opposite side of town, a sturdy tree leans over the wall in the deepest part of the woods. It'll take only a moment to climb up and drop down on the other side. He'll be safe there. Before he came to this town—properly came here—he watched from the branches of those trees for days.

He's not even halfway there, slipping through muddy back alleys that have pretty much zero foot traffic on market day, when he spots a group of soldiers with a woman and a little girl. The soldiers face away from Tory. He tries to slow down so he won't attract attention, but the woman glances over the officers' shoulders, mouth slackening with shock when she sees him.

"You said he ran this way?" one of the soldiers asks.

"Ah. Yes, well," the woman's attention snaps back to him. "You can take this path to get almost anywhere. It's not a big town, Hulven. I'm afraid I can't be sure where he was going . . ."

The girl clinging to the woman's leg clearly doesn't catch on to her mother's game. Just like her mother did, the girl peeks over at Tory, but instead of deflecting, she yells, "Ah!" in gleeful recognition, revealing a missing front tooth.

The girl who broke his fall. Shit.

"Mommy, it's the nice man!"

Tory runs full tilt, muscles screaming. If anything will save him, it's his familiarity with this place.

He skids around a clump of bright mudbrick houses moments before the soldiers do, dives into the shadows between two of them, and bolts through. He slips out front and takes a quick left, but a strong hand seizes his shirt and pulls him into the next narrow passage before he picks up speed. He jabs his attacker with sharp elbows, but the arms immobilize him before he does any damage.

"Tory! Thank the stars, I've been looking everywhere for you. Found Thatcher but he said you'd already left. Figured you'd be on the back roads, so—"

The fight drains from him. "*Hasra?*"

She lets go. "The Madam saw what happened at the market and recognized you. Long story short, I'm unemployed."

"Shit, I'm—"

"That's not why I'm here. Belmin's sending someone to extract me, shouldn't be more than an hour. Come *with* me."

He wants to, that's the thing. Her perfume—like the sun-warmed earth beside rivers—blends with the spice of her pipe to slow his pounding pulse. *Three days*, he told her, because he could hardly bear to leave. Wanting is a sharp ache in his stomach. He's not supposed to give in to it. It's what got him in trouble in the first place.

But it's fine, isn't it? If he goes with her, she'll take him someplace safe.

Yells and footsteps from nearby and a flash of that awful navy uniform shock him from his foolish dream. "I shouldn't."

She pulls him closer, out of sight. "No, all the more reason you *should*."

Maybe she's right. She's his best chance at escape. What would his mother say? Despite everything, she'd probably tell him to go with Hasra. No sacrifice is too great for freedom. But he imagines Hasra cuffed and carted away, tattooed like Tory, and he can't. "You go ahead."

"Tory, don't be like this."

He sets his jaw. He knows it's a terrible decision. He won't defend it to her.

She takes his stubbornness in stride like always. "*Fine.* Find me at Serpentshead when you're out. I'll wait for you there."

Tory swallows past the knot in his throat. He lived in the caves down at Serpentshead Rock as a boy, crawled up the sturdy stone and bathed in sunlight far above the trees. She's the only one he's ever told about it. "You don't have to do that."

Another shout. Another soldier. Closer. "He went this way!" someone calls.

"You hear me?" Hasra grabs his jaw and makes him face her. "Serpentshead. If you don't show, I'll tear this whole country down to find you."

Tory bites his tongue. He needs to leave, *now*, or he'll do something stupid like stay.

He shoves away and into the light, pushing his legs as fast as they'll go. He won't make it to the other side of town. The woods on this side are sparse and rocky, but they'll do. There's another tree out here, a flimsy thing that bows over the wall like a mourner.

The soldiers follow, their huffing breaths and the crack of twigs far too close. The air grows earthy with the tang of coming rain. The first drops spatter cold on his nose and cheeks.

"We can do this peacefully," a low voice calls—nearer than the rest, gaining on him.

Not if Tory has any say in it.

The dainty spatters shift from a hum to a roar, water falling in gray sheets. The cloak isn't wrapped right and he can't stop to fix it. Ice cold rain drips down his neck and into his shirt.

He reaches for the tree and swings up, palms slipping on bark that sloughs off into his hands as he hooks his feet over a low branch.

Cries sound behind him. He grabs the sturdiest branch and throws himself over the wall.

He has time only for half a gasp and the adrenaline rush of horror when he loses his grip too soon. Both palms and one knee crash into wet leaves and grind into the rocks beneath. His jaw snaps shut on his tongue, but he has no time for pain. He stands and runs, mouth full of copper and heart clambering in his chest. The yelling behind the wall grows distant.

Tory pushes his aching body faster, trees blurring past, and maybe, maybe—

A thud. A smooth landing. Footsteps pick up behind him. "I don't want to use force!"

Funny. Those are the last words he hears before something buries itself in his neck. His legs knock and lurch, fingers reaching to grab at whatever it is. A needle? Tory drops, rain choking him and tunneling his vision.

He can stand. He has to. This can't be how he loses the freedom his mother died to give him. A desperate flight, a clumsy fall. No strength to fight—the only blood in his mouth his own. Tory hits the ground, head cradled between the roots of a felted oak. He blinks up at its wide branches. Its presence hums warmly against his mind, and he spares a moment to curse the thing, so smug and confident planted right where it is.

It's so easy for trees, being rooted. They rarely have reason to run.

The comfort of the forest crumples to an echoing emptiness as footsteps scrunch the fallen leaves. Stars crackle across his vision, and he blinks to dispel them.

The soldier who took Tory down looms over him, his presence like electricity skittering over Tory's skin. Weapon-studded belt, crisp undercut, and that double-breasted navy uniform. Powder blue trim and silver buttons, like the soldiers who watched the weak and wounded die in the labor camps. Tory quivers, muscles tensing to attack.

He spits the blood in his mouth at one of those perfectly polished black boots.

The soldier sidesteps and kneels, offering Tory a close-up of the man he'll kill one day. The guy's downright *delicate*—unmarred skin and fine features, a fan of dark lashes over amber-brown eyes bruised with exhaustion. The black hair tumbling over his forehead, plastered to bone-pale skin with the rain, nearly obscures his left eye. He'd have been eaten alive in any city Tory survived.

He could almost be Arlunian. Laughter tears from Tory's throat. Arlune. Tory wanted to run for it, but instead it ran for him, wrapped in prison colors. The vines that climb the trees dangle purple blooms down at Tory, just out of reach. His numb fingers twitch against the thing buried in his neck.

The asshole says, "You shouldn't touch that."

He touches it anyway, closes fumbling fingers around the thing and pulls. Pain, hot and sudden. A flood of warmth. His vision narrows, rimmed with crushing dark.

"Fool. It's *barbed*," is the last thing he hears before blackness swallows him.

*

Unfamiliar noise—rhythmic clattering and a clanking like chains—tugs him from the fuzziness of drugged rest. Vertigo and darkness do their best to lull him back, but it doesn't take long for the memories to resurface.

Icy rain, blood in his mouth, bruised amber-brown eyes.

That *uniform*.

Fear sharpens Tory's vision. He wiggles his fingers, his toes. He's unbound, on his back on some sort of bench, shoulder blades digging into wood. Shifting, grayish light sifts in from three tiny squares near the top of the wooden walls. An unlit lamp swings from a hook in the corner of the small, rectangular room, its walls so narrow they could close in and crush him. Too much like a holding cell, like the camps. It smells like them, too—unwashed bodies and something like hay.

Desperation drives Tory to his feet, where he staggers, vision shuttering and dizziness rocking him like the earth has liquefied. He finds his way to what he guesses is the door and throws his weight against it. No give.

He drops back on the bench, ears ringing. The sky-blue shackle of the tattoo around his upper left arm burns. He tugs up his sleeve to make sure they haven't laid the red ring over the blue while he slept, but there's only unblemished skin, no hot ache from a fresh needle.

"I won't go back. Those bastards can throw me on the front lines instead. I—"

"You hardly have a choice," a cold voice says, startlingly close.

A figure sits cloaked in the darkness beneath the swinging lamp.

Tory growls, "Don't I?"

"You will not be going to the labor camp. The Grand General wouldn't waste your skills at menial labor." There's a bitter note in it—some joke at Tory's expense, no doubt—and Tory's eyes narrow, because he *knows* that clipped and cultured tone. That chill, the condescension. It's *him*. The pretty-boy bastard who sniped at him about the needle after shooting him in the neck.

"Where am I?"

"We're on our way to a place for people like you."

On our way. With that, the odd, untranslatable sounds slot into place: the cottony hush of the rain; the clopping of horseshoes against gravel; the grunt of a driver. A cough. The vertigo makes sense. He *is* moving.

"People like me?"

"Unregistered Seeds."

It could be a lot worse. He's heard of these places. People like Tory are sent there to learn and then assigned somewhere Westrice can make use of them. Like the mines, the Houses, and the labor camps, Vantaras won't pass up the opportunity to make use of any resource.

It could be worse, but it's not ideal. Tory takes stock. They're on the move. He's probably in a carriage of some sort. Given the hay smell, maybe even some rudimentary livestock transport car. Less sophisticated than he'd expect from Vantaras' soldiers who like to show off in their brand-new fuel-belching vehicles, but good for Tory. He might be able to find a way out. Movement in his peripheral vision draws his eye.

The *lamp*. If nothing else, he could use it as a bludgeon.

The soldier's eyes follow his. An eyebrow arches. "It's chained in. No glass."

"I could still kill you with it."

"Could you?" the soldier deadpans. "You're hardly in a position to make threats. You might have noticed you cannot access your Seed at the moment."

What's he going to do with his *Seed?* Heal the lamp?

He doesn't need it, anyway. He has hands. That's all anyone's ever needed to take a life or piece one back together. Tory could wring this bastard's elegant neck.

But healing isn't why he's here. That carriage—the way it stopped so smoothly it was like it never moved, that wasn't healing. It wasn't anything Tory's heard of. Now is a bad time to regret slipping away from conversations about people like him for fear that his pointed interest might out him. If there's a name for what Tory did, he never learned it.

The soldier sinks into silence, arms crossed. Without anger to warm him, Tory shivers. Icy autumn wind moans through the openings at the top of the carriage. Tory buries himself in a corner as far from the soldier as he can get, clenching his teeth to stop the chattering. He reaches up to close Thatcher's cloak around himself, but they've taken it away. He's unmoored without the weight of the treated leather, bare and frozen through. It shouldn't matter. He's been cold like this before.

He's gotten soft, being loved.

He can't make that mistake again. Lingering in Hulven—holding onto the people there—is what got him into this situation.

He squeezes his eyes shut and lets himself drift, startling awake only when the carriage creaks to a stop. The doors at the back swing wide, and Tory hisses as the cloud-smeared sky sears itself on his vision.

Up ahead, a black road snakes through yellowing grass toward a wall as high as any Tory has ever seen. As soulless, too—seamless, ash-gray stone. Shadowed suggestions of weapons crouch atop it like carrion birds. The forest sits well apart from it, like nature knows to lean away. It's very *Vantaras*.

Two soldiers wait outside. "Sir?" the first one says.

"I'll escort him," the delicate soldier responds. Except—the outside light glints off a smart set of bars on his uniform. Tory sneers. Not a soldier, then. An *officer*. They're the worst types, bloodying hundreds of hands with their orders while their own stay clean and soft. He's even wearing white gloves, impeccably clean but frayed at the knuckles and fingertips.

"This way." The officer walks up behind Tory so he has no choice but to get out of the carriage, then steps around him.

Tory plants himself where he is. First order of business: testing boundaries.

The officer walks up the road, measured strides slowing and stopping about halfway up. "You can choose not to follow."

Two soldiers idle on either side of him, hands on their belts. Tory doesn't miss the implied threat. "Then what?"

"You learn what happens to the ones who make trouble."

"What, you gonna kill me?"

The officer's expression, by form alone, should be a smile. "That might be kinder."

Tory's pounding pulse tells him to run. It's all he's ever done, all he knows how to do. "What do you mean?"

"Try it and find out."

Tory was born in a prison crueler than this one. He escaped at eight; he *will* escape again. Snapping at this bastard would be salve on a burn, but the relief would be temporary. Sharp words won't free him. Sharp eyes might.

He needs to bite his tongue, observe and absorb. Tory swallows bile and follows.

As soon as he's within a few strides, the dark-haired officer continues to walk.

The words *STAR Compound #7* loom ahead, engraved on the plate above the wide mouth of a massive gate, and underneath it: *Seed Training, Assessment, and Registration.*

The officer says, "You will be registered and typed, though the process is merely a formality at this point. After that, you'll be informed of the expectations in the facility and allowed to acclimate. Your training will begin tomorrow."

"Training for what?"

No answer.

The officer stops in front of a window set into the watchtower. A guard on the other side springs to his feet when he sees them, snapping into a sharp salute. "Lieutenant Vantaras."

The name hits Tory like a slap. *Vantaras*, king of this land of prisons. Tory knows Michal Vantaras has two sons, but they have a decade and change on Tory and are built like their father—musclebound, walking fortresses. The exact opposite of this guy.

It has to be coincidence.

Vantaras says, "I've returned with the alleged Channeler."

Tory examines the soldier in the booth. Dull smile—distractible. The stone wall is imposing but not impassable.

Vantaras follows Tory's gaze, eyebrows rising. He opens his mouth as if to speak but just shakes his head, mouth curling into a cool expression of disdain.

The watchtower guard pulls a clipboard from the wall and draws a thick red line across the page. "You're authorized to enter, Lieutenant; your re-entry has been logged and your permit to leave has been withdrawn. Welcome back, sir."

Vantaras nods, exposing his neck. A long white scar snakes from the fine, short hairs at the base of his skull, down along his spine until it disappears into the high collar of his uniform.

The gate whips up into the wall with a sound like a gunshot, tooth-like serration at its base, and Tory clenches his fists and makes himself move.

This is strategy, not surrender.

Inside, a wide path leads toward a squat, round building like a sleeping serpent, the same seamless gray stone as the wall. High, dark windows stretch across the front, but the rest of the building has only slit-like windows or none at all.

It's nothing like homegrown Hulven. Nothing like the labor camps, either, cast in dusty browns—rickety shacks with bedrolls set edge to edge and towering fences—but it's not altogether different. It's another kind of cage, the precision of its construction a testament to wealth. Vantaras falls in behind Tory as he enters.

Too late, he catches the silhouette of the weapons atop the wall and sees why he couldn't make sense of them before. They're cannons—and they're not pointing outside to punish intruders or escapees.

They point inward, barrels low and at rest. Glasslike circles on the sides glow with wan, eerie light as Tory passes, like empty eyes watching him.

The door falls like a guillotine as soon as they're inside.

CHAPTER FOUR

THE INTERIOR OF STAR Compound #7 reeks of clinical cleanliness that burns Tory's throat. Stone hallways extend in both directions. The one to his right looks marginally less miserable, so Tory goes right.

Alarm bells kick up before he's three steps inside—a relentless clattering against his eardrums.

Vantaras claps both hands over his ears and jerks his head in the opposite direction. "*This* way."

Tory steps back, but the alarm doesn't stop.

A device clipped to Vantaras' chest crackles—no doubt some newfangled invention from the big brains in the capital. A voice emits from it. "*Lieutenant, report.*"

Vantaras peels a hand from one ear with a glare at Tory and presses the surface of the device. "False alarm, sir. I'm taking the new Seed through Intake now."

A long pause precedes the knife-like response: "*I'll expect an explanation.*"

"Yes, sir." Vantaras jumps to attention, like the guy on the other end can see him. Maybe he can. The alarms taper out, and Vantaras' hands return to his sides. "Registration," he snips.

Tory's tired—*still* tired from helping Kelly—and all he wants is to kick this officer's face until it caves in. "What kind of registration?"

Vantaras strides down the opposite hallway in lieu of answering, shoes ticking against the cold floor. Brushed metal covers the bottom half of the walls. A thin, guiding line of powder blue sits below another line, painted a white so bright Tory's head hurts to look at it.

No, not painted.

It's a light, somehow. Blindingly illuminated, the thin line goes on forever. The mere sight of it raises the hair on his arms and makes his stomach twist, and that's how he knows what it is.

Stellite. Vantaras has kitted this whole disgusting place out with stellite lighting, that rich bastard.

The first time Tory heard that Vantaras had captured lightning inside a stellite sample, he didn't believe it—not until he saw it with his own eyes. Even Hulven's pleasure house, the only building outfitted with stellite *anything*, only has a single, small lantern set into the chandelier in the main hall, and it's only illuminated for special events.

But this—the wastefulness sickens Tory. Is this what the miners break their bodies for?

It feels wrong, too. It's nothing like the raw stellite in the mines that makes Tory's head spin and his mouth go dry. This stuff feels dead. It looks it, too, milky like corpse eyes.

"In here." Vantaras indicates an open door.

Tory paces into a wide room to the stares of at least six people.

"Alleged Channeler," Vantaras says. "Here for typing and registration."

A woman in a powder-blue uniform pushes him into a bleached leather chair and straps his wrists to its arms. Before Tory thinks to free himself, another nurse arrives with a needle.

"Just need a blood sample." He kneads Tory's arm and swipes at it with a cold cloth.

"I need to be tied to a chair for *just a blood sample*?"

"A precaution."

"Against what?"

The nurse frowns, and Tory clenches his fists, testing the bonds. No give.

They won't look at him. No one, save the Vantaras guy, has looked him in the eye since he arrived. Tory's always relied on remaining anonymous and invisible, but there's something wrong with this.

He sucks in a breath. It's fine. *Observe and absorb.*

Tinted windows line the far wall—the ones he saw from outside. If they open, they could be a good escape route.

"Relax. It's only a prick."

It's two. One in the tip of his finger to draw a generous globe of crimson, and one in the crook of his elbow to fill two vials. They press his finger to a square of parchment with a bullseye in the middle; the thick paper sucks up the blood.

A nurse pulls out a black mat. Another dons goggles and lifts a dropper with a tiny measure of yellow fluid at the bottom. Everyone's attention turns toward the paper.

Tory can't say why. As far as he can tell, they're about to squeeze an eyedropper of piss onto a piece of paper saturated with his blood.

More and more nurses don goggles, and several hold clipboards at the ready. The nurse with the fluid squeezes out one careful drop. It falls, lands—*explodes.*

A blue-white flame puffs up, devouring the bullseye and both rings outside it. The fire then fades to a dimmer navy and fizzles out in a hiss of cerulean sparks. The parchment curls up, ashy at the edges.

Hushed voices burst out around him.

"Did you observe the reaction?"

"Reaction recorded. Patterns confirm preliminary type report: synergistic Source. Channeler."

"Confirmed." It elicits a chorus: *Confirmed. Confirmed.* "No additional tests required. Archive the sample and prep a compass."

Tory wrenches his bound wrists, but the straps won't budge.

"So you *are* a Worldseed."

Tory twists toward Vantaras at the dry remark. "And you're an asshole."

The burn of satisfaction fades as fast as it comes. Vantaras' eyes sharpen on him, and Tory clamps his teeth on the soft flesh of his cheek until the sting clears his head. That was foolish. It's better if they think him docile.

A nurse clicks her tongue at him as she works at the straps. Another pulls the needle from his arm and secures a folded piece of gauze with white tape. The straps fall off one hand, then the other, and he's ushered to his feet.

"Finished, Lieutenant." The nurse doesn't look at Vantaras, either, but at least he gets the honor of direct address.

Vantaras turns on a heel and strides out the door and down the hall.

"Next, you'll receive a Core." His pace increases with every step, until Tory has to jog to keep up.

His body protests the exertion, but if Vantaras notices, he doesn't care.

If not for him, Tory would be free. Something ugly stirs inside him, clawed and sinuous, forged in flame. It'll crawl up his throat if he opens his mouth.

Vantaras leads him to a door and knocks. When a voice calls for them to enter, he doesn't go inside with Tory, just waits in the doorway with his arms crossed. The room is cast in silver and white, filled with strange tools.

A redhead in a white coat with sharp cheekbones hunches over a stack of notes, tapping a high heel on the floor. She could kill a man with whatever instruments she's stabbed into her messy bun. Spinning on a cushioned stool, she glances at Tory over a pair of thin spectacles. Her gaze shifts to Vantaras, plum-painted lips curling to reveal an unsettling predatory smile.

"This our Channeler?" She pushes toward them with two quick steps.

Vantaras retreats, speaking to the wall behind her. "Here for a Core, Dr. Helner."

Oh, how delightful. She *intimidates* him. Tory can work with that.

"Good, good. This way. Time to put the shackles on."

Tory isn't sure he likes her tone, pleased and a little off-kilter. He follows anyway, shooting a glance back at Vantaras.

"On the table, Channeler. On your belly. I'll secure your wrists here." The woman gestures. "The procedure will be painless."

"People keep saying that and strapping me to chairs."

Dr. Helner bustles into a corner to open the lid of a small wooden box. Fog billows out, and she extracts a corked vial half-filled with muddy fluid. If it weren't for the faint light pulsing out to illuminate the liquid, Tory would have said the vial contained the bulb and roots of a tiny plant.

"Ah, see, when I said *painless*, I meant it should not be excessively pain*ful*. The straps are for your and my safety. Reaching is harmless as long as I mean it to be, but some Seeds may react adversely to our energies, injuring themselves or the Reacher."

"Reacher?"

Her voice is terribly cheery. "You'll see."

The table angles upward, cushioned to raise his shoulders. There's a hole for his face and strong, thick straps for his hands. More straps coil from the bottom for his ankles, his torso. He can't tear his eyes from the vial.

The heat of anger in his belly vanishes, leaving a static-rush of cold. "What is that?"

"A Core. It'll be your best friend for the rest of your life."

Vantaras flinches in the doorway, lips thinning. "A Core is a . . . tracker, a personal identifier, and a precaution against escape."

"Tracking?"

"A drop of the blood they took in Intake is being linked to a stellite compass. That compass will be engraved with your identifier code and matched to your Core. If you escape, they can be used to hunt you."

Helner isn't armed aside from the implements she's stabbed into her bun, but Vantaras is. No windows here to escape through, but the door to the hallway remains open.

He's not bound yet. Tory calculates his odds.

He doesn't get the condescension he expects when Vantaras understands what he's considering. Instead, he shifts to the left so he's not filling the doorway. When Tory catches his eyes, he looks away.

Like invitation. Like absolution.

Or *mockery*. Helner's hand winds around his arm before he can run.

"You don't want to know what happens to the ones who try to escape. A NOVA is far worse than this. On the table."

Her bruising grip, tight over the cloth of his shirt that covers the tattoo, guides him down. "On your stomach," she says. When he doesn't go immediately, she pushes him down.

Her other hand locks around the base of his neck. She takes her hand from his arm—blood floods back in with a rush of pins and needles—and buckles the straps around his forearms, then strains the neck of his shirt to expose his right shoulder. The hole in the cushioned table offers a view of a small stretch of floor and nothing else.

"This may feel strange."

A crack, a hiss, and the drip of cool liquid on his shoulder. Helner's fingertips trail around to his neck. He waits for the sharp edge of a scalpel, but she only palpates the area with her fingers. "Ready?"

The air around him ignites before he finds words, the pressure no longer on the surface of his skin but inside him—ghosts of her fingertips on his vertebrae. He can't see it, but he feels it—somehow, impossibly, this woman has shoved her hand into his body as though flesh is as easily displaced as water. Tory bucks against the restraints.

"Damn it, Channeler." Another strap across his lower back. "You know what? Keep writhing. I can do this for hours."

"What . . ." He drags ragged breaths in through his nose. "What . . . are you *doing*?"

"I already told you: I'm a Reacher. I'm inside you. Surgery without incisions. I could tear out your spleen if I wanted—or if you distract me. So be quiet."

Tory squeezes his eyes shut against the ringing in his ears. His stomach rolls.

"Gonna be sick."

"Please recall what I said about your spleen."

Tory swallows thickly. *Happy things.*

His thoughts turn to Thatcher, but that makes him sick in a different way. He hopes the soldiers went easy on him. And Hasra—surely, she got away safely.

When he comes back to himself, his body thrums with waves of heat and ice. Blackness dances at the rim of his vision.

Pressure at his back, short and firm. "I said sit *up*. It's finished."

The straps are gone. His shoulder and neck blaze as he lifts himself. Dizziness washes over him, and Helner grabs his arm before he tips off the table.

"Burns," he says.

"Not surprised. Don't know much about Channelers, but the other Source has a history of not playing well with other Seed energies."

He waits until his feet are likelier than not to hold his weight, then starts a coltish walk toward the door.

Helner snickers. "See you later."

Not if Tory can avoid it. He stumbles over his feet, stomach lurching.

Vantaras reaches to right him, face creased with what might be concern, then tears his hand away. There's fear in his eyes—then something like disgust, then nothing. Whatever shreds of pity Vantaras has earned burn away. He's wearing gloves and still can't stand to touch him?

"Follow me." Vantaras steps through the door, hands stiff at his sides.

The hallway goes on forever. His mouth is dry, shoulder throbbing, but there's no wound when he reaches back to touch the place Helner put the Core in.

"When," he rasps, and Vantaras' strides slow to even the distance between them. "When can I get rid of this thing?"

"Never." A pause. "We will arrive shortly in the changing room."

The changing room is as clinical as everywhere else: slate-gray lockers, slate-gray walls, floors tiled in white and the by-now-familiar powder blue. No windows. Vantaras leads him to a locker numbered #2417.

"You may change into the clothes inside. The things you're wearing will be incinerated. Any items on your person deemed dangerous will be disposed of."

Tory tugs out a pair of slate-blue drawstring pants and a loose, short-sleeved shirt of a slightly lighter shade. He crosses his arms, tugs at his long sleeves to dip his closed fists inside. "They're too short."

"Excuse me?"

"The sleeves."

"All detainees in the Compound wear this."

Don't make waves. Hide the tattoos. His mother never told him what to do if following one rule broke another. Tory dangles the shirt by a fistful of the coarse cloth. He forces air into the reed-thin tube of his throat. It's a big shirt. The sleeves will be long enough, surely. "Privacy?"

"Transition upon arrival must be monitored."

Tory turns so his marked arm faces away, pulls his clothes off, and tugs the ugly shirt and pants on. The shirt dwarfs him, yet the sleeves are barely long enough to cover the tattoo. Tory ties the strings on the pants into a tight knot to keep them up.

"Those markings." Tory flinches at Vantaras' cold voice. "You're the child of an interned laborer."

Tory bites his lip almost hard enough to taste blood and keeps his silence.

Vantaras looks away as Tory tugs at the shirtsleeves. "You won't have time to shower, but there's a bag of supplies in your locker, replenished monthly."

Next, Vantaras takes him to another room with a sad slit of a window at the back and a dull metal table and chairs, bolted down. Tory sits; Vantaras retreats to stand against the wall as red-headed Dr. Helner strides in, heels clicking. A younger man, mousy and unarmed, half-asleep, stumbles after her with a notepad.

Tory shifts in his chair as they settle. "What is this?"

"Standard protocol." Helner offers a sharp smile. "Told you I'd see you soon." She waves a slender hand, and a silver bracelet swings with the motion. Its centerpiece is a flat plate with a series of letters and numbers stamped into it. "We don't get so many inductees that I install Cores full-time. I also supervise dietary and lifestyle requirements for unique Seeds and advise the Grand General on arranging training regimens to best suit them. Not that the rancid meathead *listens*." She smiles at the young man with the notepad. "Tell the General I said that, and I'll pull your kidney into your throat and leave it there."

The young man makes a pathetic noise.

Helner laughs. "The skittish little turd over there is filling out your file and will generate your ID number. Let's get started. State your full name and birthplace for the record."

"Tory Arknett."

The man in the corner scratches out notes on his pad.

"And?"

Tory resists the urge to pull at his too-short sleeves.

"Your *birthplace*."

"Why does it matter?"

"Fine. We heard you were performing healing in the southwestern mining town of Hulven. Is that true?"

They think he'll just admit to a crime? Tory raises an eyebrow.

"Doesn't matter. It was stupid, considering your abilities, but we can move on. I'm sure you've suspected by now that you're one of the Sources."

"The what?"

"No need to play coy. We have first-hand testimony of that kinetic energy redirection incident. Witnesses say you stopped a rampaging carriage. And what a performance! The concussive force you stole off it wiped out a copse of trees in the forest nearby. You been practicing for long?"

"I don't know what you're talking about."

Helner laughs, short and sharp. "Hulven's not too far from the border, is it? Perhaps you small-towners still use the old terms. Does *Worldseed* ring a bell? First Children? We would call you a Channeler, synergistic Source."

"*What?*"

Helner stares. "You really don't . . .?"

Tory stares back.

"Oh, come on. *Surely*, you've heard the stories. Shit, it went something like—I don't know. Once upon a time, there was a weird dog god who died, and the first-ever Seeds grew up out of its ashes or something?"

"You could not be more wrong." Vantaras sounds disgusted.

Helner snorts. "Didn't ask you. Anyway, you're one of those. The first ones. We call them Sources. There are two great big umbrella types of Seeds, see? Intrinsic and synergistic. The way the stories go, it all started with two Seeds—one of each type. The originals of those two types are long-dead, but once every generation or three, a Source gets recycled into the mix again, and people make a fuss. You're the synergistic Source."

"What does that *mean*?"

Helner's hands fly up. "Fuck if I know, but I'd like to figure out. The comparative rarity of the Sources means we don't fully understand their particular skills. You following?"

Not in the least. Tory's eyes burn, lids weighted, shoulder throbbing where she reached inside him. *Observe and absorb*. If he can get her to tell him what she means—what he is, what he *did* with the carriage, he can keep it from happening again when he's free. He waits for her to speak, presses his lips together, longs for dark and sleep. The dead stellite lighting in the wall casts thick shadows on the table in front of him.

"Right, you've been living under a rock! Let me explain it like this: regular old synergistic Seeds work with energies outside of their own bodies, and they work with only *one* type of energy. Pyros with fire, Healers with life—you get the gist. They amplify those energies and use them to affect the world around them. *True* Healers amplify life energy to close wounds or heal ailments, but they can't fix a corpse because a dead body has no energy they can use. Kineticists work with objects or bodies in motion. Typical bruisers. They can strengthen their own attacks, increase their speed, or accelerate projectiles at a target, but the thing they amplify must first be moving. Pyrokineticists start with a spark and make it an inferno, but they're useless without that spark. Useless to us, too, really. They have a reputation for hotheadedness and a habit of being unable to control the breadth of destruction they cause, so we don't keep any here. But it's like that. Electricity, heat, movement, the energy that fuels the growth of plants—any flavor of energy you can imagine likely has a synergistic Seed that can handle or enhance it."

She doesn't wait for him to nod, just lashes a hand across the table, points its fingers like a spear, and shoves it not only straight through Tory's hand but through the whole table. Tory only half-swallows the yelp that tries to escape him, and Helner grins like a sated beast as she pulls back and wiggles her fingers.

"Intrinsic Seeds, meanwhile, are exactly what they sound like. The energies *we* use are intrinsic to our bodies and usually enhance a sense or ability we already possess. Many people can reach, but few can reach through solid objects. Illusionists can manipulate people's senses to make them see or hear or believe whatever they'd like. Other intrinsic Seeds can do party tricks like taste the truth or hear the past, but the Grand General has little use for games, so we don't stock the party-trick types here, either."

"Okay . . ."

Helner's still smiling. "So, synergists enhance external energies. Intrinsics use their own."

"Not sure how this relates to me."

The smile widens, and Tory bites his tongue. "Oh? Why?"

"When I heal—" He cuts himself off. Was this her goal? Admitting to being unable to amplify healing energy is admitting to having and exercising an ability to heal.

"You can't amplify energies," she guesses, smug. "Don't look so shocked. Firstly, it's because you're not a Healer."

Tory's aching bones and Kelly's closed wounds beg to differ.

"It's a shame. These meatheads would mine the core of this rotten planet to get more of them. What you *are* is a Channeler, the synergistic Source. Channelers can't amplify energies like other Seeds, but for that sacrifice they gain something far greater. They don't just interact with one energy. They're supposed to be able to interact with *every energy*. What you did when you stopped that carriage in its tracks was a compelling mimic of a Seed type that can redirect concussive force. Make sense?"

"I'm not sure."

"Not my fault. You don't make sense. The short version of all of this is that you can do more, work longer, spread your energies farther—but you lack the ability to amplify them. I'd love to find out why, but alas, the *Grand General* is more interested in putting your skills to work than learning about them, to my eternal frustration. In practice, it means you're a terrible Healer. Worse than terrible. You're—" Helner's eyes sharpen on the door as a petite, dark-haired girl strides by, fists clenched. Helner calls, "Open the door, open the door!" to the mousy man with the clipboard, then yells, "You! Niela, right? You're a Healer. Get in here."

"Absolutely not. Someone in CFR just lost their *eye*."

Sighing, Helner tugs something from her hair—a scalpel—and flings the cap off. She drags its blade over her palm, splitting the skin gruesomely. "Oh no! I'm wounded."

The dark-haired girl growls and stomps in. Before Helner's palm can fill all the way up with blood, she lays two fingers on it, and the wound seals.

Tory gapes.

It's *instant*. One moment, the wound is stretched wide. The next, it's gone. Helner flings the blood onto the ground, to the chest-clutching horror of the man with the clipboard, and shows Tory her hand. There's no scar, not even a thin pink line to show where the cut used to be.

Even for an injury so small, it would've taken Tory a minute to get it closed.

"Tory, my dear foolish faker, meet a *real* Healer."

The real Healer in question snorts and stomps away. "I have work to do."

Helner sets the scalpel down (too far for him to grab it, and the grin on her face says she knows it) and considers the slick of blood on her palm before wiping it off on her coat. Vantaras shudders. "That's what I mean by amplification. True Healers take even a trickle of life energy and amplify it into a flood. You can only manipulate energies that already exist. But where was I? The intrinsic Source is similar to the synergistic Source in that it's theoretically quite powerful but also non-traditional. Where you handle all energies but not enhance them, the intrinsic Source has a frankly *unimaginable* amount of intrinsic power, but the result of that power is unstable and destructive. There's supposed to be some sort of balance the two types can strike together or some sort of . . . something, but it's been eighty years since the Sources were born in the same generation, so no one knows how. Kineticists, true Healers, Reachers—we're *specialists*. The Sources, meanwhile—" she gestures vaguely over at Tory "—are hot messes. But *interesting* messes. I think there's more to you than we know."

Tory tears his eyes from the scalpel. "So, what does that mean for me?"

"Nothing good, I'm sure! It's been *generations* since Westrice has had a Channeler, so our documentation on their abilities is pretty light. There are so many things I'd like to *try* with you." Helner leans forward, messy bun unraveling where she pulled the scalpel from it. Her grin curls up, sickle-sharp. "See, Healers are limited to amplifying the patient's own healing energies, but *you* can use anyone's. I'll bet you could heal a corpse! Vantaras, we got any stiffs here? I'm sure we do. We should try! Tory, don't you want to try that?"

Over his dead body—or whoever's dead body.

The wild grin fades. "Of course, there are downsides. You feel wrecked after healing someone, right?"

Understatement.

"Fever, nausea, cold sweat, the works? The worse the healing, the worse the symptoms? It's because traces of their energies remain behind in you."

That's ridiculous. If he has their healing energies, he shouldn't feel like shit.

"Honestly, they'll probably forbid you from healing while you're here. You couldn't be *any* worse at it." Tory bristles, but Helner just sets her elbows on the table and drops her chin onto her steepled fingers. "Your Seed treats foreign energies as invaders—thus the flu-like symptoms. It's why you were so damn wriggly while I was installing your Core. But that's not all. Because you can't amplify the energies, you're gambling with your life every time, with a very narrow margin for error. The increased heart rate, weakness, clamminess, and pallor during the initial act of healing, if you're foolish enough to let it go that far, are your body going into shock. Normally, shock is a response to physical trauma, but what you're losing is life energy. Shock is your body's last warning. If you were to go farther, you'd fall into what we call an exertion coma. In Hulven, you'd have died, and it would have been a damn shame. Lucky for us, our grumpy lieutenant was called in because of the stellite resonance incident—I heard you made the whole *mine* light up!—and he recognized your type as soon as he heard the report about the carriage."

So it's Vantaras' fault. "*You*—"

Helner twists Tory's chin back toward her. "Do pay attention. You'll receive orientation tomorrow. Sena here will be your supervisor."

Vantaras—*Sena*—steps up beside Tory, posture rigid. "With all due respect, supervising does not fall under my—"

"Colonel's orders. He said supervising a new Seed will remind you of your place."

Vantaras twitches. "Is the meeting concluded?"

Helner flaps a hand at the door. "I'm sure Kirlov is eager to hear your report. Hurry back. Your *supervisee* will be waiting."

Vantaras stalks out before Helner has finished speaking. She laughs. "Ah, well. I'm out of here, too. Corpse-hunting! Maybe I can get permission from the general . . ." She trails off, already at the door. "Anyway, follow this guy. He'll finish you up!"

And she's gone. She's gone—but the red-tipped scalpel she sliced her hand open with isn't, blending into the innocuous silver of the table. That's it. That could be his salvation.

The guy with the notepad, eyes half-mast, yawns and heads toward a gray door at the back of the room.

Adrenaline pumping through him, Tory swipes the scalpel from the table on his way past, clamping the cutting edge between two fingers of his left hand so the grip is concealed in the cup of his palm. Another reason to hate the assholes who trapped him here: no pockets to store the thing, and he's not stupid enough to stick it in his waistband. Just as he's situating it, the man turns, and Tory almost drops the thing. He jerks away from the table.

"Look, we're almost finished. Hurry up."

Heart pounding with some hybrid of terror and joy, Tory obeys.

Inside the adjoining room, the man pokes and prods Tory, weighs and measures him, examines his teeth, the tattoo on his arm, and the small scar on one side of his neck from when he was a child. "Luckily, you have some distinct traits," he concludes. "Harder to identify bodies on the battlefield without 'em."

Fear sears his veins. "What?"

The young man frowns. "I thought you knew. STAR-7 is the nearest training facility to the border. It's the battle-specialist facility. All Seeds trained here are sent to war."

Sent to war. Tory presses the scalpel tighter between his fingers, mouth dry. He breathes the bitter odor of chemicals and doesn't twitch, doesn't smile.

The man taps at the scars on Tory's palm absentmindedly. "Mind you, all the identifiable traits in the world won't help you if you come face to face with a Legion unit. Which is why you get one of these." He grabs Tory's wrist, wrapping his fingers around it.

Tory stands frozen, mind racing and fingers numb.

It's fine. This is fine.

The thud of pain in his shoulder, the lingering aches from healing, the weight of his limbs, this man's *words*—they're all easier to bear because he has a plan. He'll cut the tracker out and escape tonight.

"Legion?" he tries, forcing his voice to sound conversational.

The man says, "Hmm, I'd say medium. You're almost a small right now, but you'll fill out some when you're not killing yourself with healing."

Humming under his breath, the man pulls a scuffed silver plate—about as long as his thumb, with a length of dense chain on each end—from a box. He places the plate into a bulky metal contraption, fiddling with a few dials before pulling a lever so the top half of the machine slams down. When he lifts the lever, the plate is stamped with a series of letters and numbers: (S-S)WS/2417

He seizes Tory's wrist again, and Tory barely flinches when the chains close around it.

"Welcome to the Box."

CHAPTER FIVE

THE STOLEN SCALPEL warms between Tory's fingers as Vantaras leads him to a sterile hall labeled *Residence Quarters (C)*. "You'll soon have a stellite tab to access your room and other public areas. For today, you'll need to knock on the door and get your roommate to let you in."

"Roommate."

"You'll be sharing with another Seed. Sword corps—the offensive branch. A Kineticist, I believe."

Helner said Kineticists are bruiser types. *This'll be great.*

"You'll be in C114, at the end of the hall."

Tory peers down the short hallway. The space between one gray door and the next doesn't bode well for the size of the rooms. If he's going to cut his tracker out tonight, he'll need someplace more private. The changing room could work. "Then why aren't we down there?"

Vantaras' lips thin. "I didn't wish to make a scene."

Adrenaline floods Tory. "Make a—?"

The stellite lighting along the walls shifts red before Tory can finish, pulsing in beats like a living heart. Vantaras stiffens and turns to go. "Stay here."

"What's wrong? What's happening?" Tory grabs his arm before he can walk away.

Vantaras twists out of his grasp, withdrawing a wicked black baton and pressing it against Tory's chest. The force of his forearm behind it knocks the breath from Tory's lungs and gives him a terrible close-up of Vantaras' amber eyes, visceral and vibrant in this light, brighter than flame. "Stay *here*. I'll deal with you later."

The pressure leaves Tory all at once and Vantaras backs away, the communicator on his chest flickering brilliant blue. A cold voice comes through. *"Infiltrators in Intake. Rebel Seeds. I trust you'll put an end to them."*

Infiltrators.

The *rebels*. Hasra's stories swirl in his mind, and terrible joy flickers to life in Tory. If he can get to them, he can free himself. Maybe even join them. The impulses he's crushed down for years roar back all at once, unstoppable. He has a weapon, meager though it is. Now is no time for keeping his head down, for not making waves. If ever there was a time to fight, it's now.

He's following after Vantaras before he knows what he's doing, scalpel clutched in hand.

Vantaras is already at the end of the hall, cranking a lever as he passes. Some sort of mechanism creaks and clanks, and a thick door begins to close from both sides of the hallway.

Tory barely makes it through before the thing can crush him.

Vantaras is too far ahead—Tory can do little more than chase whispers of his shadow around corners and the taps of his running feet on the polished floor. It doesn't take long for him to lose Tory entirely, but by then he's close enough to find the fray by sound.

When Tory first arrived here, there was something eerie about the wide, bright cleanliness, all stark lines and cruel precision. The red light does no favors to the place, turning the halls dim and nightmarish. Tory misses a step and catches himself on the wall when an ear-piercing boom splits the air, then another.

Gunshots. Someone cries out.

Tory rounds the corner and takes the chaos in.

Arms extended, gun gripped in gloved hands and hair dusting over one eye, Vantaras is something otherworldly in the flare and fade of the light. With everything painted red, it takes Tory a moment too long to recognize the blood—a vivid smear of it on one pale cheek. It pools on the floor ahead of Vantaras and marks the ground with spatters and smears for a few more feet before stopping abruptly. Strange. There's no one else in the hall, but judging by the blood, they didn't make it to the door.

Relaxing out of a shooting stance, Vantaras holsters his handgun. They're gone.

Tory grips his scalpel harder.

He's *this close* to the entrance. He could make a run for it. If the rebels are still out there, he could catch up. There's only one person between Tory and the yard.

"Report." A tall, lean figure paces toward Vantaras from the opposite direction, too obscured by the light for Tory to make out his face. Tory grimaces.

Two people, then, between him and freedom. Worse, but not impossible.

"Five infiltrators, Sir," Vantaras says, unmoved. He withdraws a kerchief from his pocket and wipes the blood from his face. "I wounded one of them, two shots to the gut. When they realized they would make it no farther inside, they evacuated."

"They *escaped*," the emotionless voice says. "You let them escape."

"Sir!" Vantaras pockets the kerchief and stands rigid. "Intake holds incredibly important records and resources, and Dr. Helner and the sensitive equipment in her lab are nearby. It seemed wiser to preserve the Compound's resources and its sole Reacher than to pursue them and put STAR-7's inhabitants at risk." He pauses. "They had a Teleporter, which I assume is how they got this far. I cannot pursue and wasn't near enough to prevent them from 'porting away, but I don't expect the Seed with the abdominal wound to survive for long."

Vantaras' full attention is on the lean officer. His weapon is holstered, gloved hands clutched behind him. Tory might be able to sneak by before he can draw it. It's worth a shot.

Tory sucks in a breath and moves.

A steel-solid grip closes on his upper arm before he gets far.

"Sir," Vantaras grits out. "It seems my new supervisee was in a hurry to arrange introductions. Colonel, this is Tory Arknett, STAR-7's new Channeler."

Tory tries to free himself from Vantaras' grip, but it's stone-solid.

"He should have been secured," the so-called colonel says.

The coldness of his voice is what makes Tory look. Standing in a well-ironed dress uniform with platinum-pale hair in an undercut, the colonel is unremarkable at first glance—willowy-tall and fine-featured. Early forties, maybe, just enough for crow's feet.

That's where the normalcy ends.

He offers Tory a cursory smile. It has all the necessary tweaks—the upward turn of the lips, the crinkling of eyes paler than the silvery edge of a blade, the flash of white teeth—but it's cracked-mask cold and soulless. It falls too fast. He doesn't rock or shift where he stands, statue-still like his heart doesn't beat.

Tory knows this kind of man, has cleaned up after his type in the Houses when they left one of the employees bleeding and half-conscious.

"Seed," the colonel says with a thin-lipped nod in Tory's direction.

Tory spits on the floor to let the guy know what he thinks of the greeting.

"Insubordinate." The colonel retreats like Tory spat on him, expression warping with delicate distaste.

Vantaras goes still, grip on Tory's arm going bone-crushing. "I'll see to it that he's put away in his room."

Put away. Like a weapon, a thing. Tory seethes.

"See that you do. Your father will be hearing about this, Lieutenant."

"Yes, Sir." Vantaras turns so quickly and pulls so hard that the socket of Tory's arm shrieks with pain and he has little choice but to follow, a potent mix of helpless rage boiling in his belly. He looks back, wondering if he can free himself and make for the door, but the colonel has moved to stand in the middle of the hall, deadly sharp gaze narrowed on Tory.

Vantaras yanks harder, his too-fast stride nearly pulling Tory off his feet. He hisses, "Do you not understand the meaning of *stay*?"

They wait for what feels like an eternity until the massive, mechanical door that closed the inhabitants of *Residence Quarters (C)* into their hallway clanks open again. No one left their rooms to see what was happening. The single person standing in an open doorway yelps and retreats inside her room at the sight of Vantaras.

Once they're inside, Vantaras pulls Tory to such an abrupt stop that he nearly overbalances.

Face beaded with sweat in the eerie, flashing light, Vantaras shakes his gloved hand like he handled something wriggly and wrong instead of holding Tory's arm through an additional layer of cloth. "When I give you an order, I expect you to obey it."

"Do you really?" Bile burns the back of Tory's throat. He was so close he could smell fresh air. He could see the light of the outside, yellow-dim and warm. Those rebels had a Teleporter. They could have gotten Tory out.

But he still has the scalpel. "You said my room's at the end of the hall?"

"I did."

"Good. I'll find it myself. Thanks for nothing."

"No." Two quick steps. An extended arm stops Tory from advancing.

Turning, he bares his teeth at Vantaras, but the asshole's impassive expression doesn't even twitch. He's clearly been taking lessons from the colonel.

"I'll need you to hand it over."

Tory's fists clench—a mistake. He hisses as the scalpel's blade sinks into a fingertip. "Hand what over?"

"Whatever it is you're holding."

Blood tickles a path between his fingers. Tory presses them tighter and forces out a surprised laugh. "I don't know what you mean."

The plink of his blood on titanium-white tile betrays him.

Vantaras' eyes follow the path of another drop—two, three—that make a trail as Tory shifts that side of his body away.

"Surrender it willingly, or I'll take it by force."

Anger and humiliation make a wreck of Tory's gut. If his mom were here, she'd tell him to let it go. Maybe she'd be right. But Tory's been beneath the heel of men like this all his life, and he's had a *perfect* smile for every one of them. He's been so very, very agreeable.

"Why don't you try then, *Sena*." The words burn on their way out, equal parts thrill and adrenaline.

"If you insist."

It happens too quickly to process, between the moment the red lights sink into darkness and when they blare bright again.

Darkness: a hand on his opposite shoulder makes him jerk away, exposing his left side.

Red light, making something cruel of Vantaras' silhouette: he seizes Tory's upper arm again in a manacle-tight grip and lifts it, snatching the handle from his fingers.

He releases Tory's arm and retreats, white gloves immaculate, scalpel dangling from two fingers. With an elegant flick, he tucks the pointed edge into the holster at his left side, against the gun he used to shoot a fleeing rebel in the gut.

Lights out. In darkness, Vantaras says, "In future, you'll call me by my rank." They flare again. "We won't speak of this further. Find your room."

"If you really think—"

"Insubordination gets you hurt here. There's enough trouble in a day; only fools make more."

Tory nearly staggers at how wrong those words are on this officer's lips. How *familiar*.

Don't make waves, his mother told him, and he took it as scripture. Now, Vantaras says *don't make trouble*.

Why did he never realize it before? They're both such pretty ways to say *lie down and take it*. Tory has practiced appeasement so long it's his native tongue, and for what?

All these years, all that effort, and maybe he's not in the labor camps but he's still in a windowless box barely large enough to breathe in. They have him, locked up and marked up and numbered and tagged, an animal for their use.

All at once, the red lights die and the brutal, blinding white comes back. Tory flings up a hand to block it, but Vantaras' bitter sneer is seared on his eyes.

He never asked for this. Never asked his mom to free him, never asked to be able to heal, for Thatcher or Hasra or—whatever they called it... redirection. For this delicate rich boy who's taken his freedom *twice*. His mother begged Tory to keep his head down because she thought it might save him—thought it could have saved her when she was free. But it's clearer now that he's hearing those words on his enemy's lips: Tory's obedience would only be a favor to Vantaras, and he's in no hurry to make *anything* easy for this bastard.

Tory rasps a shattered-glass laugh and whips his wounded hand out to grab Vantaras' glove. He leaves behind a slash of red, and he can't push down the smile that warps his lips. He hopes the things are ruined, hopes they never wash clean.

"Enough," he says.

After years of aching, it's time for Tory to *fight*.

Lucky him, he knows exactly who his opponent will be.

Anger uncoils in him, sharp and serpentine. Tory pushes forward in one long stride, lowering the hand that covers his face and baring his teeth. "It'd be convenient for you, wouldn't it, if I didn't make trouble?"

Vantaras blinks at his sullied gloves, face paling to something a half-step shy of horror. His lips press thin, and he glances back the way they came. A smooth turn, and he retreats with an urgent *click-click-click* of polished boots on tile.

"Find your quarters," is his final pronouncement. "I'll see you tomorrow."

The terrible thing inside Tory doesn't leave when Vantaras does. His insides roil, ears attuned to every mechanical click and grind of his prison. He loses time outside the door. When he inhabits himself again, his blood is cold and tacky on his palm, the cut on his finger beginning to clot.

This *won't* be his last chance to run. He'll find another. He needs darkness, quiet, rest. Anything but the all-seeing light in the hallway. Tory twists at the knob on the door, but it won't budge. Right. He'll have to knock. He beats at it until someone inside rouses to open it.

He's immediately the target of three cool stares. Two men sit on a mattress to the left of the door, cards in hand and a messy pile of blue and red chips between them.

Tory must be glaring, because their gazes grow cooler.

The one who answered the door, square-jawed and thick with muscle, spits, "Who're *you*?"

Tory waves his bleeding hand at his uniform. His muscles protest the movement, bones weighted with iron from healing Kelly. Fat lot of good that did him. Vantaras probably took all his money along with Thatcher's cloak when he arrested Tory.

The cloak. He pushes its weight and warmth from his mind. It's gone now. He doesn't need it. doesn't need the connections that tied him to it—and to Hulven.

"Roommate?" the muscled guy growls.

Tory stares at the other two men. Both solidly built. Could probably kick his insides outside of him without breaking a sweat. The gray room is as narrow as he feared. In the back, a single, dim-yellow strip of lighting fails to illuminate anything.

Tory blinks and his eyes long to stay closed.

His roommate retreats from the door and slaps his cards down on his bedding. "Thought I had this place to myself."

"Not anymore." Tory slides into the room before the door slams on him. His shoulder throbs where Helner installed the Core, the vinegar-bite of nausea sharp on his tongue. A mountain of papers, strange tokens, and miscellaneous mess buries the bed to the right of the door.

"Mine?" Tory flicks a crumpled ball of paper across the room.

"That's my desk." The guy laughs.

He could give it up, could sleep on the floor under the tall beds. It's what he would've done before. He's slept in dirtier places, shared breath and space with ten others in a room this size. He's probably never slept in a place this clean. If he has to share this space with someone, he should make nice.

Anger feeds the nausea inside him. Like Vantaras and so many before him, his roommate would be overjoyed if Tory kept his silence.

Fuck that.

"Look." Tory gathers the junk in his arms and walks to his roommate's bed, dropping it on top of the cards and tokens. A stiff, balled up tissue bounces off his roommate's knee and falls to the floor. "I feel like I was chewed up and shit out twice. I'm going to sleep."

That thrill again. Freedom of expression—the only freedom he has left.

The bed has nothing but a mattress, dark blue. The color does its best to hide the crusty edges of some milky fluid or another. He's seen worse. He tips horizontal and curls up facing the wall. Tucking his knees close to his chest, he wraps one arm around them, pillowing his head on the other. The wound on his finger twinges, hand empty without the scalpel clutched inside.

This place is nothing like the labor camp with its dust and dirt and high fences, nights punctuated by groaning old men with festering wounds on nearby bedrolls, too weak for the soldiers with their sharp uniforms and full bellies to bother treating. It's clean here—cold and clinical. It's *different*. He makes it a mantra. The room is small and gets smaller as his breaths speed up.

It may be different, but it's just another set of walls.

Tory's done making himself small enough to step on. He'll get out of here—and until he does, he'll make Vantaras' life a living waste.

Across the room, the guys whisper, rough and pointed. They're talking about him.

Yesterday, he might have cared.

PART TWO:

Fight

CHAPTER SIX

THE UNRELENTING CLATTER of an alarm bell rips Tory from rest at an hour no reasonable creatures crawl from their holes. He sits up on his naked mattress and looks to his roommate for cues. No luck. The man's dead to the world.

The bell keeps going. It's coming from behind a metal grate close to the ceiling at the back of the room, which means Tory can't beat it into silence.

The first thing from his roommate's lips when he wakes is, "Dammit."

"What's happening?" Tory chances, rolling out of bed.

"Breakfast. Training."

That's something. He can follow the guy to wherever they eat.

His roommate tips out of bed and glares muzzily at Tory. "You were rotten last night, y'know that?"

Tory grimaces. That might've been a bad move. He's not here to make friends, but he knows *exactly* where he needs to point his cutting edge, and it's not at people trapped here like him. "I felt it. Bad day."

His roommate grunts and tugs the door open. "Fair. Food's this way." The cardplayers from last night, hunched and yawning, wait outside. "Normally you'd need to make your bed before leaving the room, but . . ." He flicks a hand at the bare, disgusting mattress.

"Yeah. Where can I get blankets?"

The second point on the card-playing trio, a tall guy with rat-like features, offers, "Closet two doors down has bedding. It's locked, though. Your supervisor didn't give you the stuff?"

Vantaras, that *bastard*.

His roommate laughs. "Who'd ya get, Menden? Fella's senile."

They stop in front of the closet door.

His roommate gestures to the third cardplayer—short and thick, with a clumsily shaven head and a scar that makes a furrow through his left ear and cheek. "Rendt here's got your back; he can break in and no one'll know. He did it for some of Menden's other supervisees."

"Don't know Menden. My supervisor's this guy Vantaras. And nah—I can do without a blanket until I see him next. Wanna make him work."

The men go quiet.

"*Vantaras* is your supervisor? What's your type?" Tory's roommate snags his wrist. "Synergistic. And . . . WS? What the—?"

Tory pulls his wrist away. It might be better to keep his cards close to his chest, say only a little. What was it Helner said, about the carriage? "Something about kinetic energy."

"Nah, man, I'm Kinetic." His roommate thrusts his hand at Tory, baring a tag that reads (S)K/2084. "You don't have the K."

"She said I threw concussive force."

Scar-face smirks. "Oh," he says. "Oh, man. You got Seedbait for a roommate. You'll get the bed back in no time."

Tory doesn't like the sound of that. "What's Seedbait?"

"Come on, they send you people to the front lines to catch bullets for us. You're cannon fodder. Corpse corps. *Seedbait.*"

Tory shudders.

"Ain't they CF, though? This guy's WS."

"Wouldn't be the first time the idiots in the labs fell asleep on the job." His roomie shrugs. "Well, look. I'm Gavin."

"Tory."

Gavin shakes his head. "Seriously, why'd they put the Lune on *Seedbait?*"

Scar-face punches Gavin in the shoulder and levels a look at Tory that could melt glass. "Pick up the pace. If we're too late for eggs and gravy, I take it out on your roommate here."

They speed up, dodging sleepy Seeds through nondescript halls. It's hopeless to memorize the route. "What's the deal with Vantaras, anyway? It's not like he's actually the big guy's son."

All three men look at Tory like he's sprouted a new head. "You can't be serious."

"As a sucking chest wound."

"You think there's any *other* Vantaras who'd dare to bear the Grand General's name? 'Course he's the guy's son."

"But he's not . . ." Tory makes shapes with his hands. Bullish, boxy. Old.

"Nah, it's a whole thing. He's half Lune, half Vantaras. Not good enough for Daddy, so he got shipped off to the Box. When his first wife died, Papa Vantaras picked up some chick from across the border, married her. Rumor has it he wasn't just after her *assets*. He wanted information, connections—whatever it is those bastards use to slaughter us so well when we've got three times the fighting force. The way her kid got tossed in the Box, I'm guessing Mama didn't fess up. So the General went to war for it, and he sent Mama's boy out to the ass-end of nowhere to make sure it all ran smooth."

"Real smooth," Gavin's rat-faced friend mutters. "He the one that caught you, Seedbait?"

Tory nods.

"Join the club. They send him out to catch all the escaped Seeds—the suspected ones, too. He's never failed, not once. *Perfect* capture rate."

"Yeah? Well, fuck him very mu—"

He rounds the corner and runs straight into Vantaras, who jerks back, lips pressed tight. Hair neatly brushed, dusting over one eye. Uniform flawless, while Tory stands in rumpled prison clothes. Vantaras with his prim posture and his white gloves, pressing people like Tory into unspeakable prisons and onto battlefronts for his father's pleasure. Shame and anger make a bonfire in Tory's belly. The finger his scalpel nicked aches.

"Good morning, Arknett," Vantaras says.

Tory crosses his arms.

"I'm expected to show you to the mess hall."

"I can get there on my own."

Vantaras' eyes pass over Gavin and his gamblers, cold. He doesn't even have to speak to make them scatter.

Tory glares at their retreating backs. "Or not."

"You won't be entering with the rest. Follow me." He strides away before Tory can respond.

Down the hall they go, past an endless line of people in washed-out gray-blue. It terminates in front of a set of wide double-doors. Dr. Helner waits on the far side of the doors, flanked by a straggly-haired middle-aged man on one side and the blond officer from yesterday on the other.

Vantaras stands at attention. "Good morning, Sir."

"At ease, Lieutenant." Blondie turns his gaze to Tory. "I don't think we had the opportunity for proper introductions yesterday. I am Colonel Erwin Kirlov. I oversee the First Lieutenant."

Heat spills through Tory's chest. Vantaras needs *oversight*, does he? This guy seems like a real stickler, too.

Kirlov turns his flat gaze on Dr. Helner. "You may leave, doctor."

She smiles. "And miss the chance to guide our Channeler? No, thank you."

The doors of the mess hall creak open, and Seeds pour inside in neat rows. Helner watches like she's observing a colony of ants. Kirlov watches like he'll gun down the first man to step out of line.

Inside, people fill their plates with a *feast* of different foods. Tory moves to follow, but Helner surges forward and clamps a hand on his shoulder. "Wait a second. I'll be supervising your food intake, remember? Same for Prentice here." Helner gestures to the straggly fellow with gray-streaked brown hair.

"Supervising our food intake?" Tory winces.

"The higher-ups want to make good use of both of you and will work you especially hard given your aptitudes, so they've made allowances regarding your allotment of tokens. We'll be packing your diet with nutrients. Can't have you getting ill before we have our fun with you."

Prentice smirks. "Degrading, ain't it? You'll get used to it."

That's what he's afraid of.

"Hey, I'm Prentice." The guy extends a sun-darkened hand. "Teleporter. Had a cushy gig in the priority mail service up in Maran—folks don't like to wait for their packages there—but they called me back to the Box to train for the battlefield. Desperate times, you know?" He grins. "Anyway, you're in good hands . . . probably.

Just watch out for needles. Our doctor here has ideas about how the Box should categorize and organize Seeds. Revolutionizing the process one experiment at a time."

"The current process serves," Kirlov grits out.

Helner laughs, flat and brutal. "If losing thirty percent of your shield corps every time they run into a Legion unit *serves* you."

There that word is again. Legion. Before Tory can ask what it means, the last few sleepy stragglers pace into the mess hall, and that must be their cue to enter. Nearly everyone else is seated when Helner leads Tory and Prentice through the lines, talking loudly about nutrition and wise choices. By the time she finishes, Tory has studiously ignored at least three calls of, "Hey, *Special Diet!*"

At least he has a heaping tray to show for his humiliation. There are a few times in his life Tory would have killed for a meal like this. A whole room of full plates, and the food's not even gone. He could go back for more. He starts stuffing his face before he's seated.

Vantaras and Kirlov settle in at the same table. Vantaras begins to daintily cut into his own food with his knife and fork held just so, and a plan hatches in Tory's head.

He needs bedding, anyway. Carving a rift between Vantaras and his stickler overseer will be a satisfying byproduct. He doesn't need that scalpel to draw blood.

He leans in, pitching his voice bright and curious. "Hey, where should I get blankets and pillows and stuff? I made do with the mattress last night, figured maybe you just forgot when you ran off to deal with those intruders and left me in the hall."

He offers Vantaras a sweet smile with all the poison he can inject into it.

The fingers of Kirlov's right hand drift over his watch, tapping the dial with sharp notes like gunshots.

Oh, yes. He's hit a nerve.

Kirlov speaks first. "Yes, I believe we need to have a conversation about you leaving your supervisee unattended last night, Lieutenant."

Vantaras swallows, a dry click. "It was an oversight. I apologize."

Kirlov frowns. "Lieu*tenant*."

Vantaras' spine straightens. "Sir! It won't happen again. I'll be sure to prepare bedding for the Worldseed after breakfast."

A stickler indeed. Tory suppresses a grin. The more fraught they are, the less effective information exchange will be between them. Little drips carve rifts in mountains—wide enough to escape through, if Tory's lucky.

He chirps, "I'd love that. I don't want to be an inconvenience."

"Not at all," Vantaras grits out.

Kirlov turns to Tory. "The lieutenant's negligence aside, I believe the Grand General has decided to train you for Concussive Force Redirection."

Seedbait. Gavin was right.

Helner stabs her fork into a pile of eggs. "Against my explicit recommendation. There's so much more we could learn about the Sources if we took the time to test them."

"That time is better spent defending our borders. Arlunian incursions have increased as their holy holidays approach, and the Channeler's abilities could turn the tide of the war."

"You're *wasting* him in CFR! Next week he could be a smear on some minor battlefield, and all the things we could have learned from him will be gone."

"The Grand General feels the risk is worth the potential reward."

"Your *general* knows nothing about how to make proper use of the Seeds here."

Kirlov arches an eyebrow. "Your many failed experiments say the same of you."

"*Thirty percent.* You want to play with those odds?"

Kirlov spears a baby carrot. "It's not my game, Doctor. Or yours."

"It should be!" A blotchy flush crawls up Helner's neck. "This is ridiculous. Sena, isn't this the biggest farce you've ever seen? You know it, too. I saw you."

Vantaras turns away and says nothing.

Kirlov taps his watch again. "Yes, Lieutenant. I'd be interested to hear your answer."

This is so much better than Tory could have hoped for. He tosses a bite of thick-cut bacon in his mouth and chews with relish.

"I—I don't—" Vantaras' left hand snags his right sleeve, and he rubs his thumb in circles over the textured fabric, fast enough to burn the skin off. "I believe the Grand General has his reasons."

"*Coward*," Helner spits. "And they call me a traitor."

Kirlov ignores her. To Tory, he says, "You'll sit in on CFR type-training this afternoon." Then he turns to Vantaras, cold eyes reflecting no light. "Lieutenant, I know you will not make mistakes like these again. Report to me when you've settled Mr. Arknett in, and we will review your duties toward your supervisee. I will *not* tolerate delay."

"Of course, Sir."

Tory digs into everything that remains on his plate with gusto.

Vantaras goes at his with calculated slowness, lining up the steamed carrots before eating them like they're his personal firing squad. Despite his smaller portion, he finishes shortly after Tory and stands up. "I'll take you to get bedding."

Tory almost has to run to keep up with Vantaras' inhumanly long strides. The way he glances back, lip curling, Tory's certain he's doing it on purpose.

When they arrive in residence quarters, Vantaras tugs from his breast pocket a milky-pale slice of stone enclosed in a metal setting and attached to a chain. Stellite? It looks like it, but it's faint and flawed. Whatever it is, it responds to the corresponding sliver above the door's knob with a brief pulse of light, and the lock on the supply closet clicks open. In short order, Vantaras shoves a pile of linen into Tory's arms. "One bedsheet, one fitted sheet, one blanket, and a pillow. You'll receive new bedding on a weekly basis and must make your bed each morning. Uncleanliness may result in penalties or withdrawal of privileges." He pulls something from his pocket, another slice of stone like the one on his ring. "This is your tab. Keep it with you. It has been keyed to your blood, which is now keyed to your room and all doors that have been marked as public access. Do not lose it. Do you have any questions?"

Vantaras drops the stone slice on top of the bedding in Tory's arms.

It *is* stellite, but even from this close—close enough to press the tip of his nose to it with little effort—there's barely any of the crushing strangeness he's learned to associate with the stone. Like the lights, it feels ruined. Dead.

"I said, do you have any *questions*?" Impatient.

Ah. The Kirlov guy said he wouldn't tolerate delay. Ever so slowly, Tory tries out the strange tab on his door. It does, indeed, unlock it. "Let me think," he says.

Vantaras taps a finger against his opposite wrist in an agitated rhythm while Tory flips his crusty mattress—he'd have done it last night if he'd had his head on straight—and puts the bedding on.

"What's next for me, then?" Tory finally drawls.

"You'll attend basic training after breakfast each morning, though you'll be missing it today. Type-training—which we'll observe today—follows lunch. You'll have maneuvers after that. Trainees receive meal tokens for compliance or find them withheld for lack thereof, but given the higher-ups' interest in your abilities, they will be motivated to keep you healthy. You'll face other penalties for noncompliance."

"Looking forward to it."

"You shouldn't. Will that be all?"

But he's already walking away.

"Hey!" Tory calls, and Vantaras clicks to a stop, shoulders taut. "That blond guy seems like a real piece of work. Why do you listen to him?"

"*That blond guy* is Colonel Kirlov. You'd do well to call him by his rank."

Social niceties serve only the strong. He'd do well to have given up on them years ago.

He hates this place, hates this man, hates being trapped here. Tory's body has never been less free, but there's still something thrilling about not having to gulp down ugly words.

His mom was wrong. Silence never saved him. Or if it did, it carved other, deeper wounds.

He sneers at Vantaras. "You don't want me making waves, you should have thought of that before dragging me here."

The look Vantaras gives him—silent and impossibly still—sends a shudder through Tory.

He strides away without another word.

*

When Vantaras returns after lunch, something's wrong. That oddness—and Tory's inability to make sense of it—raises the hair on the back of his neck.

"The colonel apologizes," Vantaras bites out, leading Tory down the hall. His usually blistering-fast pace is slower, smooth strides truncated. "He would have liked to accompany you to type-training but was called away by other duties. He sent me in his stead."

"In his stead," Tory echoes.

Vantaras slows, turns, blinks. He's sweaty under the savage light, and Tory can't tell whether he's glaring or squinting. "He asked me to send his regrets."

"Come on, where'd you learn to talk like this? In his *stead*. Where's the dial that turns you off?"

Vantaras' lips twist in a mockery of amusement. "Ask the colonel."

He stalks forward without explanation.

"*What?*" Tory scrambles after him. "You regret dragging me here yet, *Sena?*"

"Lieutenant Vantaras."

"Lieu-what?"

"The way you will address me."

"*Will* I?" Tory picks up his pace, racing until he's side by side with Vantaras then alternating fast walking and almost jogging to stay there. "Where are we going, anyway?"

"The yard." Lips quirking up, Vantaras adds, "Don't fall behind."

They step out of a set of double doors to a wide stretch of yellowed, pitted grass and a collection of people in clothes like Tory's. The cannons mounted on the walls around the Compound spit black spheres at them. Some stop midair and drop before reaching their targets. Others drive into the yard and kick up mud. A man with a shock of white hair stands in the midst of the chaos, waving his hands like a conductor.

Before they get close, he grins, scurrying over to meet them. "Isn't it positively *symphonic?*"

Vantaras stands straighter. "Lieutenant-Colonel Menden."

Menden—precisely as decrepit as Gavin said he was—waves both hands. "Retired, I'm retired! It's just Menden. And *you* must be our Channeler."

Menden must've left octogenarianism behind decades ago, his pale skin thin and liver-spotted but his eyes bright and aware. The trousers he wears look to be military issue, but his long-sleeved shirt is wide open at the neck and dyed every color Tory has ever seen and then some. He encompasses the training field with a sweeping gesture and arches bushy eyebrows. "So, what do you think of Concussive Force Redirection, Tory?"

A black sphere slams into the earth and explodes in a splash of cold water all over Tory's pant leg. He jerks away. "*Water balloons?*"

Menden laughs like this is the best joke he's heard all week. "What did you expect, explosive rounds? No use killing all our CFRs *before* they're deployed! But don't look down on them. We have to match the velocity of the projectiles our unit might face in a real-life situation, which necessitates a more durable casing for the balloons. Packs a bone-breaking punch." His eyes light up. "Jeffra told me her infirmary would be all but empty if it weren't for my people! Keeps her and the rest of the support corps on their toes: Healers need training, too!" Menden dodges another projectile, gently pushing Tory out of the way as two more crash into the ground, kicking up mud and bits of grass.

Menden spins to the small group trying to stop the projectiles. "Step it *up*," he yells, voice high and rattling. "You're the *shield* corps, damn it! Act like it! The sword and support corps will rely on *you* for protection on the battlefield. Next time I see one of these hit the ground without being redirected, I move you ten yards closer and put you at the front of the pack for maneuvers!"

Tory shivers. "And everyone in this unit ends up on the front lines?"

Menden has scurried away to yell at the trainees, so it's Vantaras who responds. "Without exception. The first through sixth STAR Compounds train Seeds to serve in Maran and other major cities, but STAR-7 was built here specifically to train battle-capable Seed types to hold back Arlunian incursions. Every Seed here is a type useful in war."

Menden paces back and waves a hand at them. "Vantaras, my boy, over here. Can't have you getting in the way."

Vantaras is well apart from any of the Seeds in the yard, but he sidesteps until he's shaded in the sparse grove of trees from which Menden supervises training.

"You know I don't mean anything by it, but there are always more injuries when you're here."

"I understand."

Menden claps a hand on Tory's shoulder before he can parse that exchange. "Glad to have you, Tory! Don't think I'll let you get away with just watching today! After the break, we'll see what you're made of, hmm?"

An awful groan drags Tory's attention back to the yard as a balloon nails one of the trainees in the stomach, driving him back a couple of feet before he doubles over, retching.

Menden sucks in a breath. "*Ohhhh*, the gut's the worst."

"I . . . I don't think I can . . ." Tory's not even sure how he did it the first time.

Menden flaps a hand. "Boy, we can train you in simulated situations for years, but it won't do any good. If I want you to survive a day out there, I need to throw real obstacles at you. Real harm. You and I, we'll start slow today, but we *will* start."

CHAPTER SEVEN

Watching water balloons barrel toward people and being in the middle of the fray when it's happening prove to be two entirely different things. After a brief break, Vantaras directs Tory to enter the yard and settles in beside Menden.

Figures the bastard would stick around to watch him suffer.

As promised, Menden has the others move in close, the wall-mounted cannons aimed steeply downward. Only two cannons lob the balloons farther out.

"These'll have sort of a lazy arc to them," Menden says. "It's the easiest they'll ever be for you. Good luck!"

That's all he gets before the cannons open fire, eerily precise.

"Stellite targeting system," Menden chirps as Tory barely avoids a balloon barreling toward his face. "Precision at its finest; stellite is drawn to almost every flavor of Seed energy, so you can't run from it. It'll just follow you!"

Tory trips to the left to avoid a projectile.

"Don't dodge them, fool boy! *Stop* them."

"I don't know how!"

"Well, then. Carry on!"

Vantaras leans back against a tree, arms crossed.

One to the shoulder doubles Tory over, choking and gasping. For an instant, with the force of the blow, the water feels hot. It's *freezing*. Another explodes against his thigh with the tissue-deep throb of a nascent bruise. Tory reflexively lifts his hands and closes his eyes, but it's useless. This is nothing like healing.

Tory lurches toward Menden, grabbing his shoulders and steering him toward the cannons. *Precision* indeed. The cannons follow Tory even with Menden as a human shield between them. "Tell me what to *do*!"

A projectile barely misses them, and Menden issues a shriek that tapers into high-pitched laughter.

"Harness it! You—if you let yourself, you can feel the energies. You *especially* should be able to feel them. Regular CFR Seeds work based on sight alone—simple recognition and transference of energy. You're a Channeler, and the world is *made* of energies. If the old records are right, you should be able to handle them all, which means you can—" they duck away from a balloon that would have nailed Menden in the face "—certainly handle the energies that drive these!" Another balloon splatters a foot away from them. "These things? Plain old kinetic energy. When you've improved, we'll have Kineticists accelerate a slew of projectiles at you so you can get practice redirecting natural *and* Seed-enhanced energies!"

They skitter back as two more balloons drive into the grass, spitting water up Tory's ankles. He closes his eyes, but there's nothing to *harness*. Just a biting wind and his body begging him for rest. "Seed enhanced? A *slew*?"

"Oh, yes! You'll be a great asset on the battlefield. See, the Arlunian soldiers—"

Tory drags them left.

"*Merciless*. Every weapon they use is Seed-modified—made faster, more powerful, more lethal." Menden skips them back, far too graceful. "This is terribly inefficient, Tory, please. Anyway, I'm sure you've heard what they call this unit."

Seedbait. The *Corpse Corps*.

"We've had *no* Seeds capable of redirecting Seed-modified attacks before you, and our enemy knows it. CFR Seeds cannot handle the volume of energy that you can. We've had to trust our Fielders' shields to repel the weapons they fail to stop—and they fail to stop a lot! They don't have the Channeler's rumored ability to discern energies and can only affect what they can see, so by the time the attacks get close enough to *stop*, they're also close enough to cause damage when they fall, which in turn leaves far too heavy a burden on our Fielders. With Seed-enhanced weaponry hitting them from all directions, it's only a matter of time until their forcefields fail." Menden runs them ahead of the next balloon. "But if you can do what we expect you can, you could *single-handedly* free the Fielders from that burden by redirecting massive volumes of both kinetic and Seed-directed attacks. Better still, you won't tire as quickly. Handling different flavors of energy should theoretically be like using different muscles—you'll have both wider range and greater stamina. Fewer fatalities, more opportunities to mount an offensive." Menden laughs. "You could change everything!"

"That's bullshit!"

He pushes Menden away and runs backward. The unblinking eye of the cannon follows him, belting balloons that nip at his heels. He tries to do what Menden told him. Sense the energy. It's the stupidest thing he's ever heard.

The water makes sludge of the ground and slicks down the yellowing grass. Someone up ahead gets pounded in the chest with a full-speed projectile. The cold wind freezes Tory and locks his muscles. It's useless. There's no energy that sings to him, nothing for Tory to hold onto.

"If I may." Vantaras' cool voice rises from Tory's right. He strides onto the field like it's nothing—dry and warm in his tailored uniform. The cannon angles away as he enters the field. He must be wearing something that stops it.

If Tory could see straight, he could steal the thing. Instead, he shivers, doubled over and gasping, when those perfect, polished boots stop in front of him. He glares up, soaked to his skin, and whips wet hair from his eyes. "W-what . . . do you want?"

"This is painful to watch."

"Then *stop watching.*"

"I've been ordered to observe."

"And you're s-such a good little soldier."

Vantaras' lips thin. Direct hit.

It feels good, being on more equal ground. "You listen to everything that guy tells you? *Come, sit, stay?*"

Something burns in Vantaras' fire-bright eyes. He pulls a kerchief from the front pocket of his uniform. Rich blue-green, it catches the stormy gray light with a low shine, like it's silk or something. Snob.

Carefully, he folds it—maybe two inches wide—over and over itself.

Tory's stomach flips, brain registering too late what he plans to do. "What are you—?"

Vantaras' lips twist up in a vengeful expression quite unlike a smile. He shifts behind Tory, and before Tory can make his cold-clumsy limbs move, Vantaras has pulled the cloth over his eyes and knotted it behind his head. A landscape of perfect darkness spreads out.

Vantaras says, "I think you should try it like this."

Tory reaches up to tear off the kerchief.

"I'll rephrase." The voice comes now from Tory's right side, low and cold. "You *will* do it like this. I don't believe you'll like what happens if you remove the blindfold."

Tory spits in his direction, but he can't know if he hits his mark.

He does, however, know the moment Vantaras leaves. There's a distant whine as the cannons recalibrate, and the barrage continues. Tory hears a whistling *whoosh* an instant before all breath is wrenched from his chest and he falls back into the mud. He inhales water and chokes it up, shuddering as he forces himself onto his knees.

Tory will let this petty punishment slide. He'll play at docility for now—and only for now—so Vantaras won't see it when Tory comes for him.

After a while, it's not so bad. If he listens for the whistle of their passage, he can dodge the balloons well enough. Most times, anyway. One nails his knee, and agony stabs through him, sharper than the dull gongs of cold. He staggers.

"Try harder!" Vantaras calls.

It's like the deal he made in Hulven for healing. He can do nothing but agree, without even the freedom to negotiate the terms of his surrender. The ache all through him feels like the pain after a healing, too. He misses everything he used to have, and he hates that he misses it, because healing hurt and Hulven, too, was a prison—and he a fool for willingly remaining in it—but it was better than this. One or two fewer walls, wind charms, and prayers to dispel the choking fuel fog. Two mugs of steaming tea on the table: the fumbling care of a man who could not fix Tory but tried. Warm arms and the sting of pipe smoke in his nose.

His foot twists in a rut and he's on the ground, splayed hands sinking into frigid water.

Healing. When he's *healing*, he finds the energies just fine. The low electric rhythm of a body at work, the warm pool of possibility he can focus and direct toward closing wounds, urging the body to recall and return to a state pre-injury. He knows, intimately, the struggle to direct that last fizzling wisp to the work of restoration.

He doesn't know this. He doesn't belong here.

He finds his feet in time for a balloon to pummel him in the gut, wrenching a shameful noise from him and suffusing him with sick, visceral pain.

Menden's voice: "Lieutenant, that's *enough*."

"Not nearly, sir."

"That wasn't a request, boy, it was an order!"

"On what authority? You're so fond of reminding me that you're retired. He is my supervisee, *Mr.* Menden."

Bent double, Tory coughs until his ears ring, until the roar of his pulse swallows sight and sound. Something explodes against his shoulder, knocking him onto his side in the mud.

"Up, Arknett! We're not finished."

Rage. The heat of it clears his head of exhaustion and pain. When his senses lash out, hunting for Vantaras, he finds something else.

In the dark, awareness trickles in. Something trails after the rush of the balloons in the air: a presence with all the blunt-force heft of a rock to the chest.

The *dark*. Sight was a distraction when he first started healing, too. When he was young, he'd always close his eyes.

These energies are nothing like the wild-warm pulse of life. They're destructive, without intention.

No wonder he couldn't find them before.

He rolls to his feet too late to avoid the balloon that nails him in the shin, but he *recognizes* it before it does. He identifies the clumsy energy of the next projectile the moment it leaves the cannon. It's a matter of a step to the left. He barely has to move to avoid the one that follows—a dip like a bow, and it sails over his back.

"Stop them, fool boy! Don't dodge!" Menden's voice.

"Good." That one's Vantaras, voice dripping with arrogant pride.

The wind kicks up, and Tory's teeth clack in his skull. He extends his hands and reaches for it. The balloon falters midair—he almost tastes the sputtering there-then-gone-then-there of its blunted presence—but it keeps going, splattering over his shoes.

"When you have it, *throw* it! Preferably not at me or any of your fellow trainees."

Now there's an idea. Where's Vantaras? But while he can sense his fellow Seeds on the field—CFR energy has a unique fizziness to it, and now that he's looking for it, their presence is like a busy hive on the periphery of his senses—he can't sense any energy from Menden or Vantaras. The space to his left is a void. He'll make Vantaras suffer later.

He gets back to work, closing his eyes and extending his hands.

He singles out the energy and imagines moving it, opening his eyes as he lobs it in the direction that offers the least resistance—back where it came from.

Tory wrenches the blindfold off to the sight of one of the cannons spinning wildly on its axis. Triumph pumps through him. He flings the kerchief into the mud.

"You happy?"

Vantaras' lips twist up.

Tory wants to punch them—once for this whole damn farce and again because it worked.

"I am." Vantaras bends in a graceful arc to pick up the kerchief as he passes, and a pendant tumbles from his uniform jacket—a raw stellite crystal, star-studded even in the day's gray dimness. It's bigger than Tory's thumbnail, colorful with the galaxy-like glow of nebulescence that only the highest-quality specimens show. It lacks the faceted polish of the Madam's earrings in Hulven, but it's five times bigger—magnitudes more valuable and dizzying with its brilliance. Vantaras stuffs the thing back into his jacket before Tory can tear it from his throat. "That's all I needed to see. I'll take my leave."

Tory shakes mud from his arms and stumbles over to Menden. "Can I stop now?"

"Oh, no. Keep going. We'll move in when you can drop them all without being hit once. Maybe I'll put you with the midfielders later for maneuvers!"

*

Maneuvers multiply the chaos of type-training by ten. The balloons still fly, but that's the least of it. Strange, mechanized spheres—polished metal and over half Tory's height—roll over the field at bone-breaking speeds, and the CFR unit is forced to maintain formation in spite of them.

"They won't kill you!" Menden chirps. "You'll only wish you were dead!"

One of them bowls over a nearby trainee, and Healers—lingering at the edge of the field—rush in to drag him away. He's bleeding everywhere, crying for people Tory doesn't know.

"What are they *for*?" Tory yells.

"Realism! It's fine. They only go at half-speed for the midfielders!"

This is half-speed?

Menden steps back, humming a cheerful tune, and opens a well-worn book.

"How do I kill them?" Tory yells, but Menden doesn't answer.

A man with a floppy thatch of mouse-brown hair, a mess of freckles, and a perpetual smile responds instead. He introduces himself as Randall. "Oh." He laughs. "You don't."

"*Why?*" Tory steals and throws the momentum from one of the wind-up abominations, slowing it for a moment.

Randall's answer is the same as Menden's. "Realism!" he says. "Or as close as they can get, which isn't very."

"What do you *mean?*"

Randall laughs again and keeps talking, like multitasking in a field of projectiles and death-spheres is an everyday occurrence. "Uh, just because? I mean, you don't kill them. A Legion unit kills *you.*"

"Legion?"

"Yeah, 'cause one of them is as good as a whole legion of soldiers," Randall offers. "Not that I've seen a real one! But I visit my girlfriend in the infirmary and sat with one guy the other day while he—you know."

Tory can guess.

"From what he said, these things here? They're children's toys."

A nearby trainee screams as one of the children's toys crashes into her and breaks bones. Tory doesn't have breath to respond, but Randall keeps going.

"The real ones are nothing like these. They can just . . . change shape. Any shape. Heard of one that could disappear, one that killed people before they even saw it. You see one of these things on a battlefield, you're dead. You and everyone with you."

Children's toys or not, the things are ugly. Any trainees unfortunate enough to encounter them are dragged off the field and sent back once their broken bodies have been sealed by the waiting Healers. Tory puts what he's learned to use and steals the kinetic energy off one of the mechanized spheres. The weight of its stolen momentum pushes against his hands like a boulder. Tory trembles at the heft of it, then pushes back, so the energy crashes into the rolling bastard he stole it from. Knocks it back a good few feet when he does it, and Randall laughs like it's the best entertainment he's had in years.

"Oh, do it again!"

Tory does it again, and again, until sweat stings his eyes. He manages to mess up the embedded tracks on one of the spheres so nicely that it spins itself in circles for a while.

Randall talks about everything—the quality of the cafeteria's meat, the weather, Menden, his family, his girlfriend—and the smile never goes. If this guy's midfielding, Tory can't imagine how good the ones closer to the gate are. He barely manages monosyllabic grunts while he works and still misses as many balloons as he drops.

"Sorry!" Randall jumps in front of Tory and takes a balloon to the chest, clipping Tory's shoulder as he stumbles back.

"I could've gotten that."

"That's why I apologized! I needed to take that one." Randall shakes water from his hair.

"You . . . like getting hit?" Some folks in the Houses were into that. Giving or taking it.

"In a sense!"

When the bell for the end of training sounds, Randall tells him the cooks are making corn hash soup tonight (a good thing) and guides him to the front of the line for healing. Barring medical emergencies or returnees from the battlefield, theirs is always the first unit allowed into the infirmary, apparently.

"My girlfriend works here," Randall informs him, waggling his eyebrows. "Sight for sore eyes." He rolls his shoulder and hisses. "Sore everything."

Tory can't hold back a laugh.

First dibs or not, the line is eternal and the wind blows ice-cold. It's not worth the wait. Tory slips between storage buildings to head inside and hit the showers. Hot water—as much as he can stand—will beat the cold from his bones and the ache from his limbs. A feast of food waits for him when he's done.

Today, he learned how to defend himself with his powers—and how to attack with them, to throw stolen energy where he wants it to go. He can learn from these people.

As training wore on today, Tory advanced closer and closer to the wall. The best folks are at the front already—near the matte-black cannons and the saw-toothed gate Tory entered through. It opened once or twice during training to let soldiers in or supplies out.

Soon, he'll be there with the best of them, and he'll have all the time in the world to figure out how to escape through the gate while these bastards provide him with training he can turn against them when he's out. The infiltrators Vantaras scared away are probably the rebels Hasra told stories about. They were *close*. If Tory can find them, he can join them.

His petty resistance against Vantaras has felt nice, but Tory wants to try his hand at a real fight. A meaningful one.

These walls would look awfully good as rubble.

CHAPTER EIGHT

RANDALL FINDS HIM at dinner, toting a bowl filled to the brim with corn hash soup. "I save my tokens for this," he confides, sliding into the seat beside Tory. "Keep going back for more and stuff myself 'til I almost puke." He opens his hand to show two more of the white-rimmed purple coins. "I will *feast* tonight."

Tory smiles, sipping at his soup. A bit salty, but savory and filling. "It's not bad."

"It's *glorious*. Just like home. I love her for it, but Niela—my girlfriend, remember? She's Mrs. Jeffra's daughter. Healer, just like her mom!—she can't cook to save her life. She's always sayin' I need to work harder 'cause she doesn't want to see me back in there." Randall's eyes crinkle. "Don't think she knows I let 'em clip me so I can visit."

"That's, uh . . . sweet?"

"Her uniform's so cute. They have those little *hats* and I just—her hair, and the things the apron *does* to her waist! You get me."

He doesn't. In the House, Tory met people who welcomed sex and all its trappings and trimmings, people who enjoyed only the physical aspects, people who approached it as a transaction, and people who were actively appalled by it and served their clients in different ways. He talked to them all, learned young that he wasn't alone in his indifference. He learned young, too, that his preferences didn't matter—if he wanted to keep himself happy, healthy, and alive, being what other people needed mattered more than understanding what he wanted.

Randall might understand if Tory told the truth, but Tory would be a fool to cultivate friendships after the mess he made of his time in Hulven, so he just hums agreeably, which seems to be all Randall needs.

"So." He nudges Tory, conspiratorial. "You're new here, huh?"

"First day training, second day here. How'd *you* get taken in?"

Randall shrugs. "I was a late bloomer, didn't even know I was a Seed until this one day I was working in the smithy and me and this other apprentice almost got nailed by flying knives when a display tipped. I did my thing and saved both of us, swore him to secrecy."

"He sold you out," Tory guesses.

"Nah. Gus? Stellar guy. I just felt weird staying there, you know? Secrets make shackles, and all that. Applied for work in Maran. Should've known not to go to the *capital*, but I never said I was clever! They were doing examinations at the checkpoint before the outer wall, some sort of blood test. Figured it was for a sickness or something, but, well. When my blood lit on fire, I kinda knew it wasn't. They sent me here."

"Sucks, man. I'm sorry."

He shrugs. "I was tired of hiding it, and it's not so bad here. This is where I met Niela. If we get married, we can apply to be placed together whenever the whole war thing's done."

Optimistic of him to believe Vantaras will ever let it end, but Tory doesn't say so. He's heard conversations like this one enough to know what's next. "She a keeper, then?"

Randall gets that look again. Soft—so awfully soft. "She says she was a bit of a—a delinquent, I guess, before she came here. Says she'd never have pegged herself for a Healer, but I think she's plenty nurturing. Anyway, we didn't get along real well at first, but then we saw each other every day in the infirmary, and . . ."

"You are a walking cliche."

"Tried and true methods, my man. Tried and true."

The silence goes on a beat too long.

Randall chuckles, awkward. "So, you're real good for a newbie!"

Tory stabs a kernel of corn with his fork. "Not exactly a newbie. I've been doing something that—uses the same theory, I guess?—for years now, so once I made the connection it came pretty easy."

Randall leans close. The smile stays frozen on his face, eerie as he whispers, "Don't get too good, okay? Way I hear it, the talented ones, they're the first to be deployed. Make some mistakes. Hang back. I've been here six months, and half the folks I came with are gone. Not like gone, but *gone*-gone. Being 'bad' has worked pretty well for me. The things I've heard about what's out there . . . I don't want to see it. War's gotta end sometime. Wait it out if you can."

Tory's mouth goes dry. "Okay."

Randall claps him on the back like he just told a joke. "Good man! Coming here is a bit of an upset, yeah? You been to the rec room?"

Tory shakes his head.

"Let's go! The Kinetic guys go there to spar, but I like the game tables. We can play cards or something, unwind. People gamble meal tokens sometimes. You got any leftovers from your first allotment?

Any you don't want? They trade all sorts of stuff at the tables. I got an extra pillow there once."

Tory grins. Thanks to the bastards here and their *high hopes* for him, he certainly has no dearth of tokens.

*

The rec room is wide and packed with people. That's the first thing that rubs Tory the wrong way.

The air tastes of sweat from the roped-off sparring ring and smoke from the crude card tables. Curses and conversations and laughter meld to create a steady buzz, broken occasionally by a cry or a chorus of cheers. Tory watches the fight in the elevated ring for a while. He nudges Randall.

"You gonna try? Bet you could knock 'em on their faces."

"What? No way! Who do you think I am? Balloons are hard enough. People *choose* to move. Too much going on for a CFR."

Well, Tory isn't a CFR. Maybe he'll try stepping into the ring one day.

Watching the fight makes him tense instead of calming him down, so he lets Randall drag him to a rickety wooden card table. Old, mismatched chairs make a ring around it, and off to the left, several dart games are going on. One woman guides a dart to the bullseye with her hands behind her back. Tory's pretty sure that's cheating.

Randall scoffs. "Sword corps. All the offense guys think they're so special. Don't give 'em any attention."

The creepy stellite lighting adorns the walls in here like everywhere else, but they've made it dimmer, somehow, so the light is as dull and smoky as the air. When Tory finally turns back to the table, Randall gives him a drink, has a big guy deal them in, and they start to play.

He has an overabundance of tokens, thanks to Helner, and this isn't a bad way to spend them. People talk in non-threatening environments. He might learn something useful. Anyway, he hasn't spent his whole life corralling his emotions for nothing. He has a killer game face. It's nice to use those skills for his *own* benefit for once.

It only takes a few hands until he's loose with relaxation, guarding a generous pile of tokens and more than a few scraps of paper with scribbles on them, representative of whatever these men are gambling in lieu of tokens. Two extra pillows. A sweater that will cover his arms.

He startles as a voice bursts out close to his ear. Gavin.

"Whoa, man! Didn't know you had a tattoo. Where'd you get it?"

A hand closes around Tory's upper arm. His cheeks burn, pulse clamoring. He shouldn't have let go of himself. He jerks his arm free, dropping his cards. "Don't."

"Come on, Roomie, I'm just trying to get to know you." Gavin shrugs, stepping back.

"Maybe I don't want you to get to know me, *Roomie*."

Grinning, Gavin telegraphs a reach but then catches Tory with his other hand. Strong fingers close around Tory's arm. "See? That wasn't so hard—"

Tory throws the first punch without thinking, fist landing on Gavin's stubbled jaw. Pain explodes over his knuckles.

Gavin curses, stumbling back. He grabs for Tory's shoulder, wrinkling his shirt and tugging the sleeve up to reveal the blue ring. "I was just trying to say hello. You wanna be like this? Fine. But you should know what you're getting into."

"Oh, man. Those are labor camp tats, aren't they?" one of the guys around the table says.

The unnatural energy from the stellite strips on the walls combines with the zing from the fighters in the ring to sharpen Tory's senses. All he can focus on is Gavin's grip and the awful, unwavering stares. Ragged breaths saw in and out of his chest. He's dizzy with it, the edges of everything crisp and bright.

Gavin laughs. "What, mama popped you out in the camps? I hear that means they *own* you."

Gavin's unyielding grip underlines Tory's ugliest memories—the helplessness, the things he did to himself and for others in those first years after his escape. Tory tries to shake it away. He's out. He's free of that now.

Except he's not. He's owned again. Penned in, laughed at, *again*.

Tory aches, an unpleasant reminder of today's training, and though he likes Menden, he knows the smiles will be gone the moment Tory steps out of line. The bruises over his body have settled and spread, converging into a singular throb, syrupy and electric.

Like when he did healing.

Like when he worked in the mines, when he mucked out stalls from sunup until twilight. The reminder that maybe it's always been this bad—maybe the actual, physical prison walls are the only difference—sets him alight. He breathes in the electric air, grabs Gavin's hand, and twists. Something cracks.

He jerks away. He didn't mean to break bones.

Gavin crouches, groaning, fingers loose around his dangling wrist. He swings with his uninjured hand, landing a punch on Tory's chin that sends streaks of color dancing over his eyes.

Gavin grabs a dart from a nearby game, grinning awfully before he throws it. It accelerates midair.

Tory weaves left, and it whizzes past to crumple against the wall. And that? That's cheating. It would have gone right through him. "You don't want to get into this with me."

"I think you got it the wrong way 'round, *Seedbait*."

Tentative fingers settle on his shoulder from behind.

It's Randall, wide-eyed and tensed to run. "They're right. I—I don't think you want to fight with them. They're . . . I mean, and fighting in the facility is—"

"You go on. My winnings are yours if you want to keep playing." Randall doesn't deserve to get caught up in this. "I'm just gonna settle this first. This guy thought it was a good idea to start something."

Another dart digs a furrow into the side of the table before breaking against the wall.

Randall careens from the room with a few others.

That wasn't what Tory meant when he told Randall to go on, but it works. The twinge of regret—maybe he just lost the one ally he has in this place—lasts only as long as it takes Gavin to pick up a third dart.

Tory puts the day's training to work. He gets it now: the dart's velocity has two distinct flavors—that blunted kinetic heft and the skin-tingling energy he's been breathing since he got here. He tears both of them away, stealing the combined force and throwing it at Gavin's chest. The dart stops midair, falling with a faint clatter.

Gavin is blown back a couple steps as the stolen energy crashes into him. He curls around himself, retching, and Tory smiles. This whole shitshow has been worth it for teaching him *this*. For the first time, he's not under someone else's boot. Holding a life in his hands is a potent thing. He could *hurt* Gavin. A small part of him—the part that worked so long as a Healer—balks at the harm he's caused, but a bigger part, a growing part, wants to cause more.

The ever-present hum of voices dies all at once. One moment, the room brims with them. The next, it's silent enough to hear the scuff of boots on the floor.

Then, "Arknett."

Behind him.

He spins, vision still sharp, unspent anger like acid inside him, and *there's* the person who put him here: there's Sena Vantaras, the one he really wants to fight.

"Perfect timing." Tory's cheeks ache with the grin that stretches them.

Gavin stumbles upright. "I didn't—"

"I'll deal with you later." Vantaras' gaze flicks to Tory. "You, on the other hand . . ."

He grabs the neck of Tory's shirt and jerks him off balance, taking advantage of the confusion to drag Tory out of the rec room. "Be grateful," he hisses, "that your friend Randall came to me. Had the colonel been disturbed, you'd be well on your way to getting a NOVA."

"Grateful!" Tory reaches to shove Vantaras' hand away, but he retreats before Tory can make contact. "I don't care—"

"If you don't, you're more of a fool than I gave you credit for, and I credit your intelligence hardly at all. Return to your room." Vantaras walks away.

Oh, he's had enough of this. Tory stalks after him, closing a hand around the sleeve of his dress uniform to grip a surprisingly thin wrist. "What gives? I get you're a constipated rich kid with a stick up his ass, but what's *with this*?"

"With what?"

Tory spins Vantaras around. "*This*. These gloves, the way you can't stand some peasant touching you."

"I assure you—" Vantaras tears the hand from his grasp, face flashing disgust.

Tory lunges.

Vantaras avoids it, and when Tory looks up, he's a ways down the hall, spine straight as he stares down his nose. "You misunderstand," he's saying. "If you'd—"

Tory could break that nose. "I don't care." He does, he does, he does. "You did this."

"*Me*? You're doing this to yourself with your recklessness."

Tory shakes his head, advancing. "Why me, you bastard? I was fine out there!"

"I was under orders. If you hadn't been so *obvious* with that display with the carriage, I could have pretended not to notice and reported the stellite resonance incident at the mines as an inexplicable phenomenon, but you made such a mess that my competence would have been in question if I didn't apprehend you."

"Competence?" Tory's vision bleeds red. "It was my *life*!"

The Seed energy in the rec room lights Tory up as it passes through him. The fight in the ring must have restarted. He bears the destructive force only long enough to sling it at Vantaras.

Then—nothing. He doesn't even realize he was tracking the energy until it's gone.

Vantaras stands untouched, uniform just so and not a hair out of place. "You'll have to try harder than that, Worldseed."

That *word*, like he's a thing and not a person. *Worldseed*, they say, with the same odd reverence with which some people once reached for the mark on his arm. He's something strange, precious. Precious enough to use but unworthy of freedom. Two can play that game.

"You know what? I've had enough of your Lune-ass self telling me what to do. *Vantaras*. I'll bet your hands are rich-boy soft under those things. Bet you grew up painting pretty pictures while I *bled* to assemble your weapons. I could kill you right here."

"Could you?"

Tory swallows up the few steps between them and knots his fingers in that flawless, starched uniform to slam Vantaras against the wall. Vantaras shudders with the force of the collision, hair dusting into indifferent amber eyes. He must have bitten his bottom lip—and *oh*, it's satisfying to have made him bleed—because when his mouth opens, there's blood on his teeth, and his tongue darts out to stop a bead of it before it can slip down his chin. His left hand lashes up to grab Tory's wrist, impossibly strong for how slender he is.

"Whether or not my *Lune-ass self* appeals to you or anyone, I am your supervisor and superior. My origins have nothing to do with my abilities. Considering the altercation I just broke up, I'd have assumed you might understand that, but instead you seem to be ashamed of the woman who gave you life." Vantaras' free hand hikes up Tory's sleeve, exposing the tattoos before Tory growls and pins that arm against the wall.

There's a faint jingle, a sound he's heard before. His eyes fall to Vantaras' wrist, catch a glint of silver.

(I-S)VS—

It takes a moment to understand what he's seeing. The bracelet . . . just like Tory's.

"*You.* You're a fucking *Seed*. My superior? You're right down here with the animals, Vantaras. No wonder Daddy didn't want you, sent you all the way out here to this dead-end piece-of-shit place—"

The world tips. His nose aches, teeth gnashing together with the taste of chalk, and agony shoots through the shoulder that's suddenly and inexplicably wrenched behind his back.

"You know *nothing*."

Tory blinks to find the wall cool against his cheek. Vantaras crushes him against it, and Tory's breaths wet the titanium-white surface.

"I never hid my abilities. They simply weren't relevant to any of our conversations. And I am, in fact, your superior. Respecting authority won't kill you."

"*Authority?*"

Vantaras twists Tory's captive arm until all he can do is curse and whine, standing on his tiptoes so it won't tear from the socket.

"Insubordination only gets you hurt here. I outrank you and always will. I would suggest swallowing that pill sooner rather than later."

"*You* can swallow—"

"And Arknett?" Another twist. Sadist. "It would behoove you to know that the penalty for using your abilities with the intent to harm an officer of the Westrian military, even one so low-ranked as myself, is death. Next time, think before doing something stupid. It would be tragic to die for dealing an attack that *couldn't even hit its target*."

Vantaras twists his arm once more and lets go. The limb falls back against his side, and Tory cradles it, hissing in pain. He turns around to say something—he's not sure what, yet, but it'll come to him when he sees Vantaras' smug face—but he's already gone.

Anger (at Gavin, at himself, at Vantaras and this whole damn mess) crashes around inside him and leaves him shaking. He doesn't know how long he stands there until his pulse stops rushing in his ears.

Tory falls against the wall and lays ginger touches on his arm; nothing's broken or dislocated, but he'd put money on something being torn. He swears into the silence around him.

He's done with this place. Next chance, he's getting out.

CHAPTER NINE

His chance comes the following afternoon.

"Ready!" Menden cries. The assembled Seeds brace for impact.

Another set joins the mix for today's maneuvers: the Fielders, forcefield-makers deployed to the battlefield in groups of five to set up a huge, one-way barrier.

"Protect them like your life depends on it," Menden yells, "because it will!" And then, pacing and muttering, "We have a lot of work to do if they expect me to have you placement-ready in three weeks."

Placement-ready. Tory shivers, then braces himself. Doesn't matter. He'll be gone before then.

The volley begins, three of the Legion-spheres rolling over the scarred yard at three-quarters speed. Tory and his unit protect the Fielders until they've raised the shield. Once it's up, the shield repels the Legion unit, and Tory's team takes care of all other projectiles. Ten minutes without a major injury or a single balloon breaking on the shields, and they'll earn a break.

"Spread out! You want something to get through and kill one of your Fielders? You're the only thing between them and early death, and *they'll* be the only thing between you and whatever horrors come your way. Act like it!"

Tory drops three balloons before they reach him, directing their force at the wall. He hopes it slaps some unsuspecting officer in the gut. He huffs a laugh when his lapse in concentration almost earns him a high-speed balloon to the face. As training wears on, the difficulty level increases, bringing them closer to the wall—close enough to see the lit-up stone slivers embedded in the cannons' sides.

Close enough, finally, to make a run for the gate.

He just needs the right timing. A returning soldier. A new arrival. A supply truck. *Something*. It opened a couple times yesterday, a quick whip up and down. It hasn't opened at all yet today.

Just once. He needs it to open *once*.

But this close, the balloons are deadly. There's no gentle arc to them. If they land, they won't knock the breath from him and leave a bruise—these ones rupture internal organs and shatter bones. There are more than a few stories of unfortunate trainees who took a hit to the skull or spine and were gone before a Healer could reach them. Tory *shouldn't* split his attention like this, but he can't help it. As long as the gate opens—

"Arknett!"

He startles, reflexively releasing the balloon he'd started to grab. It sputters mid-air before plummeting to burst on the shield.

The group groans as a whole, which isn't fair. They weren't *that* close to earning a break. He gets a few sharp elbows and curses from his fellow trainees, and a cheerily chirped, "You've got this!" from Randall.

Menden paces and mutters from his position away from the barrage. "Pay attention!" he calls. "On a real battlefield you'd be dead by now!"

I know that, Tory wants to retort. *That's why I'm getting the fuck out of here.*

Maneuvers wear on. The gate doesn't open. Tory's focus splinters. He loses them at least two more breaks, to the group's mounting fury, Menden's exasperation, and Randall's embarrassed glee. Randall slides close enough, once, to whisper, "When I told you not to be too good, I didn't mean you had to *suck*."

Eyes glued to the gate, willing it to open, Tory feels a little bad for not grinning and sharing in the joke. Randall protected him yesterday when he didn't have to.

Tory should probably caution him against that. His last kindness.

"Randall?" he says, and Randall makes a thoughtful *hmm?* "You're right. I've got this. You need to watch out for yourself instead, all right?"

He doesn't catch Randall's reply, because that's when it happens. The whip-like snap of the front gate rising at *last* hits him with a rush of adrenaline.

Tory doesn't hesitate. He breaks formation and skirts the forcefield, feet pounding muddy earth. There's a wagon stacked with boxes approaching the gate. Tory won't have long. The second it's safely through, the gate will snap closed like the maw of a beast.

Menden makes a startled noise when he notices Tory running and reaches for the strange device on his chest with its blue-lit stellite. The same sort of communicator Vantaras wears.

Tory can't let him use it.

He grabs the force from two balloons and directs it at Menden, trying to spread it out—he doesn't want to kill the guy. Menden makes an ugly cry as he flies back, but the delicate device shatters, its clean light flickering out.

The wagon is a mere finger's width through the gate when Tory arrives in its shadow. When the thing snaps closed, it nearly bisects him, but he makes it through. In a stroke of luck, it cuts him off from the small clump of uniformed soldiers who thought to pursue Tory. He runs through almost backward, stealing the momentum from a few of his pursuers and using it against them before they can call for the gate to open again.

Surely it will only delay them for an instant, but it's an instant more of free air for Tory. He's outside those ugly, impenetrable walls and the cannons mounted atop them, and for the first time in days he breathes and it fills him to the brim. A hysterical laugh breaks from him as his legs pump, bringing him farther and farther from the cold cage of STAR-7 and Sena Vantaras with his flame-bright eyes. If Tory ever meets him again, they'll stand on equal ground, and Tory will make sure Vantaras doesn't walk away from the encounter alive.

He's *out*. He did it. He made a mistake lingering in Hulven, but he knows better now.

He's down the gravel path, running free.

Then he's in the cool embrace of the forest, running and running like his legs never learned how to stop.

*

He's probably been racing for hours through the sparse trees, long enough to forget he has bones.

His legs pump, numb and mechanical. Pain is an odd, distant thing—and thought farther still. His brain says *run*, a blazing imperative, so he runs long after no footsteps beat the ground behind him. Long enough that when he catches sight of a tower of rock through the trees, he trips over his own feet and rolls twice when he tries to stop. He ends up on the ground, pulse pounding in his aching legs.

There it is, visible between the trunks: a natural outcropping of rock looms over the treetops, its odd peak reminiscent of a snake head.

Serpentshead Rock.

Tory's only thought when he came to a fork in the road and went left rather than right, which would've led him past Hulven, was that he wasn't sure he'd be strong enough to see that place and resist checking in on Thatcher. It didn't occur to him that the other road went through Serpentshead.

Hasra. She promised she'd find him here.

Old instinct urges him to keep moving. Stopping anywhere, even here, could get him caught.

But when he finds his feet, he heads deeper into the woods instead of farther away, filling his heaving lungs with the sweet, damp rot of decaying leaves. The murmuring trees drop puddles of light onto his shoulders as he weaves between them, until he steps into Serpentshead's cool shadow. His body still remembers this path.

He arrives at the mouth of the wide cave he slept in for months after fleeing the labor camp. The murmuring of the nearby brook joins the rustle of leaves, and he breathes in rhythm with the world around him, deep and slow.

He looks up at the head of the maned serpent. The hollows that would have been its eyes once glinted with stellite crystals, the stories go, but now, they sit empty. What might be age-old paint in shades of blue, red, and purple lies in the deepest pits in the rock, worn away everywhere else. Everyone pretends Serpentshead is a mystery.

Fools, all of them. They're barely a few hours from the border at a sedate walk, and this land didn't always belong to Westrice.

Tory stills at motion to his left, but it's only light—prismatic shards of it flickering over the ground with every sigh of wind.

From a tree branch, faceted clear, amethyst, and pale-green beads dangle on a fine cord. Tory's first instinct is a rush of fondness, but he crushes it before it can take root.

That's a wind charm.

A wind charm all the way out here, too far from the fuel fog they wish away in Hulven to be a coincidence. Tory approaches it. It's not just *similar* to the ones at Hulven's House. It's identical, down to the chip in the largest bead.

Hasra.

At the base of the wind charm, a rectangle of paper swings in the breeze. Hasra's bold, blocky writing tells him, *wait for me.*

She was here. His pulse rushes in his ears.

That's probably why he doesn't hear the men approaching until it's too late. They freeze as they pass the mouth of the cave, canteens slung around their shoulders and a huge bucket in each hand. They must have come from the brook.

The man nearest Tory drops both of his buckets with a splash and reaches for a revolver at his side, eyes widening. "He's from the Compound!" the man yells. "Mr. Belmin! Scouts in the area!"

Belmin? *The* Belmin?

Tory barely has time to process the name before someone bursts from the woods and tackles him. He lands on his back with a painful whoosh of breath. On top of him, face set with intent to kill but hands free of weapons, sits a girl. Short and slender with offensively vibrant red-blonde ringlets angled to follow the line of her chin, she sports a splash of freckles over her pale nose that reminds Tory of nothing so much as blood spatter. She wears a delicately embroidered vest in the same hazel-green as her eyes over a flowing white blouse, and men's trousers. The fragments of light from the wind charm swing over her face.

"You didn't see us," she hisses.

What is she talking about? He absolutely did—did . . .

What did he do?

The edges of the girl become indistinct, fading into the forest, and Tory's mind drifts on an ocean of peace. Someone bursts from the trees, though, and the girl returns with startling clarity, the peace vanishing.

"Ariana, *up*! Damn you, I told you I was waiting for a friend! Tory? Tory, look at me."

A familiar hand thrusts into his field of vision and helps him to his feet, then bends to brush leaf litter from the back of his ugly slate-blue clothing.

Tory's head clears, and he stops her, lifts her with a hand on her wide shoulder. There she is: eyes pinched and black hair loose, a dark blue robe embroidered with interlocking spirals tied at her waist. Hasra looks just like the day he left her.

Tory must not look the same at all, because her face crumples at the sight of him. She exhales a raw, disbelieving noise, crushing him against her, and as Tory inhales the spice of her pipe, a knot inside him unties itself.

"Hey," he whispers into her robe, eyes burning. "Glad you got out safe. How've ya been?"

Hasra thwacks the back of his head and lifts his face to examine it. "Worried! How'd you think I'd be?"

He muffles a laugh into her shoulder. "Sorry."

Her hands flutter over him. "Don't apologize, just take care of yourself. Have you been eating? And you're *bruised*! Tory, you're bruised all over! What have they been doing to you?"

Tory blinks fast and hard. "Just training. But I'm out now."

"You are. We'll keep you that way."

He just needs something sharp and to figure out where Helner planted his damn Core so he can scoop the thing out.

The girl with the murder-freckles interrupts. "Hasra, this is . . .?"

Hasra steps in beside Tory, arm warm around his shoulders. "Ariana, this is the Tory I keep telling you about. Tory, this is Ulenn Belmin's daughter. She's the brashness and boldness behind his operation. Still haven't found out who's the brains."

"Hey!" says Ariana, but then shrugs. "Honestly? Probably Wyn."

The men who were carrying the water stumble from the trees with a third man. Belmin, if Tory had to guess, rags-to-riches merchant and smuggler of Seeds. He's . . . not what Tory imagined. Sweaty and red-faced, with barely an inch on Tory and a thinning head of light-brown hair gone gray at the temples, he sports a bombastic plum-and-maroon jacket embroidered like his daughter's. Tory imagined him differently.

Belmin stares, eyes wide. "You need to leave."

"I . . . What?" Tory staggers back on boneless legs.

Hasra pulls him close again. "Don't you dare, Ulenn."

Belmin shakes his head. "Get out! You have to leave, now. Those clothes, the bracelet. They'll track you here. There's a group of rogue Seeds by the border. Find them, mess things up for *them*. I don't care. Just go."

"I won't let you do this," Hasra says, and something unnameable swells in Tory's chest. "We're so close to the border. They wouldn't risk crossing it to apprehend him, even with the tracker—he'll be safe there as long as we hurry. Ulenn, please."

"It's too risky." Belmin spears her with a solemn gaze. "If they're tracking him now, they could realize he's escaping via our trade routes. If you must defend him, you can leave with him."

She presses her lips together, and shit, Tory knows that face. "Hasra, no. This is your—"

"This is my *nothing*. I'll get my things."

The girl named Ariana steps up between them. "Hasra's right, Dad. And anyway, from what she's been saying, he's probably a Worldseed. Wyn will *lose it* when I tell her!"

"Ari, it's far too dangerous. We can't risk our current and future work for one boy."

She smiles—a disturbing look beneath her blood-spatter freckles. "Please?"

Off to the side, Hasra lights her pipe, taking one unsettlingly deep drag and then another, like she's starving for smoke. She squints suspiciously at Ariana.

"I've made my decision. Go back to our *guests*," Belmin says.

"Not yet." Ariana's eyes widen theatrically and she points toward the road. "Daddy! They're coming. We need to *move*."

Fear jolts through Tory, but when he examines the area Ariana is indicating with her finger, there's nothing. Her father stares, though, like he's seeing his own execution. "Prepare for departure!" he cries. "Hurry!"

Ariana spins, graceful, to face Tory. "Where were we, then? Tory, right?" She dances out of the way as someone barrels past. "I'm Ariana Belmin. Part-time student of medicine in the capital, full-time Seed smuggler. Call me Ari."

Tory's still squinting between the empty road and Ariana's father, who has burst into motion like there's fire on his feet. "What did you just . . . ?"

He's heard the stories, here and there, in whispers: that there are some Seeds who can change people's perceptions of reality. Mostly, the stories are whispered in fear if they're whispered at all, but there was a girl in one of the Houses, an older woman, who protected the employees with a power like this one.

"Oh, this? It's nothing much. Only visual and auditory. But enough about me. Hasra's told us so much about *you*! We've been dying to meet you." She grabs him by the bracelet at his wrist and examines it. "Score! I knew it! Wyn's gonna flip. We just need a Voidseed for a matched set."

Hasra, flustered, takes another long drag on her pipe. "By the stars above and fire beneath, Ariana—"

"Hasra, shouldn't you be preparing to depart, too? You know, *considering*?"

The same strange urgency takes hold of her for a moment, but she shudders and shakes it off. She spears Ariana with an unblinking stare while she inhales deep on the pipe and exhales a lungful of smoke in Ari's face. "When will you stop trying to pull that shit on me? You're a horrible person, Ariana Belmin."

"Comes with the job." Ari coughs in the cloud of smoke. "And that's a horrible habit."

"You've said. Useful, though, if you're going to keep messing with me." She inhales again, looking to Tory. "I figured out the pipe smoke lets me resist her illusions."

To Tory, Ari grumbles, "Any mind-altering substance makes it less effective, unfortunately." She starts walking. "This way."

He'd tolerate weirder and wilder personalities than hers to be free. He hurries after her, through the thinning woods and toward a dirt road. "I don't have any money."

"Didn't expect you to."

"Then why are you helping?"

She smiles. "Consider it an investment. We're in the business of shaking things up, and historically speaking, when the First Children are born into the same generation, the world's overdue for a shakeup. Now that we know *you're* here, we've got our theory more than half confirmed. Just be aware that we might end up asking you for a favor at some point."

They pass Belmin, putting up water buckets and preparing the horses. Caravan cars packed with goods blur by. In the first, paper-wrapped lamps with bubbled shades huddle in covered boxes, blown into dream-shapes and dyed with streaks of blue and gold. Tory knows them: the House in Hulven has three. Carallian glass from Belmin's hometown. His big break, or so the stories go. The second car is packed with shocks of cloth dyed in rich colors and decorated with maned serpents and prints of stars and vines enwrapped. Arlunian designs.

The third is a closed car, windowless. Ari leads him to the back, where two wide, wooden doors wait.

A man in long brown trousers and a ratty green sweater leans against them, eyebrow raised. His hair is red as a summer fox's and just as wild even with a token tie trying to pull it together at the back, his eyes wine- or blood-colored in the low light. His smile's vulpine, too—toothy-wide and hungry, though it sours at the sight of Tory's uniform.

"Picked up a stray pup? They bite, you know. I wouldn't recommend it."

Tory shouldn't, given that the guy has just insulted him, but he trusts the man immediately. He tugs at the bracelet locked around his wrist. He'll need wire-cutters to remove it. "My teeth are plenty sharp, but I'd rather turn them on the bastards who did this to me."

The smile returns, broad and warm. "Oh, Ms. Belmin, I *like* this one. Can I keep him?"

It's Hasra who answers. "Absolutely not, Larsen. He's going to Arlune."

"Who is he?" Tory whispers. When Hasra only presses her lips together, he meets the redhead's eyes. "Who are you?"

"Riese." The man extends a hand to envelop Tory's. "I lead a ragtag group of Seeds based close enough to the border to keep us safe. You might have heard of our work. We and our allies have been haunting their supply routes. We even got inside that damn Compound of theirs hoping to cause some problems, short-lived though it was. Their security was stronger than we expected."

Tory's stomach flips. The rebels. These are the rebels Hasra told him about.

The fire that flickered to life in him when Vantaras stole his scalpel—the hunger to *fight*—flares again in his belly. In Hulven, it was an idle dream. Now, he could make it real. No more whittling himself down, no more hiding.

Hasra snags his wrist. "Don't even think about it. I want you safe. This man is not safe."

"Nothing worth the time ever is," Riese says. "How long you been in?"

"In where?"

"Their little pen of pet Seeds. Too much time under their thumb rots the brain, but I'm getting the impression you're quite fresh."

"A few days," Tory says.

"Wonderful." Riese's eyes glint. He pulls the doors wide and gestures inside with an elaborate *after you* sort of flourish. "Forgive my unkind words earlier. In my experience, the creatures in the Box are either rabid or tragically domesticated. It's rare to meet one like you." He says it like it's an honor, like he sees something amazing in Tory. The fire flares brighter. "If it's tearing throats out that you're after, I think we can accommodate you." His wide grin goes dangerous, and Tory can't help echoing it. "It would seem we've all gotten lucky today. I happened to be out west doing some reconnaissance and caught up with Ariana here to hitch a ride to the border."

West. Hulven is not far west. "There's a mining town out there," Tory blurts, foot half-lifted to get him into the car.

Riese's smile warms. "I saw it. Cozy little place. Vines are doing a number on the wall."

Tory wants to say *did it look well?* but he forces his lips to close around the words. "You could use someone like me?"

"We *need* someone like you. Take your time thinking. I have to speak with some friends across the border about a little joint mission of ours, so you can mull it over until we arrive, but I think you'll say yes."

"No." Hasra pushes Tory up into the car. "Riese, leave it."

"You leave it," Riese snaps, and sighs when Hasra just scowls. "Why? He yours?"

"He is." Hasra climbs up and guides Tory to join a huddling crowd against the back wall.

Riese leaps into the car after them and pulls the wooden doors closed with the moan of ungreased joints, plunging them into darkness. "My apologies. I don't see the resemblance."

"Doesn't have to be blood to be family. I failed to keep him safe once. I won't let it happen again."

Tory's chest warms, comfortable and suffocating in equal measure, because he *wants* freedom. All the stories he's heard burst to life in his head: the clear blue Sea of Thorns to the east in Arlune, lethal and beautiful in the light; smoky sandglass talons curling from the seabed to prevent naval attacks. Night-black cliffs to the west. Terraced crops in the highlands, spilling impossible harvest after impossible harvest. Arlune isn't perfect—Tory barely speaks a word of the language—but perhaps it's a place where he could be free.

But the simple freedom he used to hunger for doesn't feel like enough anymore. He's sharp and primed to fight, and Riese's offer speaks to a hunger he's been denying for years.

"Hasra," he says, and she stiffens at his side. "Remember at the House, how you said you could watch out for yourself?"

He doesn't need to see her face to know she's deflating. "*Tory.*"

"I'll be fine."

She huffs. "Keep telling me that. One day it'll be true."

He leans against her shoulder.

Tory might keep his silence until they get to the border, but he knows his answer.

"We'll welcome you," Riese says. He seems to know Tory's answer, too.

They lapse into silence, which makes the noises around them all the louder. Someone taps a foot or a finger against the floor with a drumming noise. To his right, a small group murmurs, low and nervous. A child cries in quiet gulps to his left.

Ari whispers, "Shh, little one. Soon we'll be somewhere you don't have to be afraid."

The child's breathy sobs punctuate the quiet as Tory's eyes adjust. He makes out movement, then shapes with growing distinctness. Gray light sifts through the spaces between the wood that makes up the walls.

Ariana plants a kiss on the child's forehead. The boy only cries harder.

"Papa," he whispers.

"Your Papa wanted you to grow up happy."

"Don't wanna," the boy whimpers. "Want my Papa."

Tory's stomach twists. Fresh from the camps, he wanted a lot of things, too—his mother most of all. She bought his freedom with her life, so he tried to repay her with obedience. If she were here, she'd urge him to listen to Hasra. But he can't. This time, he can fight. Tory knows how to use his abilities now. He can turn them on the people who caught and caged him. So many walls in this filthy country. With Riese, maybe he can break them down.

Cries of *whoa, whoa* jolt him back into humid dark.

Everyone goes stiff and still, breath suspended.

Ariana hisses, "We shouldn't be stopping."

But the caravan's wheels creak and whine, car jerking and twisting with too-sudden deceleration.

Ariana hunches over the boy in the dimness, hushing his cries. "Shh, you're okay. I'm an Illusionist—I won't let anyone see you."

Quiet, Riese promises, "We'll keep you safe."

Ulenn Belmin's voice echoes from outside.

"*Of course, gentlemen. I'm merely traveling to the trading posts on the border to pick up a shipment of Arlunian lacquerware before we head north to Maran.*"

"*Then you won't mind if we take a look. We can tell he's somewhere in the vicinity; we need to be thorough.*"

"*Whatever you need. This one just has lampshades—here. Step up.*"

Clattering, the thunk of heavy boots.

The voices fade and re-emerge, coming closer.

"This one has fabric. You can look inside if you'd like."

"No need. The animals are well trained."

The grind of boots on gravel, then what Tory recognizes as the skittering of canine feet.

"Well, gentlemen." The voices are louder, closer. Too close. "This one's empty, as I said."

"All right," Ariana says. "Here goes nothing."

Tory bears no weapon that would matter. Hasra grabs his arms and pulls him to her, heart thundering against his back.

Ariana covers the boy's mouth and leans forward before the door opens, blinding them.

She stares straight into the eyes of the soldier holding the door. His dog erupts in snarls and scrambles up, baring its teeth.

Ariana's father makes a distressed noise, but his face remains impassive. His eyes find Tory and widen.

"See? I told you it was empty," Belmin says, faint. He trips to the left as the snarling dog snaps near his elbow.

"I see." The soldier leans in.

The dog claws halfway inside, growling deep and deadly, dripping saliva.

The soldiers *do nothing.*

"Ari," a petite girl with short, spiked black hair whispers. "The dog."

"*Wyn,*" Ariana echoes. "You know how I am with animals. You take care of it, if it's bothering you so much."

"Fine." With a playful kiss to Ariana's cheek, the girl she called Wyn sprints to the front, dodging the frothing dog's teeth to lay a feather-light hand on its head.

It slumps, weak and whimpering, falling back to the ground.

"Well, then!" Ariana's father booms, looking studiously away. "Mr. and Mrs. Rost are waiting for their lacquerware, and Yarana Vantaras *personally* requested three bolts of fabric for her daughter's Dedication. I don't want either of us to stand in the way of that."

"Certainly not, Mr. Belmin."

"Good! Please, gentlemen. I'll walk you back."

Belmin, flustered, pushes the doors closed in the wrong order. The left one creaks open a foot or so as the soldiers retreat. That was too damn close.

Tory gestures at the door. "Should I . . .?"

"I'll get it as soon as I can feel my legs again." Ariana slumps against the wall, the girl she called Wyn already sinking to the ground beside her. "That was a mess."

Riese scrubs a hand down his face. "Never a dull moment with you, Ms. Belmin."

A hand grabs the door from outside, and Ari calls, "Thanks, Dad! I would've got it—"

No.

Tory has a half-second advantage on everyone else, because the hand doesn't push the door closed, it pulls it open.

And it bears a far-too-familiar white glove.

CHAPTER TEN

Tory holds his breath as Vantaras pulls the door wide. The boy in Ariana's arms breathes voiceless sobs against her skin. Eyes steady on the door, she pats his hair and murmurs nonsense.

Vantaras examines the dark interior, face impassive, left hand tracing the shape of the handgun holstered at his side.

The crunch of gravel precedes the reappearance of one of the soldiers from earlier. He salutes. "Sir? We cleared this one. Empty."

"Did you."

Tory shivers at Vantaras' thorough, silent examination, but Ariana stays focused on her task. The dog is gone. It's fine.

The soldier stands straighter. "It's awaiting a shipment of Arlunian lacquerware. Sir, your—uh. The Rost and Vantaras families specifically requested material from this shipment, so Mr. Belmin is eager to move on."

"I see. Any irregularities?"

"None, sir. Except . . . Yaqi."

"I'm sorry?"

The soldier flushes vibrant red and stands at mortified attention. "The dog! I named him after my baby sister, sir, 'cause he's always making trouble and eating things he shouldn't. Actually, he, uh.

He ate something in the woods a while back and it must've hit him wrong. He's not acting like himself."

"That's . . ." Vantaras tilts his head. "Unfortunate. You may return to the vehicle and allow Mr. Belmin to continue preparations for departure. Convey my apologies for the inconvenience. There are a few things I'd like to check before we depart."

"Yes, sir!"

The boy in Ariana's arms sniffles and wraps his arms around her neck. The soldier doesn't respond to the noise or the movement.

Vantaras does.

And *shit*, Tory's abilities didn't work on him back then, either.

His eyes, unerring, find Tory's. His hand clenches on the door, but he says nothing.

The soldier peers into the darkness to where Vantaras is looking. He squints. "Sir? Is something the matter? I can go in and make sure there are no hidden compartments."

"You're dismissed."

"Yes, sir!" The soldier strides away.

Tory slides to the side. There's a trapdoor beneath him—he's assuming for situations like this one, when evacuation is unavoidable—and he slides off it and twists his fingers in the loop of twine. The trapdoor creaks as it lifts.

When they're alone, Vantaras lets go of the door. "I wouldn't do that, Arknett. You won't get far. You can come out, or I can come in and apprehend you."

"How about neither?"

"Anything you do will end with your capture, but if you don't exit on your own, you run the risk of drawing attention to Miss Belmin and these other Seeds. Miss Belmin may be able to put them off for a while, but her power seems to be intrinsic and effective only within the range of her sight. If they see or hear too many things they can't reconcile with the illusions she crafted for them once they're outside that range—for example, a Seed escaping from the direction of *this* caravan, they'll be back. I was sent after *you*. If you wish to see children in prison, go ahead and make noise, but their arrests will be on your head."

"Like you care." Tory's stomach twists. Inches from freedom, and *Sena Vantaras* is here to steal it from him again. But he's right. Tory couldn't live with himself if Hasra and everyone else here ended up in the labor camps or the Box.

"Remember that your Core is a tracker," Vantaras says. He lifts a glowing, compass-like device, the stellite set into its surface shining a steady, blinding white. "We found you with it once, and we can find you again."

That wouldn't have mattered if he'd made it across the border. Tory nearly suffocates on a swell of helpless anger. It grows until he's a bare inch from choking on it then bursts, leaving him empty and cold.

"Fuck you," he says. "I hate you."

It's childish, and the words make him sick even as he speaks them. They're surrender. They're an acknowledgment of failure. His fingers unwind from the loop of twine, and blood floods back in.

"Miss Belmin, I'd appreciate if you'd maintain your illusions until Arknett is outside and into the woods."

Tory stands, his legs barely willing to hold him after his long run, but Hasra seizes his hand and pulls him back. "Tory," she says. "I'll—I can . . ."

He forces his lips into a bright, irreverent smile. At the choked noise she makes in response, Tory's chest pangs like something's broken. He didn't sign up to leave her behind again. He aches to hug her or stop up his ears with his fingers or push her away. He does none of those things.

"You know me." Tory frees his hand from hers. "I can take care of myself. I'm . . . it was good to see you."

Her warm hands lift his chin, and he doesn't press into the touch. "Don't do this again. It's okay to rely on people, Tory. It's okay to let them fight for you."

It isn't, though. His mom fought for him, and it got her killed. Tying himself to anyone only leads to hurt, in the end. "Don't worry about me."

"Then stop giving me reason to worry! I'm not a patient person. Take too long coming back and I *swear* to you, I will break down those damn walls and drag you out myself. I swear it by the earth under my feet."

Vantaras shifts his attention to her at last. "You'd be safer if you didn't."

She laughs, raw and angry, then stomps forward to spit in Vantaras' direction. It lands on the floor a few inches away from where he stands, but he doesn't step back or touch his weapon.

"Colonel's orders," he murmurs.

"You and your orders can rot."

Tory walks ahead of her, gait wooden. "I'll be okay," he lies again. He smiles at her nose. He won't be able to leave if he sees how she's looking at him. "I'll find you when I'm out."

"Kid." Riese's voice stops Tory before he steps out. "We'll meet again, I'm sure of it." Tory glances over his shoulder, swallowing hard, to find Riese wearing a sharp, sorrowful smile. "Think of us when you're free."

Tory steps out of the car without answering and bends his knees to absorb the shock of impact. He tosses a lazy mock-salute at the folks inside. "Have fun."

He should say more, but his throat hurts like he gargled rocks.

"Where do you want me, Vantaras?"

Vantaras tips his chin toward the interior of the car as he closes and latches the door. "It's better to forget about family. It would be safer for them and kinder to them if you never crossed paths again."

"*Where do you want me?*"

Vantaras points into the woods, and Tory follows his finger behind a tree, far enough that he could probably make a run for it.

Your Core is a tracker.

He wouldn't get far.

He forgot how much his legs hurt from running, but they barely move to get him into the woods. When he gets deep enough, knees shaking and skin greasy with cold sweat, he leans his head against a tree's solid trunk and tastes bile.

Everything happens quickly after that. Vantaras yells something and darts toward Tory. No syringe this time—though it would be more merciful if there were. Vantaras twists his hands behind his back, locks a pair of cuffs over his wrists, and directs him to a covered truck that sputters and rattles and belches fuel fog like the machinery in Hulven. He points to the back. Tory goes.

Vantaras climbs in behind him after conferring with the two soldiers. He settles on the opposite side, as far from Tory as he can get, and doesn't speak a word as they drive away.

The dog lies on his side between them, breathing like he's broken.

*

When Tory's led back inside, everyone is busy at maneuvers. It's like he never left.

For a sick moment, motion on the field suspends itself, and Tory is the unfortunate recipient of a hundred angry stares.

As the razor-toothed front gate slams closed behind him, he's led up the hill, shrouded by uniformed guards, with Vantaras at the helm. The guards are overkill. Tory's legs will barely support him. His head throbs, lips parched.

"Ah, there you are!" Helner skips from the facility's front door in a haze of red hair, messy bun pinned today by a sharpened pencil and what might be an icepick. She snags the sleeve of Vantaras' uniform. "What a good little hunting dog you are, Vantaras," she sneers, and lets him go to grab Tory by the chin. "I hate to say it, but I *am* glad he caught you. My plans for the week would've been ruined, otherwise."

Vantaras gestures to a guard, who peels Helner's hands off Tory's chin and pushes her away. "I have somewhere to be."

"Don't we all." She paces around the group to throw an arm out in front of Vantaras. He skids to a stop before reaching it. Any other time, Tory might take pleasure in seeing Vantaras off balance, but today the frigid wind dries his sweat to him and tugs shivers from his core, his muscles so utterly dead it's all he can do to keep on his feet.

He hates them both right now.

Helner, after all, is the one who installed his Core. It's not *only* Vantaras' fault that he's in this mess.

"*Leave*, Dr. Helner. The colonel is waiting for my report."

"Lovely!" She claps her hands. "I'll tag along! Tory, don't you think it would be nice if I tagged along?"

"How can you stomach it?" Tory manages, tongue thick. "Betraying every Seed here, making them serve the Grand General? You're a Seed, too."

She flinches. "We all have to survive."

"Maybe not all of us."

She chokes on a startled laugh. "Get some sleep, asshole. I may be the Grand General's puppet, but at least I'm not a *coward*." She pokes Vantaras' chest, and he shoves her away. "The fact that I'm not the lowest worm writhing around in this place does help me sleep a little better at night. I'd have no one to trap if this one didn't bring them to me, now, would I?"

"I asked you to *leave us*, Dr. Helner," Vantaras says, voice low and dangerous.

"And I think I'll have to decline."

Vantaras lifts a finger, and the guards are ready to jump into action, but Helner raises her own hand. "Ah, but Lieutenant, you forget that I have *eyes*. The other day, when you brought this feisty little thing to me for his Core, I was watching you. Do you think your colonel would like to hear what I saw then? Because I think he'd be *fascinated* to learn how—"

Vantaras starts walking. "What do you want?"

Tory forces his legs to cooperate. It's so much harder to put them into motion after a moment of pause. Nausea is slick in his belly, his vision growing gray as the sky overhead.

"You know what I want, Sena."

The soldiers' boots echo on the floor like gunshots, counting out the moments between Helner's words and Vantaras' answer. "I do not."

"I need you to arrange me some time with the Channeler. There's something I want to try with him."

Vantaras sounds disgusted. "There's always something you want to try."

"I've put a lot of thought into it, and your report about what happened in Hulven corroborates my theories. If the Channeler can handle every energy, he should be able to control captured Legion units. He's the answer. I know he is."

"If you're coming to me, it means you've failed to get permission from Colonel Kirlov or the general. It's not my place to offer what they've denied you."

Tory bites his tongue as they walk. If he had the energy for it, he'd say *I'm right here*, or maybe *I'm not a token to be bartered*, but all his energy goes to keeping his feet underneath him, so he imagines chewing through both their throats at once instead.

Helner says sweetly, "Please recall that I can have a *delightful* conversation with Kirlov this evening if you don't accommodate this simple, reasonable request of mine, Lieutenant."

Vantaras' footsteps falter.

"I'm asking for a tiny favor. You'll arrange it, won't you?"

His fists clench so hard the bones creak. ". . . I'll arrange it."

"Wonderful!" She's already walking backward, stepping out of sight of the group and fading down the hall. "And make sure—"

Vantaras paces ahead so fast they're too far away to catch whatever comes next.

He stops the group, at last, in front of an unlabeled room, its door flanked by two soldiers. He knocks.

"Enter," calls a hollow voice from inside.

The whole group, minus Tory, seems to steel themselves, but Vantaras turns to the soldiers behind him. "You're dismissed. I'll be in contact if I have questions."

They don't *literally* sigh, but their bodies are sighs in motion as they sketch salutes and retreat like their asses are on fire, leaving Tory with an empty hall behind him and no strength to flee down it.

With a nod to the impassive soldiers flanking the door, Vantaras gestures for Tory to go inside. Glaring, he obeys.

The door closes behind them.

The lights in the hallways were bright enough, but they're *blinding* in here. The room is wide and mostly empty, windowless aside from three of those narrow, bar-like windows. It looks like an empty lab of some sort, and Tory wonders if Kirlov chose it for the counter that stands like an island between them. He takes Tory in, expressionless.

"Your supervisee nearly got away from us, Lieutenant."

Vantaras stands bone-crackingly straight. "Yes, Sir. He made it as far as Serpentshead."

It hits Tory only then that he hasn't mentioned Belmin or his Seeds. He assumed, earlier, that letting them go was part of some larger plot on Sena's part, just like he cleared space in the doorway for a second before Tory's Core was installed—a predator taunting its prey with freedom before trapping it between its teeth again. But Helner said something was up with *that*, too, didn't she? Tory grits his teeth. He's too tired for this. Vantaras keeps talking, tone steady and dry. "Private Jemmes informed me at the gate that Menden and three guards are recovering with the Healers."

"I'm aware."

A person should not be able to stand *more* at attention when they're already doing so, but Vantaras somehow manages it. "I accept responsibility. Arknett's actions are as mine."

Tory wants to bite him. Throw him out a window.

A research subject for Helner, and now not even his choices are his own.

He was so close. To Arlune. To freedom, and people who could show him how to fight to keep it.

"Do you bastards even hear yourselves?" he blurts, and the way Kirlov's eyes narrow makes him think this was a bad choice, but he's already taking a short step forward and can't stop himself mid-stride.

Or perhaps he can. His foot, when it lands on the floor, finally gives up its token effort to keep him standing, and he lands hard on one knee.

At least it takes those icepick eyes off of him and turns them on Vantaras. "Lieutenant, you *injured* him?"

"No, Sir. I believe it's exhaustion. I was hoping to deliver him to the Healers . . ."

"Do it. I expect you'll make it absolutely clear what will happen if he continues to act in this way. You are *lucky* you managed to recapture him so quickly. The Grand General will be visiting tomorrow, and if he were to see the Channeler in anything but pristine condition . . ."

"My fa—" Vantaras' hands fly behind his back, clasping each other so tight Tory's surprised something doesn't break. He shakes himself, paces to the door, and opens it. "Please escort Mr. Arknett to the Healers."

Tory isn't sure he's going to be escorted anywhere. Now that he's no longer putting weight on them, his legs have gone like jelly. Two apathetic soldiers enter to drag him out.

He hears, just before the door closes, "The Grand General will be coming *here*?"

*

He isn't sure how much time has passed when the infirmary door opens, searing Tory's aching eyes. Vantaras steps inside to whisper with the nurse, his face beaded with sweat and gait uneven.

Tory's lips curl.

The room is barren, just a nurse, the bed with straps looped around one wrist because he's a *flight risk*, and the blue-toned strips of lighting along the wall that paint the room in calming underwater colors. Relaxing colors, the young man who healed him said, while Tory nearly dozed at the euphoric rush of warmth as his tired, torn muscles repaired themselves.

Relaxing colors.

The darkness in the caravan with Hasra had the same muffled quality, but all Tory can remember is that gloved hand wrenching the door open. Hasra's eyes as she watched him go.

He's got energy, now, to feel all the shame and rage he was too drained for, earlier.

At the sight of Sena Vantaras, Tory *burns.*

Vantaras sucks in a breath, shallow and erratic. The heels of his shoes tick on the floor as he approaches Tory. "Forgive me for the delay." A demand, not a request. "I made the grave mistake of not explaining the full function of your Core the moment you received it. Naively, having never had supervisees before, I believed it would be merciful to allow you a few short days to acclimate to STAR-7 before making you aware of the breadth of the control it has over you, but I failed to take into account your stupidity and recklessness. I won't make the same mistake twice."

Tory scoffs. "You, *merciful?*"

Vantaras doesn't take the bait. He's never met Tory's eyes so steadily before. Even in the *relaxing light* of the infirmary, they're molten golden-brown. Tory aches to look away but refuses to give Vantaras the pleasure.

"You might recall that the thing implanted in your neck is a tracker."

Tory flinches.

"That's not its only function. What I failed to mention before is that it's a sort of lit fuse—stellite-powered, so your Seed energies sustain the very device that imprisons you and can kill you if you step out of line."

"What?"

"As I explained before, the matching compass in the Monitor Room, having been fed a drop of your blood and thus a sample of the Seed that powers your Core, resonates with the Core inside you and can be used to hunt you, which accounts for the tracking and identification features. But they thought it would be funnier still if the Core literally took root inside Seeds, so they employed an altered version of a vine that responds to stellite. Any attempt to remove the tracker will result in the roots it has spread in your body breaking off and remaining behind. Those roots produce an extraordinarily toxic compound when they decay, poisoning your blood and killing you."

Tory swallows, body tingling with cold. A frenzied rush in his ears mutes the noise of his breath and dyes the dim world darker. Maybe he really is underwater. His hand goes to his shoulder where his Core was planted.

"If you escape, they will track you with it to find you. You die if you take it out, so they *will* find you."

"Stop."

Vantaras does not stop. "If for whatever reason they cannot reach you, they can disable it remotely using your compass. The Core's decaying roots will kill you, but the decay of the Core itself will kill you far faster. It's a graceless, agonizing death. If you leave without permission or fail to maintain regular contact while performing an authorized mission and they judge the risk of your capture or escape higher than your use to them, they may disable your Core. Your only choice—the *single choice* remaining to you—is to do exactly as they ask of you until you die or they kill you. You cannot escape, Mr. Arknett. The second the Core was placed in your body, you signed over everything you are to the Vantaras family."

Tory laughs to cover the other sound that wants to escape him. "You have one, too?"

"Of course. As you've observed, I am also a Seed."

"Even your big connections couldn't get you a pass?"

Vantaras chuckles, low and cold. "Had my father compromised for his own son, what would others have said?" He turns away, baring the long scar on his neck. "Do not try something like this again. There are worse things than the Core. You don't want to find out what they are."

Tory knows walls. He's beaten his hands bloody against so many. This is something infinitely more terrible. Walls can be climbed or burned or broken down. Some of them, like the ones in Hulven, are silly things. From far enough away, any wall is laughable. His Core, though, is like the tattoo on his arm—a prison he carries with him.

Tory stares at his blankets. The implantation site for his Core stopped hurting shortly after it was installed. He wants to pinch it, prod it, make it bleed or burn—make it announce itself for what it is.

Vantaras' gloved fingers rasp at the material of his uniform slacks in quick, precise circles. "This incident has been noted on your record. Security won't increase for you this time, but make no mistake. They're looking for excuses to put you further under their thumb. As a Worldseed, you already have the generals' attention. It's unwise to give them reason to look closer. If you try to escape again, especially if you make as much of a scene as you did this time, they might decide you need a NOVA."

"You keep saying *they*," Tory hisses.

"Pardon me?"

"*They* may disable my Core, *they're* looking for excuses. *They* might decide. You're one of them."

"Is that what you think?" Vantaras scoffs, one gloved hand skimming the back of his neck. "You're wrong."

"I doubt it. You know, you keep giving me all this advice, *Lieutenant Vantaras*."

Vantaras flinches.

"'Don't make trouble, don't invite attention, don't make them hurt you.' All these rules to make me a smaller target, a perfect little soldier. When do you—do any of you—tell them to stop hurting *us*?"

Vantaras stands there, wordless and stricken. "I—"

His mouth snaps closed and he turns to go without a word.

"That's what I thought," Tory spits at the door that slams closed behind him.

CHAPTER ELEVEN

A ROGUE SHOT OF energy from behind drives Tory into the mud and grass of the training field.

"Damn, sorry!" Gavin calls.

Beating the guy down in the rec room hasn't been conducive to friendly relations.

It's their first day doing maneuvers with Gavin's unit. The Kineticists and other sword corps Seeds aim attacks at moving targets along the wall while the shield corps—CFR and Fielders—manages defense. The support corps—mostly Healers, with one or two Porters for emergency transport, evacuation, and reconnaissance—lingers along the periphery. This, Menden promises, is where everything comes together, each unit acting in concert.

Hardly. This is where everything falls apart.

Tory crashes into the mud halfway outside the forcefield, hands slipping out from under him as a Legion-sphere passes. He has a fraction of a second for horror—not long enough to move away—before thousands of pounds of metal roll over his hand.

He doesn't scream, not while Gavin stands behind him, snickering. He doesn't hug his wrist to his chest or invite the attention of one of the Healers. He pushes himself up with his opposite hand and keeps working. He can't prevent this pain, but he can deny Gavin the satisfaction of his suffering.

It's a nicer idea in theory than in practice. By the time training ends, his hand is horribly swollen, mottled purple and red. Drumbeats of agony throb with every heartbeat. Normally he'd skip the Healers and hit the showers, but not even Tory can shower off shattered bones.

Randall fusses over him as he gets in line, and Gavin settles in behind him, glare palpable.

"Hey, Special Diet," someone calls. "Heard you did a runner. How'd that work out?"

"At least I *tried*." He fixes his eyes on the door.

Tory's unit has mastered coordinated force redirection, and the Fielders know their jobs. With a small unit of Healers waiting on the outskirts to deal with debilitating injuries, the line to the infirmary is half its normal length.

It's already taken twice as long as it should.

Chill wind dries sweat to Tory's skin and rips a shiver from him. He longs for his usual hot shower. Resentment—if not for Gavin, he'd be enjoying it right now—pulses through him.

The guy at the front of the line when this whole thing started still stands at the front, though. The door hasn't opened once.

"Something's wrong," he whispers to Randall.

"I know," Randall whispers back. "Your arm's as big as a balloon. You want me to tell Menden what went down? I saw that jerk laughing. We're supposed to be working *together*."

"Not that," Tory hisses. "It's taking—"

The door opens before he can finish, and what might have been a spark of relief dies inside him.

"Niela . . ." Randall breathes.

The Healer who opens the door, compact with brown skin and dark hair cut at the same angle as the scar that lines her left cheek, wears blood like a robe. It dyes her apron, cascades down the front of her powder blue uniform, and sits on the tops of her white slippers. Her hands shine with it.

Randall pushes through the crowd. "Niela! Are you—?"

She just shakes her head.

Perfect silence accompanies the unit into the infirmary. Every bed lies empty. None of the Healers talk about what caused the delay, but the solemn nurses carting out blood-soaked rags and the stains not quite washed from the floor tell a story no one dares to speak. The Healer who takes care of Tory's arm still has blood under his fingernails.

The urge to run hits him with an urgency that steals his breath, but Vantaras' warning floats back into his mind. "Hey," he says. "What's a NOVA?"

The Healer's hands jerk against his arm. "You don't want to know."

He gestures at the boy's fingernails, at the stains on the floor. "Can't be worse than *that*."

Silence scrolls out, and the boy glances twice at the door before whispering, "You'd think so, wouldn't you?" His fingertips press too hard into Tory's forearm, creaking against not-quite-healed bone. "It's *inhumane* is what it is. It's part kill switch, and it just gets worse from there." The Healer pales. Far too slow and careful, he says, "Don't tell me one's been ordered for you."

Tory swallows. "Not yet."

At dinner that night, he forces food into his mouth. He can't make himself return to his room, to Gavin with his thinly veiled hostility, so he wanders.

Every time he wanders, he learns. He files away each shred of knowledge.

The guard at the front sometimes steps outside to smoke. The light in Dr. Helner's office in Intake stays on at all hours. She never sleeps, never leaves—except when she disappears, and no one can find her. Everyone has a filthy rumor to account for that. Someone said they saw her shoving a cute guy into a closet once. The only thing the nasty rumors agree on is that she's always the boss.

The asshole general who runs this place sings in the shower. Once, Tory catches Menden reciting a love poem to Jeffra from outside the door of the infirmary.

It should have occurred to him to wonder why the building is circular, but he stumbles on the answer by accident. After weeks of gray halls, the unnatural glow from the dead stellite lighting, and the nose-burning scent of cleaning solution in the hallways, he doesn't know what to do when he inhales and tastes earth.

The scent leads him to a closed door.

He tries his tab on the off chance the area is public access and jolts back when the door unlocks. He opens it to a wide-open, circular garden, like the building itself is a wall made to trap it inside. At night, the garden is alive with insect songs, and above it all is the *sky*, deep blue and cloudless, strewn with stars. It's been too long since he's seen them. He knows none of their names, but the round gravel of a cobblestone path massages his feet through his slippers, the grass on either side of it thick and soft.

Woody vines climb the walls that hem the garden in, throwing off serrated, heart-shaped leaves and a profusion of flowers in shades of indigo and violet. Aside from the colors, they're just like the ones that crowd over the walls near the mine in Hulven. The bell-shaped blossoms perfume the air, honey-sweet.

It smells like home, as much as any place can.

A massive tree rises from the center, leaves misted with droplets from the rain that blew through after dinner. It's a beast of a tree, its trunk ash-brown and gnarled. The vines live here, too, twining around the branches and dropping willowy strings of blooms between the leaves.

That night, Tory falls asleep against the tree and misses the bell for breakfast, waking with just enough time to run to training. Vantaras is less than pleased, but Tory doesn't care.

Even the mutters of *Hey, Special Diet!* don't ruin his evening, because out there in the dark there's a canopy of stars and that old tree with its blanket of moss and grass, where he can be alone. He eats quickly and disappears, his knowledge of the halls working in his favor when the distinct, staccato ticks of Vantaras' shoes echo against the floor. He ducks into a dim and dusty storage room until the footsteps pass, then continues on his way.

He gets out to the garden before the sun sets. It's narrower in daylight—more prison, less paradise. Fine netting on the skeletal dome overhead shields the space from open sky.

Sunset golds settle nicely on the tree, though.

Perhaps the gardens were cultivated at some point, but the place has reclaimed a sort of fenced-in wilderness. Tory inhales the evening damp and treasures how night leeches warmth from the ground as the insects start with their scratchy songs.

Some nights, he doesn't go back to his room at all.

*

Other nights, he doesn't even make it to dinner.

Vantaras corners him outside the mess hall, breathless and distracted. "Dr. Helner sent me to find you."

Right. Their bartering the other day with Tory as the item of interest.

Randall waves from a table in the corner, grin half-eating his freckled face and finger pointing aggressively at whatever's in his bowl. He mouths something Tory doesn't catch and waves for Tory to join him. Then he points to a ragged strip of paper dangling from his pocket and waggles his eyebrows. He's been gambling again. Tory takes a step toward him without thinking, but Vantaras' extended arm stops him.

"I need you to come with me."

"And I need you to leave me alone. I'm hungry."

"Eat later."

Tory rounds on Vantaras. "Why should I listen to you? Whatever Helner has on you, it's got nothing to do with me. Why should I care if you keep your end of the bargain?"

"Because if she tells the generals what she alluded to, I won't be the only one on the chopping block. They'll look closely at you, too, and as I said before, you don't want that."

Tory paces as close to Vantaras as he dares, balled fist aching at his side. "I want to punch you in your smug mouth."

"You're welcome to try as soon as we're finished."

"What is it she wants to do, anyway?"

Vantaras' lips thin as he leads Tory down the hall. "One of her experiments, I presume."

"That's it?" Tory scrambles to keep up. "Hey! You've got to give me more than that."

"Ask her when you see her. The doctor loves to talk."

"Tell me, *Sena*, what is it she has on you?"

Vantaras' eyes narrow at the use of his first name. The bastard walks faster. Soon, they arrive at a door marked with a simple, hammered silver plaque: *Lab #1*. It's not particularly ominous, but neither is it any more helpful than Vantaras has been. He snaps his fancy tab from his pocket and hangs it in front of the chunky locking mechanism with its inset crystal. The crystal flashes white and clicks to unlock.

The laboratory blinds him—polished metal and white walls made cutting and cruel with brilliant light.

Surrounded by murmuring technicians in the center of a gleaming silver table, a ball of tightly wrapped, peeling vines waits, at odds with its clinical surroundings. A few serrated, heart-shaped leaves sprout from it. They're identical to the leaves on the vines in the garden and the ones in Hulven with their organ-red blooms.

Pulses of energy—violent and vibrant, like something living—barrel into him. *Da-dum, da-dum,* like an electric heartbeat. Tory shakes with it, knees knocking, breath frozen in his chest. He traces the energy to its source.

To the nondescript ball of vines.

The scientists mill around like it's *nothing*. Helner stands less than a foot away, tapping long, sharp fingernails on the table. She's close enough to touch it.

Even from the doorway, Tory can barely stand. His vision tunnels.

It's like that eerie feeling he got from the mine in Hulven except so much worse. Better?

He'd die to touch this thing.

"Breathe," Vantaras reminds him, dry.

Tory manages a blurry glare. "Can't they *feel* that? Can't you?"

"They're not Seeds."

Tory notes the fine tremors in his clenched fists. "Helner is."

"Dr. Helner isn't human," Vantaras snips.

Tory doesn't mean to laugh.

At the sound, Helner turns. "Ah! Knew I could count on you, Vantaras. Such a good boy." She invites them over with two scalpel-sharp gestures.

It's not that he doesn't want to go, but there's no way his legs will carry him there.

He manages a few toddling steps, and the energy intensifies, filling every empty place inside him. He looks back, vision swirling. "You're not coming?"

At least if Vantaras was going, he could hide his jelly-limbed staggering behind him.

"I've been the subject of this experiment more than once." A quick, mirthless smile. "They didn't like the results."

"Tory! We don't have all day!"

He clamps his mouth shut on the questions he wants to ask. Halfway to the strange sphere, he goes down on one knee. There's a shuffle behind him, and when he manages to turn, Vantaras is halfway across the floor toward him.

Helner growls, "Lieutenant, move *one* step closer and I will trash you to the colonel."

All color fades from his face and he's flat against the back wall again, an inch or so from blending into it.

"Arknett, up."

Helner grabs his elbow when he gets close.

His blurred vision clarifies when he stops mere feet from the table, the world etched with sharp lines and painted in colors Tory has no names for. Dr. Helner and Sena are revelations, galaxies, the Seeds within them unspeakably bright.

"He's high," Helner says. "How sweet."

Pain blooms on his cheek like a flower, sharper and duller than any sensation he's felt.

It could be hours later when he manages, "Ow?"

Helner lowers the hand that must have slapped him and curls it into an elegant fist. "Hilarious though your reaction may be, you have work to do."

He's outside himself. His lips don't belong to him. "Work . . . ?"

"What do you feel?"

"A lot."

"Your specialty is in recognizing and handling energies—which accounts for your extreme reaction to proximity. It also increases the likelihood of your ability to help us. You've done this before—there were reports of the stellite in Hulven glowing, a clear resonance response."

"I didn't . . ." But he remembers the strange, impossible energy that leapt into his hands when he was healing Kelly. It was nothing near so intense as this, though.

"Don't bother denying it. The color of the glow matched what the analysts saw during your typing. In any case, meet Legion unit #2. Shari here calls it *Joe*, but we don't listen to Shari."

The scientist beside Helner crosses her arms. "Joe is one of only *three* in our possession. We used to have six." She glares at Sena.

Legion. Isn't that what those huge things in training are supposed to emulate? This is melon-sized and kind of cute. It has *leaves*. It's a toy compared to what Tory has faced in training. But those bone-crushing spheres are supposed to be the toys? Someone is confused.

"Legion units are the thorns in Westrice's side. They're Arlune's strongest weapons. Their stellite cores are locked to the unique energy signatures of their users, and no standard Seeds have had any luck awakening them. Zero response to proximity or touch. They're *so simple*, but we haven't been able to reverse-engineer them, either. General Renstein put a stop to our attempts after our third potential pilot bit it. Anyway, there's clearly something they're doing to the vines or the stellite we can't replicate." She sniffs. "We've had a hard enough time getting stellite to hold *any* energy for a significant amount of time." She gestures to the lights along the wall with their milky, cracked crystals. "As you can see, Westrice's attempts have met with less-than-perfect results. What do those lights feel like to you?"

Tory scowls. "Dead things. They're wrong."

"Ha! Wait until I tell the generals they've *killed* the stuff trying to process it. Anyway. So we discovered—" her eyes flick to Vantaras again, "that the Sources may be able to . . . *interact* with the ones in our possession in certain ways, but we still haven't managed to get anyone to form a proper connection with one and make it move. Your abilities should be well suited to controlling one. If I'm right, those assholes will finally listen to me."

"It's . . . cute."

"It can take many forms. Just hope you don't have to see them." Helner extracts a small wooden device with a clock-like hand that swings back and forth. "We've exhausted all avenues of research with the lieutenant. Thus, your turn."

"How do you know I won't do something worse?"

"I assure you, that's impossible. Step closer. You'll need to touch it. It might be overwhelming at first, but once you've settled, I'll provide further instruction."

He reaches out, and the roots pull back like a curtain, like they've been waiting for him.

"That's new," Helner breathes.

A huge stellite crystal sits at the center, flaws sparkling like a field of stars in the Compound's merciless fluorescence. Alive.

Tory's hand trembles, body throbbing with a beat out of time with his own pulse. If it's this bad being *near it* . . .

"By the Beast, just touch it." Helner seizes his wrist and presses his hand to the crystal—

—and Tory breathes for the first time in his life. His blood sings with it. A map of light and texture and sensation unfolds itself across his awareness.

The tang of citrus and the bite of woodsmoke and the brush of silk against his skin fade out, a farewell kiss to every sense. The crystal beneath Tory's hand glimmers with the same galaxy of blues his blood shed when they typed him, casting light like ocean waves onto its cradle of roots.

The roots *shift*, too, like they're eager to listen.

"Good!" Helner could be outside the room, outside the Compound, for all her voice matters. "Yes, this is—" She gulps. "Try a shape, an easy one. How about . . . a sphere that goes all the way around you."

"Dr. Helner, I don't know if that's—"

"Cork it, Vantaras."

Tory imagines it—a sphere to embrace him. The roots lift, tentative.

"You have to *visualize it*," Helner says.

He closes his eyes and sinks into the image: the closeness and darkness of it, claustrophobic. A cage of roots to lock him in, each one a bar in a living prison. Adrenaline scorches him, and the crystal sears his palm. He twists away, but it won't let go.

Heat mounts. Sound fades. The light grows until it burns his eyes.

Roots explode in every direction. One spears the ticking instrument and impales it against the far wall where it spills wood splinters and cogs onto the floor. A strip of the inset stellite lighting bursts when a root punches through it, throwing glass-like shards through the air.

The white-coated assistants duck and cower. With awful, hollow *thunks*, more roots crash into stone walls, the floor, the ceiling, burrowing like they want to break through. More stellite slivers fly. The roots writhe, curling deeper. The ceiling falls in chunks.

Tory stands in the midst of it, safe and far away, senses swathed in wool. Two or three roots over his head deflect debris.

Red light kicks up in the strips along the floor—burst and fade, burst and fade. Tory staggers when something pulls at him from behind. He tips his chin to peer at whatever it is.

Helner.

She's screaming in his ear, but she could be whispering from another room.

Let go, she's saying. *Tory, let go of it!*

He can't. It's part of him now. Tory tries to pry his fingers away with his other hand.

Pipework tumbles from the ceiling, and water sprays down in a fine mist.

Sound returns in a roar. Twist of metal, crash of glass. Screams. The discordant clatter of an alarm bell. The instruments the vines didn't topple or destroy hum and sing and tick around the crystal. The assistant who bemoaned how few of these were left sobs at Tory's feet, hands bloodied from stellite shards. Tory meets every eye, but not one has an answer, until—

Vantaras strides toward him, backlit in red, a study in purpose and fear. The roots shy away, like they know something Tory doesn't. Like the cannon did on the training field.

"Move," he whispers, but Tory hears it loud and clear.

"*Damn* it, Vantaras," Helner growls, but she doesn't stop him.

He pulls the glove from his left hand with his teeth and lets it drop.

The air electrifies. There's no other word for it. Static raises the hair on Tory's arms and neck. It's nothing he can feel or touch, nothing much of anything—it's the silence before a lightning strike, and it's coming from Vantaras.

Vantaras apologizes just before he lays a shaking hand on the roots.

The energy shifts at his touch. It's something, nothing, everything— the bright burn of a star before it dies. The root beneath his hand goes still and gray. The color spreads, and vines crumble to ash, unable to bear their own weight. The crystal cracks, gray-black at its core, stars winking out. Tory staggers, freed from its hold and hollow with its absence.

Reality rushes in. A light flits on and off, a dying smoke-gray in color. The bell shrieks louder, earth-shattering and consuming.

Sena drops to one knee to grab his glove, shoving his hand into it before pressing both palms to his ears. The communicator on his chest flickers blue. "*I* said *alarms were triggered at your location, Lieutenant. Respond.*"

Kirlov's voice.

Sena doesn't answer, probably doesn't hear it.

Ash-like flecks floating on the air are all that's left of most of the roots, or little fragments in the shape of roots that crumble at the touch of Tory's foot.

Red light throbs in and out with the cacophony of the alarm, and on the floor, in the center of it all, Sena says, *sorry, sorry, I'm sorry* and rocks into the cradle of his knees.

CHAPTER TWELVE

I T TAKES A FEW moments, once Vantaras staggers to his feet and flees the room, for Tory to follow. Out the lab, down the hall, *around, around, around* the wide circle of the Compound, past places he's never been, and through a door—at last—into a clearly not-public-access hallway he can only enter because Vantaras' tab unlocks the door and Tory grabs the knob before it closes.

The hallway is empty when he steps inside, but the door to one of the rooms hangs open. Naturally, the thing is twice as large as the glorified closet Tory shares with Gavin. Inside, Vantaras sits on the end of a bed made with unsettling precision, gloved hands in his hair.

"What *was* that just now?" Tory demands, pacing inside.

He's a few steps away when Vantaras finally looks up, wide-eyed. His hands leave his hair to push out in front of him. "Don't!"

He's shaking, and after a moment he seems to realize how close his hands are to Tory, because he makes a noise and drags them back, wrapping them around himself and tucking them under his arms. "Don't," he whispers again. He rocks forward—toward a window, the bastard has a window—eyes fixed on its light. "You can't be in here."

It occurs to Tory, with a sudden lurch in his belly, why Vantaras has so carefully avoided touching him all this time. What happened in there—what he did with those hands—Tory takes a reflexive step back. "I'm not leaving until you tell me what you did."

Vantaras flinches. "It doesn't matter."

"I think it does! Could you have done that to me? Could you have just, like—fucking *erased me*?"

Vantaras bows toward his knees, hands still tucked around himself. "*Stop.*" It might've sounded like an order if his voice weren't frayed, his breaths coming too fast. "Leave."

He wants to, is the thing. This is wrong. This isn't what Vantaras is like. This isn't what *they're* like.

Sena Vantaras captured Tory, brought him to this disgusting place. He's taken his freedom several times since, in large and small ways. But right now, he's trembling so bad his teeth are chattering and his hands look less like he's hiding them and more like he's trying to hold himself together. This isn't the untouchable Lieutenant Vantaras. This, Tory supposes, is just Sena.

Tory crosses his arms, pacing to bleed off nervous energy. "You need to stop breathing like that or you're gonna pass out and I won't get any of my answers."

"S-stars forbid I should inconvenience you." *Sena* sucks in a shallow breath and shakes his bowed head, and Tory can't help noticing how that long, thin scar snakes between the short hairs at the base of his skull and down his neck into his uniform. Tory wonders who did it to him, how far down it goes. He wonders, for the first time, if Sena deserved it.

"If you want me to calm down," Sena manages. "Then *move out of the way of my window.*"

That's when he notices it. A pendant hangs from a hook above the narrow window—the pendant he saw when Vantaras put the blindfold on him. Even from where Tory stands, it's easy to tell that the crystal is the purest specimen he's ever seen outside of the Legion unit he touched today. The rare nebulescence that stellite is famed for creates a river of color at the crystal's center that puts everything in this cold facility to shame. The fading sun shines through and casts its light onto the floor—star-specked galaxies of it in blue and magenta and forest green, transforming as the crystal twirls and swings; Vantaras' hands must not have been steady when he hung it there. The light paints itself onto Tory's simple shoes and up his slate-blue trousers.

He steps out of the way of the light, and Vantaras doesn't say anything. He just stays where he is, hunched forward and staring at the shifting array of vibrant nebulae. His breaths gradually slow.

Tory shuffles, clears his throat to scare away the sudden silence. "Come on. That level of purity? You're just bragging."

"It was a gift," Vantaras says, wooden. He sits up and begins to unbutton his uniform jacket. Tory has the strange urge to look away. "From my mother. It was for my Dedication."

Tory sniffs. "Rich kids and their fancy parties."

"Fancy," he repeats, but doesn't elaborate.

Tory could go, probably, but he came all the way here and he still doesn't have any answers. "About that thing with Helner—"

Sena isn't looking at him. "You made it work."

Tory startles. "I didn't make anything work. It went batshit on me."

"No." Sena sits up. "Whether it was subconscious or not, it was under your control the entire time."

"It fucking *wasn't*—"

"I noticed when I first apprehended you. You don't like being contained, do you?"

Tory's skin crawls. "What do you mean?"

"The vines arched above you and kept even a single piece of stone or debris from hitting you. They weren't destroying indiscriminately. They ruined the instruments meant to measure you and went at the walls that contained you. They didn't kill anyone. You were panicking, so their movement was violent and damaging, but . . . Dr. Helner was not wrong. You're uniquely suited to controlling them.

"The first thing you did when you woke up in the livestock cart, when you shouldn't even have been able to stand, was to get up and beat at the doors. Helner's mistake was not in testing your ability to control them, but in asking you to make a sphere all the way around yourself."

"Then why did you—whatever you did. Destroy it like that?"

"Because you were making a mess. And because I'm not sure it's a good idea if *they* know what you can do."

"We've talked about this. You're one of them."

Sena doesn't answer. He slides his dark jacket off, and the stark white of the button-up makes the dark circles under his eyes seem even darker.

Tory turns his attention to the room. It's wide and mostly empty, aside from the crystal hanging on its hook in the window and two small ceramic pots on the sill. The contents of the first pot are clearly past saving but seem to have been freshly watered, and the plant in the second—a squat, furred, unkillable little thing of the sort that thrives in rocky dirt in high places—seems to be holding on. Vantaras' bed is flawlessly made, the table beside it empty of anything personal. The door in the corner—a full closet, Tory imagines—is closed, and nothing hangs from it.

There's one thing, though, as he completes his slow revolution. Something at odds with the otherwise perfect organization. A letter pokes through the mail slot on the door, fat with its contents and addressed with looping blue ink on fancy, cream-colored paper.

"Oh?" Tory lopes over to snatch the letter from the slot. It smells overwhelmingly of perfume.

"Give me that." Vantaras trips to his feet—he's halfway out of his boots, one unlaced and the other standing beside his mattress.

He kicks the second one off as he strides toward Tory, but Tory lifts the letter away from Vantaras' grasping hands, reading the sender's information by the light from the window. "Hina? Who's *Hina*? Would *not* have pegged you as the sort of person to be loved by anyone—"

"My little sister," Vantaras grits out, grabbing for it.

The letter sags in Tory's grip as he processes that, and Vantaras takes the opportunity to snatch it from his lax fingers. He tightens his grip at the last moment, and the force, between the both of them, rips the top corner of the envelope.

Pressed leaves and flowers tumble out, and Tory feels abruptly guilty. "Sorry," he says, though it's more an old impulse than anything.

"Apologies are useless," Vantaras spits, kneeling to gather the pressed flowers in one gloved hand.

To fill the weighty silence that ensues, Tory says, "You're not allowed to have a sister. That's just weird."

Vantaras scoffs. It's the usual holier-than-thou coldness, all sharp edges, but it fits wrong in this room, where the only light is the fading sunset through the window and the gently rocking nebulae from the pendant. "I'll be sure to let her know, if I see her again."

Tory rolls his eyes. "You're not allowed to be funny, either. I still hate you."

"As long as we have that settled."

Once he's gathered all the flowers, Vantaras sets the small pile and the unopened envelope on the table beside his bed.

Tory frowns. "You not going to open it?"

"I imagine she'd like me to attend her Dedication. I'll need to decline."

"*Why?*"

"I can't—" Vantaras doesn't turn. "I'd prefer they remember me as I was before."

Restless heat surges in Tory. "That's ridiculous."

He didn't even say it loudly, but Sena looks away, wincing. "You don't understand."

"Don't I? You have a living mother and a *sister* who wants to see you, and you're—what? Hiding from them?"

Sena's gloved hands clench at his sides. "The last time I saw them—"

"I don't care if you've grown horns since the last time you saw them! You should—" Tory cuts himself off, and shame is a sick thing in his belly. Does he have any right to talk? He left Hasra and Thatcher behind like they meant nothing, and even if his mother could be in front of him right now, he's not sure what they could talk about. His eyes find Sena's window.

Plants, maybe. When the meals in the camp weren't nearly enough for a growing boy, much less a *working* one, she'd take him into the woods. Whenever he lingered too long on the high fence visible through the thick trees in the distance, she turned his eyes to the ground instead. She taught him the names of every wild edible inside that fence. It saved his life more than once when he was free. His mother acted like the trees were the wall between him and all the ugly things in the world, but she was.

He doesn't know the names of the plants in the pots on Vantaras' sill and hasn't learned any new ones he could share with her.

Stubborn, he finishes his sentence. "You should still see them."

Jaw set, Vantaras tugs at the cuffs of his shirt.

It's weird. The gloves are still on, and even though the double-breasted uniform jacket is gone, the undershirt's starched collar is just as high despite the few buttons he's undone. And the boots are off, but Vantaras' dark socks still snake up beneath his uniform trousers, so he's no less covered than he's ever been in front of Tory. There's no excuse for the way Tory's stomach flips, the way he feels like he's *intruding* when he sees the shape of Sena Vantaras' slim ankles and exposed collarbones.

He looks human.

That's it. *That's* the whole of it. He looks like a person, and for once in his stars-damned life is acting like one, too. It's distracting, like Sena having a sister and a sense of humor.

Tory came here for a reason, though. He reminds himself of it as Sena paces past him on socked feet toward a small cage hanging from the ceiling to the left of the window, covered with a sheet.

"Don't think you'll distract me," Tory says. "I'll keep bothering you until you tell me what your power is."

"Was it not obvious?" With a tug, Sena removes the sheet from the cage and Tory gapes at the sight of something inside, delicate and yellow and—

"Is that a *bird*?"

A knock on the door grinds Tory's sputtering thoughts to a halt.

Just the one knock, like a gunshot.

Vantaras goes still, spine taut and expression carefully blank. "The colonel," he whispers. He bursts into motion, pulling his jacket back on and buttoning it with unsteady fingers.

Another knock, loud enough that it bounces in Tory's skull.

"I can get that . . . ?"

"Don't!" Vantaras skids across the stone floor toward his boots while buttoning the last button on his jacket and stops, clearly distraught, staring at the complex laces on the nearly knee-high boots. There's no way he's getting those on again in any reasonable amount of time.

He wrenches open the door in the corner (a full closet, as Tory thought) and pulls a pair of offensively fancy shined dress shoes off a rack, shoving his feet into them with desperation a hair short of violence.

In the breath before the third knock lands—two knocks, this time, and if knocking can be a threat then this third knock is the most bone-chilling threat Tory has ever heard—Sena looks toward Tory, hair in slight disarray, eyes wide like Tory's must have been when that carriage was bearing down on him.

He pats his hair, strides toward the door, and stands at perfect attention in front of it.

"Sorry—" He pulls the door open. "—Sir."

Kirlov, unbreathing-still, waits on the other side. "What have I said about apologies, Lieutenant?" He doesn't wait for Sena's answer. "You didn't respond."

"Sir?"

"The alarms. I expected an immediate report, but I had to hear about the incident from *Dr. Helner*."

Sena was in no position to give a report, the way Tory found him, but Sena says nothing to defend himself. "It won't happen again, Sir."

"See that it doesn't."

Tory has no reason not to be loving this. Vantaras is off-kilter, and Tory still quite likes the idea of that, but he really shouldn't have followed him here, to his *room*.

Now he knows that Sena off-kilter can look like he did in the lab—on the ground, rocking toward his knees with ashy roots falling to dust all around. It can look like he looked in here, like he was a bare inch from shaking apart. Sena is a jerk with a stick up his ass, but he handles pressed flowers so gently he didn't break a single one picking them up from the ground.

Enjoying this would feel too much like kicking a wet, wounded dog. He hates Sena for that.

Kirlov's expression twitches as he peers into Sena's room—from the boot knocked on its side halfway across the floor to the still-swinging light show from the stellite and the sheet discarded on stone and the twittering, awakened *bird,* and then to Tory in the midst of it all—and says, "Non-officers are forbidden from entering this area."

Vantaras adjusts his stance and doesn't tell Kirlov how adamant he was about Tory leaving. He just looks at the floor like the world's wettest noodle of a person. "Yes, Sir."

"We will discuss that later. For now, come. *Both* of you. The Grand General has arrived, and he wishes to see you."

Kirlov strides away, forcing them to lurch into motion to follow him. Vantaras' always blistering pace makes more sense, if he has to keep up with Kirlov's.

They pass Helner in the hallway and she hurries to catch up with them, pointing a finger like a knife at Kirlov. "You're a bastard," she says, half-running in heels to keep pace.

Tory's eyebrows rise.

"Just heard the news. You weren't going to tell me, were you?"

Kirlov's shoulders draw up. He stares ahead, like ignoring her might make her disappear. "It wasn't relevant to you."

"Wasn't relevant! Did you hear nothing I said about the incident in the lab?"

"Did I *hear*." Hollow, mocking, darkly amused. Kirlov's footsteps keep time on the floor, lending extra weight to his words when he speaks again. "I heard you damaged both property and valuable tools with your ill-thought-out experiment. I heard you drew Lieutenant Vantaras—whom I oversee—into your unauthorized test. I *heard* that due to your recklessness, yet another of the Arlunian weapons our men have died by the hundreds to procure for STAR-7 has been destroyed. I've heard more than enough today, Doctor. If we were capable of preventing you from removing it on your own, I'd have recommended you for a NOVA long ago."

Helner extends her fingers, graceful, and pushes them against her opposite hand until her Seed allows them to slip through it. Of course: NOVA or Core, she'd just remove anything they tried to saddle her with. She turns her cutting smile on Sena. "Lucky me, to get the carrot instead of the stick."

The corners of Kirlov's mouth tick downward, a monumental shift in expression, in Tory's experience. "I have no patience for your antics. Leave."

"And go where?" Helner spits. "The Grand General summoned me, too."

*

The Grand General, ruler over all Westrice, turns slowly when they enter an over-bright, too-empty room. The only thing inside is a short table with a chair and a closed silver briefcase.

Michal Vantaras, a pale, compact man with a thick head of graying hair, examines the group as they settle. If the unchanging tightness of his lips is any indication, he's not impressed. Everything about him is square, from his big-boned hands to the muscled torso that strains the buttons on his uniform and the thick, black vest over the top of them. He bears little resemblance to his son.

Kirlov and Sena—his son; his *son* is saluting him—snap to attention to greet him, and Michal Vantaras accepts it as his due.

This is the man who made Tory's mother's sentence lifelong. He's the one who made conscription of Seeds mandatory. This man built *every* wall that has ever caged Tory.

Reflexively, he reaches for energies he can grab and throw at the man, but he can't sense even one. The world is muffled and silent. Tory's fists clench. The room is empty aside from the briefcase, which might work as a bludgeon if he can get to it. If not, he has teeth, at least.

"At ease," Michal Vantaras says, blessedly unaware of what Tory is considering. He skims over Helner and his son like they're not there. To Kirlov, he says, "I assume you've been brought up to date?"

"Yes, General."

"And the others?"

"I prioritized speed in bringing them to you."

"I see. I'll make it brief, then. We've been losing supplies along the routes," he says. "Medical supplies. Rations. They were intercepted farther inland than we've ever encountered Arlunian infiltrators, which is . . . concerning."

Tory's ears perk up.

Could it be the rebels? When Tory was with Ariana Belmin, Riese mentioned some of his allies intercepting supplies. Tory keeps his face blank while joy sparks a fire in his belly.

"We shifted some of our forces toward guarding the supply routes, but that proved unwise. Our most recently deployed unit was massacred en route to the Arou Cliffs outpost before the Fielders could lay down shields. A Porter managed to bring sixteen wounded back here to our Healers. Only two survived. We've lost several smaller scouting units, as well. We think the increase in aggression is due to the nearness of Arlune's Dedication Day and the Arou Cliffs' historical significance in past celebrations of the event. They are likely attempting to reclaim the cliffs. We can't allow that."

Tory doesn't like where this is leading.

"We must send out the new recruits."

"General!" Helner says. Michal Vantaras twitches like a big cat might, to dislodge a fly, but Helner keeps going. "Our *Channeler* is a new recruit. He's not completed his training."

"He's close enough."

"There's so much more he could be doing! Today's experiment—"

"Was a failure."

"But he elicited a meaningful response from one of the Legion units. He made it move! No one else has been able to do anything like that."

"Then let him do it again on the battlefield, where it will be useful."

"You're not *listening!*"

"Doctor. Your wife sends her regards from STAR-1."

Helner pales, teeth clenching. "*Sir*," she grits out.

"We won't speak of this further." Michal Vantaras turns to Kirlov. "The reports regarding the Channeler's ability to target Seed-enhanced projectiles have been extraordinarily promising. It's just a matter of time before we push those slippery sons of bitches back over the border for good. Naturally, we'll take every precaution to keep this investment of ours safe. Erwin, I bestowed a great honor on you, tasking you with overseeing my son despite your less-than-ideal family circumstances."

The press of Kirlov's lips says he doesn't see the honor in it. "Yes, sir."

"As the Channeler's supervisor, Sena must follow him to the battlefield. I'm sure you understand what I'm saying."

Kirlov's inhuman stillness belies his displeasure. "As his Overseer, I will of course accompany the lieutenant."

"Sena." Vantaras turns to his son. "The Channeler's use redirecting Seed energies is unfortunately indispensable if we want to defend our border. If it comes down to it, his life takes precedence over your own."

Tory catches a flash of something in Sena's eyes—a bitter twist of his lips—but then it's gone. "If I may ask, Sir, when will we depart?"

"You'll get your papers soon enough. Don't get comfortable."

"Understood." Sena subsides, teeth clenched, and Tory wants nothing more than to push him, poke him, do whatever it takes to make him *act*.

The smile Vantaras directs over Sena's shoulder is a cold, calculating thing. "Go knowing you will always be the strongest weapon in my arsenal, Sena. We couldn't have gotten this far without you." The general flicks his bulky black vest. "Like this vest. It mimics the Neutralizer's ambient energy to an extent and nullifies any Seed attacks that come near."

That's probably why Tory couldn't find any energies to attack him with, earlier.

The General smiles. "We've made so many advancements. All because of you."

It's sick. This man looks at his son like he's a gun, not a boy. And Sena just *takes* it.

When Michal Vantaras says, "We'd like STAR-7 to perform tests with some of our prototypes, and we'll mass-produce them if they're effective. I expect your cooperation," Sena only stands straight and says, "Yes, Sir."

"Dr. Helner," the Grand General says, joyless smile still fixed on his lips. "I look forward to your reports."

"Of course." Her returning smile is tight. "If you reconsider my request—"

The smile vanishes from the General's lips. "Ah, Doctor. The reason I brought you here."

He snaps open the briefcase, which contains a section of tubing that ends in an excessively thick needle on one end and a tall glass bottle on the other.

"Sena, take a seat."

Sena obeys.

Tory blinks at the wicked needle.

Surely, they don't intend to—

"Dr. Helner, as you always do," Michal Vantaras says. "The samples we have are surprisingly stable, but our researchers are curious whether freshness conveys any special benefits, so I promised I'd bring something back."

"Of course," Sena says, quiet.

Idiot. *Coward.*

Nausea surges in Tory. Is this what he looked like back in Hulven, head bowed, accepting every pain? Sena Vantaras is a fool. He has to know he's only making it easy for them, laying down a carpet so they don't dirty their feet when they step on him.

Sena unbuttons his uniform jacket for the second time in an hour. This time, his fingers are steady. He slips his right arm from the jacket, loosens the sleeve of the button-up beneath, and carefully rolls it up. Tory startles at what it reveals, but neither his father nor Dr. Helner show surprise at the array of needle scars that dot his pale skin.

Without speaking, Dr. Helner dons a pair of gloves, arranges the tubing, and pierces Sena Vantaras' skin when she finds a vein.

No one speaks while he bleeds for his father. The Grand General looks not at his son but at the container that grows full and red beside him.

Sena is sagging to one side by the time his father finally says, "Stop."

Once it's been capped, the Grand General lifts the bottle filled with Sena's blood, and his fingers twitch around it, like he expected his own child's blood not to be warm.

"This will do." He tucks it back into the briefcase. "I'll need to get this back to my scientists as soon as possible. Doctor, the promised shipment of prototypes will arrive soon. I'll await your report."

Grand General Vantaras strides away, leaving ruin in his wake: Kirlov stormy-faced, Helner pale and furious, and Sena half-slumped over the table, folding the sleeve of his shirt down to cover the still-dribbling needle wound.

Tory will kill that man. One day, he'll look into Michal Vantaras' eyes as he dies.

CHAPTER THIRTEEN

TORY FINDS AN envelope torn open and thrown on his bare mattress when he swings by his room after dinner. Gavin regards him with a predator's smile, his card-playing buddies stone-faced beside him, as Tory skims the single page. Deployment orders, as promised.

CFR unit, of course. *Corpse corps.*

He has two days.

One of them snickers. "Not so special now, huh, Special Diet?"

Tory throws the papers down with numb fingers.

"Ready to bleed, Seedbait?" Gavin sing-songs.

Laughter follows him from the room and into the claustrophobic and ever-narrowing halls. Every short, sterile corridor looks like the next. It figures that when he *needs* to find the garden, he gets lost around corners.

He could run, but he wouldn't get far. They'd deactivate his Core. Vantaras' words mock him: *a lit fuse,* he called it.

There's got to be a way to take it out. Maybe Vantaras is misinformed. He's the type to follow orders without question. He'll bet another Reacher could do it. They may not be as rare as they're said to be. Maybe not *all* of them work for the military.

Tory has survived so many things. He'll survive this, too.

At last, he pulls the windowless gray door to the garden open.

His heart slows; his eyes stop roving. Life thrums through him.

He trades the acrid bite of chemicals in the hallway for a honey-sweet breeze that carries the smell of herbs and earth. Echoing stone shifts to irregular cobbles and springy, sun-warmed grass. His feet lead him to the tree with the gnarled trunk.

Sunset—fiery yellow and fading—sifts through the netted dome and sets the tree's leaves aglow. Specks of greenish-gold swim over the grass with every whisper of wind.

In the Compound's neglected garden, flowerbeds lie devastated, long since gone to seed and crowded out by weeds and wild things. Woody vines cling to every crack in the concrete, stubbornly blooming and straining toward the sky. Tory sits back against the massive trunk, yawns, and closes his eyes. The rustle of leaves and the distant calls of birds blend into a white-noise melody. His fingers, outstretched, trace roots that wind out of and back into the ground.

Tension slinks from his body like an unwelcome visitor, and he sighs as he drifts.

"Do you know the story of this tree?" The voice comes from his left, tearing him from his peaceful haze.

Vantaras.

Speaking of unwelcome visitors. Maybe he'll go away if Tory doesn't answer.

"You might like it."

Or maybe not. "What, you're stalking me now?"

"If you're referring to the garden, I've been visiting since long before this place was graced by your presence, Worldseed."

"You know you're a hypocrite, right? You're one of us."

"You treat the word like it's an insult."

Tory cracks open an eye. "They made it one when they locked us in here."

Silence.

"Yeah, I thought so."

The light shines red through his eyelids, but Vantaras pipes up again before Tory can sink too deeply into rest. "Have you seen the plaque on this tree's trunk?"

Tory rolls his head until he has Vantaras in sight: he sits on the half-circle of stone benches around the other side of the tree.

"There is no plaque."

It's only because he's looking that he catches Sena's dry smile, there then gone. "Exactly. They drove it into the tree so long ago the trunk grew around it and swallowed it up. Remind you of anything?"

Tory thinks of the Core spreading poison roots inside him, a mark of their ownership and power.

"They say Westrice's founders, Anton Chimre and Ramus Vantaras, followed the capital's Golden River to the southeast corner of the country while they were seeking to expand their territories. The land at the time was heavily wooded, so thick with blooming kuhlu vine that they could see nothing. This tree stood taller than all the rest, so Ramus made use of it, climbing its trunk and standing on its branches to look out over the land. He saw trees blood-bright with kuhlu blooms bowing over the Golden River and light glinting in every color off a vein of stellite by the water, and he fell in love, made it his goal to bring prosperity to this place." He gestures to the strings of flowers in all shades of blue and violet, only a few of them gray-maroon. "Kuhlu vines bloom only in proximity to stellite—the richer the vein, the closer to red. This place was once the richest mine in the country. It's dry, now, like all the other border mines. Within a few years, these vines will bloom bright blue. A few years after, they'll stop blooming entirely."

The vines in Hulven bloom purplish for miles outside the town and maroon close to the mine. Maybe it, too, is on its way to emptiness. "That's depressing."

"Yes. So when my father chose to mine his territory for *Seeds*, he had STAR-7 established here. They have a joke about the tree: it's us, penned in by the Compound, marked with their name. We're the thing they stand on to get to the top, the strength that supports their ambitions. They discarded all the old stories about how Seeds came about. Seeds, they decided, exist only to bring glory to Westrice."

Tory's mouth twists into a grimace. "Why did you think I'd want to hear that?"

Sena laughs. Actually laughs, for the first time since Tory has met him. "Where do you think the founders are now?"

Maybe he's supposed to have some profound answer, like *they're within every citizen of Westrice*. "Probably rotting in the ground."

A quiet chuckle. "And this tree?"

Tory can't help laughing when he realizes what Sena's driving at. The tree just keeps growing, alive and spreading, roots running up against the high walls of the prison they built for it and pushing through cracks in solid stone. It may well outlive the Compound.

"Yeah," he says at last. "I guess that's not so bad."

A smile flickers over Sena's face, lazy and satisfied, and Tory finds himself sharing it.

"You could work on your storytelling skills, though." He leans against the trunk again and closes his eyes.

*

The first hit takes him by surprise.

It shouldn't, after Gavin's stunt during maneuvers and his eerie warning when Tory received his deployment orders.

After maneuvers the following day, Tory takes his usual shortcut between a couple of storage sheds while everyone's waiting to be seen by the Healers. The moment he steps into the narrow walkway, hands grab him from behind and fling him into the wall of the shed. Gavin, his cardplayers, and a couple others Tory doesn't recognize glare at him as he rights himself.

The first hit lands on his jaw, snapping his mouth shut on his tongue. They waste no time with words.

If he wasn't swallowing blood, he might respect that.

He spits onto the ground. "What's this about?" He pushes forward, and the group tightens around him.

"It's about you going around like you're better than everyone," Gavin says.

Someone hooks a foot around his ankle and yanks, and Tory crashes against the wall of the shed. Another punch—despite his attempt to block—batters his solar plexus. Breath rushes from him, and Tory tips, a laughable attempt to right himself foiled by a push from his left. His right ankle wrenches as he falls.

Tory realizes, as hot pain stabs up his leg, that he can kill them.

He wouldn't even need to do much. Bodies are so easily broken. The force from a punch dropped into their skull or spine would do it.

He could rupture a spleen with just a little effort if he could remember where spleens are.

He's thinking about that when someone grabs him and pulls him back up. Assholes. They worked so hard to get him on the ground. It's not like he *wants* to be on his feet.

"You know what?" He sways and swallows more blood. "I'm done with this."

They must think so, too, because he doesn't see the last blow coming.

*

Tory blinks awake to pressure on the side of his face and a pair of appraising amber-brown eyes. A blurred figure crouches beside him. His world rocks as a hand tips his chin this way and that.

"Unequal dilation," a familiar, dry voice observes, "and sustained loss of consciousness. You really did it this time, didn't you, Arknett?"

Tory groans, head throbbing.

Sena Vantaras is the last thing he needs. Clever stories about Seeds and trees or no, it's hard enough to deal with the guy when Tory's operating at peak condition.

"Go 'way," he says.

He thinks he says it, at least. His tongue pulses with pain, sausage-sized in his mouth. But it doesn't matter if he spoke clearly. He at least made an unhappy noise.

He gets no response except that *stare*.

". . . to Jeffra, just in case," Vantaras is saying. "Can you stand?"

Tory grunts, hoping Vantaras will take the hint. When he gets closer instead of farther away, Tory licks dried blood from his lips and puts effort into enunciation. "Back . . . *off*."

Raising a curious eyebrow, Vantaras does, standing and retreating until his back presses against the other shed's wall.

Tory takes stock of his injuries. His head is a spongy mass of agony, and he thinks he might have done something to his ankle. All other pains are secondary, but his ribs, stomach, and back have a few things to say when he tries to sit.

He sucks a breath through clenched teeth as he pulls his knees up, testing his ability to put weight on his right ankle.

The ankle is having none of it.

Vantaras crosses his arms as Tory slides up the shed, pushing with his left leg and right arm until at last he's upright. Burnt orange and purple clouds beyond the Compound's wall indicate that it's probably past dinner time, damn it. He'll be lucky to catch a shower tonight.

Without warning, the sun sinks. The earth goes muddy and liquid, and he's freefalling.

A startled curse bursts out beside him, and something catches him under his arms.

"I suppose that answers my question."

As the haziness fades, he finds the sun is, in fact, still setting, the ground is solid, and his cheek is squished against the buttons of Sena Vantaras' uniform.

"Now. Can you stand by yourself?"

That's Hasra's question. Hasra—glitter smeared over her cheekbones, pipe-smoke spice, and lullabies murmured when she thinks he's asleep. His chest aches, deeper than the pain from bruised ribs, and he remembers her eyes when he left her behind for the second time.

The hands under his arms hike him up higher. "I'll be taking you to Mrs. Jeffra. If you feel confident in your ability to make it there without assistance, I'd be happy to leave you here."

"Ankle," Tory mumbles. The grass under his feet sags, gray-brown and trampled. "Can't put weight on it."

Vantaras looks down to where Tory's right foot hovers over the ground. "All right, then." He moves to Tory's right side, then positions one arm around his shoulder, tugging one of Tory's arms across his back. "This will have to do. Tell me when you're ready to move."

"Just move."

"You'll get yourself killed like this."

Tory is uniquely skilled at *not* dying, thanks very much, it's just that Vantaras ruined his lifetime record of avoiding unfortunate run-ins with authority figures, so really it's his fault that Tory ended up like this, isn't it?

Vantaras gives Tory a second to get used to standing before he takes a step. Tory follows, nearly landing them on their faces. A few more tries, and their steps are more coordinated.

"Do you know who did this?"

"Five of them," Tory says.

Vantaras takes the news with as much emotion as he takes anything. "If you know their names or recognize their faces, I can warn them that such behavior won't be tolerated."

Tory snorts. "Like that'd help."

"You'd be surprised what privileges we're allowed to revoke. They'd get the message."

Tory shakes his head. "Gonna be out on the battlefield soon. No point."

"If that's what you want."

Another wave of dizziness forces them to stop, and before they continue, Vantaras speaks up, quieter and tentative.

"It might be humiliating, but when they're serious about causing harm, it's best to curl up on the ground to protect your head and core—prevent serious injury as well as you can."

Bitterness floods Tory's mouth. Another commandment to add to the ugly scriptures of staying alive. *Don't make waves, hide the tattoos, keep your head down.*

Curl up tight so they don't kill you. "More of your *advice*?"

Vantaras breathes out a noisy sigh. "I can't control their actions and cannot discipline your attackers if you refuse to tell me their names. I meant to say, as someone who has been in your position, I know what to do when people are intent on hurting you."

"*You?*" The upbringing Tory imagined for him was all money and faceless cronies smiling deferentially and . . . riding, or whatever rich people do in and out of their dreary gray fortresses. Parties with faceted glasses and very nice cake.

Sena stops, gives Tory his full attention. It's . . . a lot. He's too dizzy for this. "More often when I was young. My mother gave birth a few weeks early. I was slow to hit my growth spurt, slow to make friends. My health was . . . an issue, and I was clearly different from my peers. I was an almost laughably perfect target."

"Was?" Tory smirks. He finds him a perfectly satisfying target now.

Sena looks away. "You wanted to know about my Seed? I destroy things. My Seed blossomed when I was nine. A boy . . . lost a leg. It ensured my attackers would think twice before targeting me again. Since then, my physical health has been near flawless."

"Braggart." It should be illegal to be rich *and* healthy. Tory is too tired to get irritated, but he manages a weak scowl in Sena's direction.

They're silent the rest of the way, until Sena extends his free hand to rap on the infirmary door. "Room for one more, Healer Jeffra?"

Tory hears bustling from inside, and a heavy-set older woman opens the door. She's somewhere between Tory's height and Sena's, salt-and-pepper curls held back with a bright yellow headband. She's dressed in the usual uniform, except she has a huge yellow apron tied over the top, with vials and papers and pads tucked into the multitudes of pockets. "Well, if it isn't Sena. I don't see you around here often enough." Her warm gaze travels to Tory. "And *you*, son. Didn't we just discharge you after you did a runner?"

Tory winces.

Sena lugs him over to a reclined seat. "He was attacked by a few Seeds from his unit. Concussion, sprained or fractured ankle as far as I can tell. Probably bruising on his torso. Think you can fix him up?"

The older woman gives Sena a mock-withering look. "What, you think I can't?" She waves over at the corner, and only then does Tory notice the Healer from the other day with the scar on her cheek—thankfully no longer covered in blood—sprawled over a chair. "Niela, dear, I thought I told you to see to the slice wound in the rec room. You need practice on stimulating the body to produce more blood."

"C'mon, Ma . . ."

"I'll tell your young man where to find you if he drops in. Go."

Jeffra strides over to Tory as soon as Niela leaves. "Lift up your shirt, then. Let me assess the damage so I know where to focus."

When Tory isn't fast enough, she does it herself, clucking and tutting.

"Need to eat more," she says.

He can't keep the bite from his voice when he retorts, "I eat plenty."

"Don't sass me," Jeffra warns. "You like having regular bowel movements?"

Tory stares.

"Do you?" She pushes him back onto the chair, elevating his legs.

He blinks at her, not sure what she expects him to say.

"I thought so," she huffs. "No backtalk."

Sena snorts out a laugh.

"And *you*, kiddo, need to keep your distance if you want me to be able to do my job."

Sena takes a few long steps back until Jeffra nods.

"All right, then. Let's start with your head. I daresay Sena was right. It looks like you took a real good hit."

Tory shifts on the seat, but Jeffra stops him. "Relax and close your eyes. Don't wiggle. Don't talk."

Tory obeys, though he's sure that sound is Sena snickering from his place by the door.

Warmth envelops him, and the ache in his head fades. The focus of the warmth shifts gradually downward, erasing the pain in his ribs and the bruises from training until she gets to his ankle. It's weird being on the other side of this. Weird to sense, without really trying, how *different* the energy of a true Healer is, how differently it works. Tory works backward, toward the body's memory of wholeness pre-injury. Jeffra works forward, toward repair. A Healer's energy is . . . warm, expansive. Like sunlight on stone. He recognizes the sharp edges of his body's natural healing energies, but they're softer and larger in her hands. It's nice.

He's almost asleep when it fades.

"No napping in the infirmary." Jeffra tugs him to a sitting position. She peers into both of his eyes, one at a time, nodding at whatever she finds. "You still hurting anywhere?"

"No." He feels amazing, actually, buzzing with energy. "Uh . . . thank you."

Jeffra nods firmly. "'Least he remembers his manners," she quips at no one in particular.

Tory stands and bends to brush dirt from his clothes.

"Whoa there! Wait up!"

He stops, hands frozen two inches from the clump of mud on his pants. "Uh . . .?"

"You wanna clean my floor?"

He shakes his head, seeking Sena's eyes. He gets only an amused shrug.

"Then don't primp yourself in here. You can shake off that filth on the Grand General's bedsheets for all I care, but don't you make a mess in my infirmary."

Sena snorts.

Jeffra slants a guilty glance at him. "I trust you won't tell your father I said that."

"Not a word, ma'am."

She laughs. "Good! You get on out of here, then, both of you. For your sake, I hope I never see you again."

That seems to be the end of it.

Sena spares him having to walk around the entire building and leads him through the officers' quarters and around the front, past Intake, until they reach the mess hall. "Most of the stations are closed down, but you may be able to get some leftovers. I'll speak to the head cook."

In the end, he manages a sandwich and some still-warm soup, and Sena sits opposite him in the dimly lit room. Only the faint illumination from the kitchen reaches them.

"Are you ready for tomorrow?" Sena asks.

The food goes down heavy.

That's right.

Tomorrow morning, they depart.

CHAPTER FOURTEEN

Tory creeps back into his room while Gavin's away at breakfast. There, he finds a pile on his bed with a note. The note has no name, but the straight rows of precise, delicate lettering scream Sena.

Beneath the note is Thatcher's cloak. Tory traces the shapes of vines sewn with such care along the bottom—kuhlu, with its serrated leaves and delicate blossoms—and his chest aches.

This seemed to be important to you, the note reads. *Few of us have the ability to go to the battlefield with something that reminds us of home. There should be room in your pack if you wish to bring it. If not, hide it. Were someone to find this, it would be confiscated and incinerated.*

He shoves it in his pack and readies himself to go. While the rest of the Compound's occupants head to breakfast, around eighty Seeds march into personnel trucks and are shipped off before the sun rises above the trees.

The torturous monotony of basic training comes in handy when the personnel trucks drop them off. They walk in formation over the scrubby hills until they're close to the border and Tory's legs are liquid fire beneath him. They have their orders: they'll continue in the general direction of the Arou Cliffs after addressing some problems in the area. Rumor has it that multiple small cells of Arlunian soldiers have pushed into Westrice, much farther than they'd usually travel. A support corps scouting team—two Porters, dressed for stealth—identified the location of one group. That group, they're informed, will be their first target.

Just like in maneuvers, the shield corps takes the lead, prepared to repel surprise attacks. Prentice joins them, straggly hair pulled into a ponytail, and teleports short distances to examine the terrain so they don't fall into anything unexpected. It doesn't take him long to close in on the enemy camp: about fifty Arlunian soldiers in the forest, just beyond the tree line, he reports.

Resting.

The first attack from Tory's unit comes from the Kineticists. It hits three infiltrators napping against a tree, killing them instantly. Then the battle begins in earnest.

Tory and the CFR unit work interference, dropping whatever attacks come close. Too many consist only of Seed energy, so Tory is left to handle them. The others crash against the forcefield the Fielders maintain. Maneuvers served them well: Tory's unit works like they've been doing this for years.

In the chaos, it takes too long for Tory to notice that the Arlunian infiltrators aren't *fighting* them. They're distracting them.

In the background, an Arlunian Porter evacuates people and stacked boxes of supplies. In a flash, Tory recognizes the text stamped on the sides: *STAR-7*. Perhaps these are the people who intercepted the supplies the Grand General said were stolen. The boxes disappear in clumps as the Porter flickers in and out.

Tory doesn't say a word, doesn't want anyone to notice, but the space behind them is getting emptier and emptier. Soon enough, someone will see.

When they do, Tory's hands are too full deflecting a barrage of Seed energy coming from the Arlunian forces to do anything about it.

"That *bastard*, he's getting away with all the stuff!" someone yells. Gavin, maybe. Kinetic energy builds with a crackle.

Tory gasps as an overwhelming wave of the same sort of energy builds on the Arlunian side, incandescent on the fringes of his awareness. The Arlunian Kineticists push several large rocks at Tory. They must have noticed he's the one keeping the shields clear. But he's already pushing a different attack away—heavier than any he's ever held, hands literally full with it as he forces it away. He can't help a noise of shocked horror as the rocks gain speed. They'll tear right through him.

Protect the Fielders like your life depends on it, Menden said in training, *because it will.*

He hopes the shield holds up to such a concentrated attack, or he's ground meat.

Something dark blurs in front of him before the rocks reach him, and all Tory can see is the rocks dropping midair. One of them crumbles when it comes into contact with his protector's bare hands.

Sena?

But that's not the only effect the interference has. Tory's awareness of the energies around him blinks to nothingness. The section of shield in front of him crumbles away. And the kinetic attack Gavin was about to sling at the Arlunian Porter fizzles out and falls. The Porter evacuates with a great clump of boxes and a huddling group of people.

Sena turns, shoving his bare hand back into his glove and fleeing the front lines, but for a ridiculous moment, Tory can't help wondering if he had ulterior motives for stopping the attack.

The Porter blinks back in, but Sena isn't here to interfere this time. Before he can gather another group, a rock accelerated with a Kineticist's energy slams through his chest.

Tory practiced every part of battle until he could've puked most days, but nothing prepared him for this—for the hole left behind, for snapping bones and blood flooding out to thaw the razor-cold frost on the fallen leaves. After that, it's an easy victory.

They leave eighteen corpses, all told. When the battle is finished, Kirlov orders them to reclaim any remaining supplies and secure anything else they discover.

They retreat to an advantageous position and set up camp: flimsy tents—twelve Seeds to each with the thin rolls of bedding from their packs—and then people mill around. Near-hysterical laughter and uproarious celebrations abound. Adrenaline sharpens the world for Tory, too, but he can't join in their happiness. This isn't his fight. It never has been.

The look on the Arlunian Porter's face just before he died was innocent surprise. Tory and the other Westrian Seeds wear heavy vests, but the Seeds they killed wore only tunics and olive-toned jackets to keep out the cold. No guns, no bombs. No armor. Tory has understood all his life that Westrice is not a victor. It's a conqueror. He should not be so unsettled to see the truth in action.

"Tory!" a voice calls.

Randall scurries up, dragging the Healer from that day in the infirmary that necessitated their deployment, her dark hair swept back into a ponytail and the scar on her left cheek dimpled with a dry smile. Tory doesn't know when he'll stop expecting her to be covered in blood, but her clothes are clean today.

Randall grins. "It's long past time for formal introductions! Tory, this is Niela, best girl in the world. Niela, Tory, my sullen training mate and pal. Today was wild—"

Niela shrugs. "Support corps had nothing to do. It was actually a bit boring."

"—and it's time to *drink*. Found this thing of Arlunian wine in one of the tents, and I don't know about you, but I plan to drain it."

"Weren't we supposed to return everything we found to the—"

Niela presses a short finger to Tory's lips. "What they don't know won't hurt them." She throws an arm around Randall, who glows with happiness. "Taught you well, huh? I'm about to blow your minds. The illicit stuff *always* tastes a thousand times—"

Vantaras rounds the corner before Niela can finish her sentence.

"Arknett!"

Wide-eyed, Tory finds Niela, who has somehow vanished the entire wine bottle into her shirt. She quirks an eyebrow at Tory when he gapes.

Vantaras sighs. "*There* you are. I need to report to Colonel Kirlov about the supplies we gathered, but then he'd like to speak with you. Stay here. I'll be back."

He stalks off, and Niela grabs Tory's wrist and runs around the back of the tents until they're well cloaked in shadow before she tugs the great bottle from under her shirt and works the cork out. Randall pulls the cap from the canteen clipped to his fatigues and fills it, knocking it back in a few quick gulps. He fills it again, and they take turns.

After three capfuls, Tory hears Vantaras calling for him, but he shrugs it off and waves his hand for another cap. By six, the *I survived, but I saw that Porter's chest collapse* feeling stops hounding him.

Of course, that'd be when Vantaras finds him.

Randall yips an apology and scrambles. Niela is already gone, and Vantaras twines a gloved hand in the neck of Tory's shirt and pulls him up.

"The colonel *hates* to be kept waiting," he hisses, and drags Tory along at a near run.

*

Kirlov stands stiff as a board in a large tent—the same size as the one where twelve of Tory's fellow Seeds sleep, except it has only a single bed—looking like he'd happily burn them alive to roast tree nuts over their corpses.

"I asked you to return *promptly*, Lieutenant."

"*Sir.*" Vantaras snaps to attention and salutes. "Arknett was not where I ordered him to remain. My initial concerns were unfounded. He had merely wandered off to . . ." Vantaras shoots Tory a look that could wither flowers, ". . . speak with some friends."

"Your neglectfulness of your duties sickens me." Kirlov's right hand crosses over his left, fingers closing around the watch at his wrist.

Sena shudders, eyes flickering closed like he's going to be sick.

"And *you.*" Kirlov's eyes narrow, shifting toward Tory. "You reek of spirits. Whether or not you intended to run, you engaged in frivolous acts and disobeyed direct orders from your supervisor. Your insubordination disgusts me."

"I, uh . . . I'm sorry, I guess?"

Sena shudders again.

"Action speaks louder than impotent apologies. This is why I've brought you here. I've been displeased with reports of your recent conduct. Creating rifts within your unit. Reckless behavior. Destruction of property." Kirlov's lips curl, and Tory takes a moment to consider role models. Vantaras can be irritating, but he has nothing on this guy. The stick up his ass must go on for miles.

Kirlov turns to a basin and washes his hands with infuriating slowness, like he needs to scrub off their presence. Tory stalks forward, mouth opening to give the guy a piece of his mind.

"*No.*" Sena's hand twists in his sleeve and pulls him back.

It's not the word that makes him stop. It's the bone-white knot of Sena's hand in his sleeve, the pitch of his whisper—not an order but a plea.

Tory crosses his arms and waits for Colonel Germophobe to finish.

After a while, Kirlov dries his hands on a rag folded over the basin and turns back.

"It is my judgment that both of you should be disciplined. Have you heard of a NOVA, Seed?"

So that's where Sena gets the wretched nickname. "Yeah."

"I am an officer. You will address me as such."

"Yeah . . . sir," Tory drawls, because fuck if he's going to acknowledge the guy's rank.

"You are well on your way to being fitted with one. If I lodge a complaint, you'll need only two more marks on your record until you, too, are assigned an Overseer. That won't take long if I don't want it to. Are you aware of the device's function?"

A kill-switch. "Yeah."

Kirlov's gaze slices through him.

"Yes, sir," Tory corrects himself.

Kirlov lifts his wrist. He touches the dial.

Sena's shoulders go up, chin ducking. Tory's stomach plummets at the uncharacteristic display.

"Perhaps you are. I certainly can't know what you've heard. But words are only words, Seed. You need to see in order to understand what you'll have to look forward to if you don't shape up. Lieutenant," Kirlov says. "Don't you agree?"

Sena pauses, swallows hard. By the look on Kirlov's face, he pauses too long.

"Yes, Sir," he whispers.

Tory found such perverse pleasure in creating a rift between Sena and Kirlov when he first met them. Now, his insides twist with sickness, and Kirlov is Sena's *Overseer*, and Tory desperately doesn't want to find out what that entails.

Kirlov sighs, and at the same time Sena hauls in a frantic, shuddering breath, turning away as if from a blow. His eyes meet Tory's for a single, terrible moment.

Kirlov's long fingers stab at one of the buttons on the watch, then he twists a dial around its face.

Sena goes impossibly straight and still. A sound starts in his throat, like he's trying to breathe out and can't. A rending, high-pitched keen makes goosebumps erupt on Tory's skin.

Before he can open his mouth to ask what's happening, Sena drops. The keening turns to an awful scream that cuts off almost before it starts. Kirlov, expressionless, twists the dial higher. On the ground and on his back with his eyes wide open, mouth stretched wide with no sound coming out, Sena jerks like he's seizing.

The bile-bite of fear paralyzes Tory, rips strength and thought from him. His knees hit the ground, the impact making his teeth clack.

He extends a hand—curls it into a fist and draws it back. He doesn't know what to *do* to make this stop.

The keening starts up again, broken by ragged exhales with no inhales, and it's wrong, all wrong. Sena's not actually *breathing*, his skin bluish, tendons corded in his neck, spine arched like he's trying to break himself in half. Blood paints his lips like he bit them on his way down.

At last, he stops. Everything. His eyes close, his body relaxes, and he falls limp.

Kirlov takes a measured step forward. "Arknett. On your feet."

He tries, but he can't tear his eyes from Sena's too-still form. Fear is a shrill thing in his ears, a pins-and-needles chill in every limb.

"On your *feet.*"

He manages it, stomach rolling.

"Look." Kirlov gestures down at Sena, like a man might gesture to a pile of garbage discarded a few feet from a bin.

It's wrong to look at Sena from above like this.

"*Look* at him."

Tory complies. Frozen-pale, chest still, Sena lies lax like a corpse, the blood on his lips startlingly bright.

"This is what you have to look forward to if you don't shape up. It's a graceless state, even more base and vile than your current one. I or another Overseer will be able to bring you to heel in an instant. This is merely a sample of a NOVA's capabilities. I could have let it go on for longer, but prolonged exposure can sometimes cause them to lose their bowels, and the last thing I need is to have to clean up after any of you."

Tory holds his breath only a fraction as long as Sena has held his, and his chest burns with it, blood hot with panic and vision narrowing to the third button on Sena's jacket, just above his heart. He wills it to move.

A sob-like cough of panic works its way up Tory's throat. "He's—he's not . . ."

Kirlov says nothing.

Tory jumps when Sena arches and gasps, drawing in a whistling breath like he's been drowning and just broke the surface of the water. Tory breathes with him.

Kirlov steps back and turns away. "Lieutenant," he says.

Sena moans, hazy eyes opening to half-mast and finding Tory before they squeeze closed again, lashes clumped with tears.

"Show your charge to the tents where he'll be sleeping. I received news; we'll be splitting up to take on a splinter group of infiltrators on the Arou Cliffs tomorrow. They still insist the claim to that area is *theirs*. The others will proceed to the site of the last skirmish as planned, and a portion of us will break off to handle this."

Sena's lips move, but no sound comes out. He swipes blood from his lips. Tory waits what feels like hours for him to curl onto his side, then push himself up on an elbow, onto shaky knees, and then onto both feet.

"You're dismissed." Kirlov turns to Tory. "Remember this, and learn."

He won't be able to forget.

Sena makes his way out the tent flap before he's down on one knee again. His breaths come in odd, rasping gasps, like his lungs can't remember how to work.

"Can I . . ." Tory whispers. He remembers, suddenly, that first time Sena arrived to take him to training, the way his gait looked wrong—wrong like this. "How many times—"

Sena shakes his head, doesn't even look at Tory. Tory wonders if he's aware of the sound he makes when he forces himself to his feet, a low whimper that makes Tory's body flush with shame.

"T-told you," Sena manages. "I—*told you* . . . to s-stay there."

Tory's voice deserts him as he takes small steps, trying to stay behind Sena. It's hard. The long strides that usually leave him in Sena's dust are drunken and staggering, his knees locking or giving out at odd times.

"I'm sorry," he whispers when he finds his voice. For being the reason Kirlov hurt Sena this time, and probably times before this. For standing over him and looking down on his body like he was a thing. For sassing Kirlov. For *not* sassing Kirlov, not fighting back. For things he can't put into words.

"Apologies are . . . useless," Sena whispers. He makes a sound almost like a laugh, except it's bitter and cracked and nearly voiceless, more a cough than anything. He brings Tory to the outcropping of tents where he'll be sleeping.

"Here." Sena stands stiff like his bones will crumble if he doesn't.

Tory wants—needs—to say something, do something, to explain, but he can't make his mouth work. He watches Sena go in silence.

CHAPTER FIFTEEN

A QUICK OPERATION, EVERYONE says. A chance to stretch their legs.

Just a handful of Arlunian soldiers camped in the woods bordering the wide field and picturesque Arou Cliffs that hem in the cold ocean.

What meets them is anything but small. Fog and smoke explode around them when they push out from the tree line, blotting out the salty sea air.

Prentice saw none of this. Tory has no time to wonder how.

Chunks of dirt and cutting fragments of stone rain down. Tory surges forward, squinting into the billowing wall of white. It consumes the Westrian troops until Tory is alone inside it. The fog swallows sound. He knows only the hammering of his pulse and the heave of his breaths.

The CFR unit is limited by range of sight. If they can't see what's coming—

Tory doesn't need his eyes. He reaches for nearby energies. Unlike during training, most of the projectiles out here are guided by Seeds and carry their signatures. He finds them.

Thousands of them.

A volley of arrows pierces the fog. Tory expands his awareness to the fringes of the field and takes the energy off the arrows, flinging it in the general direction it came from, but once he's done his job, gravity works as well on the arrows as it does on anything else. They stop, arrested midair—and fall.

Top-heavy, too many plummet point-first. Screams tear the air.

Alone in the impenetrable fog, Tory hears but doesn't see the deaths of Seeds like him. Young like him. Wanting to live like him.

Where are the Fielders with their forcefield dome to protect everyone? Where are the cocky Kinetics to lob projectiles at the enemy?

Someone stumbles into view, fog-dimmed and ghostly. Randall.

A shaky smile splits his freckled face. "Hey there!"

The moment of distraction nearly kills them both. Tory barely deflects a crushing wave of Seed energy before it barrels into them. "Pay attention!"

Randall laughs, half-hysterical.

Explosions swirl the fog, swallowing great gulps of it in rushes of flame. Screams pierce the air. There's no energy to the fog, nothing Tory can wrap his mind around and *move*. Every man trapped in it dies alone. Tory didn't train for this.

A few brave Healers duck low over the ground to reach the wounded just like in training—except none of this is like it was in training. A breath of peace, then—

Randall's voice, from his left, high with terror. "Niela? Niela, run!"

An explosion rocks the ground, spraying Tory again with dirt and stone.

It's wet. Tory swipes three fingers over his face and pulls them away. In the eerie, flat fog-light, the blood that turns earth to mud is impossibly red.

He steps on Randall before he notices him. He's strewn across the ground, chest a mess of broken flesh. His eyelids flicker, red-slick mouth gaping wide.

The fog rushes away as the Fielders *finally* establish a barrier (weakened; one of the attacks must have thinned their numbers), but it's too late. They worked like a machine in maneuvers, CFRs dropping projectiles while the Fielders established their barrier in record time, every time. They were so *confident* on a field where a balloon to the chest meant a bruise and Randall smiled on his way to the infirmary every day.

"Randall?" Niela's cry from beyond the wall of fog is wrenching.

Tory's breath clogs in his throat. He falls to hands and knees as the sword corps rush to the front to take their positions and the CFR Seeds retreat to do their work at the periphery. Now that the shields are up, the rest of the Healers scramble in to whisk away the injured, heal them, and return them to the fight.

Niela finds them then.

Randall's name tears from her throat as she stumbles to her knees. She doesn't spare Tory a glance, pressing her hands to the meaty mess of her boyfriend's chest, and Tory staggers back. Niela curses through her teeth. Randall's unblinking eyes stay fixed on the sky.

"No. Damnit, Randall, *no*," Niela is saying, and she leans down to give him breath, but the air just bubbles from his lacerated lungs.

Tory coughs on an exhale but manages to keep from gagging. When he looks up, the fog is thin enough to reveal a group of Fielders and fighters lobbing attacks at nothing, their practiced formation in tatters.

In his peripheral vision, there's Niela, hazy in the fog and soaked yet again with someone else's blood, giving herself away for a corpse.

She grabs Randall's face, squeezing at his chin like he might move his lax, wide-open mouth for her.

Tory screams for her to run, or maybe he just thinks it. She's an idiot. He's gone already. Tory will be, too, if he doesn't focus. He's standing here stock-still and covered in mud and Randall's blood, making a target of himself.

He tears his eyes from them and turns. Arlunian soldiers in loose shirts saunter from the tree line in pairs. Tory understands, now, why they wear no armor. They don't need it.

A small splinter group. No more than ten, the report asserted.

There are ten at the front of the line and more behind them than he can count. Seeds, all of them. Tory has learned, with practice, to pick out the faint, electric presence of Seed energy. There's nothing faint about these, each one a lightning storm. Their attacks rock the forcefield, splintering it with glowing cracks the trembling Fielders hurry to seal. They won't survive this for long.

He'll die here. They'll all die.

Either he's shaking or the earth is. Tory reaches for the next wave of attacks—massive, overwhelming—and peels off the Seed energy and kinetic energy before they can hit the shields.

He gives the entire unit a moment's reprieve. They regroup, but the CFR unit is still hindered by the fog, and Tory won't be able to deflect all the attacks forever without the support of his unit. He diverts everything he can, but he's only one pair of hands, and carrying the buzzing energy of hundreds—thousands—of projectiles is like lifting a boulder twice his size. Sweat stings his eyes. His vision swims.

The weakened forcefield bursts when he fails to fully deflect the next volley of attacks. The unit scatters. Tory ducks and runs zig-zag, weaving in and out of smoke.

This isn't how he wants to go. Not like this. Not today. He barely knows himself, is only now learning to speak the words he used to swallow. Their own weapons fly back at them, amplified. Seed-enhanced explosives carve craters in the earth.

Tory swallows hard as the trembling under his feet increases.

The earth really is shaking.

Something rolls over the hill—or rises from it—silhouetted black in the fog. No, three of them.

Legion. Every horror story Tory has heard batters around in his skull.

The one nearest him unrolls from its sphere shape and *grows*, piercing the ground with vines like spindly, spidery legs, and bursts upward, rising into the sky. At its center, the vines gather into a thorax-like platform. A Seed crouches on the platform, hand clasped around a stellite crystal glowing yellow-white while two other Seeds, beside him, attack the fleeing Westrian soldiers with flames from above.

The other two Legion units take the form of spheres—writhing and ever-shifting. They share the shape of the mechanized things on the training field, but they're so much worse. They roll over the ground at impossible speeds, vines disentangling from the sphere to spear anyone who gets too close. At this rate, they'll drive the fleeing Seeds over the cliffs.

A wave of energy nearly crushes Tory. He crashes to his knees in blood-soaked mud.

Enough of this.

Tory forces himself to his feet and runs for the spidery Legion unit. He grabs one of the braided vines at the base and throws all his energy and anger and desperation into it.

Like they did in the lab, the vines break from their curated shape. They unwind, tear apart, wrench away. The Arlunian Seeds tumble from the crumbling platform and land on the ground with awful cracks. The vines drive into the earth on either side of Tory like a doorway of bone. His vision fades, ears ringing.

Another noise fades in, discordant, distant but getting closer. "Arknett, *damn* it!"

Sena.

Yesterday's guilt is nothing in the face of his relief. Sena has a terminal case of competence. Tory could do with a dose of that right now.

"Hey, I—"

Sena's annoyed face morphs into terror. "In front of you!"

He throws the energy from an incoming projectile, body aching with the effort.

He has a fraction of a second to realize his mistake as a shell touches down, clattering once, twice on the springy grass.

It's not a cannon ball or a balloon. It won't just lie there.

The pressure from the explosion hits him before he registers the sound. A gasp sears his lungs with white-hot air.

He needs to take the energy and redirect it, preferably toward one of the Legion units, but it's useless; he's only practiced with balloons. He grasps for the swelling explosion, but it expands beyond his control. It's too large, too strong, bleeding a reckless, wild energy. The force of it drives him back and up.

They've modified the shell, too.

Of course they have.

Sena's panicked voice rises above the roaring in his ears. "Tory, stop! Behind you!"

If he can just get his hands on this, if he can contain and throw it—

Arms lash across his back, wrapping around his shoulders, and the energy is out of his hands, thrown only a fraction as far as he wanted. The force of the explosion catapults him—them?—backward.

He expects to hit the ground and get pummeled by the blast, but he keeps moving—up and over and down, down, down. The fall lasts a few seconds, long enough for him to see jagged rocks and hear the lash of salty waves.

A flash of recognition, a lurch of fear. He doesn't even have time to breathe.

The rest comes in fragments.

A crash as they hit the water, softer than he thought it would be.

Cold, sharp enough to shock the breath from him.

Fire in his nose and mouth when he reflexively inhales.

Then, blessedly, nothing at all.

PART THREE:

Fall

CHAPTER SIXTEEN

THE FALL IS a short one, the landing merciless. Sena plummets into icy water nearly cold enough to stop his heart.

It's sheer luck that he doesn't inhale. He tightens his arms around Tory, kicking his feet, but Tory's dead weight drives them deep into the churning water.

Sena surfaces to the taste of brine and the smell of smoke. Above him, fog rolls over the sharp black cliffs, illuminated by intermittent rushes of fire or the bright blare of an explosion. The noise of it grates on his ears, but it's not the worst sound: it means there are people still alive to fight.

Tory is an anvil in his arms and they're a long way from anything resembling shoreline. A wave lashes against Sena and nearly buries him in water again, but just before it hits, he catches sight of a sad stretch of sand shaded by the cliffs. He's too dizzied by the fall to know whether it's on the Arlunian or Westrian side of the border, but it hardly matters. They will be far more dead, far more quickly, if Sena doesn't swim.

His muscles still ache from yesterday's—from yesterday, but they serve him well enough to bring them both to shore. By the time he gets to the shallows, the prospect of dragging Tory across wet sand is unappealing enough that he seriously considers letting the ocean take him. He's not even sure he has the will to drag *himself* across wet sand right now. Briefly, he entertains the thought of lying face-down and drowning in a knuckle's depth of frothy water.

But while Sena is many, many things, he's not a quitter, so he drags Tory out of the surf and into the shade of the cliffs, taking only a tiny, truly conservative amount of joy from dragging Tory's dead weight over two large, bumpy rocks.

When he finally drops him and checks his breathing (three sharp pumps to his chest make him groan and expel the water he swallowed) Sena flops down next to him. Beast have mercy on anyone who calls upon him to stand.

But his reprieve doesn't last long. Now that he's not imminently at risk of death, his body begins to process its own aches, and a pain in his chest—a sharp, stabbing thing that glows white-hot with every breath—makes itself known.

Sena shouldn't be surprised. The landing wasn't kind, and Tory has very sharp elbows. Sena muses, with a careful press to his ribs that makes him grit his teeth, that he may have broken something.

It won't be a problem. Sena will not allow it to be.

Sheer stubbornness brings him to a sitting position, where he takes stock of himself. He's soaked, naturally. The rations in his pockets are still secure, but the communicator clipped to his pocket must have gotten lost in the fall—not that its delicate components would have liked the water even if it remained on him. Aside from the communicator, his belongings are intact.

By the time Sena finishes cataloging everything, Tory is groaning awake. He rolls onto his side, coughing more water onto the sand.

His voice is gravelly when he speaks. "What happened?"

"You don't remember?"

Tory rasps a laugh. "I remember . . . being about to throw that explosion, then you pulled us over the cliff."

Sena lets the silence stretch long enough to grow a personality. He grits out, "The fall must have addled your brain."

"By all means, tell me what really went down."

"*You* botched throwing the explosion and were about to be tossed over the cliff. I foolishly tried to warn you and, failing that, tried to keep you from falling. And here we are."

"You have a terrible memory," Tory mutters. "We'd be ground meat if I hadn't thrown it as far as I did." Which is accurate enough. Tory sits up with what appears to be monumental effort. "Did you send out a distress call?"

Sena waves a hand over his empty pocket. "Lost it in the fall. Not that it matters. Anyone in range is likely dead."

"Mm, love that optimism." Tory shivers for a while before he startles, looking up at the cliffs. "It's over?"

It is. No more smoke or flashes.

No more fighting, because there are no more fighters.

He makes himself stand. "On your feet. We need to move inland. We're likely still in Westrice, but that just means any infiltrators who find us will be on high alert—more likely to kill than capture us."

Tory lifts himself and brushes wet sand from his clothes. "Tired," he says.

"Tired is better than dead. We need to put whatever daylight we have left to good use. Navigating around the rocks will waste time, but there's no way we could scale them in our condition. Once we make it around, as long as we head northeast and don't get killed, we'll find the road to the Compound before long."

They start off, traversing the rock-strewn sand.

"How can you still be wearing those gloves?" Tory asks. "All . . . soggy and . . ."

"I don't notice it. I rarely take them off."

"That sounds unsanitary." Silence spreads between them, broken only by the obscene *squish-schluck* of Tory's shoes. With Tory behind him, Sena feels his gaze like a brand between his shoulders. After a while, Tory says, "So, how long have you been doing this?"

"Doing what?"

"*This*." The word is not nearly as illuminating as Tory seems to think it is. Sena lets his judgmental silence clue Tory in, and he does eventually clarify. "Being a soldier, I mean."

"An *officer*." Sena speeds up as they enter the woods. "I was sent to officer preparatory school as soon as my Seed was discovered."

"Yeah? How'd that happen?"

"As I said before, I was the target of harassment. A group of boys found joy in roughing me up whenever the teachers' eyes weren't on us. I reached out from the ground to stop one of them from kicking me in the face. Without meaning to, I . . ."

Tory perks up. "Killed him?"

"He survived. His leg had to be amputated below the knee."

"Ah. Yeah, you mentioned that. You finally going to tell me what your Seed is?"

Sena pauses. "How much do you know of the First Children? Dr. Helner would have called them the Sources."

"I know I'm supposed to be one of them. 'Til a few months ago, I'd've sworn up and down I was a Healer."

Sena laughs. "That really was unwise."

"So I've heard."

Sena slows his gait. "In Arlune, there are legends of the Great Celestial Beast."

"The what?"

"The Celestial Beast was an ethereal creature who swam among stars, the creator of our planet and many others." Sena cuts himself off. He has the words right, but it *sounds* wrong. There's something missing when Sena tries to recite them. He grumbles, "I can't tell the stories like my mother did."

"Give me the abridged version."

"Just as well." Sena adjusts his jacket and pulls in a halting breath. He'll have to get used to shallow breaths. "The first Seeds ever to appear on this planet after the Beast's body was planted in the earth were two children, the Beast's gift to the planet it loved unto death. They're the so-called Sources, because the military likes slapping its own names on everything. The First Children were the Worldseed and the Voidseed—Channeler and Neutralizer, if you use Westrice's names. Just as the world has roads and roots and the universe is flooded with rivers of stars, the First Children each carried life. From them, all other Seeds blossomed."

"Worldseed."

"That's you. The Worldseed has the ability to handle all energies."

"And the other one?"

"Voidseed." Bitterness churns in Sena's stomach. He stuffs his hands into his pockets. "That's me. Intrinsic. The Voidseed destroys all energies. It's notoriously unstable. Also the rarest, with your type coming in a rather distant second. I can break down anything I touch."

"So you'd kill me if you touched me?"

Sena laughs, brutal and short. "My self-control is better than that, I hope. But . . . I could, if I weren't careful. I also nullify foreign energies as a matter of course. It's why no Seed abilities can affect me, and why my Core and . . . and NOVA had to be surgically rather than Seed-implanted."

Tory winces.

"You remember when you came to the facility, the test they did to determine your type? It destroys the Seed in your blood when it touches it. The color and pattern of the sparks indicate your type, and the extent of the destruction indicates your range of effect. They've been taking my blood since I was eleven to develop it."

He swallows a surge of shame. Tory saw, the day his father visited. He saw Sena's arm, marked with over a decade of needle scars.

"Not only the type tests," Tory whispers.

"No." Sena has not allowed himself to feel anger for years, but heat surges in his chest when he remembers the vest his father wore, the *prototypes* he promised—all the weapons they're making out of Sena, like he's not destructive enough on his own. "When my ability comes into flesh-to-flesh contact, it neutralizes the energies that sustain the human body. The boy whose leg I grabbed when I was nine lost the limb to necrosis."

Silence falls for a long while. Tory is probably horrified. But when he finally speaks, it's not to express disgust. "So, if you can't be affected by any Seed . . . you can't be healed?"

Sena's breath freezes in his chest before he regains control of it.

Typical Tory. Since the day they met, Sena's had a beast of a time trying to predict him. He shrugs, brushing off the flutter of surprise. "My Seed has, thus far, kept me from experiencing any major illness."

Another long pause. Uncomfortably long, this time. "And physical injuries?"

Sena flinches. Heat climbs his neck. Tory must be thinking of that shameful incident in Kirlov's tent. "I've developed a high pain tolerance." He speeds up. "We need to hurry. We've got an hour or so until nightfall, and this terrain will be too dangerous in the dark."

A low wind rustles the leaves, and Tory audibly shivers. "Gonna get pneumonia."

"Considering your exhaustion from using your abilities so long without rest, the fact that you inhaled water, and your current state, it's not impossible."

Tory scoffs. "Wow, thanks. Where did you learn to *interact* with people, Sena?"

"You're no better at it, if the way you drew your roommate's ire is any indication."

"Better than being a freaking puppet."

Sena winces, but it's an accurate-enough descriptor. He saw the NOVA before they cut him open and installed it against his spine: a strange, articulated metal thing with a long, embedded strip of pure stellite. A symbolic set of strings to control him with. "Do you think you're beyond control? All someone has to do to send *you* on a rampage is mention your tattoo. I'm still not sure why."

Tory's glower is palpable. "I just don't like it. Do I need a reason?"

"You must have one. I don't need to know it, if that's what you're asking. I didn't intend to cause offense."

Laughter explodes from Tory. "Oh, you're *really* good at not pissing people off."

The sun is a sliver ahead, barely visible through the trees as they climb a hill blanketed with dead leaves. It will be dark soon. Sena stares straight ahead. "I don't mean to," he offers.

"What are you trying to *do*, then?"

Sena's chest hurts, and not only because of the fall. He never learned how to talk about this. "I've never been as . . . socially competent as my peers. I've gotten better at interpreting behavior by observation because I've had to, but not overwhelmingly so. Not enough to keep them from—" His shoulders go tight. "Never enough for it to matter. It's not my intention to 'piss you off'. The feeling is mutual, if you care to know."

"What did *I* do?"

Sena levels a dry stare at Tory. "You were loud. Reckless."

He was infuriating. He *is* infuriating. But he is also, to Sena's great chagrin, infuriatingly impossible to look away from. When he arrived at the Compound and threw himself up against every wall, tested the give in every rule, spat in the face of safety and propriety—

It made Sena furious. It was like Tory didn't know that people could only fall so many times before they couldn't stand again. Like his bones didn't know how to break.

Tory huffs. "Not everyone can have their panties in a bunch all the time." His footsteps slow, considering. There's a smile in his voice when he continues, "So I pissed you off, huh? The blindfold thing, on the training field—you did that 'cause I annoyed you?"

"No." A bald-faced lie. Sena amends, "That wasn't the only reason. I thought it might help. Seeing you bombarded with balloons was merely a pleasant byproduct."

"Didn't see the point of being nice anymore, after where it got me."

There it is again, that awful nonchalance. Sena's trembling, but that's no surprise. It's been ages since anger didn't make him shake. It's at least as dangerous as hope has ever been. "The *point*," Sena grits out, "is to not become a target. Were my heritage something

I could have disguised when I was young, I would have. If I could have matched the graces of my peers, I would have. If I could—if the colonel—" It's not fair. Tory makes rebellion look so *easy*, so consequence-free. "You invite violence and blame the ones who bring it."

"Fuck you! I was tired of appeasement!"

Sena shouldn't be glad to have gotten a rise out of Tory, but it douses some of the furious heat in him. It means, at least, that Sena isn't alone in feeling like his body is a fuse waiting for a spark.

"I was so tired, you have no idea. I've spent *every moment* since I was eight just taking it. Why don't you get it? Your dad fucking *bled* you and you let him. I—what I saw—don't you understand you're just making it easier—"

"Nothing makes it easier!" The heat surges back, foreign and horrible and frightening. Tory plucks this feeling from him so easily. He makes Sena weak and unsteady. Out of control, when control is the only thing that's ever kept him safe. Sena clamps down on the surge of anger and throttles it. Calmly, he says again, "Nothing makes it easier. I tried everything. The only thing I could do was make it happen less often."

"*Don't make trouble.*" Tory's voice is thoughtful, and Sena grimaces. He doesn't need Tory's pity. "My mom had rules like that. She was afraid, too."

Sena rasps out a laugh that echoes with a gong of pain in his chest, and he stops to catch his breath.

Tory must notice something. "Are you . . . ?"

"Fine," Sena breathes, straightening.

Afraid. It's such a flimsy, laughable word for the horror that's carved Sena hollow for years, so sharp the agony of the NOVA came almost as a relief at times: at least he didn't have to keep waiting for it.

Conveniently, they come upon a creek, and Sena buys time by kneeling to fill his canteen. He uses the excuse of his busy hands as he twists it closed and secures it to his belt so he doesn't have to look at Tory when he finally decides on, "It wasn't your fault."

"What?"

"In the tent. The NOVA. Kirlov would have found another reason, if not that. You apologized back then, but it wasn't your fault. It was at least in part because I allowed the Arlunian non-combatants to 'port away."

"I wondered if that was on purpose."

Sena shrugs. "When I can do something . . . I try. Sometimes it doesn't work. That day you arrived—with the scalpel—I meant to let the rebel infiltrators escape unharmed, but one of them went for my gun. You were right that I'm a coward, that I only give others advice to prevent their own pain."

Tory swallows audibly. "I didn't say you were a coward."

"You didn't have to."

They walk, on and on and up, until Tory finally says, "Ownership."

Sena blinks. "I'm sorry?"

"The tattoo. You asked, right? It's—it's like the Core. It's not something I want, not something I *chose*. Someone put it on me to show I don't belong to myself. People *see it* and think they know me, think they—" He stops, like maybe he can stuff the words back inside himself.

Sena knows the feeling. He gets it now, though. Warmth fills him. How strange, that they can be so different and think so alike.

Tory's looking down, shoulders up to bracket his ears, like he's bracing himself for a blow. Sena says, quietly, "I've misunderstood you."

Tory's wide eyes find Sena, tension going out of his shoulders. His gaze is a question, so Sena makes himself answer. "There's no shame in survival. Your tattoos"—his scars, Sena's scars, so many other things—"aren't ugly. Other people make them ugly."

"You're not wrong." Tory trudges up a hill behind Sena, humming under his breath. Finally, he says, "You know, I fucking *hate* people."

The suddenness of it shocks a grin from Sena. "Yes."

He doesn't interrogate the warm feeling that fills him at the brilliant smile Tory offers in response. They sink into silence, and for the first time, it's comfortable.

The sun sets fast. They find a defensible resting place before the last of the light leaves—a nook in a jagged wall of rock that creates a right angle, leaving only the front exposed—and Sena sets to work making a small fire. Discovery is a concern but dehydration, illness, and hypothermia are equally dangerous. Sena leaves his wet gloves on.

Tory dries his socks in front of the fire while Sena boils the water from the creek. They feast on some of the dried rations in one of the large pockets on their jackets and save the rest for later. Sena keeps his handgun but gives Tory a knife, just in case.

When Tory's clothes are mostly dry, he falls asleep sitting up, and Sena gently prods him into lying on his side. It's been a long day. Sena should sleep, too.

But it's not bad, like this. The cold, open air. The heat of the fire. Tory curled like a crescent moon toward Sena, close enough to touch.

The sky above goes on forever, and Sena really should sleep, but instead he counts the stars and whispers their names and feeds brush into the fire to keep it bright. He'll enjoy this freedom, every moment of it, for as long as he's allowed to keep it.

*

Tory wakes at first light. The fire has died down, but the embers still burn bright. Tory frowns. Sena hasn't been asleep long, then.

He waits until the light sifts full and bright through the trees overhead before he wakes him. Sena barely stirs at the first nudge. Tory tries again, shaking his shoulder, and Sena jolts awake, taking in the state of the light. "You should have woken me hours ago," he rasps, and immediately tries to stand.

He fails, making a ragged, shallow gasp as he crumples.

Tory should have noticed it earlier. "When we fell . . .?"

Sena grits his teeth. "It's nothing."

He makes it to his feet this time.

Tory steps in front of him. Something strange and unfamiliar wriggles in his stomach at the pallor of Sena's face and the bluish smudges beneath his eyes. "Wrong answer. Try again."

"I . . . may have fractured a rib during our plunge."

"Hitting the water wasn't so bad. Did you land on something?"

Sena's breathy chuckle turns into a cough. "*Something* landed on me." He stretches out, winces. "In any case, the break is tender but not debilitating. It was merely unwise to move without consideration for it."

Tory swallows an apology (Sena might tell him it's *useless* again) and packs up in silence. He works fast so Sena doesn't have to—an apology in action, not words. With dry shoes, socks, and clothing thanks to last night's fire, the work is nearly pleasant.

Sena sets a brutal pace. A few minutes into their journey, he breaks the silence with a grimly cheery, "In any case, our injuries are the least of our concerns. We'll be dead in three days if we can't get back. Two days, now, I suppose."

Tory nearly tumbles down the hill. "We'll *what?*"

"Standard protocol, remember? We're high risk. Just because they don't know how best to use us doesn't mean they'll risk us falling into the hands of enemies who might. Our Cores will be deactivated after three days. If we're dead, we wouldn't notice, and if we're alive, three days without contact usually means a soldier has defected. It's reasonable, but in our case, extremely unfortunate." He waves a hand toward where his communicator would be if it had survived the fall.

The steepness of the rocky terrain increases as they go. Sena says, "It will be like this for a while. Most of Westrice is high above sea level. Be careful."

Tory isn't the one who needs to be careful. He positions himself behind Sena, not liking the way his steps weave. It's not protectiveness; it's pragmatism. Tory can't navigate for shit. He can't let their terrain expert fall and get impaled on a rock. "Doesn't sound like we have time for careful."

"True. Two days, if we're lucky and use every hour of daylight and then some, *might* get us back to the Compound. We don't—" Sena nearly misses a step in a clump of damp, decaying leaves. Tory's hands go up to catch him. He drops them with a sigh he assures himself is frustration and not relief when Sena finds his balance again. "We don't have the luxury of assuming we'll run into a patrol. We're as likely to run into enemy soldiers as any of our own."

They march to the crunch of fallen leaves, the low hum of the wind, and the staticky rush of the distant sea. Sena's looking worse and worse as the day wears on, face beaded with sweat. Silent, he puts all his focus into walking. Tory, grudgingly, focuses on watching Sena walk.

The result is that neither of them notice their pursuers until it's too late.

For almost an hour, shreds of yellowed flatlands have flashed between the trees and hanging vines. They're almost out of the woods when Sena stops.

"Tory."

Tory's hand goes to the knife on his belt at Sena's tone, but Sena shakes his head, a minute motion. "We're surrounded."

Someone emerges from the trees.

Arlunian. Short and slim, with dark hair braided and twisted into a bun. Slick pink scars cover his hands and wrists. He can't be older than seventeen, but he paces toward them like the gun at Sena's side and the knife tucked into Tory's belt mean nothing to him.

Tory recalls Sena's words. In enemy territory, they're likelier to be killed than captured.

The boy takes in their attire, lips drawn back in a snarl. He knocks two thick thumb rings together, and a shower of sparks lights the air. The sparks converge and swell into a ball of flame in the boy's hands, lighting mahogany eyes gold and red. The boy slings the sphere when it's as big as Sena's head.

With instinct born of training, Tory diverts it into the woods where it bursts against the thick trunk of a tree, sizzling and spitting. The second comes too fast on its heels, aimed at Sena's chest.

"Sena!"

Tory curses, frozen where he stands, but the ball of flame sputters out before reaching him. Relief floods Tory. Right. He spares a moment to be grateful for Sena's strange power.

Their attacker spits, "Null," at the sight of the dying flames and withdraws a wicked hunting knife. In fluent if lightly accented Westrian, he says, "You want to do things the ugly way? I will not pass up an opportunity to gut a pig."

He slashes before Sena can raise both hands and say more than, "We're not here to—"

Sena arches away from the swing, so smoothly Tory wouldn't be able to tell how much pain he was in if he didn't already know. "Tory, stay back!"

Sena flings a glove off and catches the sides of the blade on the downswing with bare fingers. He doesn't touch it for more than an instant, but it's long enough. The deadly glint of the blade goes dull, then brittle, then reddish with rust like it bore thousands of years of wear in the space of a breath. When it leaves Sena's grip, it does so in flecks and fragments.

The boy drops the useless hilt, staggering back as Sena presses a bleeding fingertip between his lips to suck off the blood. The blade must have nicked him.

"Not Null," the boy breathes. "You're—both of you are—"

A young man and woman appear behind Sena, the woman reaching out. Confusion flits through Tory. These ones aren't Arlunian. They're Westrian. Still enemies, though, if the focused malice on the woman's face is anything to go by.

"Behind you!" Tory calls.

The boy whose knife Sena ruined says, "Spark, it won't work, he's a—"

But the woman learns for herself when her hand closes around Sena's neck and nothing happens. The woman, with big dark eyes and brown hair shorn close to her skull, flickers out of sight with a curse. Sena spins, drawing his handgun and scanning the woods, but the pair reappear at his side. The woman leaps close enough to chop at the wrist holding his gun.

It clatters into the dirt. Sena finds Tory, eyes wide. "Run," he says. "I'll keep them—"

But they're gone again.

When the woman reappears, she shoves Sena—hard—in the chest. Sena makes an awful sound and crumples, curling over himself. His eyes find Tory as the pair flicker out of sight once more. Expression taut, he mouths *go.*

But there's no way Tory can go. He shakes his head, moving closer to Sena. If he can *find* these jerks, hunt them by their energies—

Sena's eyes fly wide, and Tory knows something's wrong before his own name leaves Sena's lips, breathless and urgent. "Turn around!"

A cold hand settles on his nape before he can.

The boy with the ruined knife opens his mouth but only manages one raw syllable.

A triumphant breath of laughter raises the hair on Tory's neck. The woman's energy flares against his senses, sizzlingly sharp and so close he can taste it. He has to grab it, redirect it, *something*.

They don't have time for this.

Electricity rips through him before he can do anything, locking his limbs.

What he hears as he falls might be Sena's voice, but he's too far gone to tell.

CHAPTER SEVENTEEN

Fuzzing in and out of awareness, Tory isn't sure how far they drag him before dropping him.

When clarity trickles back in, he blinks into impenetrable darkness. He's weighted down, skin buzzing, breath shallow. He blinks and blinks, but there's not a drop of light.

There's something wrong with that, with the darkness. But his brain is slow to answer, body aching in a syrupy way that's consistent with being battered, marinated in seawater and tenderized on the rocks, then fried to perfection by some weird electric lady, which is awful, really, because they're kind of in a—

Shit. It's dark.

With a lurch, Tory tries and fails to stand, but it's like his body is anchored to the ground. If it's dark, that's a whole day wasted. "Sena?"

"Tied to you," comes the strained reply. "Can you stop moving?"

"How long have I been out? If it's night already—"

"Not night. Blindfolded. You've been in and out for maybe ten minutes. Just long enough for them to tie us up and leave us here."

"Oh." Tory wiggles his nose and the prickly sensation of motion across it does indeed feel like cloth. Tension leaves him in a rush. "That's . . . not so bad, then."

"I wouldn't go that far. One of these people had to be physically restrained to keep him from killing me when we arrived. I'm not optimistic about our prospects."

"Shut your mouth, dog." The low, gravelly voice comes from Tory's right.

"Ah," Sena says faintly. "It was that one."

Tory reflexively reaches for his power—for any energies he can turn against an enemy—but the world is empty and silent. It's worse than being blindfolded. He shivers.

That must be why they've tied him to Sena.

"Who are you?" Tory says. The more he blinks, the more his eyes adjust. The cloth they've tied around his head is rougher than the water-smooth kerchief Sena used on Tory in training. He can almost make out shapes through the loose weave. A hunched, restless silhouette sits on a box of some sort, a mere few strides away from Tory. "What do you want with us?"

"Boss thinks you might be useful." The way the man spits his words says he disagrees. Something bounces with an irritated *tap tap tap* against the man's knee, catching the light on each upswing. A knife?

A terrible plan begins to take shape in Tory's head.

He pitches his voice casual. "How 'bout this hospitality, huh? Almost in line with what those bastards at the Box offer."

The man goes deadly still where he sits. "Don't you dare compare us to *them*."

A weak spot? "You're not doing a lot to differentiate yourself." Tory tries to gesture at his current state but fails again, fibers from the thick rope that binds him to Sena piercing his shirt to prick his skin. "I'd say you're about even."

"Stop talking." Irritation shows in the increased pace of the taps of the flat side of the blade against the man's knee, the way his leg jumps up to meet it.

But he's not irritated *enough*. Not yet.

The quiet stretches, nothing but the shallow wheeze of Sena's breath to break it. In this hazy dark, it's easy to remember the bursts of blood-slick dirt over his skin and the riot of his breath in his ears. Randall, empty eyes aimed at the sky. It's easy, too, to remember Sena's terribly casual, *Our cores will be deactivated in two days.*

There's no time to do this slowly. "Let's play a game."

It's a flimsy plan: piss this guy off; get him over here. In close quarters, Tory can headbutt him, maybe turn the tables. "I'll start. If I stood you and the bastard Grand General side by side—"

"*Tory.*" Sena's voice. Half exhaustion, half warning. "I hope you know what you're doing."

"I'm just saying, their hospitality is shit. Even *you're* a better conversation partner than this guy."

"Am I really?" Sena scoffs, a punched exhale that turns into a crackling cough. He stills against Tory's back, and when he speaks up again, his voice is low. "Tory."

"Hm?"

"They didn't drag us far. We're still in the woods. I've heard at least six people since we arrived here. All Seeds, if I had to—"

The man with the knife lurches to his feet and stalks toward them. "You wanna die, lapdog?"

Sena shuts his mouth, and the man retreats with a growl, but he doesn't go back to his seat. He stalks once, twice in agitated circles around the both of them, wrist flicking like he wants to set his blade against flesh.

Almost there. If Tory can get him to come nearer, if he can stun him and get his hands on that knife . . .

"Maybe you're *worse* than the bastards at the Box," Tory tries, when the man's third, angry revolution brings him close again. "After all, if you think about it—"

"What the fuck did you say?"

There. The shadowed shape of the man clenches his blade and breaks from his circle to stalk in Tory's direction.

"Tory!"

Maybe it's Sena's interjection that deflects the man's rage, or maybe it's that the guy seems to have it out for the Box as a whole, but at Sena's panicked call, the man heads for him instead.

There are few emotions more awful than the sudden, searing dread that flushes through Tory. It's Kirlov's tent all over again. It's Sena on the ground, unbreathing while Tory stares down from above.

He wrenches at the ropes that bind him, but there's no give. They only get tighter, sawing at his skin and squeezing the breath from him. From Sena, too, by the sudden, sharp noise of pain. Tory can't *see*, this time, and it's so much worse.

"I was the one who said that shit!" Tory yells, but there's terrible pressure against his back. A thud, the crinkle of leaves like Sena is trying to scramble away and can't.

"Don't think I didn't hear them talking. Don't think I don't know what you did to her, to my—"

Tory can't see a thing, can't tell if the man stabbed Sena already or is just getting started, and this is all wrong. It was supposed to be Tory. This isn't what he planned for. He hates it, hates this, hates *feeling* like this—

"Stop it! You said you had questions! Just let go of him and I'll—"

The thud of running footsteps. The low growl of a voice. Suddenly, the pressure against Tory's back vanishes, and the ropes around him tighten as Sena sags.

"Judge!" a deep voice booms from somewhere behind Tory. "I leave you alone for *one* moment. Drop the damned knife. *Now!*"

A clink.

"How many times have I told you your temper will be the death of us? You're as bad as Iri. Get over here." A grunt, the rustle of cloth. "You will *not* let your emotions ruin our mission. Sit this one out. Cool your head."

"He said—"

"I don't care what he said! We need him."

Tory's stomach flips, because he *knows* that voice—honey-smooth and authoritative. He's heard it somewhere. But his heart is a drumbeat in his ears, turning the world to ocean noise, and his thoughts are a riot in his skull. He can't place it.

Slow and casual, footsteps crunch the leaves around Tory until they stop in front of him. Tory tenses at sudden pressure on the side of his face. On the blindfold. "That was a terrible idea," the familiar voice drawls.

Then there's light, brutal as a blow to the head. Tory blinks through the ache of it, squeezing his eyes closed until they adjust.

The voice says, "You could have gotten yourself killed, provoking Judge like that. He has ample reason to be unhappy with the Westrian military. What were you thinking, Tory?"

This guy knows his name? Blindfold removed, Tory squints into the gray light. A man stands in front of him, leaning all his weight on one leg and bending to peer at Tory with an exasperated expression.

Tory takes in the man's fox eyes, his waves of red hair like flames. "You!"

Riese. The rebels. He's found them, but what an introduction.

Riese's lips curl up. "Me. Told you I'd be seeing you again, although—" he quirks an eyebrow at Tory's disheveled state "—maybe not quite like this. If I were a moment later, I'd be burying you, not greeting you. What were you thinking with that stunt?"

"I meant to get him to attack me," Tory admits with a one-shouldered shrug. "I was going to headbutt him and take his knife."

Riese laughs. "Bold! Foolish, but bold. It might have worked if you hadn't become so soft."

Tory bristles. "What?"

"*Soft.* Like spoiled fruit. All Judge had to do was apply a little pressure to that Box-dog and you were ready to sing like a canary. Where's the sharp-toothed boy I met, the one who wanted to start fires and open veins?"

Tory flushes. His mother's words echo in his skull. *Don't grow roots.*

Has he? Surely not again. Not so quickly. It's just that Sena's the only one who knows the terrain. Tory doesn't let himself look at Sena. "It's been a long day."

Riese offers a mild smile, but the sharpness of his canines ruins it. "So it seems. I apologize for the reception you received. We normally don't treat guests this way. You have to understand that we must be careful, given the sorts of creatures we find crawling in these woods." He scowls at Sena. "I'll be frank. In any other situation, I would have killed your friend here," Riese says. "We've taken in Seeds from the Compound before, which comes, naturally, with its own risks. Never have we taken in an *officer.*" He spits the word like it's a curse.

"Sena is a Seed," Tory says, and regrets it instantly. He probably shouldn't have used Sena's name. If these people want to kill Sena just for being an officer, he doesn't know what they'd do to him for being Vantaras.

But Riese just nods, unaware.

"We noticed. Iri here had plenty to tell me about that." Riese flaps a hand toward the sullen boy who ran in behind him: another familiar face. Short, angry, drowning in a knitted burnt-orange sweater several times too large for him and still wearing his hair in a braided bun. Burn scars on both hands and thick rings on his thumbs. "I'm told he tried to incinerate your friend."

"No hard feelings," says the boy, who clearly has enough hard feelings for both of them.

Tory glares at Iri, who only crosses his arms and raises an eyebrow.

Riese continues with a thin-lipped frown at Sena. "The fact that he is a Seed and the fact that he's with *you* are why he's still alive. If he attempts to betray us or I'm given any reason to believe he *might*, I'll kill him myself."

"You can't—" Tory starts, but Sena interrupts.

"I would expect no less."

Riese shrugs, and his smile is directed at Tory, not Sena. "I wanted to start out with honesty, however unpleasant it might be. In any other situation, we conduct an . . . entrance interview of sorts with any new inductees. Judge has the ability to discern truth from falsehood. Apparently when someone lies, it tastes terrible. However, your friend's unique constitution means that Judge is unable to get a read on either of you."

"Because you tied us together."

"Yes. I have enough *hotheads* here—" at this, he flicks a glance first at Judge, then at Iri "—that caution is second nature. I didn't know what state you'd be in when you woke and wanted to prevent others using their abilities to harm you or you doing the same to harm us."

Tory grumbles under his breath. Just because it's reasonable doesn't mean he has to like it.

"Luckily, my conversation with you in Ms. Belmin's caravan made it quite clear that you're just the sort of person I'm looking for, though I'm not especially pleased that you've arrived with company. Wasn't this the Box-dog who dragged you *back* when you were so close to freedom? I don't understand why you've allowed him to live."

The old anger surges through Tory, but it simmers down just as quickly. "He's—" What is he? Discomfort knots in Tory's gut. Sena is a fool, unwilling to defend himself, but he's also protected Tory, over and over, even when he didn't have to. Even when protecting Tory meant hurting himself. He's an ally, dangerously close to becoming something almost like a friend. Tory can't make himself say any of those things, so he says only, "Sena's on our side."

Riese's expression is bone-dry as he drops down on the box Judge was sitting on when Tory first woke. At eye level now, he pins Tory with an unblinking stare. "I wouldn't be so sure."

"I would."

Riese scoffs. "You've let them *domesticate* you."

Tory bares his teeth. "I didn't let them, and I sure as fuck won't let you."

Riese laughs.

Judge steps in, still glaring, but his knife, at least, is nowhere to be seen. "It doesn't have to be him. We can find someone else."

"Give him grace," Riese says. "You'll see what I saw in him soon enough. We'll sharpen him up again. As for the other one . . ." Riese's eyes flick to Sena. "I'll have to ask you to keep your dog in line, Tory. Some things, I fear, freedom can't fix."

"Maybe some things are none of your fucking business." It settles, with a dizzying lurch, that Tory would have agreed with those words mere days ago. They hit wrong, now, stirring anger in Tory's gut. "You're acting like I've agreed to whatever it is you want me to do, but the way I'm hearing it, you *need* someone like me."

Riese looks away into the woods. "We do, yes. Very much."

"Then it sounds like all the power is in my hands."

"Yes, well. Your hands are a little tied up at the moment, aren't they?"

At Tory's incredulous scoff, Riese laughs. "I apologize. We've lost many, many lives to people like your *Sena* here, and it's made us crude. We have an active mission and we're missing an important piece of the puzzle. We'd greatly appreciate your assistance if you're willing to render it. I'm sorry for treating you this way. The purpose of the bonds was to keep things civil until I'd had a chance to speak with you. We'll untie you momentarily."

"And what's to keep me from walking away when you do?"

"Curiosity?" An elegant shrug. "The things we could do together, we'd rewrite the way this whole country works. You'd change everything."

Tory bites his lip to keep from showing how good that sounds. "That's all about what I can do for you. What can you do for me?"

"You mean aside from freeing you and other Seeds from Westrian control?" Riese waves over his neck. "To start, we can help with *this*. I know someone who's had . . . *moderate* success removing Cores. She's the only Reacher in the country who freelances for the right price. I'm sure you're eager to be rid of that thing."

Giddy relief surges through Tory. He crushes it down before it can spread. If there's someone out here who can remove their Cores, they won't have to go back at all. "When? As long as it's still installed, they can track us."

Riese shakes his head. "They can't. We have something that . . . I suppose you could say it prevents them from getting close. They won't find you as long as you're with me, and the tracker won't matter for long. Once it's removed, we'll destroy it."

"But *when?*"

"Soon. I know you might be in a bit of a hurry, but I'll need to arrange things with our Reacher and carve out enough time for safe removal."

"What do you need us to do, then?"

Something glows in Riese's eyes, bright as flame. He clicks his tongue. "I don't think we know each other quite well enough for that yet, Tory. But I swear to you, I'll share the details as soon as I can. For now, I can tell you this: the things we can do together—Westrice has had us on the run for years. With you, we can finally fight back. The future I imagine would see us all free."

Tory forgets the ropes as Riese leans close.

Hiding has kept him alive for so long, like medicine that breaks a man to give him breath—but Riese is offering a chance to strike a blow against all the people who've kept him under their thumb. "I want it," he whispers. Then, louder: "Let me help."

Riese laughs. "Excellent. Let's get you out of those ropes, then. Iri, if you don't mind?"

Iri paces toward them, but Sena speaks up before he arrives. "Before you untie us . . ."

There's a sudden slackening of the rope around Tory's chest, and it falls onto his lap. Sena stands in one quick push, hands raised in surrender, lifting the blindfold from his eyes.

Tory gapes.

Iri smashes his thumb rings together to make sparks and has flame floating above his palm in an instant. Riese leaps to his feet, predator-fast. Judge must have found the knife an unsatisfactory threat last time, because he pulls a gun from his belt and levels it at Sena.

"Whoa! Hey!" Surging to his feet, Tory skids between them. He's never tried throwing the energy from a bullet, but there's a first time for everything.

Iri's flame flickers out. "That's on me," he says to Riese, quiet. "I failed to consider that he could decay the rope when I bound him. He must have found a way to put it in contact with his skin."

In the gray light, Sena is parchment-pale and greasy with sweat. "I unbound us shortly after you arrived so we could free ourselves if you proved to be a threat. That I didn't attack was a gesture of good faith."

"Judge," Riese says. "*Lower it.*"

The gun's barrel points at the ground, but the air rings with tension.

Riese breaks it. "It was my oversight as well. Don't blame yourself. We haven't dealt with a Seed of this type before. Iri, if you could escort them to the fire? Dinner should be ready soon. Do whatever you must to defend yourself if the officer tries anything."

"I did not need your permission," Iri says, lips twisted with malice.

Riese massages his temples. "*Do* control yourself. I would prefer not to have to break up a third unprovoked murder attempt. Judge? With me."

Judge's low grumbling suggests that he thinks the murder attempt was plenty provoked, but he follows obediently at Riese's invitation.

Iri's shoulders go up when Riese is gone. "This way," he says unnecessarily. "You go first."

"Tory," Sena says before he can obey.

Tory freezes. "Huh?"

"The box. Look." Sena gestures at the box Riese was sitting on. There's text stamped along the side, the same text that was on the sides of the boxes guarded by the Arlunian cell they slaughtered yesterday. This must be where they were delivering the supplies.

Iri's hands twitch, like he's aching to make sparks.

Tory shakes his head. To Iri, he says, "We ran into the people who took these supplies. They—not all of them made it out." Seventeen, was it? Maybe eighteen corpses.

"They knew the risks." Iri's expression cools. "We all do. We're working toward something more important than any one life." He gestures again to the path ahead. "Please."

Tory steps around him and walks. For once, Sena is the one trying to keep up, gait unsteady and eyes trained on the ground.

That awful, helpless dread creeps back, slick like oil. Tory's hands ache to heal, but of course Sena would be the one person his healing doesn't work on. "Your Westrian is excellent," he tells Iri, to break the silence.

Iri's voice is flat. "I was born on the border. It was not a proficiency I sought, but it has proven useful."

They pace along the leaf-strewn path toward the fire blazing between the trees, and when he turns, Tory could swear he sees the sparks of it in Iri's eyes.

"My mother lived at the border," Sena says.

Iri's eyes narrow. "We all know of your mother. A traitoress who lies in the bed of a warmonger."

Sena's mouth clamps shut, and Tory *feels* the blood leaving his face. Iri knows, then. He knows exactly who Sena is.

He must catch Tory's expression, because he scoffs. "Riese is not aware. I do not judge whole cloth for one foul stitch. I don't expect much of you since you come from rotten stock and have served them for years, but I will judge you for your actions."

"I'm sure you chose your parents, too," Tory spits. "I'll bet they're perfect."

Iri shrugs. "I would not know. Your people killed them."

Tory grimaces. "Fine. Let's play this game, shall we? My mom was a whore and I have no idea who fathered me, but the way she looked at my eyes sometimes, she knew and was afraid of him. I could ask, but she killed herself to let me out of prison when I was eight."

Iri stares at Tory, horrified. "Excuse me?"

Tory stares back. "I thought we were telling sad little stories that have nothing to do with the point."

"The point," Iri echoes.

"Please," Sena whispers, voice frayed. "It doesn't matter."

"It does! The *point*," Tory says, "Is that none of us chose our parents and this guy doesn't have the slightest idea what any of us went through to get here. I won't defend Westrice. We all know it's rotten. We're here because it's rotten. But none of us chose this."

"Didn't you? To serve that monster or to die—I know which I would choose."

"I'm sure you believe that. I did, too, but here I am, still scrambling to survive. Go ahead and blame me. I probably deserve it, but Sena—"

"Tory! I have no excuse."

"*Sena*," Iri spits the name like a curse. "Did you know your name means hope? I wonder how the bodies you left behind unburied feel about that."

Tory wants to interrupt, but he doesn't know where to start. Dread simmers in his stomach. *Soft*, Riese called him. The word echoes in his skull. He should know better by now.

Iri continues, "Do you know why your father started this war?"

Sena shakes his head.

"He and his new wife, your *mother*, were invited to celebrate the twentieth anniversary of the treaty that formalized trade and brokered peace between our nations. At the event, an artisan Seed shared a performance. She used what you call Legion. It was not a weapon. It was an expression of unity between two disparate but interconnected elements. They were used for building and bridge-making, for transportation, for many of the intricate works we traded with your country in exchange for stellite. Your father saw the artisan at work and saw a threat. A month later, he killed the stellite trade. We *relied* on that trade—for food and buildings and everything else. And when it stopped and our reserves ran scarce, we starved."

Iri pauses. "Your Grand General was right. 'Legion units' can indeed be used to kill, though they would never have been used that way if not for him."

He turns on Sena, dark eyes burning. "How can you allow him to make a weapon of you? The Voidseed is meant for growth, *protection*—it is the cosmic womb of all life, not a mindless destroyer."

Of all the things Iri has said, this hits Sena hardest.

He draws back with a wounded expression that's gone before Tory can name it. "My power *destroys* things," he says flatly. "I don't see what's protective about that."

And of all the things to deflate Iri's anger, it's that line that does it.

His taut shoulders loosen. Irritation, then confusion, then a sickened sort of wonder bloom on his face. "You do not know," he whispers.

"Know what?"

"You don't know anything. *They* do not know anything. About the Voidseed. They are warlike men, so they see a weapon in you. But both of your abilities are mere byproducts of your true skills. No wonder their names for you are flawed. They've taken the part to be the whole."

Sena must mean to respond, but he opens his mouth and says nothing.

"If telling you the truth will take a weapon out of your bastard father's hands, I will do it. It is too late to make a proper start on it tonight, but both of you, find me tomorrow."

*

Fatty meat sizzles onto the rocks around a roaring bonfire. Tents pock the ground beyond it, green as the vines that arc between the trees overhead. Riese's people bask in the bonfire's glow. The group's Porter—a genial young man with large brown eyes who introduced himself as Travin and spent the first few minutes after Tory's arrival apologizing for their first meeting—blinks in to steal a slice of meat before Judge can grab it, earning a scowl and a half-hearted swat.

Spark, the buzz-cut girl who zapped Tory into unsweet dreams, shocks Travin and steals the meat from his fingers, swallowing it almost without chewing and serving both Judge and Travin a satisfied grin.

Tory aches.

He spent his whole life hiding his powers or trading his service for silence. These people use their abilities as freely as they breathe. They laugh like they have nothing to fear.

It's absurd—it's reckless, their confident liberty.

There are few things he wouldn't trade for ease like theirs.

Riese smiles in the midst of it, and every Seed around the fire glows with his grand vision. Maybe this is what real freedom looks like. Freedom from fear. Tory's never known it, but he longs for it with a fierceness that rattles in his bones. It's nice.

But it's not complete.

Mumbling excuses, Tory stands to leave. He parts the curtain of vines strung between the trees and walks away into the woods.

Sena didn't receive the welcome Tory did around the fire. When he left, he wandered off in this direction. Twigs crunch beneath Tory's feet, and the gold tongues of fire fade from behind his eyelids, replaced with cool moonlight.

He finds Sena leaning against the knotted trunk of a massive dead tree wrapped with vines that drip strings of frail, electric-blue flowers. Sena said it before: they bloom blue in the short years before they never bloom again.

This place, too, has been mined dry of stellite.

The tree's barrenness creates a hole in the canopy of leaves. Dyed blue and ink-black in light of the moon, Sena stares at the tapestry of stars overhead.

Tory sinks down beside him. The wildfire warmth from Riese's people fades, replaced by a quieter, uncomplicated peace. The Tory of a few weeks ago would've laughed himself sick if anyone told him he'd ever choose to sit beside Sena Vantaras.

Sena goes rigid for a moment before relaxing.

Tory pulls his knees up. "Way too cold out here."

"It's not so bad." Sena tips his head back against the tree's rotten trunk. "You know, you should stop defending me to these people. It'll only make things more difficult for you."

A startled laugh rasps from Tory's throat. "Haven't you already tried to warn me against that once? Seriously, have I *ever* given you the impression that I'm interested in making things easy for myself?"

A long pause. "You have not," Sena admits. "I should have expected nothing less." With a soft huff, he tilts his chin at the stars. "Would you believe I used to think I could gather them? The stars, I mean. I learned the names of every constellation, the Celestial Beast at the core of them." His finger rises, and Tory can almost tell where he's pointing. Up above, there's a cluster of pinprick lights, serpentine and stellite-bright. A red one twinkles at its heart. "There's the one for the Worldseed. My mother says when the First Seeds died, they rose to stay beside the Beast whose sacrifice allowed them to bloom. *Thus on the earth as it is in the air*—that's why kuhlu is drawn to stellite, each crystal a scale the Celestial Beast shed on the planet in death. They say the vines are the earth's veins that once bore the Beast's mortal blood, that their blossoms are a love song our planet sings to the stars."

Tory stares up and imagines it: that distance, the loneliness of crying out for something gone. "You need to stop telling bad stories."

"You don't think it's beautiful?"

"Being torn apart, separated?" Tory scowls. "It's *horrible*."

Sena shrugs. "I've loved that story since I was a boy. Just—the way a love can last, even when the ones who felt it are gone."

"That's not pretty. It's just pain."

"Pain has to be beautiful sometimes. Otherwise, it's unbearable." The denizens of the forest fill the silence that follows with hoots and mournful calls that only sometimes find an answer. After a while, Sena hums. "Did you know that outside their use as a locator for stellite, kuhlu vines are considered a nuisance? They're invasive and destructive, not only to the trees that house them but also to manmade structures. They tear down walls or burrow underneath them. They slip into cracks in roads, in buildings, and pull them to pieces. They plant themselves in soil where nothing else will grow. I think they're a lot like you."

Tory frowns. "What, you're saying I'm a nuisance?"

A tiny bud of a smile blooms on Sena's face. "Perhaps a *small* nuisance. You certainly caused me enough problems at STAR-7. But also a tearer-down of walls. I think that's beautiful."

Tory's cheeks heat. He schools his face to neutrality and settles back against the tree. "What's your take? On what they're doing here, I mean."

Sena's gloved fingers trace the scar on the back of his neck. The chirps of insects nearly drown his whispered response. "I want it."

At Kirlov's hand, Sena dropped like a marionette, denied even the breath to scream. It's not hard to see why Sena might long for the same freedom Tory does.

It's not a bad thought, the idea that maybe they can seek it, together.

Sena called Tory a nuisance, and maybe he is. But he's more than that, and in this light, Tory understands that Sena's more than Tory thought he was, too. He's a teller of terrible stories and a breaker of falls into the sea. He begged Tory to *go* and save himself when he was on his knees on the ground. He's kind in a way Tory is only just beginning to recognize.

In the silence that grows between them, thick as vines, Sena's breaths are shallow wheezes. Guilt spreads through Tory. He owes Sena a story, too. He owes Sena the truth.

"I want it too," he admits. "I'd give anything to have it. I don't know if this is in that *file* you have on me, but I've been running a long time, just getting by. *Surviving* but never living. I couldn't let myself—" Oh, but he's not used to this. The truth feels like cutting himself open and inviting someone inside the wound. Tory's heart hammers. "Anyway, now—now we're free, right? And this feels different. It feels *important*."

"It does."

Don't lay down roots, Tory's mother begged him, and he obeyed her because her wisdom was all he knew. But his raw honesty doesn't leave him sick. Instead, he feels seen. Grounded, like kuhlu spreading roots and vines into earth and air, tearing down any walls that would cage it.

Maybe roots will make him stronger, if he lets them grow someplace solid. Maybe he can have this strange, comfortable thing that needs no words.

Tory remembers with a sudden, years-old ache that his mother used to love the woods. All he's been thinking about for years is how she was at the end. Her desperation in those last days, hands white-knuckled around his as she taught him how to survive a world without her.

But before all that, she worked so hard to convince him the earth was beautiful, that it grew trees to shelter people and food to nourish them. On bad days, she'd guide him into the small stretch of woods within the camp's high fences. She'd pull rotting leaves away from a little frill of greenery and break a bit off the end for him to sample. *This is Widow's Feast,* she'd say, or she'd come back flushed and grinning from a short walk to show him a clump of domed white mushrooms. *Raincaps,* she'd confide, *better than anything with a bit of butter.*

A purple flower: Emberdown, for infection.

A fat, veiny green leaf for him to crush and put on a wound.

She told him not to lay down roots, but all the things she loved most deeply had them. In the end, she couldn't follow her own rules, either.

Insects fill the silence with trilling, unbroken songs, and Tory lets himself settle. These woods, too, are full of things that can nourish and heal.

"I'll die," Sena says, conversational.

Tory chokes on his own spit. "*Wh-what?*"

"Perhaps I shouldn't have said it like that." Sena pauses. "I can't think of a better way."

Tory's body sings with a jolt of useless adrenaline. His pulse thrums, reckless like running feet. He pushes himself away from the hollow tree's wide trunk. "Excuse me," he says again, very slowly, "you'll fucking *what?*"

"I told you our Cores would be deactivated if we didn't return."

"How does that—you said—" Tory sucks in a lung-filling breath, but the adrenaline still wreaks havoc inside him. "You can't just *say* things like that. We'll be fine. Riese said there's someone who can help us."

"There's someone," Sena says, "who can help *you*. Riese's 'helper' is a Seed. Theoretically, Reachers can remove rooted Cores, but it's risky. They're best at identifying foreign substances in the body. That's how they remove tumors. They're distinct—malignant. The roots on the Core have been altered to make them difficult to distinguish from healthy, living tissue. They might be able to take out a Core, but you'd die if they missed a single root."

It settles. A Seed, Sena said.

". . . And they can't help you at all."

"No. And if for any reason this Reacher can't come in the next two days, you'll die, too."

"Then we have to contact the Box!" Tory sits up, shoulders squared, fists clenched, ready for a fight even though there's nothing to battle. "We can tell them . . . I don't know. That we were stranded near the border and we're coming back on foot. That way they won't disable our Cores. You'd be safe. We just have to tell them—"

"With what communicator?" Sena's glove skims the pocket that used to hold his radio.

"We'll find another."

Sena huffs, like Tory should know how absurd that is. "How?"

"We could tell Riese. He might have ideas."

"*No*. Riese is on guard for the faintest hint of betrayal from me. There's no way he'd let us contact the Compound. If they have a Reacher who can remove your Core, they have leverage. They could easily hold our inevitable Core-deaths over our heads to force compliance."

"They're not—" *Kirlov*, he means to finish, but their treatment of Sena hasn't given him reason to believe otherwise.

Something ugly curdles in Tory's gut. He blinks and sees Judge's broad back, the glint of gray light off his knife. Then the gun. Judge could've shot ten times before Riese finally ordered him to lower it. "Point taken. This'll be our secret. I don't want to go back, though."

"I'll *never* go back."

Taut silence settles between them.

"Tory." Sena looks up suddenly, eyes bright. "The battlefield, it's in disputed territory. No one will have gathered the bodies yet."

"That's . . . gross?" Tory ventures, not sure what Sena is getting at.

He grimaces. "No, the bodies. They'll have weapons. Supplies Riese could use."

It just keeps getting more confusing. "You want us to loot corpses?"

"No, I—" Sena cuts off. "Yes. But for a good cause. There will be officers among the dead. Riese can get weapons and supplies, but *we* can get a communicator. If you want to get in contact with the Compound and convince them not to disable our Cores, that's our best chance. We just have to convince them to go."

CHAPTER EIGHTEEN

Iri's words ring in Sena's head all night. He said the Void-seed was meant for growth, *protection*.

Surely, he was lying, but as soon as the first rays of light pierce the flaps of the rudimentary tent Sena was given to sleep in, he finds his feet, ignoring the growing ache in his chest—it's inconvenient, not debilitating.

The place is abandoned, all the more eerie for the many indications that it should have people. Frowning, Sena wanders. It might be challenging to implement their plan of convincing Riese to return to the battlefield if there is no Riese around to convince. Sena should be much more worried about that than he is, but it's the fear of Iri's absence that bothers him more. He promised. Tomorrow, he said. Sena forces calm on himself. He needs to investigate, find out what precipitated everyone's absence.

In the rest of the camp, there are more indications of a quick departure. A line strung between one tent and the next contains drying clothes. A half-drunk cup of tea steams on a log, and the fire still contains stubborn embers and a kettle bubbling merrily away on a metal grate.

When a hand lashes out to grab the kettle, Sena startles, but the shock is soon replaced with a flutter of anticipation. A figure, hunched over and bleary-eyed, emerges from a huddle of brown blankets beside the fire.

The chaotic poof of long, dark hair and the resting murder face allow him to place the person quickly.

Iri. It's *Iri*. "You're here."

The figure blinks, refills his cup, and takes a long gulp of tea so hot Sena is surprised it doesn't sear his throat closed. "Mm."

He should ask about Riese. "Where is everyone else?"

Iri irritatedly waves away. "Not here, mostly."

"I gathered. When will they return?"

"Who knows? They're on a *mission*." Iri cups both hands around the battered metal cup, sullen. "Riese has another Flameseed. Didn't need me."

Tory emerges from his own tent with sleep-swollen eyes and staggers toward the fire. He mumbles something Sena can't discern and doesn't bother trying to. Instead, he turns to Iri. "Yesterday—" he starts.

With a sigh, Iri pushes himself up off the stump he's sitting on, stumbling and nearly spilling his tea. He catches himself with a guttural growl that can only be a curse.

"Yes, right. Promised you a demonstration." He still looks half-asleep, clutching his drink like a lifeline, but his eyes narrow at Sena, his sleep-slack expression sharpening. "Ready to learn the things your bastard father could never have taught you?"

Sena couldn't be more ready.

After Iri dips into his tent to grab a lovely woven rug, a bowl, and other assorted items Sena can't identify—on account of them being wrapped up in the rug—Iri leads them to a leaf-strewn clearing a short way outside the camp and lays down his bounty. Yawning, he heads off to gather more supplies, then takes his time setting everything up.

He calls Tory over first, to Sena's disappointment.

While he waits, Sena cups the stellite crystal his mother sent him the year he would have celebrated his Dedication, holding it under a bubble of light that slips through the trees and casts dim galaxies onto his gloves. The pendant has never touched his skin. If he were careless, his bare fingers could crack and blacken it. But this—the reflected light of stars he cannot reach for—is something he dares, at times, to enjoy.

These stars, his mother always told him, shine because of the crystal's flaws. When things were too much, she'd whisper his favorite stories to him word for word and stroke his hair. *Oh, miokh,* she'd sigh. *My heart.* She still calls him that in her letters. *Visit home, won't you?* she always asks, and he has to come up with increasingly creative reasons why he can't.

In the northern capital of Maran, stellite is a luxury item. At STAR-7, it's a marvel, allowing his father to create weapons that target Seeds and Cores that imprison them. Sena is not so unlike stellite—all his stars made from flaws, a trinket at best and a tool to hunt his own kind at worst.

In Arlune, it's a precious mineral, borne by warriors who fear neither pain nor death. They use it to store and amplify Seed energy—the secrets of how, they have so far managed to keep from Westrice. Each crystal is a fragment of Arlune's history, a fractured scale from the hide of the Beast who birthed the cosmos, a creature star-strewn and crystalline, snake and lion in one.

There's nothing holy about Sena. He's no warrior. He is not brave. Like the Compound, he is destructive, reductive.

But Iri said his abilities are meant to nurture *life*.

Hope is a sharp and terrible thing, and despite his best efforts, Sena has cut himself on it more times than he'd like to admit.

Minutes pass, then an hour, and Sena watches Tory work.

Tory stands in the center of the round rug Iri has rolled across the ground, Sena's kerchief (offered up when Iri realized he didn't have anything on hand for the purpose) wrapped around his eyes, knotted at the base of his skull.

"Do you sense an energy?" Iri asks for the fifth or sixth time.

Each time, he hides something under a silky stretch of cloth on top of a wooden barrel, and each time he spins Tory in a wide circle and asks him to locate the energy in question. For the purposes of the exercise, Sena and Iri stand in various locations on the circular rug.

As he has done for the past two times, Tory turns first toward Sena, which makes something inside him leap. It's a strange feeling, to be found.

"This one's you, right, Sena?" Even with his eyes covered, Tory points directly at Sena's chest. "Right . . . here."

Iri sighs. "Very good, but not the object of the exercise. Try again. The energy I'm asking you to seek out will be faint."

"Seed energy this time?"

"No. It will be many times fainter than our previous exercises, but it will be the same type I've been asking you to find so far. You've done well in our previous tries. This time, it will be . . . nearly absent. The energy I'm asking you to seek is likely to be so faint it's a mere thread away from nonexistence."

"What the fuck, that's—" Tory reaches up to his blindfold. Iri stops him.

"Removing the blindfold will ruin the object of the exercise. Leave it on."

"But I can't—"

"You can. We have already done it many times." Iri sighs and takes Tory's shoulder.

"Those were easier!"

"Did you expect them to stay that way?"

Tory huffs.

Iri mutters something in Arlunian, too quiet to catch. By the tone, it's not complimentary. "Excuse me," he says, before he spins Tory a few times.

When Tory stops, he staggers, feet tangling like a drunkard's.

"All right. The cups on the end of this training rug hold stones that silence outside energies, so you are already doing this in the *easiest* possible situation. Other than Sena and I, there should be no interference. The energy lies not behind you but in front of you. If you had to guess whether it lay to the left, right, or center of your current position, which direction feels most likely?"

"None of them."

"Choose one. This is not a trick question."

Tory frowns, turning to his left, then center, then right.

"If it would be easier, Sena and I can leave the training rug so you can focus more effectively."

Whatever it is Iri wants him to find, it lies atop the barrel, hidden beneath an elegantly embroidered towel to Tory's right. "No, it's actually . . . I think it's easier with Sena here."

Tory turns again, lingering a while in each direction. One hand scrubs at the short hairs at the back of his neck, and he exhales slowly. "There," he says at last, finger pointing more or less at the barrel. "Over there feels . . . more. There's something there, I think."

Iri's eyes shine with some complicated, overpowering joy. "Yes."

Tory waves at the blindfold. "Can I . . .?"

"Not yet. Heal it."

"Heal? This is . . . that's not . . . it's not a person. I can tell."

Iri's eyebrows rise. "Can you tell me what it is, then?"

Tory shakes his head.

"You're correct. It's not a person. But you can renew it. When you heal, are you not able to sense the body's desire to return to wholeness?"

Tory stands straighter, stiller. "Yes."

"All living things have this intent—the instinct for restoration. When you handle the energy of the human body, you know where to send it without sight, because you speak the language of restoration. This is not human, but the *language* will be the same. If you let it, the energy will tell you where it wants to go. Reach out for it. Allow me to instruct you when you're holding it."

Tory's hands twitch at his sides, like they did on the training field that day.

"Do not restrain yourself if you wish to reach with your hands."

His right hand lifts. "I have it."

"You're certain?"

Tory nods.

"Excellent. Hold it. Give me one moment. I'm going to do something that should make it easier to sense and manipulate."

Iri paces over the rug with its dark metallic strands woven in, and lifts the embroidered towel.

Beneath it is a branch no longer than Sena's forearm, raised into the air at an angle by what looks to be a hurriedly hand-twisted piece of wire wedged into the barrel. The wire forms a y-hook that cups the branch at the top. It's dead, or nearly dead, brittle-looking and gray with age. A small cup, translucent blue with an iridescent glaze, lies next to it. Iri lifts the branch and tucks the bottom into the cup.

"Oh," Tory says. "That's . . . that helped."

Iri smiles. "Yes, I imagined it would. I would not ask you to do this work without assistance—it would be unnecessarily harmful to your body and in opposition to our goals. Do you understand what I meant when I spoke of restoration?"

"Yeah," Tory says, "And . . . no. Like, I get what it . . . wants? But I don't get it."

Iri laughs, a dry breath of air. "It's not asking you to understand. It's asking you to restore. Can you do it?"

"I think so."

"Then—"

Before Iri can say anything, Tory sets to work. Sena can't sense the energies like Tory can, but it's visible. The grayish branch gains color and richness and breadth. The trailing bark where it was torn from its tree goes springy rather than brittle.

And on the tips of the branches, life. Leaves, vibrant green, then flowers in full bloom, silky white with gold and pink tones at the center. It's *beautiful*.

"Stop," Iri says.

Tory drops his hand like the branch is letting go of him, not the other way around.

He falls, hard, to one knee.

Sena hurries toward him and takes him by the shoulder. "Tory? Are you okay?"

Tory's head hangs, face slick with cold sweat that darkens his blindfold and drips from the tip of his nose. "That was . . . really weird. I feel . . ."

"Take some time. Catch your breath. What you have done is not so simple as merely grasping or releasing common energies. This work can easily exhaust you. Restoration, after all, is against the natural flow of things."

Tory hunches over, breathing hard.

"Do you wish to stop? I would rather not be responsible for your death. If it helps, we are nearly done. I have only one more question."

Dragging in a breath, Tory says, "I'm okay. I'll finish up."

"Good."

Tory finds his feet. "Can I take off the blindfold?"

"You may, but only after you tell me what energy you believe you handled."

Tory grumbles. "Shit, I don't . . ."

"Reach for it again. I think it might be more familiar to you now."

After a long pause, Tory gasps. Finally, voice low, he says, "It's a tree, isn't it? It's . . . in Hulven, I'd lay in the woods, and there was this—something. This peace, like they were watching over me, you know?" He frowns. "But this is . . . so small. A baby tree."

"You may remove your blindfold."

Tory pulls the sweat-soaked strip of cloth away from his eyes and flings it to the ground like he did on the training field. Sena finds himself smiling. For all that things change, so many remain the same.

"I was right," Tory says, triumphant. "Close enough, anyway. A branch is kind of a baby tree." He stares at the branch, the infant leaves, the vibrant blooms. "Did I do that?"

Iri smiles. "You did."

Quietly, nearly inaudible, Tory says, "That's not healing."

"It never was. I told you, what you do isn't healing. It's—"

Tory traces the silky blossoms. "Restoration."

Iri turns to Sena. "And what you do is not destruction."

He walks off the rug, to the pile of items he dumped in the clearing when he arrived, and he grabs a dented metal bowl. From the bowl, he lifts a flattish, disc-shaped stone, deep blue and milky, with inclusions that catch the dim light like stars. He grimaces when he handles the stone, fingers twitching like he wants nothing more than to let it go.

"Remove your gloves." Iri walks toward Sena with the stone clutched in one hand, and Sena retreats, a shudder crawling up his spine. "It's your turn next."

Remove his gloves? Sena's hands clench, and before he knows it, he has them half-hidden behind his back.

Tory turns as if sensing Sena's unease. "Hey!" he says. "He clearly doesn't want to. Knock it off."

Iri stops, sighs. Drops the stone into a pocket and winces like it punched him. "I assure you, he'll be thankful."

He turns to Sena. "My dislike of this training method aside, I promise it will not hurt you. We use these stones for Seeds who struggle with control. Because of the stress my family endured and our nearness to the battlefront, I blossomed when I was six—earlier than I should have. Earlier, certainly, than was safe for a Flameseed. I had to train with one of these for two years after I burned down our home without meaning to. I keep them to remind me of how far I've come. My discomfort with the inkhstone is personal, not universal. It dampens powerful Seeds and will allow you to train without fear of causing wide-spread damage." Iri lifts it from his pocket and holds it by two fingers. "I'll be asking you to use your abilities, and in absence of the control this demonstration requires, a dampening of your energies will suffice."

"He's not a child," Tory blurts.

Sena takes the inkhstone immediately.

"It requires contact with skin. Remove the gloves."

Sena does, and the effect is instant. All this time, if he'd had one of these—so many things could have been easier. Unlike Tory, he can't feel his energy dropping. Instead, he feels the stone's effects like a cocoon, like a weight around his shoulders. "I . . . It's okay," he says to Tory. "I like it."

"It's harder to sense you," Tory grumbles. "It's weird."

Sena smiles. "I really like it, Tory."

Tory throws his back against the nearest tree and crosses his arms. "Fine. Do your thing."

Iri invites Sena close to the blooming branch. "Tory, I'll need you to observe this, as well. Sena . . ."

Sena's grip around the stone tightens.

"I'll . . ." Iri frowns. "Actually." Without another word, he disappears between the trees.

A minute or so later, he returns, arms packed with items: a bright copper teapot, a few blossoms plucked from a hardy wildflower, a glittering silver wristlet, a potted plant.

"All right. We're working on control. Your goal is to do your work as slowly as possible." He clears the branch from the simple pedestal, twists the wire smaller, and sets a single flower in the y-hook. "Do what you usually do but make it last."

Sena shakes his head and backs up. "I've never—"

Duration has never been a consideration. His focus has been on never using his abilities, and his uses of them, otherwise, have been instinctual. Fine control was never part of the process. No one, not even Sena, thought he was capable of it.

"You have the inkhstone," Iri says, and now his voice is softer. He's looking at Sena like he understands the fear pinging around inside him. Maybe he does. "It's all right. You won't harm anyone here. Tory is off the training blanket, see?" Iri gestures to where he's still leaning against the tree. "Watch this."

Iri hits his flint thumb-rings together and makes a massive fireball from the sparks. "Even if you tried to hurt him . . ." He flings the fire at Tory before Sena can stop him, and the ball blinks out midair at the rim of the training rug. That's when he sees it. At regular intervals along the rug are thick chunks of inkhstone in hammered metal settings. Dark chain is woven along the blanket's edge, connecting one inkhstone to the next. "Like I said. Inkhstone is a dampener. In direct contact, it dampens a Seed's power. When arranged in a ring, it creates a barrier. The ring on this training blanket means *no* outside energy can get in and no energy inside it can get out." His expression twists. "Not even fire. I will leave the ring. Please." He gestures at the flower. "The inkhstone in your hand will be doing its work as well. You have no reason to fear."

Sena extends a bare fingertip to touch the flower. It's a bright thing, purplish-blue and dense—many-petaled, like a crumpled silk napkin. It's cool to the touch, its smell lightly sweet.

"As slowly as you can," Iri says again.

Sena touches it and pushes his energy into it tentatively.

Instantly, the flower grows small, brittle, grayish-brown, and flakes away like ash. Sena jerks back, broken ribs sending a bolt of pain through him. Iri, even though he's outside the circle, jerks away, too.

"Oh, dear," he says. Setting down his teapot, his wristlet, and the potted plant along the way, he tucks the remaining flowers into his pocket and returns to the small black bowl, grabbing one more stone and bringing it over. "All right. Another," Iri says. "One in each hand."

The next flower takes maybe two seconds to become like the first.

Gaping, Iri pushes the whole bowl at Sena. It contains maybe six or so more inkhstones. Even in the morning light, they glitter like a profusion of starry nights. "More. Try again."

Four stones. Six.

With six, the decay is slower, and Sena winces, watching the bloom close and grow brown and spill its seeds. The leaves wither and crinkle and crumble. In less than a minute, it's dust.

Iri lets out a blistering string of curses before dropping the last two stones into Sena's over-filled hands and retreating. "I don't *have* any more, and I refuse to destroy the training rug, so this had better work."

On his way back, he lifts the branch Tory returned to health. Sena's stomach sinks. The blossoms are still breathtaking and fragrant with life, the end still wet with the muddy water that fed it. Again, he places it in the hook.

"Try again," he says.

"But . . ."

"This branch will not grow roots if replanted. Whether you or the natural flow of time ends it, the thing will not survive. It was . . . a good luck charm I took from my favorite tree back home before coming to your country. It has faded since I cut it. Allow it to serve one last time." An open-handed gesture at the branch. "As slowly as you can. Watch."

Before he begins, Sena shifts all the stones to his right hand. With his left, he traces the blooms, inhales the subtle sugary-sweetness of them. They're water-soft. He sighs. Cups the stones tight in his right hand. Sena whispers, "Sorry," and he touches the textured wood of the branch.

At first, nothing happens. The blooms shift, maybe. Sena turns, withdrawing his hand.

"Keep going."

He does, and indeed, his power is doing its work with brutal slowness. The beautiful petals flutter down or curl up on the branch and brown. But—

The center of the flowers grows rounder, redder, larger. Then larger still. The leaves shift from delicate spring green and unfurl, expand, flourish. In half a minute, greenish fruits the size of a bird's egg wait on the branch. By a minute, they're white and lightly furred, with a pinkish-orange that turns deep red where they meet the branch, and as large as Sena's fist.

"Stop," Iri says at last. With the quirk of a roguish smile, he brings the bowl over again. "Pick them. Put them in here."

Reflexively, struck speechless, Sena does. Iri retreats outside the circle again, bowl tucked against his chest, and bites into a blood-peach, smearing his lips with its shocking red juice. "Continue," he says around the fruit.

Sena continues. The leaves grow wide and dusty green, then vibrant red, then brown. By two minutes, the branch has crumpled into brittle chunks on the pedestal to join the dust of the dead flowers.

Tory stares, mouth open, eyes bright.

Iri cocks a grin at Sena and raises an eyebrow.

Sena looks at his hands, full of stars, and his eyes burn with inexplicable tears. He finds the fruit, fresh and fleshy and beautiful, waiting outside the ring.

"Hungry?" Iri asks. Without waiting for a reply, he throws one at Sena. Sena barely catches it, fumbling the pink-white peach against his chest and bruising it. It's a little too ripe.

As if he sees where Sena's thoughts are going, Iri shakes his head. "This is when they're sweetest," he explains, and shrugs before taking another big bite.

Sena finally forces words through his throat. He looks back at the grayish chunks of the branch.

A few of the inkhstones plummet from his numb fingers to the rug. "What just happened?"

Iri's grin goes soft again. "What do you think happened?"

"I . . ." Sena looks down at his bruised fruit. Where it was connected to the tree, it has veiny, blood-red coloring. Sena bites into it there, and his mouth floods with a sweetness just shy of offensive. It's real. "It grew."

"Clearly." Iri finishes off his peach and uses his teapot to refill the bowl on the barrel with water before dropping the stringy pit inside. He bends to claw rich, dark soil and decaying leaf bits from the cold ground and drops them in, mixing them with a finger to make an unattractive slurry of water. He takes another fruit for himself. "I *missed these*. But you see what I mean. I told you it wasn't destruction. It's just that your energy is so plentiful and so dense—" he gestures to the five stones still in Sena's hand and the three on the ground "—and you are so horribly untrained—"

Sena winces. "Sorry."

"Don't apologize. It's your disgusting, barbaric country at fault. Blunt-instrument sons of bitches," he adds in Arlunian. "Anyway, all those factors combined and your frightening amount of accessible power ensured that the work you do happens so quickly it seems like destruction. For all the beauty of life, things spend much longer in the states on either side of it—death or nonexistence. See, one inkhstone should subdue a moderately powerful Seed enough to allow for precision training. When I was training, I used two." At this, his chin rises. "When my great-grandfather was a boy, there was a Voidseed who had to use four." He waves at the stones in Sena's hands. "That is ridiculous, in case you were wondering. I'm . . . I truly don't—" he stuffs the peach in his mouth and babbles around a bite of it. "It's *obscene*. What you do necessarily ends in destruction, because that's the natural end of all things. Akaos: death is the way of all life." Striding forward, he paces past Sena and lifts the cup with the muddy water and the peach pit inside. "But it's not only death. Try."

Sena reaches into the muddy fertilizer-water to touch the pit.

With three fewer stones in his hand this time, he's not ready for the speed of it.

He wouldn't be ready for this, regardless. Something spreads in the cup, then rises from it almost fast enough to spear Sena's chin. He jerks back but fails to break contact, and then his vision is flooded with green, and then the cup is shattering—pretty shards that drip mud and bite at Sena's palms, and Iri is yelling *stop, stop,* and Sena—finally—wrenches his hand away.

"Whoa, hey, shit," Tory's saying from the corner. "That's a tree."

It is, in fact.

It's maybe three feet tall, pushing out spindly branches with a profusion of green leaves. Iri pulls the tree from Sena's hands, and the muddy residue its roots didn't consume drips to the ground, fast and thin and . . . red.

Sena stares down. "Oh."

"You're bleeding!" Tory is at his side, picking glass shards from his palm and flinging them to the ground with prejudice. He spins on Iri. "What the—"

Iri, tree in one hand and peach in the other, backs away from Tory's murderous glare. "I didn't expect—"

Sena turns toward Tory, and he must be smiling, because his face nearly hurts with it, body pumping joy to the tips of his fingers, and Tory dips to the ground and picks up the blindfold he threw earlier. He unknots it, careful, and takes Sena's bleeding hand. With one last glare in Iri's direction, he picks a few little slivers of porcelain from Sena's skin and then says, "Sorry, it's kinda sweaty. I refolded it so it should be on the outside, but . . ." and then he ties the cloth around Sena's hand and looks up. His expression freezes, stricken.

Awkward, he mumbles, "It's just a few little cuts, nothing to cry about."

But Sena barely feels the pain. He was fourteen when he last cried from pain. No, this . . . He turns to face the tree, and he *is* crying, probably looks like an idiot, but— "I made that."

Sena has never been a maker. All his life, he's broken things. Marriages, bodies, anything his hands could touch. But on the ground outside the ring, there are five or six blood peaches still in the bowl, and Iri is shaking the tree so its leaves make a pleasant rustle, and in Sena's hands there are five inkhstones, and he brought something to life.

The tears won't stop. This is ridiculous. Sena has always had better control of himself. He clears his throat and turns away. "How could I . . ."

Iri smiles. "The First Children's Seeds are so much more than— whatever your warmonger of a Grand General calls it. Neutralizing.

Channeling. When your people turned their backs on the Beast hundreds of years ago and chose to believe only in what their hands could touch, they left behind so much knowledge. Westrice's understanding of Seeds is rudimentary, warlike. Quite simply, the First Children are different variations on the same theme." With his peach hand, he waves at the tree. "*Time.*"

Iri gestures at Sena—shakes his tree-hand for emphasis. "Forward." Then at Tory, who's in the middle of digging a peach from the bowl. "And back. All other Seeds' domain is the present."

Forward. Death is the way of all life. And new life—Sena looks at the pit he made into a tree—is born from the death of other things.

Suddenly, desperately, he wants to throw his arms around Tory and feel the breathing warmth of him. If not for years of practice holding himself back, he'd probably have given in and shocked or disgusted Tory with the suddenness of it. Instead, he gingerly places a bare hand on Tory's cloth-clad shoulder, just a thin layer of fabric between them.

"I *made that*," he says again. It's not enough, not *nearly* enough to give vent to the feelings that threaten to crack him open, but it's all he can think to say.

Tory's expression morphs into something soft. "You sure did. And it's fucking beautiful."

CHAPTER NINETEEN

Time. It makes sense. Without even realizing it, Tory has always thought of his abilities in those terms—as if he's turning the body back to when it was whole. And Sena—

Warmth spreads in Tory's chest.

Today, Sena made something grow.

"Westrice has taken the byproducts of your Seeds and presumed them to be the whole of you. Channeler. Neutralizer. In naming you, they diminished you."

"Wait. Why *can* I channel energies?"

Iri shrugs. "By accident, really. The Worldseed and Voidseed exert some level of control over all energies because time affects all things. But it's much easier for a Worldseed to use their true power with life energy, because that energy is native to them. Most often, their first successful attempt to handle time is with the human body, but until they've extensively practiced with other energies, the best they can do is clumsily grasp and throw them. Like infants crawling before they walk, Worldseeds usually learn to pull or stretch or throw energies back before they learn how to *turn* them back."

"So I'm crawling," Tory says.

Iri laughs. "It has its uses, as I'm sure you've realized, but it's a pale imitation of your true power. A fortunate byproduct."

"Then why call Sena a Voidseed? How does that not diminish him?"

"In your language, it might. But think about it." Iri gestures up. "A void may evoke ruin and emptiness, but it's so much more. It's the void of space, birthplace of stars and planets and everything that lives on them—avatar for the Celestial Beast, a cosmic womb for all life. A peacefully coexisting duality: creation and destruction." Iri gestures to the potted plant he brought. "That's eliheni, by the way. Great in soups. Sena, I was hoping you could give me a nice big bush of it, but I suppose you'll want to stop and get that hand looked at."

"No," Sena says, and Tory flinches at his expression. He's never looked so young. Happy. Unburdened. Tory's chest aches. "It doesn't hurt. What's next?"

"Well, *ideally* what's next is that you learn to control your power so you're not indiscriminately unmaking things, but that's not the work of an afternoon and it's certainly not work I can do. But for now . . . I think perhaps we can do a little bit of practice letting Tory handle your energy."

Sena startles, stumbling back. "No."

"You won't be harming anyone. What I'd like Tory to handle is merely the plentiful energy you create by being alive—the field that neutralizes other Seeds. He *should* be able to handle it. All right?"

Sena settles, offering a careful shrug he instantly regrets by the way he pales. His ribs must still be giving him trouble. "All right."

Iri positions Tory several strides from Sena. "Is this far enough? You can still access your abilities? I'm not sure how far his nullifying field extends . . ."

Tory spreads his awareness out and senses a faint buzz of ambient Seed energy beyond the clump of tents. So there *are* people still here. Patrols, maybe. The roughness of it reminds him of the energy at play in the Rec Room testosterone battles. "Yeah."

"Very good. Try to find Sena. You did it before on the training blanket. It will be harder this time, since there's more to distract you."

He tries, but his senses keep swinging toward whatever's happening beyond the clump of tents, jagged and wild and so clearly *there*. The trees here hum with their quiet industry.

It really is harder to seek Sena's energy with everything else, but Tory forces his awareness in front of him, nudges it out until it runs into the shape of something. What he finds expands beyond Sena by a few feet on every side, a massive, static void.

"Found you," he says.

"Good. If you can discern it, you can use it. First, would you try to expand it?"

If he expands Sena's bubble of nullification, he'll temporarily disable any other Seeds in this camp.

Which would be pretty damn neat, actually.

He could make use of that—could've made use of it the other day. A whole *battlefield* worth of Seeds, defanged. If the assholes at the Box knew this was a possibility, they'd have been all over it.

Disable and demolish. They could have made a weapon of mass destruction of him. On second thought, Tory can't help the rush of dizzying gratitude that they didn't know. " . . . Do you have permission for this?"

Iri's eyes flash terrible joy. "I find it easier to beg forgiveness."

"Sena? You okay to try this?"

Sena gives an aborted twitch of one shoulder. "Go ahead."

When Tory reaches for it, the energy jumps to him like it was waiting for an invitation. It's slick and buzzing, pins and needles all up his arms. It's dense as anything, so heavy it nearly drops him to his knees.

This is what he felt in the lab with Helner, just before Sena reached out and ended it—that brimming possibility, the charge in the air before a lightning strike.

He starts slow, stretching it just to see if it will spread. It does—eagerly. It passes over Iri, and the burning energy at the core of him collapses. He shudders, and Tory spreads it farther, over the clearing and then beyond it, to the tents and past them. He doesn't realize how alive the camp was with energies until they die. There *are* people still here. Maybe not many, but enough. The hair-raising buzz from the patrols beyond the tents flickers out, then something shimmery-bright that made the air feel warmer. Others go like background noise. Perfect silence with Tory at the center of it, electrified.

Sena sucks in a breath.

"Okay?" Tory asks.

"Feels strange."

It spreads out and out like warm butter, easier than anything he's ever handled. It must be far outside the camp and into the woods—and he's not nearly at his limit; it would go *farther* if he asked it to—when he lets it go.

It snaps back like a rubber band, and Sena staggers.

An apology half-forms on Tory's lips, but Iri speaks before he can voice it.

"It's strange, how slow it is to come back. It's not immediate, it feels . . ."

Tory lets his eyes drift closed. It's a sort of reverse crumpling. All around the camp, like insects starting their songs again after a predator passes, distinct energies flicker or whisper or crackle back to life.

It's a *lot*. Everything feels crisper, clearer. He's not even trying and he gets the electric zap of the energies from beyond the tents flaring back, so clear they could be right beside him—

A choking noise precedes a non-verbal growl and a torrent of curses, and Tory's eyes snap open. He knows that voice.

His body flares with remembered fear as he turns to find Judge with Sena on the ground, hand at his throat. No. *Blade* at his throat, thin line of red welling around it.

"I'll kill you this time, don't you fucking doubt me."

Tory's moving before he registers the desire to.

Iri is faster. Judge has at least a foot on him, but he wrenches at Judge's arm, the fingers around his bicep too small to go all the way around. *Don't pull*, Tory wants to beg. If Iri pulls—if the hand holding the knife snaps back against Sena's throat—

Iri shoves at Judge. "Leave him alone! He acted on my request!"

"He *what?*" Judge rounds on Iri, fingers releasing their grip on Sena's throat and dropping him.

Sena levers himself onto an elbow and rolls onto his side, choking his way into a rattling coughing fit. Tory winces at the wrecked sound, the way Sena goes ghost-pale and tries to stop.

His insides knot. He can ground a carriage, drop an arrow. He disabled a Legion unit the other day, too, but there's no way to stop a body from tearing itself apart. This must be how Thatcher felt— restless, helpless hands that want to *fix*. It might be the worst feeling Tory's ever known.

But making sure no one else goes in for the kill—if nothing else, he can do that. Tory steps between Judge and Sena and holds his ground.

It's then that a group of three breathless Seeds breaks through the trees. One is Spark, soot-stained, singed, and ready for a fight.

"What did you do?" She advances on the group. "We were 'porting back and Travin *dropped* us all in the woods mid-'port, said something cut him off. He nearly split his skull open on the rocks. Two of the boxes were damaged when we landed."

Iri pales. "Shit. I didn't realize—"

Riese stalks into the clearing as Travin flickers into view, chest heaving, arms wrapped around a stack of cracked crates.

Riese checks on Travin first, a whispered exchange, but then turns to Iri. "I need you to tell me," he says, quiet in the way some murders are quiet, "what *exactly* you just did."

Behind Riese, a growing group mutters, bitter and accusatory.

Iri looks at his feet. "It was an experiment expanding the Voidseed's nullifying energies. I didn't know you'd be coming back so soon."

"And that's why we didn't take you along. You're *impulsive*, Iri. You acted yet again without considering the consequences and risked disabling every Seed in this camp. You *know* there are soldiers in the woods hunting us. I owe your father my life many times over, but . . ." Riese rubs at his temples. "You can't *do* things like this. Unrestrained emotion like yours is what cost your father his life. I was emotional, too, back then. Idealistic. And he paid the price. Unity and caution are important above all. Iri, if we're going to stay safe, I *need* you to listen to me."

"But you've said it a thousand times! Every Seed deserves to be able to understand and exercise their skills. Those Westrian fools know nothing about the Voidseed, and Sena—"

Judge turns back to Sena, bristling, the slicked edge of his knife ready to cut. Tory relaxes his stance, ready for anything.

Riese sighs. "Judge, stop."

"But he—"

"*Go.* No negotiation. You've done enough here."

Judge's scowl slips off his face and he stalks away.

"The rest of you, too. Keep your distance from him. I'll handle this."

Just like that, the taut rope of tension slackens. The crowd disperses without complaint.

All these people, they trust Riese.

Tory relaxes as soon as Judge is out of sight, and maybe that's why he only notices the boxes then.

While they were talking, Travin 'ported in with a few more precarious stacks. The damaged ones sit at the front, the wooden crates splintered to disgorge their contents onto the ground in chunks of translucent crystal. The shiver that scales Tory's spine and sharpens his senses is not just adrenaline. It's stellite. Riese's people intercepted a stellite shipment. A few of the boxes have charred corners. It clearly wasn't an easy theft. And the nearest mine to the border—

Tory catches the letters HLV stamped in black on the side of each crate, and his breath seizes in his chest.

"Hulven."

When Tory first met Riese that day he tried to escape, Riese was doing reconnaissance in Hulven.

The boxes are *burned*.

Tory's chest won't expand. He can only think of Thatcher and the huge hands he only ever uses to fix things, of the asshole miners who risked everything, over and over, to save their own. "Where'd you get that?"

A ridiculous question. He knows.

Riese blinks over at Tory. "I'm sorry?"

"Those boxes are from Hulven. They're burned. What did you *do?* The people in that town, they're innocent."

"We didn't harm the townspeople. We intercepted the shipment after it left Hulven's gates."

"Then why—how—"

Riese shakes his head. "You need to calm down. I'll explain everything, but your friend is unwell. Iri, we'll have words later, but for now—" he jerks his chin toward Sena. "Yized just arrived. Take him to her."

Sena grabs Tory's pant leg and pulls with strength he shouldn't have. "Help me up."

Tory blinks, bemused, and extends a hand that Sena grasps to lift himself.

Halfway upright, he stumbles against Tory's shoulder, close enough to his ear that Tory hears it loud and clear when he murmurs, "Get him to agree to a supply run, remember? We *need* a communicator."

"What?" Tory hisses. "How do you expect me to—"

"Tory!" Riese's voice. "Iri's got Sena from here."

Riese turns to Tory with a fatherly grin as Iri leads Sena away. "I don't mean for my people to assault you before every conversation. It's hardly conducive to meaningful discourse." His lips purse. "I won't let it happen again. My people have reasons for their anger and distrust, and Judge more than most. He lost his little sister in our recent attempt to infiltrate the Box."

Tory remembers, with a terrible sinking in his gut, red light and a fine spray of blood on Sena's face and smears of it on the floor. *One of them went for my gun*, he said. Tory swallows hard.

"So, uh, who's Yized?"

Riese laughs. "A pain in my ass, but she's useful. She'll take care of your friend. Come on. I'll explain everything, including why we had to hit up that little mining town. I think you'll like the sound of the ending we've planned for Vantaras' ambitions—and the part you'll be playing in tearing it all down."

Like last night around the fire, his words spread warmth through Tory's bones. *Purpose.*

"This way."

Tory follows.

*

"Not much farther," Iri murmurs. "Yized's just around back."

Sena measures his breaths and walks, eyes ahead. Shallow breaths in, each one igniting a blaze of pain. His throat burns, swollen from the grip Judge used to force him to the ground, and there's a tickle starting in his chest. He ignores it. At this point, he'd rather die than cough.

That's hyperbolic.

But he's had plenty of time, lately, to think about things he'd rather die than do.

With Iri in the lead, they weave through a mess of tents that would give Kirlov an aneurysm. Sena smirks at the disorder, huffing out a dry laugh. A mistake. Black spots blossom over his vision, specked with bursts of frothy white, and he pauses to get his bearings.

"Are you all right?"

He's too busy trying to breathe deeply enough to clear the spots from his vision to reply.

"We are in no hurry. Take your time."

"What you said about the Voidseed . . . thank you."

It doesn't matter, but it's nice—not only a weapon but a well; not only emptiness but the field of stars he used to reach for at night. Creation, and togetherness, like he's meant to belong somewhere.

"No need. As I said, it was selfish—if the truth could wrest you from their hands, it was worth it."

"Still. I'm grateful."

Iri's hand rings round his opposite wrist, tracing the burn scars. "No Seed should have to fear himself, not even a Vantaras. It is a shame you had to go until now without knowing that, and shame on me for forgetting."

Quiet falls between them, but Iri matches the pace Sena sets when he continues walking.

Perhaps everything will work out.

If they can return to the battlefield and find a communicator, Sena will do everything he can to secure a promise of leeway on the Core shutdown from the Compound. If nothing else, it'll give Tory a few more days for a competent Reacher to remove his Core. His odds are decent, and he's stubborn. He's the type to claw his way from the restful jaws of the Celestial Beast and live to spite the world. Tory will be fine. He'll be free. And that—ensuring Tory's safety—was the only real reason to go back.

Sena, meanwhile, has found his line.

He's a pragmatist; it would be unrealistic to envision himself surviving this. No Reacher can help him. Sena is a curiosity at best. He's no Healer, non-threatening and central to the dirty business of war—the sort of Seed who'd easily be given lenience because they're too valuable to lose. Sena knows too much, and the generals, lacking competently preserved records, know too little about the Voidseed. To them, he's an attack dog afraid of his own teeth. The only use they've found is in bleeding him, and they've taken more than enough of his plasma to make type-determination tests and *prototypes* for decades. They will not risk Sena's knowledge and skills falling into enemy hands.

They won't bother to track and recapture him. They'll disable his Core as soon as they can justify it.

To live, Sena would have to return to the Compound with its stale air. To Kirlov with his watch and a set of expectations Sena will always fail to meet. To hunting other Seeds and making a game of avoiding pain.

That's not a life he wants.

Perhaps it's like Tory said: Sena has not been living. Since he was nine, he has merely survived—until Tory came and unearthed an anger years buried, made a mirror for Sena to look into. Tory beat his hands against walls he could never climb, burned foolishly and recklessly bright even when his only fuel was himself. Sena, on the other side, dreamed impossible dreams. For all their differences, they want the same thing. Tory makes him want to believe they could have it, makes him want to believe in all sorts of things he still doesn't dare to contemplate.

He always thought death would be scarier than this, but there's peace in knowing he'll die a person outside his father's control rather than living as a weapon within it.

He's not welcomed here, but he's *free*, the night sky close and clear enough that he could walk the path of stars through the bone-cage of the Beast's belly and find his rest. Here, Kirlov can't control him. If he's lucky, Sena will die without seeing anyone from the Compound again.

With an ache, Sena remembers Hina's unopened letter, full of flowers. He hasn't seen her since she was four, Sena nine. She'll turn sixteen before the leaves fall this year.

Today is Westrice's Dedication Day—a watered-down and glitzed-up version of Arlune's coming-of-age ritual. Tonight, without Sena, Hina will watch fireworks from the highest point in the city and eat rich morsels from silver plates and think about what part of herself she needs to shed in order to grow. At Hina's age, alone in a grungy dormitory and without ceremony on the day of his own Dedication, Sena tried to shed the concept of wanting. It seemed a foolish, dangerous thing to someone whose hands were not allowed to reach for it.

He hopes she knows he misses her. Sena allows himself, for a moment, to imagine what it might be like if he were there: letting her show him every plant she cultivates and tell him its name. Sitting by the fire as she casts an effigy of her sacrifice into the flames. In his imagination, they get along as seamlessly as they did as children. Hina will do well, he's sure.

He'll miss Kierney, too, and his twittering tunes. Things were simple with Kierney: food and water and a perch close to the light.

Space on Sena's shoulder, little pats considerate of his bird bones. A blanket to close out the world when it was too much. It made no difference to Kierney when Sena said the wrong words or couldn't find words at all.

He'll miss the stories his mother whispered into his ear when she smeared liniment on his chest and counted his fading breaths when he was a boy. *You're star-blessed, miokh,* she told him when his Seed first blossomed.

Star-blessed, she said, and gave him his first set of gloves so she could hold his hand.

There's little else he'll miss. Seeing Seeds liberated, maybe. He's never really had room to contemplate it. He thought about the future in hours, before. Now he has a day, at least, to live. *Days,* if Tory can convince Riese to return to the battlefield.

He's giddy with the freedom of it. Tory asked him, after Sena dragged him from Belmin's caravan, when he'd tell the people who hurt him to *stop* instead of working so hard to avoid pain. Maybe this is where he starts.

There are more important things than survival. Here, he has a choice, even if he can only choose how he dies and where he draws his lines.

"Ah. Here we are." Iri tugs him to a stop in front of a netted tent and gestures at the flap. "Yized will get you patched up. You'll be out making history with us in no time."

That begs the question. "What does your leader even need us for?"

"I can't say. I think he's speaking to Tory about it now. He'll reveal it all in good time."

"You trust him?"

"I've not yet met anyone who offers more hope for a better future." He glances into the woods, then back to Sena, and shakes his head like he's clearing it. "Actually, find me when Yized is done with you? There's something we should discuss."

Iri strides away before Sena can answer.

He gives it a bemused moment before he opens the tent flap. "I don't know who told you I needed to be here, but I'm fine. I doubt there's anything you can—"

A too-familiar voice calls from inside, and his blood freezes in his veins.

"Doesn't matter. Riese's orders. Come on in, Sena."

Red hair, thin glasses, sharp teeth exposed in a predator's smile.

Dr. Helner.

CHAPTER TWENTY

Riese's tent is not nearly as big as Kirlov's was, but it's big enough for a makeshift table strewn with maps and pages of notes.

Tory can't let himself focus on them. "Hulven," he says as soon as they're inside.

"Yes. It was our half of the exchange with Arlune." Riese settles onto an overturned box and gestures for Tory to do the same. He grins with his sharp canines. "But it wasn't just about the exchange. It was about splitting their attention."

"Their attention?"

"The Box is always well guarded. Stocked with Seeds and soldiers, constantly patrolled. Naturally. It's the heart of Vantaras' war effort. Close enough to the border to easily deploy Seeds. Far enough that no one can easily invade. The walls are impregnable, and, as we learned when we tried 'porting in with Travin, only Seeds with Cores can travel freely within the facility without setting off the alarms, which threw a wrench in our impromptu invasion plans. But Vantaras is making anti-Seed weaponry *now*. Once it's widespread, it'll be harder than ever to make headway. We had to act fast. Our thefts along the supply routes, in addition to keeping us cozy, mean the military is looking for enemies *outside* their walls rather than inside, and they're sending every spare trainee to guard the routes. The stellite theft serves two purposes, as well. It'll allow Arlune to keep its populace alive and create more Legion units, but it means those Box bastards are also looking at Hulven, spreading themselves ever thinner."

"Clever," Tory allows.

"And effective. We've asked Arlune to increase their aggression at the border to draw soldiers and attention away from the Compound, too."

Tory remembers the infirmary that day during training, the blood beneath the Healer's nails and between the floor tiles. Increased aggression, indeed. ". . . You slaughtered them."

Riese lifts a shoulder. "It wasn't part of our instructions, but yes. I believe what happened to your unit was also part of our efforts. For what it's worth, I'm glad you survived."

"All those Seeds—" Randall, Niela, they didn't *choose* that.

"Don't let the details turn your eyes from the truth: *Vantaras* started this war and fanned its flames. He's the one feeding the bodies of his people into it to maintain power. I'm here to *end* it, and ending a war is no more beautiful than starting one. Blood paves the path to every bargaining table. I'm sorry about your unit, but I knew the sharp ones would survive. I was right; here you are. You know what all survivors know: with grit and sufficient desperation, anything is possible. It's why you'll be the one to end this."

He makes it sound so simple, like Tory was made for this. Like all the blood he's shed and the words he's swallowed and the scars he's borne have *meaning*. Warmth fills Tory, slick and spreading, like oil waiting for flame.

Sufficient desperation. Tory has that in spades. "How do you know?"

Riese closes a hand around Tory's arm, right where the tattoo rests. "Because of this."

Tory pulls back. "What?"

Riese rolls up the sleeve of his own sweater. On his upper arm, vital and sharp-edged, is a red tattoo. Just like his mother's: the mark of a convicted criminal.

Tory's reaching for it before he thinks twice. He pulls back before touching.

"It's okay," Riese says. "Go ahead."

His fingers trace the warm skin. "I've never seen one like this. Outside, I mean." He met a woman in the illegal House he worked in as a boy, bought out of the camps as an infant by her aunt. The only tattoos he's seen were like hers: blue tattoos denoting a prison-born child with an intricate design in purple to show they'd been pardoned. He's never met an escapee like himself, without the pardoning mark, and not once in his life has he ever seen a red one, freed.

All Riese's wild claims seem suddenly, terrifyingly possible.

"We're rare breeds, the two of us," Riese says. "I refused to let them keep me. Clearly you felt the same."

Tory can't tear his eyes away. "What happened?"

"I was on one of Vantaras' think tanks, if you'd believe it. I was a poor kid from the Northeast—little mining town. Coal, not stellite. But I was *smart*, and I knew Vantaras values smarts. He and his geniuses had already made their first steam engine, but I studied mechanical engineering at university and argued in my thesis that if stellite could stably store power for the Arlunians, we could work miracles with it if we could get it to do the same for us. I was put on a special committee to see if we could do just that. And the *strides* we made. There was a woman, a few years younger than me, still the most brilliant person I've ever met. We stayed over at each other's houses, ate leftovers, didn't sleep. She'd start a thought and I'd finish it. The first time Vantaras got stellite to store energy? That was *us*. We made that happen."

Tory thinks of the stellite in the Compound, brittle and dead from whatever they had to do to make it work, and winces.

Riese echoes the expression. "Yeah. See, after a while, things started falling into place for me. I'd gotten so caught up in the *theory* of it that I failed to consider the implications. When I realized that the energy the Grand General wanted to put in the stellite was Seed energy, for the purposes of tracking and identification . . . I was already too far along. I went to the woman I'd come to love and shared my fears with her. Naturally, she'd guessed the truth years ago, sharp thing. She must have reported me as a seditionist—not as a Seed, I wasn't fool enough to tell her *that*—because she gave me tea after hearing my worries, and when I woke, I was in the camps—a *mining* camp, like she knew it'd sting the worst—and they'd already marked me." He taps the tattoo.

"I realized it then, and you'll learn it the hard way, too, if you don't wise up now: love is dangerous. Being free, being a *leader* means freeing ourselves from the blinkering feelings that would let people hurt us. Lie to yourself all you want, but none of us can protect more than our hands can hold. Believe me, I tried. When I first established this group, I had such *grand* goals. I turned over supply shipments. I freed a whole wagonful of conscripted Seeds like you. I grew the group, made us a force to be reckoned with."

He bares his palms to Tory. "But it was more than I could handle. Iri's father paid the price for that. He was a Reader—he could identify Seeds at a glance. An incredibly rare and valuable Seed type. If he were ever captured, that bastard Vantaras could have turned him on all of us. Could have tried, at least. He would rather have died. He was *good*. But one of our new inductees panicked, thought it would be *safer* if Iri's father was dead so Vantaras could never use him." Riese grits his teeth. "I learned my lesson then. I've kept my group smaller ever since." He turns Tory's hands to show the scarred palms. "Learn from my mistake. Think hard about what you can't let go of. That lapdog officer of yours, you'll realize he doesn't make the cut, either now or when he betrays you."

Something flips in Tory's belly, and the warmth from Riese's confidence wars with the chill spreading from his stomach. He scans the tent, looking for a distraction.

His eyes land on a roll of blue grid paper. He recognizes the blueprints of the Compound immediately, its soft hexagonal shape covered with notes in black ink. *Archives*, one note reads. Another one says *Officers' Quarters*. At least half the rooms have labels.

Tory has done enough late-night wandering while staying out of Gavin's way that he could put names to at least half of the empty spaces. The room between *Archives* and *Intake* is a closet stocked with cleaning supplies where the night janitor likes to light up a pipe.

Riese clears his throat.

Tory's eyes jerk up to meet his.

"It's all right. We have nothing to hide. This is why I brought you here. We *need* you. We've been gathering intelligence for years, but Vantaras' anti-Seed prototypes messed everything up. Some things we hadn't expected to need to do for *months*, but if we want to get out ahead of these weapons he's making, we need to act now. We were desperate. Then you came along, like the stars led you here."

"Why me?"

"You'll know everything soon. I like you, Tory, but I hope you understand now why I'm more careful about who I trust."

Tory squeezes his fist until his knuckles creak and remembers Sena's parting words. "You want me to show you can trust me?" He says, mock-casual. "I can get weapons for you. Tons of them—more than you could ever use."

Riese's gaze sharpens. "What are you proposing?"

Tory swallows. "Scavenging. The little massacre you arranged? There are tons of bodies on the cliffs. All of them will be armed."

"Except the side effect of our work on the border is that Vantaras has this area crawling with people. Our scouts came back this morning with news that there are soldiers on the fringes of the woods. We don't have anything near the firepower they'll be packing. It's too risky."

Tory leans over the maps, fingernails biting his palms. "You *would* have the firepower if you took the risk." And if soldiers are trawling the woods, that means *someone* will be in range of a communicator. They can get in contact, buy themselves breathing room. Win-win. "What did you call it? Sufficient desperation?"

"Wisdom is important, too. We have time."

Tory doesn't, though. Sena doesn't. If Riese can't bring in that Reacher in time, Tory will be dead. "Guns are out there for the taking *now*."

"You seem awfully interested in speeding up my timeline."

"You haven't *told* me your timeline. And anyway, what I'm interested in is making sure you and not the Grand General get your hands on whatever's out there."

Riese frowns, considering. "It might not be the worst idea. We'll need to act soon to knock Vantaras off his throne, and it wouldn't hurt to have more firepower." Riese steps closer. "You and your friend will be joining us, of course."

Tory tries not to let the surge of worry and wild satisfaction show. He never considered that he might not be allowed to come. "Hostages?" He lets a wry grin twist his lips.

Riese's responding smile is blinding. "Insurance. We'll aim for this evening. For now, I have some work for you." He gestures to the map of the Compound. "With your help, I don't think liberating every Seed under their control is out of our grasp anymore."

That unshakable faith fills him with warmth like it did last night around the campfire. It blends the joy of success—tonight, they'll have a *communicator*—into something nearly ecstatic. This is what he needs, what he wants. He's spent so much of his life on the run. This—people with purpose and a battle worth fighting in—is more than he ever dreamed he could have. Laughter bubbles up in him. "Just tell me what to do."

Riese's smile turns sharp. "You can start by filling in some blanks on these blueprints. And while *you* do that, I need to have a little chat with Iri, if you'll excuse me."

*

Helner.

Sena can't turn. Can't breathe. Where Helner is, Kirlov so often follows.

She stands from the boxes she's using for a chair. "What a surprise to see *you* here." He must make a sound, because she laughs. "It's just me. Sit."

His hand is frozen on the tent flap. "You're . . .?"

"Not that sort of doctor, as you well know, but I've been taught basic first aid. I spoke to Riese about you."

It all falls together. "The Reacher he talked about."

"Bullseye! I saw a chance to spit in your father's face and took it. Money doesn't hurt, either." She gives him an odd smile. "Kinda gutsy of you, joining the enemy. I wouldn't have thought you capable of surprising me. But come *in*, come in. I don't have all day."

He steps around the mountain of boxes to perch on a cot. An oil lamp flickers on a nearby box, lighting Helner dim gold. Sena rubs his hands together. The rasp of his gloves calms him. "They called you Yized."

"Did you think *Doctor* was my first name?"

"But why are you—"

"Here?" She rifles through a box of strange tools and rattling bottles. "Money."

"Not only that," Sena says.

Helner laughs, acidic and cruel. "Isn't it enough?"

No amount of luxury is enough when you're not free. It's why they clashed with each other at the Compound—both forced to hunt and trap people like them, trying in their own small ways to make a difference—Helner by conjuring better, more efficient ways for Seeds to survive battle, and Sena by looking the other way whenever he could.

Helner keeps rummaging until she pulls a kit from the box—marked for use at the Compound. She opens it without looking at him. "Money is power, Vantaras. Perhaps it hasn't occurred to you since you've had it your whole life, but the money I've saved might mean the difference between making a successful bribe or being recaptured and killed if I ever get out. See, I don't need to save only myself. My wife is an Eraser. Made bank adjusting memories for rich folks outside Maran in secret. Free therapy and all that. Someone must have reported her, reported *us*. They took her to STAR-1 up in Maran. Couldn't have put us farther away from each other. She's your dad's leverage against me, but one of these days I'll get her out. I'll get both of us out. I'm not sold on this revolution thing—it's a bit too *selfless greater good* for me—but I hope they *do* succeed. I'd laugh to see your daddy's work burn."

"I'd like that, too."

She gives him a funny look, but it's no funnier than any of the others she's given him over the years and no easier to make sense of. She digs in the medical kit. "Bruised ribs, right?"

"Broken. At least one."

Helner laughs bitterly. "And that's nothing compared to how you'll be feeling in a few days. Here." She digs under a pile of papers until she finds a matte-black case. "I'll have mercy on you. Give me your arm."

Sena's given her his arm a thousand times. He's in no hurry to let her stab him again. "I'll pass. I have a high pain tolerance."

Her expression does a strange thing. "This isn't for pain."

"Then what is it?"

"*Antibiotics.*" Extracting a syringe, Helner draws a purplish liquid into it. "Come on. Your arm. See, usually, I'm taking something from you, but today I get to give you something. A fresh start for both of us."

"I would prefer a fresh start without needles."

"Not my call, sorry. Riese's orders."

Sena knows orders and the game of finding room to move between them.

It's a small freedom, choosing which arm they wound, but he treasures it because it's his. Better to keep his dominant arm unhindered. He offers his right arm.

"You and your good veins." Helner leans in and casts a strained smile over his shoulder. She pulls a little table closer and swipes his arm with something cold and wet. "Arm on this. No sugarcoating it. This one's gonna burn."

Before Sena can respond, the needle plunges in.

Fire blisters along his nerve endings when she depresses the plunger. The hand stabilizing his arm holds tighter, and Helner pushes the rest of the injection into him quickly.

"See?" she says. "That wasn't so bad."

Regardless of allegiance, her bedside manner remains terrible. He tells her as much.

She slants a strange grin at him. "Didn't know you were funny."

He shrugs.

She shrugs. She gestures away, the moment broken. "Go on, then. Get out of here."

Sena stands, lurching with the sudden motion.

Helner bolts to her feet to take his elbow. She gets a look in her eye, this flickering expression of doubt he can't translate. "You're not the best with drugs, are you?"

An understatement. "They don't work sometimes, or, sometimes they work too well?"

"Is that a question or an answer?" She doesn't let go of his elbow.

Sena thinks about it, but he finds he's forgotten the question.

Speaking of forgetting. There's something he's supposed to be doing after Helner's finished with him. Something . . . someone? To meet someone.

"This must be one of the ones that's too effective. I'll take you back to your tent to make sure you don't fall over, huh?"

Sena blinks to clear the gauzy glow from his vision. "S'nice of you," he says.

"Didn't you know? I'm a nice person." Helner snorts out a laugh. It's an ugly, sad sound, and also kind of funny, because Dr. Helner is definitively *not* a nice person.

All the way back to the tent, she supports him only where her hands are prevented from touching him by his clothing.

Iri! He remembers only when the young man passes by, shoulders hunched. Sena pulls Helner to a stop, stubborn when she tries to urge him on. Iri wanted to talk to him.

They stop. Iri stops. Silence in the air between them. He should say something.

"Sena?" Iri says, confused.

Helner sighs. "He's a bit out of it. High as a bird. On *antibiotics*."

"Is that even possible?"

"Apparently it is!"

"Wanted to talk," Sena says. He's not out of it. He remembers.

"You wanted . . .? Oh!" Iri turns to Helner. "He's right. I told him we'd—" He looks at his feet. "Riese just tracked me down to give me an earful about *risking everyone's lives*. Another time?"

Helner pulls on Sena's arm. "You're a mess, both of you. Come on. Let's get you to your tent while you can still stand."

Iri gives him a cursory smile so unlike the ones from earlier and nods as he departs.

Helner guides him through the flap as his vision shutters black, letting go as quickly as she can. She murmurs a cold apology before retreating.

Some things never change.

CHAPTER TWENTY-ONE

A CRISP BREEZE MUTES the sweet reek of gore and the tang of exploded shells on the battlefield.

Bent over and silent, Tory navigates a path through corpses, stepping over gummy swaths of crimson-black.

Carrion birds, startled into flight by his arrival, circle overhead and settle on the roots arching into and out of the ground. A few brave birds hop around in the distance, blinking glassy black eyes at Tory when he comes close. Some of the bodies, there's nothing to scavenge—barely enough to tell they were human. He targets the intact ones, holds his breath and swallows hard, and tries not to look at faces.

He fails. His eyes find a scar that warps an ear and part of a swollen face. The eyes have gone milky gray and flat, unrecognizable. Tory chokes and tastes bile. He knows that face. One of Gavin's buddies. Not too far behind him is Gavin. The massive hole punching through both of their chests makes them a matched set. Perhaps one tried to protect the other.

Tory takes weapons off the bodies, slings the straps around his neck one after another, then digs into pockets and packs for rations, canteens, and ammo—whatever he can find—and stuffs it into a sack strapped across his front. As careful as he is, there's no avoiding the blood that gets under his fingernails. He leaves the bracelets on the bodies, though Riese said the metal could be melted into bullets. The tags might be all they have to put names to the fallen.

He doesn't find Randall, no longer remembers where he fell. Wherever he is, maybe Niela is beside him.

Tory pulls that foolish thought out by the roots. They're dead. It doesn't matter, anymore, what these people wanted or who they loved. Those things are no use to dead men. *Nothing* is of any use to dead men.

One after another after another. It's different, being here again. Silent. Frightening in a marrow-deep way he didn't have time for in the heat of battle. Death has become something insidious and mundane, a thing that lingers. After a lifetime at the work of staying alive, the fact that Tory doesn't lie among these bodies comes down to luck. Luck, and maybe Sena warning him about that shell.

Every shift and crunch and caw of birds sends a surge of anxiety through him. The movement in his peripheral vision is only the other Seeds Riese sent to comb the battlefield, but Tory's brain rolls out images of Arlunian soldiers walking from the trees, ready to fight.

Shaded by the tree line, Sena stands sentry.

When Tory's pack is as full as he can fill it and he has two rifles slung over each shoulder, he snags a communicator from a fallen officer's belt, clipping it to a pocket underneath a heavy rifle like it belongs there, and turns to bring his loot back to the wagon.

He drops the communicator at the edge of the woods as he runs and hopes Sena finds it.

He heads back as soon as he dumps his loot. The communicator no longer lies where he dropped it. The stones and leaves where it fell are arranged in a crude smiley face, which shocks a snort out of Tory. It's still so strange, the idea that Sena can be funny.

He fills the sack again, slinging rifles across his chest three at a time.

Two more runs, and on the third he returns to Riese, barely resisting the urge to veer off and check on Sena. Sena slept most of the way here, restless against the tarp-covered back of the rickety wagon they brought. He was slow to wake when they arrived. Confused.

"Where's Sena?" Riese asks. "We're out in five whether he's here or not."

Tory searches Riese's face for suspicion but finds only impatience. "I—" His mouth is bone-dry. He won't lick his lips. Mark of a liar. "I'll get him."

Riese stares, dark eyes unwavering. "Five minutes."

Tory runs. Now that he has a sense for Sena's energy, he's like a beacon.

He finds Sena in the woods with his forehead against a tree.

"Hey!" Tory whisper-calls.

Sena doesn't do anything.

"You look ridiculous!" Tory tries again.

Sena coughs out a low laugh. "Five days," he says.

"Huh?"

"We have five days until they disable our Cores."

That's—

Tory frowns. The way Sena talked about it before, he thought their reprieve would be longer. *Indefinite.* Far more than five days, anyway. "Riese is being cagey about letting me in on his timeline. I don't know if that'll be enough." He pauses. "You didn't tell them about Riese, did you?"

Sena drops the communicator, stomps it into the ground, and kicks fallen leaves over it. "Of course not. I said we were isolated and injured near the border, trying to make our way back. They started out promising three days . . . said we should be able to rendezvous with teams scouting the area in that time. I managed to talk them into more, so—well. It could be worse."

"I mean, that's not so bad, right?" But there's something wrong with three days, with five. With a reprieve so short. It settles too late. "We can just . . . I mean, I can—" Tory goes cold. "*Shit.*"

This whole time, he's had his own Core and the battle and Riese's plans and a million other things on his mind. He's been on fire with Riese's promise, Riese's purpose, Iri's strange and lovely truths. He didn't think—

He didn't *think*. Sena has no promise of salvation waiting at the end of this.

Five days of life isn't much at all. What they've done to Sena, they've given him no choice. Return or die.

"You have to go back."

Jaw set, Sena says nothing, half-moon bruises under his eyes the only hint at his exhaustion. When they met, Tory thought him a coward, an obedient doll—Kirlov's perfect soldier. This bravery in the face of death is so much worse. A coward would *survive*. If Sena were Tory, he'd go back to the Compound. He'd smile and play nice and crush himself down as small as they asked him to, because nothing's been more important than surviving until now.

"They may change their minds, of course," Sena says, dry. "I wouldn't put it past them to disable one or both of us to prove a point, so it's best to get your Core out as soon as possible. We're only special when we're in their hands. As soon as our risk outweighs our potential contribution . . ." He waves a hand. "You looked like you had something to say?"

Desperation is an ache in Tory's throat. "It's nothing."

"It's clearly something, for you to run all the way here."

Tory swallows. "Riese sent me. Says we've got five minutes before he leaves without us."

"He won't."

"He will. He said so." He doesn't mean to snip, but the words come out rough.

"No," Sena says, matter-of-fact. "He's smart. He wouldn't leave us. He'd kill us first. As I said, we're too big a risk."

A risk.

Something swells in Tory, incendiary like the explosion that threw him over the cliff into the cold ocean—something too big for his hands to take the shape of, too frightening to name. Something that could kill him.

He tries futilely to produce words as they walk back in silence.

*

Tory swings into the back of the covered wagon to absolute silence. No one moves as he helps Sena up.

"Just in time to go down with us," Riese whispers.

Tory takes in everyone's drawn faces.

"What?"

Iri answers, trying out a wan smile. "Military patrol." His eyes dart to Sena. "They've got Null. Saw them with tranq rifles and syringes."

"Null?" Iri used that word the first time they met.

Riese speaks again, eyes cold and flat as they travel over Sena. "Not long ago, we discovered the Westrian military was testing weaponry that disabled Seeds. Iri here theorized that the military had a

Voidseed and had adapted a weapon to neutralize our energy. The results are excruciating. The effects of a single dose can last a whole day. If they have Null, it doesn't matter what our skills are. They'll slaughter us."

Sena goes ramrod straight. "I didn't know."

Riese sighs. "It doesn't matter. If they saw Iri, they'll be monitoring the roads out."

"Then we go and meet them," Spark says. "Travin and I can zap at least a few of them before they hit us with a dose of that shit, and even if I can't zap 'em, we have guns."

"And show our hand? They have communicators. Do you want to bet our whole mission on the hope that they won't be able to call out for reinforcements, won't hit one of us with Null and capture us while we're in too much pain to move? I know everyone here would promise me their silence, but believe me when I say they *would* make you talk. We can't face them head-on."

Chest tight, Tory says, "There has to be another way out."

"With our supplies? We've got cliffs on two sides and freezing ocean beyond. Woods to the third. There's only one road out. Travin could 'port us in small groups, but he can't 'port the wagon. We'd have to leave most of the supplies behind, and we can't risk losing the upper hand they give us, not now."

Shouts in the distance, drawing closer. Iri's eyes dart to follow them, fists clenching.

Riese hunches forward. "We have to give them someone to chase so we can slip away when they're not looking." He trails off, examining each silent, pale member of his group.

Sena is the first to speak. "Send me. My presence compromises everyone's abilities, and I'm injured and can't travel well on foot."

At his words—so casual—Tory's heart leaps into his throat.

He opens his mouth to object, but Riese beats him to it, eyes darting between Tory and Sena with a conflicted expression. "I can't let you do that."

"*Damn right* he can't!" Tory blurts. "What're you thinking?"

Tory startles as Travin 'ports in beside him. He didn't even notice him leaving.

"They're close," Travin says, breathing labored. "We don't have long."

Riese scrubs a hand over his face. "Damn it!"

"I'll be the decoy."

Iri. He stands, shoulders squared. Why are all the decent people suicidally reckless?

"That's ridiculous," Tory says. He waits for the chorus of agreement, but it doesn't come.

"You know what that entails." Riese's voice is solemn, steady.

"I'm not afraid to give my life for a cause I believe in. I'm the one who drew their attention. I should be the one to divert it."

"Iri . . ." Riese moves toward him but runs into a rifle. It skids and clatters over the wagon's bed. He stops.

"You know as well as I do I'm the only real choice. I'm the newest to the group and the least prepared to help you execute your plans—and look at me." He gestures over himself. "I'm exactly who they'd *expect* to see out here. You would have volunteered me if I hadn't."

Riese looks away. "Travin. 'Port him out and get your ass back here. Iri, I—it's unfair of me to ask you to do this. If your father were here, he'd kill me for allowing it."

"Then don't allow it!" Tory says. Surely Riese can't be serious. *Iri* can't be serious.

"No one's letting me do anything. I'm choosing it." Iri's expression is cocky, but Tory can't help noticing the feverish desperation in his eyes, the press of his teeth into his lips. He's too young to throw himself away. "But you know what, you bastard? I'm taking a rifle with me."

"I'd expect nothing less. Burn 'em down."

"That's the plan."

"If you take 'em all out and need a ride, light something up and we'll swing by."

Iri shrugs. "Nah, might head to the Box and get started without you instead. It'd serve you right."

Riese smiles, reaching to ruffle Iri's long hair, but then his expression hardens. "If they overpower you—"

Iri's chin goes up. "I won't let them."

"I know. But Iri, I can't put another weapon in their hands. So *if* they overpower you . . ." Riese stops, fighting a grimace. He looks straight into Iri's eyes. "Don't let them take you alive."

The brutal significance of his order hangs, scythe-sharp, in the air until Iri says, "I won't." Motions wooden, he slings the rifle's strap around his neck, leveling an even gaze on the wagon's occupants. He stops a moment too long on Sena, his humorless smile an apology. "I had hoped to speak with you more. Don't let those bastards make a weapon of you, all right? You're better than that."

"Iri—" Sena starts, voice broken, but Travin settles both hands on Iri's shoulders from behind.

"Ready to go?"

One dry, mocking bow, and Iri disappears. Moments later, Travin flickers back in.

"Let's head out!"

"Wait," Tory says, but everyone's bustling to obey.

Tinny and small from somewhere far away, Tory hears Iri's running feet fading into the distance. A whoosh and crackle of flame. The soldiers who were drawing closer call out and follow, getting farther from the wagon. Someone beside Tory sighs.

The wagon begins to move, and Tory scrambles over supplies to get to Riese. "You can't leave him out there. We can go back. This is *wrong*. Riese—"

He doesn't move. Tory grabs Riese and tries to pull him around.

A strong arm whips out and knocks Tory to the ground. He lands on rations and rifles, knocking ammunition to the floor with a shower of *clinks*.

"He's just a kid! He can't take on that many soldiers! Not with Null."

The sharp report of a rifle punctuates his words, followed by an answering spate of bullets. Through the flap, a rush of flame grows bright in the distance, then extinguishes with horrible suddenness and a shocked cry.

"No." Tory bolts to his feet, but Riese grabs his wrist.

"*Stop it*, Tory."

Tory's legs lose strength and he staggers, but Riese's grip stays tight.

"Riese, they'll look at him and see only an enemy. They won't take him, they'll *kill him*."

A final shot rings out, and Tory flinches at the unfeeling *crack* that splits the silence. If he knows anything from all his painful years of healing, it's how breakable the human body is.

Riese claps a hand around his mouth. "Exactly," he whispers, pained.

Exactly.

There's something terrible and knowing in that word. Tory can't help but recall what Iri said: *You would have volunteered me.* The words crawl like bugs beneath his skin.

Would he?

"Iri made his choice." Riese says. Then, louder, "We'll survive today because of him. Remember that."

Tory gets as far as he can from Riese, dropping down at the back of the covered wagon with Sena, well away from the rest of the Seeds.

"You hearing this?" Tory says. "He's already fucking eulogizing him."

Sena's lips thin, gaze fixed on the scenery intermittently visible through the heavy flap over the back of the wagon. "It was . . . a solid tactical decision. Iri is not the only Pyrokinetic Seed in Riese's group, and he's right—they will almost certainly shoot first rather than take an Arlunian Seed into custody. No competent leader would put a weapon in the hands of his enemy, so Riese chose to give them a weapon they would not dare to use."

Anger sings through Tory. "How can you—" He breaks off when he notices how Sena's teeth grind. He's shaking and damp with sweat, a flush of restraint high and hot on pale cheeks.

"The utilitarianism of it disgusts me. It's . . . it's exactly what my father would have—" Sena pulls his knees against his chest, buries his face in them, and dissolves into wracking coughs until Tory thinks he might shake apart. "Fuck," he moans, and wheezes out a laugh more like a sob. "It was his choice. Earlier, he told me . . ."

"What?"

He waits a bit too long before he speaks again. "He said there are causes worth dying for, said he'd do anything to see Riese's vision through. I could've saved him. Riese would have let me go if not for you. Did you see? That look. He . . . couldn't make an enemy of you, so he couldn't agree. He—he wouldn't . . ."

Tory swallows.

"It should have been me."

Tory can barely breathe. "Don't talk like that. You'll be fine. You just have to—"

Sena's words come muffled from between his knees, faint and getting fainter. "I won't go back. I *won't*. They'll have to kill me first."

"You'd die either way!" One of Riese's Seeds up front startles and glares, so Tory leans in and lowers his voice to a whisper. "If you go back, at least you'll live. If you stay here, all you can do is wait for them to kill you. That's worse. I won't let you."

Sena laughs, but it chokes off and he knots a shaking hand in his shirt, face bright with sweat. "*Let* me? You can't make me."

"This is *stupid!* You'll kill yourself to make a point!"

"I thought the same of you," Sena says, so quiet he's barely audible. "Beating at walls you could never break. Couldn't understand . . . why you'd do something so useless." Beneath the dusting of dark hair, his eyes are bright as flames, lips curling into a weak smile. "But it . . . feels good to choose it. To stop being afraid."

"Sena, please. I'd go back for you. I'd find you and get you out. I swear I would."

"You don't get it. I'd . . ." Sena shakes his head, gaze hazy and faraway. "I really would rather die than see Kirlov again. I can't . . ."

Sena doesn't keep going.

"Hey." Tory jostles his shoulder. Sena only rocks, makes a plaintive mumble. "*Hey.*"

Tory reaches out, but he doesn't have to touch Sena to feel the wildfire heat radiating off him. Sena's burning up, his breaths fast and shallow.

Tory scrambles upright and moves along the wall toward the back of the wagon, where Riese is cataloging supplies and organizing them into empty boxes.

"You guys have a doctor, right?"

"Did your friend not tell you about Yized?" Riese frowns. "Are you unwell?"

"Sena's sick. Was there anything in the supplies we can use? Or anyone—"

Riese's expression goes blank. "I doubt there's anything in the supplies, and Yized won't be back until this evening at the earliest. So far, I've only seen rations, canteens, ammo, guns—"

"Give me a canteen, then."

"*Tory.*"

There's one tangled around a rifle barrel on the ground, and he snatches it up. Several heads dart up at the clatter.

"Sorry," he says. "Sena is . . ."

The eyes move toward Sena and come back colder. They murmur variations of *should've left him there.*

He hurries back and drops down beside Sena, uncapping the canteen. "You need to drink."

Hasra used to force water into Tory when he was feeling like crap—as much as he could bear. Three sips after he healed Kelly. A cool hand guiding him down to sleep. Gotta hydrate a fever, right? Not that he appreciated it like he should've. Always too busy trying to keep himself from getting attached.

Oh, and like a fool, he's attached. To Sena with his earnest stories of stars and stubborn trees penned in by the Compound, with such steadfastness in the face of fear, with infuriatingly terrible self-preservation instincts and a bone-dry sense of humor. Sena who carried him to the infirmary after Gavin attacked him, who dragged him from the sea with broken ribs, who knows Tory's fears and dreams by name because they're Sena's, too.

What was that story Sena told? Stellite, and kuhlu, and a reckless, helpless reaching for something ages dead. It's like a prophecy. Tory's such an idiot.

How didn't he *notice?* He looked down on Randall, and here he is in the same place without realizing his feet were taking him there. This feeling is the sort that rips people open. It's the lethal landing after a short, brutal fall.

But he wants, unreasonably, to take the leap anyway. He wants—

The things he wants terrify him.

Tory healed the broken for years. But this—selfishly, awfully, painfully, he wants Sena to live, because he wants Sena to *stay*.

The realization leaves him dizzy.

Suddenly, he understands his mother's warnings in a way he never could before. He doesn't know what she wanted back when she was free, but he knows with a certainty that sucks the breath from his lungs that losing it hurt her badly enough to turn her eyes only to survival.

To want something is to give that thing permission to hurt you; it's so much easier to remain whole when you're alone. Tory hasn't even lost anything yet—stars, he doesn't even have it—but it hurts already, a dizzying throb that steals the heat from his fingers and lips and leaves him shivering, his head a rockslide of catastrophes. Tory forces them away before they can crush him.

He can fix this. Somehow, they'll fix this.

Sena's hand slips off the canteen when he reaches up to grab it.

Five days.

Tory shoves the thought someplace dark and small and far away.

"Here." Hasra did this so much better, cupping his head and pouring sip after sip into Tory's mouth when he was too weak to move. Tory's movements are stilted. He pours water on Sena's face twice before he gets the speed of it right. It's worthwhile, though, because Sena gives him one of those dry, unimpressed looks that *has* to mean he's not doing too badly. The third try, Sena supports the canteen with one of his own hands and tips it up, nearly draining it in a series of desperate gulps.

"Hey, Sena?"

The silence between question and response stretches taut.

"Mm?"

He's spent his whole life swallowing words. Turns out speaking the ones he really means hurts just as bad. "You don't get to die."

Sena hums, thoughtful. "Not your choice."

He can choose not to watch. "I wouldn't make you go back, but—something. We'll figure something else out."

Sena tries a lopsided smile Tory translates as *fat chance*. "Maybe."

"Tell me you won't go off and die. I'll—I'll keep looking for answers until the last minute. I'll even do all the heavy lifting since you're such a mess. You hear me? We'll fix this."

"In five days?"

"Promise me you'll try."

Sena mumbles something close enough to *promise* for Tory to hold him to it.

Sena's eyes slip closed, his thick, dark lashes a startling contrast to the pallor of his face. Underneath his eyes and in the hollows beneath his brow, by the bridge of his nose, the thin skin lies bruise-purple.

Tory scoots back, reaches inside himself for his healing energies. He finds them, alive and thriving. But what use are they if he can't use them? A broken rib, a fever and cough would be so easy to fix. The body is a stubborn thing. It wants to be well. Tory would barely suffer at all to make it like they never happened.

But he can't sense Sena's healing energies beyond the chaotic crackle of his Seed. He doesn't dare to expand them again and earn the wrath of everyone here, but perhaps he can crush them down instead, maybe small enough to be able to heal Sena—

"Hold on," he murmurs. "I'm going to try something."

The energy responds to him as readily as it did with Iri, but it's dense beyond imagination. It doesn't want to shrink. He pushes it, but Sena starts trembling before Tory gets it down to half its size, fingernails scrabbling at his skin like it hurts. Tory lets it go, and it snaps back. Tory grits his teeth. Maybe he can heal *around* it. Make it withdraw from Sena in a localized way so he can heal him bit by bit.

Nothing. There's too *much*. Far too much. "Damn it, Sena."

Maybe Iri will have some idea—

Tory aches. Iri can't help them anymore.

Even eight inkhstones weren't enough to fully suppress Sena's power. Tory presses his hand over Sena's uniform and reaches for his own healing energies. He's the Worldseed, one of the First Children. He and Sena are supposed to be able to do the impossible.

But there's nothing.

"*Useless.*" Helplessness carves hollows in his gut.

Sena slips forward and Tory catches him, presses him back against the wall. Tory joins him there, knees tucked up under his chin. When

Sena's head falls onto his right shoulder, he lets it stay. He unbuttons his jacket and slips it off one shoulder and then the next, awkwardly tugging it past Sena and finally pulling it off his arm. He uses his left hand to toss it over Sena. He's plenty warm, and he still has the grungy, short-sleeved undershirt on, so it's not a big deal.

Sena shakes, the depth of the tremors clear even in the brokenness of his breaths.

How did he get like this? What did Tory miss?

"Didn't you say you don't get sick? Shit. Wake up, I can't do this."

The wagon rattles along, the only sounds the whistling of the wind, the crunch of rock beneath its wheels, and Sena's too-fast breaths against Tory's skin.

Tory squeezes his burning eyes closed.

They'll make this right. They have to. Tory isn't sure he can bear the alternative.

CHAPTER TWENTY-TWO

SENA SLEEPS ON ice and wakes to darkness, on fire.

He shudders halfway-upright in his tent and chokes until he's nearly retching. Pain bursts white-hot behind his eyelids and clears the haze of confusion. He really shouldn't have slept on his back.

He's never once missed these things: the anchor-weight of his bones that comes with high fever; the whistle of breath from overtaxed lungs; the molasses-like slowness of disjointed thoughts, each its own isolated emergency. He's glad to have left them behind when he was nine.

He can't remember how he got here.

He has fragments. The communicator. Bumbling through a halfway-competent explanation of their circumstances and begging for time.

Five days.

Talking with Tory in the truck. Being dragged out, arm around someone's shoulders. A steady stream of complaints, their token sharp edges dulled by the warmth and steadiness of the hand on his waist, the way the voice would crack sometimes and say, *hey, not much farther, okay? Just keep walking.*

Getting to his feet is a nightmare in gradation, every movement broken down into steps.

This, like so many things, he's gotten better at with practice.

He finds himself on his feet and doesn't stop to wonder how he got there. He steps through the tent flap and into star-studded dark. A fire burns a little ways away, and Sena recognizes the lone silhouette in front of it. He drops down on one of the vacated stumps around the pit and focuses on breathing. Through the trees, faint blue glows at the horizon. Sunrise. He slept a long while, then.

Tory tosses a twig onto the embers. "You look like you were chewed up and shit out twice."

"Then I look better than I feel," Sena rasps.

It startles a laugh from Tory, a tightness in his shoulders easing. "Hair's a *mess*. It's like a bird's nest. You should wear it like that all the time."

Sena frowns, but Tory grins, soft, in the direction of the flames.

Sena wouldn't mind keeping that smile on his face. "You should see it in the mornings before I wet it down. Lay a towel over it. Sometimes my bird sits on the towel while I get ready."

Tory's eyes dart to him, dancing. "So your head is sometimes an *actual* bird's nest? I love that. What's its name, your bird?"

"Kierney." Jeffra always takes good care of him when Sena is away. Perhaps she'll adopt him when he can't return.

"I wouldn't . . . Wow. Yeah, I can't imagine that." Tory turns to Sena, cheerful as Sena has ever seen him, and says, "You're pathetic, you know."

Sena blinks. He dives deep into his well of standard responses and finds nothing to match that, so he stays silent. Tory will keep talking. It will make sense soon, probably.

"I've been wanting to say that to someone for *so long*, you have no idea. See, I was always the one getting variations on that theme from, uh,

From Thatcher or Hasra. Hasra, mostly. Hasra entirely, actually. Thatcher's way too nice. She'd be all, *poor little thing, legs wobbling like reeds*, or, *sad creature, what do you expect me to do with you?* It's nice to be able to try it on someone else."

Thatcher. Hasra. He says the names with such gentleness. Those are the people he left behind when Sena dragged him into this. Sena leans toward the heat of the fire and squeezes his eyes closed.

A face drifts up in his vision—graying hair and smile lines. "Thatcher," he murmurs. "The one with the tea. Terrible liar."

Tory jolts upright on his log. "You *saw* him?"

Of course. As ranking officer, Sena made sure he was the one who questioned him. "He knew you were acting illegally and still protected you."

Tory curses. "Idiot! I told him to—"

"He's fine. My report asserted he knew nothing. I had to capture you," Sena says. "No one else needed to get involved."

"I . . . thank you." Tory hums something, staring into the fire, before turning back to Sena. "Hey, what do you think you'll do next?"

Responding with *die* seems a little macabre. "What do you mean?"

"After all this. What'll you do when all this is said and done, and you're free?"

"If," Sena corrects him, gently.

"When," Tory repeats. "Humor me."

Irritation ripples through Sena, then sorrow. "Don't," he whispers. "Tory, please."

"I just want to know. It's a simple question."

It isn't. Sena's never met anything with a sharper double edge than hope. Making that tree grow with Iri—seeing the fruit he made that dead branch bear—

This feeling is a thousand times too large for him. Sena has mere days to live and hands he wants to bare before Tory. He wants to touch Tory, skin to skin. Reckless Tory, bright Tory. Tory who tried to heal Sena even when he knew he couldn't. It's such a terrible, unfamiliar feeling, one he never dared to embrace before. It's so much harder not to *want* now that he knows his hands are capable of making things grow. He's full of so much hope it could choke him, growing in his chest like nuisance vines. There's far more than five short days of it banging to get out.

"Sena," Tory echoes. "Please."

Sena laughs, and it cuts at his throat, raw from coughing. His ribs stab at him with pain that lights up his whole side. "Fine." He stares into the fire. Tory stares at him. "*If* I'm still alive five days from now, and . . ." Free. He can't say it. "I don't know. A quiet place, with trees. A friend for Kierney." Short sentences because he's short of breath.

These are easy things to hope for, because they are easier to let go of.

He can't bear to tell Tory how much he'd like to see his mother and sister and catch up on a decade of conversation he avoided because he was afraid they might look at him and see the weapon he saw in himself. He can't tell Tory *you're foolish and reckless and impossibly warm, and you make me want to hope for things again.*

Tory laughs. "Come on, that's boring! Think big. Like—you and I, we'll break down those ugly walls your dad loves so much. We'll empty the labor camps and remake this place into a country worth living in." His hands clench in front of him, firelight catching on thin, slick lines. Scars.

"What happened?" Sena says. "To your hands?"

"We're telling nice stories now. It's not a nice one."

Sena has never minded the sad stories. "Tell me anyway."

Tory shrugs. "I was clumsy when I was six, and there were lots of sharp parts on the assembly lines in the camps. If folks messed up too often or got too slow, the soldiers would *motivate* them." He taps the backs of his hands. "Never on the palms. Didn't want to prevent us from working."

Bitter rage boils up in Sena, squeezing the breath from him. "Those camps should be destroyed."

Tory grins. "Right? I'd pay to see it. You'd just touch those awful fences and turn 'em to so much rust. Like I said, we'll burn the world down. When we're done, I'll drag you to Hulven, reintroduce you to Thatcher. *Then* we can find your boring house with trees."

We. Sena could poke a million holes in that ridiculous dream. Instead, he says, "It'd take a lot of time."

It's cruel, that Tory is the past and Sena is the future but neither of them can make five short days last longer.

Tory whispers, "I suppose we'd need a lot of help."

The wind picks up in the trees, low flames flickering as ice skitters through Sena's bones. He starts shaking and can't stop.

"You cold?" Tory's hands skate over his shoulders, feather-light touches that make Sena shiver, but not from cold. Something must come to Tory as he sits there, considering. "Hey, wait here a second."

Sena's raised eyebrow does its best to communicate *I wasn't planning on moving*.

Tory retreats. Sena leans as close to the fire as he dares.

He loses time, he's pretty sure, because next thing he knows, there's someone behind him yelling, "Catch!"

His body is too slow to respond. He stares at the blurred, firelit curiosity of his empty hand until he registers that he's supposed to have something inside it. He squints into the dimness and finds something rumpled on the ground.

Tory grabs up the item and dusts it off, suddenly sheepish, before extending it.

"Treated leather," he says. "Pretty much waterproof. Warm as anything, but pretty light and thin. You can use it."

Sena examines the item. A cloak.

The cloak—kuhlu vines lovingly but imperfectly sewn along the bottom, worn slick with years of wear. "I can't. This is . . . important to you."

Tory shrugs. "All the shivering you're doing is making me cold, and anyway, I don't want you to get me sick. Go ahead. Be warm. Use the thing."

"I was the one who took this from you."

"The one who gave it back, too."

Sena sighs relief as he shrugs the cloak around his shoulders.

The glow on the horizon is brighter. No sun yet, but the promise of warmth. The cloak traps the heat of Sena's body inside and thaws the ice in his bones. "S'nice," he says.

"I know. That's why I brought it."

Sena wraps the cloak tighter around himself with his left arm. He must have done something to his right. It aches. Maybe Tory dropped him once or twice, dragging him back to his tent. He lets his eyes close, enjoys the light show of the fading fire through his eyelids. He could sleep here. This was not how he envisioned his last few days of life. He imagined it would be a quiet, dignified affair, with no one in attendance to see him struggle.

"Sena, listen."

He tries an "Mm?" Hopes it's audible over the wind and the crackling fire.

"What you said earlier, in the truck—about your Core."

Sena keeps his eyes closed at the tentative words. Tory is not used to caring, but Sena is even less used to being cared for. It's a strange feeling. Worse, it's not a terrible one.

"I get why you don't want to go back. I swear I won't make you. But there's gotta be a way, right?"

Sena inhales. Shallow, still shallow. "May not matter." He ignores the wild patter of his heart, the greedy, awful thought that he could get used to this. "You know I'm not . . . an optimist. Don't think they're equipped to treat this out here. But it's fine. There really are more important things than survival." Freedom to make his own choices, that's one of them. He won't give them a single drop more of his blood. They will not cage him, and he won't let himself be used to cage others. "If you ever find more of the stuff they've made with my blood, burn it for me?"

"Riese says Yized will be back soon," Tory says. "She can give you more antibiotics. You'll be fine." He doesn't answer the rest. Stubborn, dragging his own truth from what he hears and ignoring everything else.

It aches, deeper than the pain of broken bones or whatever calamities are happening in his chest, to have that stubbornness focused on helping him. Maybe that's why, against his will and his better judgment, a terrible confession breaks out of him. "I wish I didn't have to go."

Tory startles, as he should.

Sena isn't sure he's ever said anything with so much conviction. It's tantamount to a confession of—

He shakes his head. "I'm sorry," he says, more calmly. "It must be the fever."

The shock in Tory's eyes hardens to determination, and *no*, Sena can't be the one to do this to him. He needs to convince Tory not to hope. Pneumonia doesn't care about hope. His Core, when they deactivate it, will not be nudged away from its inevitable decay by the fact that Sena might like, for once, to not fall asleep alone.

"We'll fix it. I'll fix it." Tory grabs for Sena's gloved hands and for once he holds on. "Wait for me. I'll find a way."

Sena should say *don't count on it*. He should tell Tory that it's only in stories that heroes find the right answers on a timeline like this, that not even all stories have happy endings. Sena would know. The sad ones were always his favorites. But he barely has the strength to stand on his own two feet. He certainly doesn't have the power to crack Tory's rock-solid resolve. It's selfish to let it stand, but Tory is still holding his hands, and Sena is far too weak to resist that gentle invitation to touch. Carefully, he leans so his torso is braced against Tory's shoulder, face tucked into Tory's neck so no one can see how terrible a job he's doing of controlling his expression. Barely louder than a whisper, with Tory radiating warmth through his thin shirt like a furnace, Sena breathes, "Okay."

A foreign voice interrupts, and Sena starts at the sound, pulling away from Tory.

"Boys, if you have a moment?"

His mind scrambles to place it.

Riese.

Tory scowls. Probably angry about Iri. His loss sits like a rock in Sena's chest. Or maybe that's the pneumonia.

Silence.

Riese is waiting for an answer, eerily still. He's unhappy.

"Yes, sir," Sena says, reflexively.

"Both of you," Riese says. (But his eyes are only on Tory.) "It's time to talk about our plans. Are you all right, Sena?"

"Yes, sir." The world around Sena is gauzy and unreal, hazy with firelight. And in the distance—the first glow of sun melts on the horizon like liquid gold, turning the sky purple in shades from bruise to lavender. Kuhlu blooms sway in a breeze, such an impossibly vibrant blue they almost glow with it. Like lanterns for the dead.

Riese's voice, far away like it's coming through a tunnel: "You don't look well. Go rest. I'll fill you in when you're feeling better."

He needs to say something, but Tory speaks first. "I'm not sure it's a good idea . . ."

"M'fine," Sena says. "You go on."

Riese says something, but Sena can't focus.

He loses time again. He blinks in Tory's direction and finds the stump he sat on empty. He wracks his mind for memories.

It offers up only these: a warm pressure and a blazing bolt of strange pain in the shoulder that was giving him trouble earlier, and Tory's too-serious promise that he'll *be right back.*

Sena reaches up, curious, to his right shoulder where the ache comes from, settles his hand over the cloak and presses.

He gasps, withdraws, curls double. He makes an ugly sound and murmurs thanks that no one is beside him to hear it.

This is wrong. Sena has had pneumonia before. This is different. His whole right arm burns when he tries to move it, hammer-clangs of pain and *heat*, like it's caught fire.

It's wrong.

No—no.

It's *early.*

He finds his feet after a few tries, grabs a bright metal pitcher from the grate over the fire. It smells of coffee, turns his stomach. Reflective—it will do.

Into his tent, onto his knees.

Signal mirror from his front pocket.

Breaths fast. He won't cough.

Crackling in his lungs like crinkled paper, gray haze around his eyes, not enough air. What a mess he is.

Cloak off, buttons freed to expose his shoulder. Arm burning, burning. He loses time checking it's not on fire. A fool notion. Of course it's not, it's—

Signal mirror over his shoulder. Pitcher in front, warped but serviceable in the reflection it offers.

Unmistakable. He's seen it on a corpse or three before: purple-black lines under irritated skin.

Roots. Like a tree, the tree they stand on to get to the top.

Mechanically, he buttons his shirt again. Lets the pitcher down. Tucks the mirror into his pocket, closes the cloak around himself. Warm. Woodsy. Smell of smoke, treated against water and given to Tory by someone who loved him. Sena closes his eyes and for the first time in ages allows himself to long for home.

Oh, and Tory's clumsy promises of the world they could build. Tory's *wait*, Tory's *we'll find a way*.

Now is a terrible time to want to believe in it, a terrible time to admit, like the weak creature he is, that he wants to live. That he could be someone better, fuller—together. Sena wasn't lying before. There *are* more important things than survival. Living, now that he's found someone worth living for, is one of them.

It could have been, anyway.

The flap of his tent shifts open—Tory returning, no doubt—and Sena doesn't dare open his eyes. He rarely has the right words for anything. Finding the ones to tell Tory *this* might be impossible.

He does not have five days, or a day.

His Core is already dead.

*

In the flickering lamplight in Riese's tent, Tory perches on a box, ready to kill.

"You *what?*"

Riese flips placidly through a pile of documents in the far corner. "I wanted you to meet Yized, since she'll be helping you. Sena didn't tell you about her?"

Sena's had a lot on his mind and is a half-step shy of delirium. Sena is not the one Tory blames for not telling him. "She's from the Compound! The Core you said you'd remove? She put it in me!"

"Funny thing," Helner drawls. "You're from the Compound, too."

"I'm not—"

"Give her a chance," Riese says. "I've known her much longer than I've known you. She's saved a lot of lives for us . . . though she's a real bitch about it. Keeps asking for money."

Helner smiles sweetly. "If you think anyone gets a single thing in this world for free, you're delusional, dear."

Riese purrs, "I can be very persuasive."

"Oh, I know. It's why I never linger. I hate sticky men."

Tory stands. "Are we finished here?"

Riese keeps ruffling through papers. "Sit. Give me a minute. I could tell you, but it's better if you see."

Tory drops back down on the box, kicks his knee up and down, runs the pads of his fingers over the coarse slacks of his combat fatigues. Wishes for a change of clothes. Wishes he were back by the fire—wishes he were as far as he can get from all of it. It's the most relaxed conversation he's ever had with Sena, but that's what made it so wrong.

Sena told him about his fucking *bird*.

Tory's mother was like that in her final days. She stopped paying attention to the big things. Her focus narrowed to him—to them. To the final meal they foraged from the woods for themselves. She held him close and alternated between sweet melancholy and fear. Told him stories, told him (again and again) how to protect himself once he was out. Stroked his hair and kissed his forehead and promised there was a wide world out there full of every wonderful thing except her.

If I'm still alive five days from now, Sena said. He, too, is already telling stories of a future he doesn't expect to share with Tory.

Tory was eight the last time he felt such dread. No wonder he didn't recognize it. It's been a lifetime since he got so close to someone he could lose.

Years have dulled the grief of his mother's loss, but *this*—Sena who wants a quiet house in the trees with his dumb bird, who has five days to live free or a lifetime to live under torture, in servitude. Sena shaking on that log, fevered and fading. The tentative way he leaned against Tory, like nearness was something he would have denied him. Who's to say he even has five days?

It's worse than any pain Tory can recall, like hot ropes strung around his chest, tightening.

That's why this was stupid.

He's stupid, just like Niela. How could he let it get this far?

He kicks his knee harder, brings a thumb to his mouth to chew at it. He pulls a strip of dry skin away with his teeth, hisses at a spark of pain. Blood wells up, and Tory presses his tongue to it, tastes copper.

He wants, and he wants, and he *wants*, but right now, he wants not to hurt. To be able to walk and not look back. He couldn't even do that with Thatcher, though.

What a fool he is, to cling to things that could break him.

"Tory, hey. You hearing what I'm saying?"

He shakes his head, taste of blood still sharp on his tongue. "Huh?"

"I can take your Core out today. We know you've been worrying about it."

Tory jerks from his haze. Shit, does she know what he and Sena did on the battlefield? Is that why Riese made him leave Sena behind?

He spins to face her, searching her eyes . . . and finds nothing. Just the quirk of her plum-dark lips.

"Why didn't you tell us before? We were pissing ourselves wondering if—"

"Shhhh." A cold finger settles on his mouth. "Everything in time. Riese didn't know if you would betray the group. He wanted to watch you, see if you'd be a good fit."

"And if we weren't? You'd just let them disable our Cores?"

A pang. *Five days.*

Riese chuckles. "We live in a world where everyone wants to kill us. A little ruthlessness doesn't go amiss. You think nice people spearhead revolutions? If they do, you think they live to see the other side of them?"

He's right. Of course he's right. Nothing comes without a cost.

Helner interrupts. "Anyway, it's messy. I don't have good lighting here, barely have passable instruments. Even in carefully supervised removals, we can lose more than 10% of patients. This *isn't* carefully supervised."

"What are my chances?"

"I'm no slouch. I'd give you 80%."

A one in five chance of death.

"You don't *have* to have it removed," Riese says from the corner where he's shifting boxes and sorting through papers.

Tory scoffs. "I really think I do."

Riese stands bolt upright, brandishing a stack of pages. "Found it!" He covers the distance with sure strides, navigating the mess of the tent with effortless grace. Backlit by lamplight, his unbound hair is a conflagration. "You *don't* need your Core removed, and I'll tell you why."

Helner stands. "That's my cue to go. I'm all about plausible deniability. I don't want any part in this if it crashes and burns. If it does, that awful place needs at least *one* person interested in limiting casualties. Can't stay gone too long or they'll notice. I've irritated Kirlov enough that he won't ever seek me out of his own free will, but better safe than sorry. Be back soon."

Riese waves her away. "I asked Travin to take care of something, but he'll 'port you back as soon as he's free."

When she's gone, Riese drops a series of maps and documents on the table. "This," he says, "is our plan." The document on top bears a stamp he recognizes as the letterhead for the Compound. It was on Tory's deployment papers.

"What's all this?"

"It nearly bankrupted us, but this is one of many bits of information we've bought from Yized. Read it."

The contents of the letter are simple, detailing the process by which Cores are tracked and how the information is backed up:

Simple stuff. Overload the stellite security core and the compasses in the Monitor Room and the Cores will be useless. Without the compasses, no one could track or disable the Cores, and without the Security Core that's been fed a drop of blood from every person within the facility, the security measures that allow only employees and Core-bearing Seeds to travel freely inside the Compound would be inactive.

It includes a postscript, marked with a mocking smiley face. *I say this because you paid me to tell you, not because I think you could do it.*

Stapled to the back, a map.

As requested. Have fun.

He examines it, finds the circled area marked *Monitor Room* in red ink.

Riese taps it. "That's where the compasses used to track escaped Seeds are stored. That's what I meant before. If you don't want to worry about the risk of death from a botched Core removal, just leave it in. Once we've finished our work, it won't matter."

"I don't care. I need it out of me." Tory traces the area on the map Riese pointed out. The Monitor Room. Tory *passed* that door on his walks. "I could do this."

"I know you can. I'll send you back with everything you need. Michal Vantaras built on *my* work to make the Cores, and I'll see them unmade, no matter the cost." Riese presses a small slice of stone in a metal setting to the table. "You'll need this."

A tab, larger than the one Tory was given. It looks like the one Sena used to let Tory into the linen closet.

Exactly like it. Tory picks it up.

On the side, stamped into the metal setting: VANTARAS.

Riese rubs the back of his head. "Don't be angry. I pocketed it when I helped you carry him to his tent earlier."

Tory blinks, frowns, opens his mouth. Closes it. It's an asshole move, but the irritation fizzles and fades in him. He didn't even notice it happening.

To be fair, he was tuned in only to the whistle of Sena's failing breath and the heat of fever that radiated through his clothes. Riese could have taken it off *Tory* and he wouldn't have noticed.

"He'd have given it to you if you asked," Tory mumbles.

"He wasn't in any condition to answer questions." Riese taps the stellite tab, scraping a thumb over the engraved name. Mildly, he says, "You didn't *tell* me he was Vantaras." Oh, he's irritated. "The leverage we could've had! If I'd known, I might have done some things differently."

"Yeah, well, you took your sweet time telling me things, too," Tory says.

Riese sighs. "Fair. It can't be changed now, and either way, we have everything we need. For a while, we've been trying to figure out a way to infiltrate." His lips press together. "I couldn't force anyone to take on a Core. But someone *already* in their database, already with a Core, and willing to help us?" He smiles. "You might see how you were the answer to all our problems. If you're willing—"

It's not even a choice.

"I'll do it. And Sena—Sena can help with—" He smiles, hands shaking. Relief blazes through him, leaves him razed clean. "Sena! He..."

He can go back, stay safe. They'll destroy all the compasses and get out. He won't have to listen to Kirlov. If they can't track him or disable his Core, it won't matter that they can't remove it. He'll live. He'll *live*.

This is it. This is their way. Tory hardly believed himself when he promised it, but it's here, just in time and almost too good to be true.

"Bastard," he hisses at Riese. He should be mad that Riese stole Sena's tab, but he's grinning. They'll be safe. He'll be free. This strange, terrifying, overwhelming thing between them, he can have it. He'll have plenty of time to hold it up to the light and make sense of it, put a name to it if he dares. "You're a rotten bastard, you know that?"

Riese laughs. "I am what I am."

Tory lurches to his feet. "I have to tell him."

CHAPTER TWENTY-THREE

RIESE SCRAMBLES OUT behind him, calling his name, but Tory outpaces him. Riese might have been on the run for the last few years, but Tory's been running almost as long as he's been alive. It's nice to move toward something, for once.

Helner can take his Core out. They'll trash the Monitor Room so Sena won't have to worry about being tracked. They'll figure this—this *thing* out, whatever it is, and it'll be fine. Sena will get better and Tory can stop having to worry because worrying sucks and he's over it, can't imagine for the life of him how Thatcher put up with it.

But things will be good. Near-perfect.

Nothing is ever this perfect, but maybe he's due an easy win. Maybe they both are.

"Sena! Hey, listen! You won't—"

He's not by the fire where Tory left him. The embers flicker livid red. Sunrise makes spindly shadows of the silent congregation of trees.

He hurries to Sena's tent, hesitates only a second before pulling open the flap.

He coughs. Smoke, sweat, and the biting tartness of coffee heated too long make his eyes water. There's a pitcher on its side, its sludgy contents poured over a circular singe mark where the pitcher's heated bottom must have set the edge of the blanket alight.

If Sena were there in the midst of it, maybe Tory could laugh, joke about how Sena isn't allowed to touch anything even remotely hazardous while sleepy or unwell.

But his stomach sinks, mouth sour.

Sena is gone.

This is the most awful feeling yet. An acid, wrenching emptiness. The worst part is, he goes straight to bargaining. *Surely, he'll be back. Maybe someone needed to talk with him; maybe he was confused—*

Or maybe he bailed.

Sena's pack, after all, is also gone.

The sizzle of relief in Tory fades to numbness. He forgot that his choices have so often been whittled down to these: leave or be left behind.

Maybe Sena knew it, too, decided to make it easier for both of them. He probably did. It hasn't been easy for Sena, either. Like Tory, he can't afford the pain of holding onto things that could ruin him. Maybe he was afraid, too, of wanting. Those last words he said before Tory left with Riese—"You go on." He was sick. He was so awfully sick.

Maybe that was a benediction. Maybe those stories were his way of saying goodbye.

Five days, he promised, and Tory believed him.

This should be a good thing, shouldn't it? An easy break, bloodless. It *is*. It's just that there's not nearly enough air out here.

Something sharper and more caustic than shame burns in his belly.

A hand settles on his shoulder, heavy and warm, and like a traitor, his mind jumps first to *Sena?*

He crushes the thought and turns.

*

Sena can't stop running—doesn't dare.

Fresh blood slips in lazy lines down his right arm and dyes his glove red. His hands—he feels the urge to hide them, even more than usual, and there's a reason why, but his buzzing thoughts refuse to yield an explanation that makes sense.

This is why he runs: an acid burst of horror; the flap of his tent slipping open behind him; grasping hands; frightened, wide eyes mirroring his own; light glinting off metal; pain, localized and sharp like a bee sting; an apology.

This is why he runs: like a fool, he wants to live.

His blood roars in his ears and his uniform rasps at fever-hot skin. He's never wanted anything more than he wants to rest, but he can't. If he does, he won't rise. He forces leaden legs to move. *Away* is the only way that matters.

It's light and dark and then light again, like a magic trick, and acid nausea bubbles through him. Branches and eerie blue flowers sway in front of his face, and roots lash out of the earth to grab him. His skin strains over his bones, like he might burst.

Fading vision fixed on the ground, he finds a path and follows it.

His feet twist in deep ruts. *Wheel tracks*, his head tells him after he's followed them maybe for miles. Sena staggers past whispering trees, between rocks like blades, and out into open air and hills wreathed by low fog.

Roots rise in the distance, a cathedral or a great ribcage—the bones of the Beast inviting him to his final slumber among the stars. If Sena passes through them, he can be at rest. But what a lonely rest it would be.

No, he's running for a reason. Toward or away from something, to keep or to save something.

Tory.

Sena turns away and loses his breath at the wasteland beneath and beside and all around him. He chokes on the sour-sweet odor of blood and decay and the tang of saltwater, blinks and opens his eyes to a deathscape pocked with bodies like flowers, swollen and cold on red-dyed grass. Somehow, he's walked himself all the way to a graveyard.

It's appropriate.

He forges a path through the dead, their faces rigid with fear, eyes flat and whitish. Dull, bruise-colored sunrise glints ghostly silver off hundreds of bracelets just like his. This place is a mortuary of numbers, not names.

(I-S)VS/0001. Sacrifices to a war of his father's devising, Sena the first of thousands—not a son but a sword. He'll lie among them soon. Maybe he already is. Fog plays around his ankles and beads on his skin. He shivers.

He burns from the inside out.

His eyes settle on a gangly figure near the trees, face covered with a scrap of cloth. There's blood in a long, wandering line in front of it, like someone cared enough to try to drag the body away.

Whoever the boy is, he is loved.

The thin wrists, folded over the ruined chest, look so much like Tory's. The tone of the skin, pale like the sun never touched him a day in his life, the spatter of light freckles—

It can't be Tory. This land of the dead is no place for him. Tory is achingly, awfully alive.

Sena staggers toward the still figure, breath stopped by the knot in his throat, and stumbles to his knees beside the body. He wheezes and tastes rot. His fingers find the edges of the cloth over the boy's face and sit there. A voice inside him tells him of *course* Tory is fine. He's—somewhere. The details are hazy. Firelight and warm smiles and a cloak—that cloak he loves so much.

It warms Sena now, and there's a *slice* in it and Sena's dirtying it with his blood and—

Tory is not the boy underneath this cloth. Sena steels himself to lift it. One, two . . .

"Don't you touch him!"

A shadow races out from the tree line, knife in hand, and Sena's head whips up. His vision does an awful cartwheel at the suddenness. The angry stranger rushes up. She and the ground and the grass and the body tip and roll, but Sena catches the important things.

The girl—short and uniformed and bloodstained from hands to chest—crouches over the body like she'll die beside it. "Don't you dare touch him."

Then she goes still, and her face is as much a muddle as the rest of the world, but her voice comes out odd and cautious. "L-Lieutenant Vantaras?"

He squints. "I . . . do I . . .?" Then, with a flap of his hand toward the body, "Tory?"

The girl huffs. "No."

From the woods, a young man's voice rises up, slurred and faint. "Niela? What's happening?"

The angry, bloodstained girl's eyes flick toward the woods. She shifts to stand between Sena and the voice. She calls, "Stay where you are. Don't move again. You know what happens when you do."

"My friends, are they . . .?"

"Long gone, thank the stars. Stay there."

The voice in the woods goes silent.

The girl—Niela—frowns. "This is Randall. I tried to heal him, but . . ." Her lips go tight and thin, bloodless.

"I'm sorry."

"You should be. You *and* the bastards who sent him here."

Sena flinches.

Niela hisses a breath in, mouth opening like she's not finished with him, but before she can start, a petite young man, barely upright with a tangled mess of long wavy hair, stumbles through the tree line and collapses against a rough trunk on the fringe of the woods. He sways where he stands, eyes dipping closed in a slow blink. And that determined set to his mouth, the burnt orange sweater several times too big for him, the burn scars on his hands that Sena now knows must be from the fire he set when his Seed blossomed at six—

Niela throws her bloody hands up. "You'll reopen it! *Why?* I only *just*—"

The boy breathes, "Knew it was your voice I heard."

Sena's vision tips and turns and maybe he's turning with it, but he finds his feet again. "*Iri?*"

Just like he last saw him, except the sweater is more black-red than orange, pocked with five or six holes, his skin the bloodless bluish-pale of the dead. He's gone because of Sena.

Words stumble from his lips and his eyes burn. "Sorry," he slurs. "Sorry I couldn't . . . save you."

Iri makes a sound like a laugh and lifts a shoulder in a shrug. He winces, turning his smile to a grimace. His free hand flutters over the holes in his sweater.

Sena doesn't realize the flesh beneath the holes was smooth until it opens in front of his eyes like a ragged mouth, weeping blood.

"I'm so sorry." Sena presses a gloved hand—already wet with his own blood, from a wound he doesn't remember getting—to Iri's red-soaked sweater. Blood seeps through the cloth and warms him, but all he can do is shiver.

Iri smiles at him with the forgiveness of the untethered dead.

"It's okay," Sena offers. "I'm dead, too." Dark blots close in from the corners of his vision.

"Oh, you really are a mess, aren't you?" A hand reaches for him.

He rears back before Iri's cold fingers make contact, and Iri staggers, shocked. Sena trembles where he stands. This must be his punishment, to watch Iri die again.

"Oh. Oh, no." Iri's eyes widen, bloodless lips parting, and he grabs Sena's hand, ignoring his flinch and clinging with a grip both vengeful and desperate. "Sena, I wanted to tell you before. I *tried* to—listen to me. Riese is lying. I didn't—my thoughts are a mess but they're *clearer* now that I'm away, see? Tory," Iri murmurs. "They're going to kill him. You can't . . ."

No.

He can bear any punishment but that. His tongue fails him when he tries to speak, vision blinking to a seamless darkness. His bones are molten, eyes burning dry. The ground tips up to meet him.

When he falls, no one catches him.

*

The sun blinds Tory as he turns.

It wasn't that high a moment ago. How long has he been standing here?

He rubs his eyes to clear the sun's flickering after-image and squints at the man behind him.

Riese waits, foxlike eyes creased with something gentle. "You ran out and never came back. I got worried."

Tory swallows. "Sena . . ." The name sticks in his dry throat.

Riese's expression hardens. "That's what I need to talk about." The hand on his shoulder guides him away from Sena's tent and toward the fire. "Take a seat."

"I'm fine like this."

"*Take a seat,* Tory."

The words land twice as heavy as the hand on his shoulder, and Tory's body obeys the order, falling onto a stump next to the fire so hard he's surprised his legs kept him up so long.

Riese watches him. Finally, he says, "Travin and Yized were attacked."

Tory tries to stand, but Riese's hand goes from calming to controlling in a second, clamping around his shoulder to keep him down.

"Who . . . ?"

"We think it was Sena."

"He wouldn't—"

"He did."

Tory's mouth moves, but he can't find a single word of argument in the jumble of his thoughts. "*Why?* What happened?"

"They heard a sound and pursued it. I'm sure you understand. We're all sensitive to unexpected noises here. They found Sena, attempted to talk with him, but he was . . . *confused.*"

Tory pushes down a surge of concern. Of course he was. He was confused beside the fire, too. Tory shouldn't have left him there. If he'd stayed . . .

"Combative, as well. Travin said it was like he didn't recognize him. He tried to use his Seed to escape, but of course . . ." He sighs. "I don't want to say this, Tory, because it's been clear to me from the start that you're quite close—"

"We're not." It tastes like a lie. *Again.* "We're not. Tell me."

Riese sits on the log across from Tory, the one Sena used earlier. "I tried not to make a big deal of it while he was here, but I didn't trust him. I meant what I said before. Being under the thumb of the Westrian military rots the mind. Some dogs bark on command for so long they can't forget their masters." He peers into the dying fire. "I would see all Seeds free, but sometimes that's not the merciful choice. Some Seeds don't know what to do with freedom."

Sena wasn't given the chance to know what to do with it. Tory can't help the ugly surge of hope. "Did Travin catch him?"

Riese shakes his head. "He got away. It's for the best. I sent a couple of my people to look for him, but . . . if they didn't find him immediately, I advised them to pull back for their own safety. They can't use their abilities against him, and I won't lose more people for that—" he closes his lips on whatever he was going to call Sena. "I don't imagine he'll get far."

Tory steers his thoughts around the wrenching feeling those words bring. *It's for the best. It's for the best.* It becomes a mantra in Tory's head. He doesn't say, *shouldn't we go after him?* Or, even worse, *I'll go after him.*

He could, though. Tory promised—five days of looking for every answer at Sena's side, not giving up. It wouldn't be hard, with Sena like he was, to find him and drag him back.

He *could.*

"I'll—" The words die on his tongue. *It's for the best.* He still can't help saying—hoping, "I could look. Don't we need him? For your plan?"

"Not as such."

Tory bristles. "What do you mean?"

"We'll discuss any revisions to our plans later. It's time for breakfast."

Tory turns away. "I'm not hungry."

"Understandable, but you should eat. Taking care of your health is important. This is a setback, but you're like me. You'll take it and use it to make yourself stronger. Come along."

Tory's following a few steps behind Riese before he realizes his legs are moving. A setback. It's a nice word, packaged with the hope of moving forward. "Sorry," he mutters.

"No need for apologies. It's understandable to be upset, but it *is* better this way. This way, you're focused."

Tory grabs those words like a handhold in a flood. Maybe Riese is right. He has a job to do, a mission to fulfill.

They don't need Sena for this. *He* doesn't need Sena. It really is better this way. His mouth is dry when Riese leads him to where Judge, ever-present frown on his face, is distributing bowls of reheated stew to the assembled Seeds. Travin, sweat soaked and shaking, sits on the ground while someone wraps up his arm.

Sena. *Sena* did that. Did Sena do that? Confusion and frustration and all manner of unsettled feelings bubble up in Tory, shredding the cloak of fragile peace he's pulled around himself.

Sena wouldn't do that, would he?

Tory averts his eyes and speaks up again only when they're in line. "Riese."

Riese turns to face him, eyes shadowed, face dark with stubble.

"Tell me what I need to do," Tory says before Riese can open his mouth. "I'll do anything."

He has a mission, and doing it will free Sena—even if it's too late for it to matter.

Riese smiles. "I knew I could trust you. The effects of freeing Seeds from Westrice's control will echo far beyond today. Westrice will no longer have captive Seeds to stock their hospitals, run their most sensitive mail, and fight their battles against others and against *us*. With one move, we strike a killing blow against Michal Vantaras and his war effort. You have *no* idea the kind of role you'll be playing for us."

At that, Tory can't help a wan smile.

Sena was right.

There are things more important than survival. He can change the world. He'll make all of them free.

*

Hands on his neck, his shoulder.

Sena shoves them away, scooting back until he runs into the solid trunk of a tree, hands scrabbling at its roots. His jacket, unbuttoned, hangs halfway off his shoulder. He tugs it up.

Fog and a tomb-like dome of leaves squelch the pale sunlight overhead. Two blurred blobs resolve into people-shapes as he blinks.

Where *is* he? Where was he?

Images flood his mind, sharp and free of context: surprise, pressure, and *running, running, running.* Broken images. And *fear*, not for himself but of himself. Nothing before that, but plenty after, ghostly and dreamlike. Blood and the bodies of the dead. Roots arching from the ground like something sacred.

Iri.

He found his way back to the battlefield on the cliffs.

"Iri!" His last words ring in Sena's head: *They'll kill him.* "Tory, where's . . ." Those hands again, reaching for him. *"Don't touch me!"*

His head throbs, too full. The hands retreat, and Sena drags in a shaky breath, vision wavering. He forces himself to his feet. "H-have to find Tory."

Tell him—something. He didn't mean to leave. He wants to live, to *stay*.

Sena wants so many things he can't have. All he can do now is choose to chase them.

"Yeah, I don't think you'll be finding anyone in your condition," a no-nonsense voice offers. "You're bleeding, by the way. Stab wound, looks like, though you didn't give me enough time to assess it. I tried to heal it, but no luck. Both of you, problem patients. I swear . . ."

Sena blinks down to his right arm and the blood soaking his glove, oozing from a wound he doesn't remember getting. He falls back against the tree, sliding to the ground again. "S'fine."

"It's not," says the voice. Niela. That's her name. Niela who loves the freckled boy with the cloth over his face, who couldn't save him. Sena hopes that's not a prophecy. "But it *is* the least of your concerns right now."

"Please. Iri said . . ."

Another voice echoes toward him from farther away, so faint the wind nearly overcomes it. *Iri*. "Welcome back," he says, and Sena squints until he sees him—forcing himself upright with a shaking hand cupped over a still-bleeding wound, skin nearly translucent with blood loss and shot through with green-blue veins.

Niela grumbles and moves across the clearing again, pressing her hands to the wound. She growls as she lifts Iri's bloody hands away and replaces them with her own. "You won't make this easy on me, will you? Gimme a break, I'm an *apprentice*, I'm not—" She wipes her forehead on her upper arm. "*Something's* neutralizing my work, and it circulates the more he exerts himself. It's almost out of his system, but it's a bit of a game now to see which will last longer—his life energy and my ability to force his body to produce more blood to replace what he's lost, or the toxin that's preventing my healing from sticking."

Null. It has to be. Sena must make some sort of noise, because Niela's eyes dart to him.

"You know something about this, Lieutenant Vantaras?"

"I'm sorry," he whispers.

Iri's chin falls against his chest like he can no longer support it. "S'not your fault," he murmurs. "S'your asshole dad."

His blood oozes between Niela's splayed fingers and floods over.

Sena might not have to be a weapon—but Null *is*. The tests used to expose Seeds, made from his blood, have become a sharp weapon in the Grand General's hands. Iri showed him beauty and creation and crushing hope, showed Sena how he could make things grow, but it's the compound made from *Sena's* blood tearing open his wounds over and over.

Sena presses the heels of his hands to his eyes and pulls his knees up to his chest. His breath quickens, vision bursting with color from the pressure. He shouldn't be here.

Iri's voice, far away and gentler than he deserves: "Sena?"

"Don't you dare move and undo my hard work again. You should stay well away from him right now, anyway. Look. *The tree.*"

Sena looks. Beneath him, the dark, healthy roots he clung to sit grayish-brittle and pitted, aged a hundred years in a moment. He brushes a twig growing from the tree as he turns. It cracks and crumbles, drifts down on him like ash.

"I didn't—"

His hands are gloved, the right one stiff with his blood. It should be *safe* with them on.

His head throbs, iron-weighted but cotton-filled. His eyes burn. He's breathing in and in and *in* and he's dizzy with it, unsafe and surrounded by people he could hurt. "This isn't . . ."

"You need to calm down."

He draws a breath in so fast he loses it in an agonizing fit of coughs and reflexively pulls his hands back to himself. He tucks them against his belly and curls over to hide them.

Niela walks toward him on her knees, and Sena pushes himself farther back. Sena's *never* done anything like this through a barrier before. His whole life—all this time—

"Breathe. You're making it worse." Iri. "Believe me, I know from experience. Panic does *not* help an unstable Seed. It will likely calm down once you do."

He forces shallow breaths into his uncooperative lungs until his spotty vision clears.

"Like that," Iri says, whisper-light.

Sena shakes his head. "Tory! You said he would . . ." He can't make his lips shape the word. "I have to go back."

"By the time we could get back, they will have moved on." Iri leans toward him. The wound on his shoulder stretches open again at the movement, but it's only the surface—shallow, bleeding pits. Niela sighs and heals it again. This time, it stays closed.

"Moved where?"

He laughs, breathless and tired. "Can't you guess? Riese will want to get started."

The Compound.

"And that is where the problems begin. Without you next to him, Tory is probably singing Riese's tune right about now."

"What do you mean?"

"Riese uses . . . a form of persuasion to ensure group harmony. His type is relatively rare, but I think you'd probably call him an Orator. As long as you were near Tory, Riese was unable to affect him. When I was around you, it wore off for me, too." He grimaces. "That's when . . . I'm sorry, I tried to tell you, back then. He wasn't always like that. I doubt he needed to use his abilities on me at the start. I was *angry*. I wanted to hurt everyone in this awful country. My father was accepted into an exchange program in Maran's largest university. That's where he met Riese. My father was old for a student and Riese was young for it. They were the odd ones out, so they became friends. My father confessed his abilities to Riese—he was a Reader, capable of seeing Seed energies on a person. He had known Riese was a Seed from the moment they met. They were friends until graduation. But Riese went on to seek a higher degree, and my father went back to Arlune, where he met my mother and had me. This was just before the war."

He had assumed, given that an Arlunian scholar was admitted to and graduated from a Westrian institution.

"And Tory?"

"I'm getting there. Riese got in contact with my father many years later, thanks to the help of a certain gutsy merchant's daughter. My father was a gentle man, always, but my mother had just died and he was lost. Riese . . . something had changed in him, too. He was harder. Angry." He shakes his head. "He came to my father with a plan. If he would help Riese find Seeds who might be open to joining him, he'd lead them in liberating the Compound from Westrian control. STAR-7 houses *all* the battle-capable Seeds. No Compound, no soldiers . . . no war. Or at least a great pause while your father reconsidered his approach to warcraft."

Niela speaks up. "That's not sounding too bad."

Iri shakes his head. "It isn't, is it? My father went all in, helped Riese gather Seeds for his goal. But they couldn't get inside: the wall was too high, the security too tight. They kept losing people—to Westrian soldiers, Westrian Seeds, recruits whose loyalties had been addled by their time inside. That's how my father died, betrayed by one of our own. They never found his body, never even told me that he'd gone. I tracked Riese down after my father's letters stopped and decided to join the fight. I had nothing else left. But Westrice kept pushing us back. And when Null appeared, it just got worse."

Sena flinches.

"That's when Riese changed. The dogs were using our own to kill our own. He started talking about conscripted Seeds like they were animals. He said . . ." Iri presses his lips together. "Releasing domesticated Seeds would be a cruelty. He started talking like it would be better if they all died. I would gladly kill any of Vantaras' soldiers myself, but to kill *our own*—it was against everything I believed. I went to share my concerns with Riese . . . and then I wasn't concerned anymore. Riese barely has to imply something to make you believe it. Then you came and cleared my head—it's why Riese warned us all away from you, I'm sure. Your neutralizing field seems to affect anything within a couple of paces from you. I wanted to tell you what was happening, but Riese spoke to me before you finished with Yized, and I forgot again, until . . ." He shrugs. "Until I got here. His manipulations are subtle—like a splinter in your brain. He's the same as any illusion-type Seed. The more ideological dissonance, the easier his work is to unravel. But the thing is, we all agree with him on almost everything. He just has to sand down any sharp edges. I'd have gladly sacrificed myself for a worthy cause, but it took me too long to remember that this is *not* my cause."

"What about Tory?" Sena leans forward.

"Tory is a sacrifice, a tool in his bid to stop Westrice from hunting Seeds. Riese will use him to lower the Compound's defenses. Once he lets them in, it will be a massacre."

Sena laughs into his hands, the cruelty of it settling into his bones. The only way to save Tory is to save the Compound, the root of all their pain. He can't go back. He won't spend his last days alive in their hands, forced to be their perfect soldier. But Tory will be there, and he has no idea what he's walking into. "We need to get to Tory first."

Pain stabs at Sena's chest and the grind of broken bone against bone makes his teeth itch. Stars pop in front of his eyes, and he falls.

He doesn't hit the ground. Warm, small hands press against his shoulders and lift him.

Reflexively, he pushes them away. "What's *happening* to me?"

"You're . . ." Niela winces. "It's just that—shit. They only taught me to heal people and toss them back into battle, not how to talk about this stuff. You know about your Core, right?" She gestures to his still partially unbuttoned jacket. "That thing's *rotten*."

"I know, but—"

Niela winces. "No, I mean . . . your Seed's going haywire because your Core is deader than dead and your body's shutting down. A Core like that's been dead for days. Maybe a week."

"That's impossible."

Iri interrupts, quiet. "It's not. I've seen dead Cores before, and yours . . . yours is as bad as I've ever seen."

This is—what, the third full day since the battle? Fourth if he counts the day of. They'd have to have disabled his Core *days* before he even went missing. "That doesn't . . ." It makes no sense. "I haven't even been gone for a week."

Niela hums. "There are substances that can break down the organic matter of the Core and speed its death. Did anyone give you anything? A pill, a serum, an injection?"

Sena shrugs—and the pain of it travels up and down his right arm. "Oh." He tugs up the sleeve. "Here," he says. "Antibiotics."

The site where Helner injected them yesterday is inflamed and weeping pus. He didn't even notice, what with his ribs, his Core, the wound on his shoulder—

The *wound*. The memory of how he got it comes back in a frantic rush:

The flap of his tent shifting open in the dark, showing Travin when Sena expected Tory.

Sena dropping the metal pitcher onto his blanket in surprise, unable to manage even a greeting as Travin lurched forward with some tarp or bag or bundle of cloth and shoved it over Sena's face. (Suffocation, of course. Easy to explain away, in Sena's condition.)

Travin's eyes, wide and afraid. Sena reaching up with gloved hands, with the same focused burst of desperation he felt at nine years old. Travin avoiding his grasp but not flinching away when Sena's left hand seized his wrist. Of course. He shouldn't have been able to do a thing with the gloves on.

Then a muffled yell. Withdrawal. Travin clutching an arm going sunken-thin and black where Sena touched him.

Fear—from both of them—thick enough to choke on. The smell of smoke, splash of coffee as he upended it in his hurry to run.

Travin scrambling away from the tent and away from Sena.

Then Helner, who smiled wryly and gave him painkillers the other day, running into him as he tried to leave the woods. A scalpel plunged in his shoulder and wrenched out, then raised again. An apology, barely audible. Regret, maybe, or some adjacent breed of feeling—hard to discern in the low light of morning. An elbow to her chin as he found his feet and ran until he couldn't run another step.

Their fear and hesitation.

They were asked to do it. He wants to believe that, anyway. It's easier to believe they didn't choose to hurt him.

Niela says what he's thinking. "There's no way what they gave you was antibiotics."

Sena closes his eyes.

"I don't want to be the bearer of bad news, but . . ." She shrugs. "All I can suggest is you don't use your Seed. It could make this worse. Sorry. I wish I could . . ."

Sena shakes his head. "It's enough. Thank you."

"We need to hurry. My mom's back at the Box and she doesn't know what's going on. I already lost . . ." She stands, squares her shoulders. "I'm not letting anything happen to my mom, too. If we can find a Porter—"

"I can't be 'ported. But . . . there were soldiers in the area. If we find them, they'll have a way to get us back."

First, they'll find the patrols, and then they'll aim for the Compound Sena swore he'd never return to. He bites his lip against the surge of fear and hardens his resolve.

He's dead either way. If he can save Tory, it will make all this pain worth it.

CHAPTER TWENTY-FOUR

TORY SPRAWLS ON a makeshift operating table in the center of the gutted camp. The tents have been torn down, the stolen supplies packed into the truck, the boxes of stellite long since 'ported to the border. Everyone else departed, at Riese's order, before the sun reached its zenith. Only Helner, Tory, and a curling wisp of smoke from the snuffed-out campfire remain.

Clouds rush in with the afternoon wind, darkening the light to an eerie and shadowless gray. Helner presses Tory onto a "treatment table" made from a stack of empty boxes and gets to work removing his Core.

It's about as pleasant coming out as it was going in—fire and ice where she's rooting around in his body. When she's finished, Helner lays the Core on a platter in front of him, purplish-red and fleshy, dark roots spreading from the central sphere like veins. "Lovely, right?"

His stomach flops, and he turns his head to the side. "Beautiful," he manages.

His skin burns, but when he slides a hand over where Helner extracted the Core, it's smooth and unmarred. No long scar for Tory.

"Hey . . . what you did with Reaching, could you have done it with a scalpel?"

She goes still. "Aside from the fact that I am a *Reacher*, so cutting people open is not my specialty—unlikely. Remember I said Core removals via Reaching have a 10% mortality rate? It'd likely be the reverse for surgical removal. And that's generous. A 10% survival rate would be a miracle."

Tory closes his eyes. He feels sick because of the Reaching, not because—

"Why do you ask?"

"No reason."

The silence that falls between them is palpable.

"I'm . . . sorry," she says, "About Sena."

"I don't want to talk about it." Prickling-cold waves of nausea roll through him, his skin itchy and too tight, tongue thick in his mouth.

He opens his eyes, seeking a distraction, but only finds Helner's face. The right side is swollen, the skin along her cheekbone ragged and rust colored. She catches him looking, shifts the uninjured side to face him.

Travin and Yized were attacked, Riese said. There's the evidence of it, but his brain refuses to parse it.

"Stop staring or I'll pull out a lobe of your lung."

Tory turns away.

She's the one who ends up talking, voice quiet. "What happened to Sena was a mercy. I wasn't his biggest fan, thought he was a coward for the longest time, but I wouldn't wish that bastard Kirlov on anyone. Death was the kindest possible choice."

"But it wasn't! If Riese's plan worked—"

Helner whacks the back of his head. "I don't want to know. Plausible deniability, remember?"

"Fine. Are you finished?"

After a pause that feels eternal, she pokes his Core with a finger, and it rolls over with an unpleasant *plop-squish*. Tory doesn't gag, but it's a near thing.

"I'm not seeing any broken-off roots, but . . . you know. If you die, think of me fondly." She shrugs. "I need to get back. If they notice me gone, your little gig will be up, too. Travin better hurry. He's my ride."

"Mine, too, I think."

Without fanfare, she plucks a scalpel from a tray of instruments to his right and plunges it into the Core. Blackish fluid oozes out in rhythmic rushes, like the thing has a *pulse*, and—

Yep, that's Tory's breakfast.

Helner sidesteps and pulls the Core away before he can defile it with scrambled eggs once removed.

"No appreciation for my fine arts." She withdraws a sliver of pure stellite from the fleshy mass with a pair of tweezers. "I have to put this back in you."

"You *what?*"

"You can't get in without it. This bit of stellite, charged with your energy, is what allows you to move around freely in the facility. Only place anyone can walk without it is Intake."

She laughs. "But maybe you knew that, what with setting off the alarms as soon as you arrived by going down the *wrong hall*. But anyway. Right or left?"

It's so different from the first time. No straps. No Sena waiting in the corner like he'd rather be anywhere else. "Neither. I'll put it in my pocket."

Helner makes a production of her sigh. "Fine. You lose it, don't blame me."

He's situating it in his jacket pocket when Riese reappears out of nowhere, Travin at his elbow.

"Tory," Riese says, regal and warm. "Glad to see you're all right."

"For the moment," Helner says. "I see you brought my ride. Tory? I'll see you later. Got some tests I'm going to propose to the generals, so be ready for that."

She takes Travin's arm and makes a shooing gesture, and they blink away, leaving Riese and Tory alone in the hollowed-out camp. Tory tries on a smile, lips tilted into just the right shape. It fits wrong, but he knows from years of experience what Riese will want to hear. He says, "I'm ready."

"I know you are."

Warmth spreads through him, like a reward. He *is* ready. He can do this.

Riese drops a small, canvas-wrapped bundle into his hands, and Tory peeks inside to find three small devices. Smoke grenades, perhaps.

"Remember what I told you?"

Tory ticks the list off on his fingers. "Residence quarters, intake hall, and the room marked #004."

"Good. Activate them *in order*. They'll create a distraction so we can slip in."

"And the Cores . . . ?"

Riese lifts a stellite tower, pure and a few inches tall. "Push as much energy as you can spare into this thing. If you use enough, given your unique abilities, you should be able to resonate with all the crystals in the room, your energy essentially overriding what's already stored in them."

Tory considers that. "Doesn't that mean they all could be used to hunt *me*?"

"Yes. That's why you continue putting energy into this crystal until you hear it begin to crack."

"Do I want to know why?"

"It will explode *catastrophically*. The compasses won't be a problem after that."

"And me?"

"Sufficient desperation, remember?" Riese grins, vulpine. "If you get caught in the blast, your desperation wasn't sufficient enough. You'll need to run like there's fire on your feet as soon as you hear the first crack."

"I can do that."

"I know. Don't let anything distract you. Remember, wait until closer to evening to get started. Travin can't 'port the wagon, so we need the travel time. You have everything?"

Tory kneels to shove the bundle of supplies into the bottom of his pack. He has plenty of room—it's nearly empty without Thatcher's cloak. Something coils around his lungs, and he *doesn't* think of Sena shivering by the fire, doesn't let himself contemplate the future he dared to imagine for them.

He's been fine alone for over twelve years, and he'll be fine now. "Everything I need."

"You'll do well. You don't have to be afraid."

The miserable knot of nerves uncoils.

Travin arrives again behind them and chugs something from a canteen at his side.

Riese laughs and claps Travin on the back. "Sorry to make you work so hard. Just one more. Back here when you're done. We have work to do."

No-nonsense, like when Travin 'ported Iri out and left him to die. The anger the thought brings slips before it can find purchase. He's got this. He'll do well.

Travin executes a sloppy salute. "You got it, boss."

One hand is bandaged, and Tory remembers Riese's words. Sena hurt Travin when he left. Tory squints at the bruise between the bandages, blood-flooded blue—nearly black, halfway up his forearm and creeping to the tips of his fingers. He winces. Tries, again, to imagine Sena hurting Travin. His mind won't even unspool the images for him, the concept is so absurd.

Travin grabs Tory's elbow, and before he knows it, the world shifts. One moment, an isolated road covered with trees. Tory nearly loses his footing on the slope of the earth beneath him. His feet were angled for level ground.

Again—the rocky bank beside a creek. Tory does lose his footing this time. One knee goes into the creek, startling a lazy school of minnows. He curses and glares.

"Oh, I apologize. You new to 'porting?"

Again. Thick woods beside a familiar road, well worn and expertly paved. Tory arrives on his knees, and Travin lets go of his elbow, laughing. "Sorry, it's just so fun to see how the new ones take it."

Tory left his sense of equilibrium behind at the last jump. His head spins.

"And—for this, I'm *actually* sorry."

Tory has no time to ask what for. Travin's fist collides with his face, and pain bursts in bright colors as he crashes into dirt and leaf litter on his side. He tastes blood. His tongue darts out to find a split lip. "*What?*" he demands, belatedly.

Standing above him and shaking his left hand, Travin shrugs—only halfway apologetic. "Realism. You think they'd believe you found your way off a battlefield and all the way back looking so clean and put together?"

He's hardly *clean*. Tory wipes his expression blank. Stares at Travin until the guy shifts his weight and pushes out an awkward chuckle.

"Okay, fine," he confesses. "But listen, it was like . . . a really flimsy punch, because I had to do it left-handed. Spark made me promise to mess up your pretty face. You're not her target of choice, of course. That would have been—uh." He lifts his bandaged hand. "Anyway. Good luck."

Then he's gone, and Tory is alone.

He's fine. He has a job to do. Sitting up, Tory wipes blood from his lip and brushes mud and leaves from his clothes, for all the good it does. They're filthy beyond help, stiff with seawater and three-plus days of dirt, sweat, and worse. Given the option, he'd kill for a shower.

Tory stares through the woods and up the road where the sleeping cannons and the high walls around the Compound wait. Home, unsweet home.

He'll tear this prison down himself.

*

Sena and the others find the patrols faster than they hoped. A pillar of campfire smoke gives them away.

He and Niela refine their plan as they travel. If there's a full unit, they'll commandeer the services of its Porter to get Niela to the

Compound. With her Core, she'll be able to travel freely within its walls to warn her mother and maybe even Tory. Iri and Sena will use whatever other means of transport they find.

They come to the camp from the trees, the dampness of fallen leaves muffling their steps.

A couple soldiers playing cards on an overturned box startle as Sena walks from the woods. He shouldn't be surprised. His arm and shoulder are dark with blood. He probably looks more like a corpse than most corpses.

The soldiers jerk to clumsy attention. A few cards flutter to the ground, and Sena digs deep to find the perfect soldier Kirlov created in him. It doesn't fit well on him anymore, if it ever did. "At ease," he says. "Where's the officer in charge?"

"Out on a search, sir. We—uh, reports of activity in the area. Are you . . . ?"

"Your Porter," Sena barks. "I've come into possession of information I urgently need to convey to General Renstein. I need immediate transport to the Compound." Hopefully they don't know much about him, don't realize he *can't* be 'ported.

"Sir . . . ?"

The nearest soldier, thick and dark haired, steps forward. "Our Porter's out scouting. She'll be back in a few hours."

The Compound will be burning in a few hours, and Tory with it. "I said *urgent*, soldier."

The second guy speaks up. "Why not radio? You—where's your communicator?"

Sena's gloved hand slides over his empty pocket, and the soldier's eyes linger on the blood dried stiff into his glove. "It's gone. And the information is sensitive; better to deliver it in person."

The soldier casts a narrow-eyed glance into the trees, and Sena's stomach twists. He *knows* he looks suspicious, sounds suspicious.

"Sure, all right. Sir," the dark-haired soldier adds. "Gimme a second, maybe they can send someone." He paces over to the long-distance communication rig set up in the rear of the personnel truck. Sena hears snatches of conversation. "Yeah, ours is out on patrol," and "Yessir, says it's urgent. He's a real mess, too, so I'm inclined to believe him. If you have anyone you could spare . . ." He waves Sena over.

The first step nearly fells him. His vision blanks, knees wobbling, but he stays on his feet.

He has to. They have so little time. The world flickers back in, grayed-out and flat, just as he's arriving at the truck. He grabs the back of the truck to support himself.

"Got some questions before they'll send a Porter out." The soldier lifts his clunky headphones off and passes them over. "Here, I'll trade you."

Sena steps in front of the bulky rig, dropping the hand not holding him up over the dials.

The earphones blanket the ambient noise of the world in sweet silence—so when the voice comes through the headphones and pierces Sena's eardrums, it's everything.

It's his whole world.

Cold and crystal clear, Kirlov's voice says, *"Our Porters are indisposed. I've been informed there's urgent information you wish to convey. This is a secure channel. Report."*

Sena's heart staggers, stabs at him with a spike of whole-body pain. He shudders, knees giving out, and grips the back of the truck.

He makes a noise, he thinks—a whimper of reflexive fear he swallows before it can escape him.

Sound flees. He's *freezing*—dunked underwater, the rush of a mad river all around him. He's drowning, hauling mud into his lungs with every failed breath. His vision wavers.

"*Soldier, report.*"

Irritation, knife-sharp, from miles away, from somewhere above the water.

Water everywhere and his lips are bone-dry.

"*My pa*— . . . *nce is limi*—"

Crackling. Fragmentation.

Blissful silence.

Rust flecks floating away on the current, blood red.

"Shit!"

The earphones tear away from his head, and the world floods back in. The soldier stares wide-eyed at Sena, somewhere between horrified and lost. "What did you *do*?"

Beneath his hand, the massive communications rig has aged, polished chrome dials flaked away, metal body rusted through and pocked with holes. Its exposed innards share the same fate, tarnished and wrinkled and rusted-out in turns. Something fails, spits sparks over Sena's skin. They hiss out on the still-wet blood on his sleeve.

Sena tears his gloved hand away and stumbles back. "I . . ."

Iri and Niela burst from the woods at the commotion, and the soldier raises his gun and swings wide.

"Don't!" Sena manages, just as Niela yells, "Will *someone* tell me what's going on?"

The soldier grips his rifle, but he can't seem to decide where to point it.

Niela, still blood-smeared from front to feet, glares at him. Iri, glancing narrow-eyed between the soldiers, rolls a little ball of flame from palm to palm.

It's almost funny. It should be funny.

Fear hollows Sena out, and the laugh that escapes him is hysterical and hollow.

Going back to the Compound means going back to Kirlov, with the watch that could still kill Sena, with brutal expectations he can never live up to. Breath whistles in and out of him. Pain crashes cymbal-loud and all-consuming in his chest.

But Tory's at the Compound, too.

"I need . . ." He finds his way around to the driver's seat of the vehicle. Keys on the dash. He snatches them. "I need to take this."

Part of his training was learning how to operate one of these back when the first ones were manufactured. It's been a long time, but he'll make do.

The soldier's expression goes from slack shock to belligerence in an instant, grip on his rifle tightening. "Can't let you do that."

Niela stalks up behind him. "Don't think you can stop him."

The engine growls to life, too loud, like nettles on his skin. His vision fizzes gray and he swallows a surge of sickness. Niela pushes him out of the driver's seat. "Gimme the keys, Vantaras. You're in no condition to drive."

"Have you used one of these?"

"Nope. But I saw someone else do it, once."

Obligingly, Sena shifts the gear that will allow the vehicle to move forward.

Niela wiggles the steering wheel and shifts her feet until she finds the acceleration pedal. "Ah, yes, this'll be easy. Iri? Get the med kit. This boy needs help."

Then she floors it, tossing both the unsecured communication rig and an enterprising soldier attempting to climb into the back of the vehicle with a crash and a guttural yell.

"Come on, come on," she mutters. The truck jolts over every bump, the needle of its speed gauge shivering into the red zone. "We don't have *time* for this."

CHAPTER TWENTY-FIVE

HELNER FALLS IN beside Tory as soon as the soldiers drop him off inside the Compound's door. "You'd better have your story straight. Kirlov wants your report *right now.*"

The weight of the pack Riese gave Tory, stuffed with contraband, increases a thousandfold on his shoulder. "Can't I swing by my room first? Or—or wash up, at least?" He could put the pack in his locker. "Surely it'd be disrespectful to face the colonel like this."

But Helner with her *plausible deniability* has no idea what she's making him do.

"No time." She pulls him to a stop at a nondescript gray door and, before Tory can explain, tugs it open and shoves him inside. "Brought the Channeler!"

Colonel Erwin Kirlov waits on the other side of a gray table, hands steepled and posture rigid.

His cold eyes pin Tory. "Arknett."

Ice rushes through Tory. He quells the instinct to lean the shoulder carrying his pack away from Kirlov.

"Sit."

Kirlov's gesture exposes the watch he used to hurt Sena, and heat floods Tory. He should probably greet Kirlov with his rank. Should probably say something—anything at all. But Sena isn't here for Kirlov to punish for Tory's mistakes, so Tory just drops into the uncomfortable chair screwed into the floor on the other side of the table.

He slides his pack from his shoulder—as casually as he can while his heart drums double-time—and tucks it between his knees. He white-knuckles one of the straps when Kirlov's eyes go to the bag but unclenches his fist from the thing, bones creaking, to offer the man an unkind smile. "What's so important I wasn't allowed to shower?"

Kirlov's expression doesn't change in any way Tory can pinpoint, but the air in the room goes thin and frigid. "We'd like your account of what happened to Lieutenant Vantaras."

Matter-of-fact, without mercy.

Tory's fists ball, stomach churning acid.

It's fine. Whatever they see on his face, it'll only help him sell the story. "We were pushed over the cliffs by an explosion from a modified shell. We survived the fall, but Se—Lieutenant Vantaras was injured." The title comes easily, so far removed from Sena as Tory knows him that he can almost imagine he's telling a story about someone else. "It worsened as we traveled. We made it back to the battlefield to get our hands on a communicator, but . . ." After all the people he's healed—people whose names he can barely remember—"I couldn't heal him. I *tried*." He twines his hands together under the table and squeezes as tight as he can. He wants to move, not think, but he can't mess this up. Fidgeting will get him pinned as a liar, could draw attention to the pack between his knees.

"And the body?"

Wouldn't you like to know? It probably shows on his face, because Kirlov's eyes narrow. Tory wipes his expression clean. "In the woods."

"Which woods?"

"Ones with *trees*. I'm crap at navigation. Sena's—" He closes his teeth on his lip, lets the sharp burst of pain clear his head. "The *lieutenant* was the one who knew the terrain. I just went where he said. I . . . before he—" He's so weak. He can't even say it. "He said as long as I kept going northeast, I'd hit either the Compound or the road, so I kept going. I got here."

Helner ticks the sharp heel of her shoe against the floor. "If we're finished . . ."

"I believe we need a more thorough account of the lieutenant's decline. Arknett?"

Thorough like Sena's gentle smile by the light of the fire—apology and farewell in one? Like the way he tried to dissuade Tory from hoping he'd survive?

Like the whistle of air in his chest, maybe. He never once had hope for himself, and this bastard is the one who denied him that. Anger sits bitter on Tory's tongue. Back in Hulven, Tory had Hasra and Thatcher behind him, feeding him kindnesses he never let himself embrace.

Who did Sena have?

Helner paces over to the table. "Colonel, enough. This is getting morbid."

"*Doctor.* I did not ask your opinion. You will not be the one writing the report to the Grand General informing him of his son's passing. Arknett, as much as you remember."

Tory forces himself to speak. "When . . . when we hit the water, Lieutenant Vantaras took the brunt of it. Broken ribs, at least. He kept moving, said we needed to get back or we'd die." The words come out rote and flat. That's probably bad. It probably sounds like he's lying, but he can't make himself linger. "He was fevered on the second day, delirious. Coughing. I could tell it hurt. The last time I saw him, he was—" he chokes the words back. His head feels too full, a bare moment from cracking open. Lungs too small, air too far, bones too big. Tory pushes up from the chair. "I can't do this."

Because here's the awful truth of it: Sena had *him*, and maybe only him, and Tory promised to stay. Sena wasn't well. Maybe he didn't even know what he was doing when he left. Riese said he was confused.

It's easy to blame Kirlov, but Kirlov never played at being a friend.

"Sit *down*, Arknett. I will inform you when you're free to go."

But he can't. He's not sure his legs would bend for him if he tried.

"He's fresh from a slaughter, Colonel," Helner says. "The only person who survived with him is *dead*."

"That's the question, isn't it? Arknett, how are you sure he's dead? Before you left him, did you check for pulse and respiration?"

"I—" Tory's spread hands blur and waver on the table. The room grows smaller.

A hand seizes his arm. Helner? "We're leaving. This is going nowhere. Track the corpse if you need it so badly."

"I might. But we're not finished here. Once he's calmed down, bring him back."

With any luck, Tory will be long gone by the time Kirlov thinks to accost him again.

They make it to the door before Kirlov's voice stops them.

"Arknett."

"*What?*"

"Do you intend to leave your pack here?"

Adrenaline sears him. Tory snatches the pack from the floor and stalks out with Helner at his side, Kirlov's eyes following him the whole way.

*

Helner tracks him down after his shower. His hair's still dripping into his eyes, skin livid pink with the blistering heat of the water.

"Sorry to hit you with this, but for once in my life, thanks to some of the reports we've received of your performance in the field, I've gotten permission to run you through some exercises to see whether you'd be useful in the sword corps. I don't plan to waste the chance." She leads him down the hall as he towels his hair dry. "I really do think, if the generals stopped defining Seeds in such restrictive ways, we could change things for the better. Can you imagine Fielders doing offensive maneuvers? Creating a dome forcefield around a group of enemy soldiers and—" She makes a dome with her hands and collapses it with an accompanying squishing noise. "—just *crushing them*? There's more to all of us than they think."

She pauses, steps slowing, in front of a door. "I'll have to leave you here for a minute while I gather some things. I truly wasn't expecting to get permission this time—"

Her voice dies in her throat as she tugs the door open.

Tory's traitorous heart lurches at what's inside.

A dark-haired officer stands inside the room. Familiar undercut, dress uniform. A familiar stance.

But the officer turns, and he's too short, and too solidly built, features squished onto a mundane face. His expression is flat, lips pursed like he's bored. "Ah, Doctor. I'm sorry to interrupt, but you won't be performing your experiments today."

Helner's eyes narrow. "Won't I?" Her hand doesn't fist at her side. The fingers narrow to a spear-point, like she's considering Reaching into the officer's throat and pulling out his trachea.

"Change of plans," the officer drawls. "I was ordered to accompany a shipment of prototypes by the Grand General himself." At this, he stands straighter and gestures to encompass the high-ceilinged gray room. At the back, a massive pile of boxes has been stacked. A large, round target with red and white concentric circles has been mounted above the boxes, and a small group of Seeds stands facing the back wall. One wears a strange, bulky vest, like the one the Grand General wore when he visited.

Tory's knees knock. Back then, he didn't know how to recognize the static-sharpness of Sena's energy, but it's a beacon, bleeding off everything in those boxes. Off the target. The vests. He was never anything but an object to these people.

The officer gestures to the boxes. "You were informed they'd be arriving."

"A lot's happened since then."

"Well. General Vantaras' priority is to test these against battle-trained Seeds and see how they hold up. I've spoken to the sword corps and called away a few of their Kineticists to start."

"Why not do that in the capital?" Helner says, the kind of sweet that hides a sharp point.

"The other STAR compounds house Seeds with primarily non-offensive abilities. STAR-7 is our best bet at getting proper feedback."

"I'll take care of it, then. You can go," Helner says coldly.

"I'm afraid not. I've been asked to observe."

"You don't trust me."

"We simply believe two sets of feedback will be best. Besides, I'll be able to give my report in person. You may provide notes and offer suggestions, but I'll be taking the lead."

Helner's hand twitches at her side, and Tory wonders what organ she's daydreaming of removing. "Lieutenant—"

"*Major*," the officer corrects her, smile strained. He looks back to the gathered Kineticists. "Gentleman, please continue. Ah, hmm... #1, please throw an attack at the target. #2, direct an attack at #3. This time, please use all your strength."

The trainees must have gotten used to being referred to by numbers, because they obey. Their energy is a sizzling, electric thing. Tory can't help his reflexive flinch, but both attacks naturally fizzle out before landing, the small metal balls they're using as projectiles slowing and dropping before they hit their target.

The officer's eyes dance, and he lifts a clipboard from his side and jots urgent notes. "Excellent. Oh, *excellent*, this is better than anticipated." He smirks at Helner. "As you may have noticed, Doctor, the material used to create the target and the vest has... unique properties."

"I noticed," Helner bites out.

"In addition to the vests and targets, we've also sent some of what we're calling N001, a nullifying agent. We have it in injectable syringe form, dart form, and gaseous form, to disable enemies. Naturally, we'll need to test all varieties and record the effects. The Grand General is especially interested in how the gaseous form works in both enclosed spaces and open air and how long we can expect enemies' abilities to be inaccessible after exposure."

"Enemies," Helner echoes, hollow. "Both Arlune and Westrice's fighting forces are Seeds. These weapons will disable both sides."

"Yes," the man says, thoughtful. "But we need to think of the future."

Helner says what Tory's thinking, fiery as ever. "*Lieutenant,* what future could we possibly be preparing for with anti-Seed weaponry? Civil war?"

"Doctor!" The officer's spine goes rigid. "I'm not at liberty to discuss that."

"And he's using his son to do it. That boy really is better off dead."

Tory closes his eyes, but the feeling growing in him is closer to rage than sorrow. How dare these people? How *dare* the Grand General turn someone as gentle as Sena into a weapon?

The officer straightens a uniform that's not in need of straightening. "A minor inconvenience, that, but nothing we can't work past. Luckily, the compound in the Neutralizer's blood is stable and powerful in very small doses. Our existing stock should serve us for *years.*" He brightens. "Ah, forgive me. Is this the Channeler, then? The Grand General believes it would be wise to repeat the experiments but have the Channeler gather and combine the attacks before directing them at their targets. We'd be interested to see if the unique skills of the Channeler change the way the neutralizing component reacts to attacks."

He pauses after he speaks, like he expects Tory to leap to attention and execute his orders.

"Channeler?" The officer says again. It's weird to recognize how different it is from how Sena said *Worldseed*. The officer says Channeler like a person might say hammer.

"I have a name."

"And I would use it if it were relevant to our work here."

Anger coils in Tory's stomach, and he strides over to where the officer has indicated.

"Good. Kineticists, please accelerate attacks toward the Channeler as a group. Channeler, redirect those attacks toward the target."

A long pause. The officer's pen waits, poised over his clipboard.

"I'd appreciate verbal affirmation."

"Fine," Tory says.

When the three Seeds throw attacks at him, it's child's play to steal the energy. It takes a bit more focus to combine and direct them, but he already did it during his escape attempt, and he handled energy on a much larger scale on the battlefield.

As expected, the attacks die before reaching the target.

The officer jots a few more notes. "Very good. Keep going. Kineticists, give it everything you have. Don't let up—once one attack is redirected, send another. It's important that we discover whether the target's effects are static or exhaustible."

The sizzle of their energy approaching fast in the periphery says they're obeying, and Tory steals and slings those attacks, as well. Sena's energy neutralizes them.

It's nothing like his actual presence. Even with every prototype they've made—the Null and the neutralizing vests and the targets and whatever else waits in those boxes stacked at the back of the room—the energy is negligible. If *this* were the extent of Sena's energy, Tory could have crushed it to a pinprick and healed him, easy—soothed his fever, sealed broken bones. He could have saved him. This is *weak* in comparison. He could lift and move it, could expand it.

The next attack, he tries. The energy jumps to do his bidding as readily as it ever has. Tory spreads it until it's riddled with holes, nothing like Sena's energy that unfurled over miles of forest. He wonders, with a pang, how far he'd have needed to expand it before it showed holes like this. Which one of them would reach their limit first?

It's a silly question, and not one he'll ever be allowed to find the answer to. He was so stupid. He should have stayed, should've *looked*.

The more he thinks about it, the more his insides knot up and his flimsy self-justifications flood away. They seem so childish, a transparently thin veneer over his own cowardice. Why didn't he scour the woods, reach out for that beacon-like energy? Why, when he wasn't too late to save him?

He'll free every Seed with what he's going to do today—every Seed except the one they had most thoroughly under their thumb. It doesn't fill him with the same glowing purpose it did when he talked about it with Riese. He expands the energy farther, then directs the kinetic attacks at the back of the room.

The target—and the wall behind it—burst where the energy stretches thin. The wall craters, spilling stone. The boxes explode with the force Tory throws at them. Vests shred. Vials burst. Slivers of stone and wood and whatever the target is made from slice at him as they fly past with the force of the explosion.

Blood drips from at least four fine cuts on Tory's face and arms as silence settles over the room, and it's not enough. It's not satisfying, but it's something.

Sena asked him, after all. If he saw any of the weapons they'd made from Sena's blood, he was supposed to ruin them.

It's Tory's turn to smile, a hollow thing. Next time, he'll turn every last item they've made from Sena's stolen blood to dust. He won't stop with STAR-7. Everything here, and then everything from here to Maran. The Grand General thinks he's so clever, cutting Sena open to torture him, bleeding him to subdue other Seeds. Tory will track every sliver of that lightning-storm energy that calls to him like a song. None of these people deserve to have any part of Sena. "Keep it coming."

The officer glances, mute, between Tory and the shredded target and blown-open boxes. A clear fluid that must be Null spreads out along the ground at the back, mixing with stone-dust. After a moment of gaping, the officer bursts into a flurry of motion. "I—that—there's clearly been a mistake. This is—this shouldn't *be*—"

The Kineticists scatter as chunks of concrete crash down.

Tory executes the most mocking bow in his arsenal, loose as a sated predator. He pastes on a concerned expression, too sweet. "I think they might be broken. Maybe you should run back to Vantaras and tell him he'll need to try harder next time."

The pen slips from the officer's lax fingers. He doesn't bend to retrieve it.

Helner clucks her tongue and scurries over to Tory. "Oh dear!" she says, playing it up. "You're bleeding! I should take you to the infirmary, can't let the General's best weapon bleed out on the floor . . ."

The officer's mouth opens again, but Helner has already seized Tory's elbow and begun to pull him from the room. "Stars!" she muses, performatively loud. "No idea what went wrong. That was horrible, wow!"

But when she gets him a ways down the hall, she rounds on him, eyes glittering. "*Fuck yes.* Absolutely stellar. You'll have to tell me what you did after we get Jeffra to clean up your pretty face. What have you been *eating* since I saw you last?" She ushers away her own question with a wave of her hand as she stops him in front of the infirmary door. "Tell me later. I'd better get back and smooth things over in there."

Then she's gone, heels ticking down the hallway.

The thrill he got from destroying everything in that room lasts only as long as it takes Jeffra to notice him standing in front of the door and open it.

The silence presses between them, suffocating. Last time he was here, Niela was sprawled on a chair in the corner, avoiding work. And right over there was where Sena—

Tory retreats. "Sorry, I'll just—"

She drags him inside by the wrist. "You're bleeding on my clean floor."

He could be bleeding on someone *else's* clean floor if she'd let him.

She gestures to one of the treatment beds. "You know the drill."

"They're superficial. They'll scab up in a minute. I'll just go."

Jeffra pushes him down onto the nearest bed. "I insist. We need to catch up, don't we?"

Tory isn't so sure. What is there to say?

She heals him to the tune of cheerful birdsong, closing cuts and flinging splinters into the trash as she urges his flesh to give them up. A small cage hangs in the corner of the room, close to the west-facing window. A vibrant yellow bird twitters and swings as the warmth of healing spreads through Tory.

"Glad to see you safe," Jeffra says, quiet. Her hands linger too long. Twice, she opens her mouth like she wants to speak. Tory's eyes keep finding the bird.

He doesn't mean to say it. "Sena's?"

Jeffra follows his eyes. "Sweet, isn't he? I think he's a good addition. Music can be as healing as anything. His name is Kierney."

Kierney who makes a nest of Sena's hair, who made Sena smile like a child by the fire. He can't push words past the stone in his throat.

Jeffra bustles over to the other side of the room, where she begins to make an already made bed, smoothing out invisible wrinkles. Back facing him, she says, "I know you were out there. I heard about the battle." He knows the question is coming before he watches the tension coil through her spine. At last, she says, "Niela, did you see her?"

Tory winces. "Jeffra . . ."

"I asked because I wanted an answer."

". . . All right, then. I saw her."

Jeffra waits.

"Randall was—he was." Tory can't look at her. "Niela tried to heal him."

"Fool girl," Jeffra whispers.

"It was chaos. I didn't see her after that, but . . ."

Jeffra nods, hands riding over the blanket on the cot in a long, gentle sweep before she pulls herself up. "All right. I asked because I wanted an answer." She sets her shoulders, sets her mouth into a grim line. "I've done enough blubbering, so I'm going to ask you to give my hands some work to do. What else hurts?"

"Jeffra. You don't have to."

"I always have to! It's our job. It was *her* job. Doesn't matter how we feel. We go out and fix things."

"Not today," Tory says. "I won't tell anyone."

Kierney continues his cheery tune.

"Just tell me what else hurts. Don't make an old woman go looking."

"Nothing much."

Her hands settle on either side of him, brown eyes unsettlingly close and steady. "Don't *nothing much* me. Pain is your body's free warning system. I'll thank you not to ignore it."

That damn bird won't stop singing. Tory throws his arm over his eyes, muffles his next words into his elbow. "I just need to *focus*. I don't have time to be weak, to think—" He has a mission. He gulps a breath in, exhales the disgusting heat of it against his face. "I don't need this."

Jeffra tuts, and the warmth starts up again, seeking out little pains. After a while, she says, "I don't think you have any idea what you need."

"It's *over*, it's not important anymore—"

"Did you hear a word I said? If something hurts, it's *because* it's important. My girl was important. Sena? He was important. The important things are ugly. They leave scars. What you're feeling, that's how you know it mattered."

It mattered. The truth is a horrible thing in retrospect. Mattered, past tense, because he turned away to save himself. He doesn't feel saved. He feels eviscerated. "I left him there. I left him behind."

She lets his words sit between them. "Then hold on tighter next time."

He's not sure why he says what he says next. Jeffra's matter-of-factness, maybe. The birdsong. The underwater dimness in here, hazy as a dream or a secret. The words slip out before he can stop them: "I hate how the world looks without him. I'd take his place, if I could."

The words strip him bare. He wishes he could stuff them back inside.

Jeffra just nods. The healing energy fades out, slow.

"Tired," Tory murmurs. His vision blurs anew, and that cursed bird keeps singing. He squeezes his burning eyelids closed.

He waits for Jeffra to tell him she's plenty busy without a lazy-ass dodging duty in her infirmary, but a heavy hand smooths his hair down.

"Sleep, then."

He could, easily. He wants to, but he makes himself stand. He can't save Sena, but he can save a lot of other Seeds today. *More important than survival*, Sena said.

Tory can do this for him, if nothing else. An apology in action. He'll do this, and then he'll go back. He'll search those woods and find Sena, even if the only thing left to do is bury him. Grieve for him, without hiding.

"There's something I have to do."

Jeffra waves him out, smile slow and sad. "Stay out of trouble, all right?"

"Can't promise anything."

The devices Riese gave him to create interference wait at the bottom of his pack. Intake, residence quarters, and the room marked #004.

First those, then the Monitor Room.

A swell of Sena's energy stops him in his tracks as he paces down the hall. Tory's stride falters, a surge of foolish hope nearly tripping him over his own feet.

He pauses in front of a closed door and pulls Sena's stolen tab from his pocket, dangling it in front of the stellite slice in the door until it unlocks.

There's more than one source of Sena's energy inside, but the most intense one is a small cube of dull gray metal on a crowded, paper-strewn desk, the seam between the box and its lid barely visible.

The type-determination tests, the targets, the vest, Null, and now this cube. Tory snatches the box off the desk and tucks it under his arm. It's his, now.

The density of the energy coming off the thing is ten times stronger than that off the targets. The familiar buzz of it warms him as he stalks down the hall. He tips his pack off one shoulder and swings it around front. It'll be a tight fit, but he can probably fit the cube inside. He stops before dropping it in, curiosity getting the better of him. He gets why they'd use Sena's energy for the type tests, for Null. But why a *box?* What is it they're neutralizing?

Tory pries one corner of the lid up and nearly drops the whole thing as a billow of crushing, disconcerting heat rolls through him. "Shit!" He punches the lid back on as something inside the box stirs, like it's moving from sleep to slow wakefulness. Vines.

Of course. Of course they'd store a *Legion unit* in a box like this.

Tory shoves the thing deep into his pack and hurries down the hall.

*

Sena shakes awake to haze in his head, heavy-limbed slowness, and the shadowless solid gray of an overcast sky.

At Niela's bidding, Iri pumped Sena full of whatever was in the med kit before he fell asleep. Painkillers, antibiotics. Ointment and a simple dressing for the scalpel wound and another for the blistered injection site in the crook of his elbow.

Niela must notice him stirring. "Feeling any better?"

"Yes, thank you." He's feeling a different sort of worse, so it's not a lie. "How far out?"

Her lips turn up in a determined grimace. "A few minutes if the fuel lasts that long."

The meter shivers on empty.

Niela taps her foot on the accelerator, but she's already flooring it.

A few minutes.

They crest a hill, and the world spreads out beneath them. The great, cold mass of the Compound and the sea of trees with their fading, yellow-brown leaves block the sight of the Golden River Anton Chimre fell in love with and the rocks beyond it, mined bare of stellite. In the sterile Compound's high walls, pinprick-sized Seeds scurry to training, to dinner, to the infirmary.

"The sun is almost down. Riese and the others are likely already there." Iri squints down the road. "No smoke, screaming, or other signs of chaos, so whatever he's making Tory do, it hasn't happened yet. That's good. I am going to kill him." The words come out soft and strangely thoughtful.

Sena's NOVA winds around his spine tight enough to crush it. The man who can use it to kill him waits beyond those walls, but Tory's in there, too. What a rotten choice to be left with.

"How will we get in?"

They're hardly an impressive fighting force.

Niela frowns. "You'll have to convince them to let us in the front, then you can find Tory and convince him to stop whatever idiocy this Riese guy's put him up to."

Sena has never been convincing. "I don't know if that's the best idea."

"We don't have time for better ones." Niela's knuckles show like blades from her bloodless grip on the steering wheel. "You've got this, right? Tell me you've got this."

Trees swallow the Compound and its suffocating walls as they descend the hill.

Sena breathes while he still can. "I've got this."

"You're a terrible liar." Niela pulls off the road at the rim of the forest, and they get out.

Even with the drugs softening the edges of his pain, it thuds up through Sena's bones. The earth pulls him down, pulls his eyelids low, begs him to sink into a long sleep.

"I've got this," Sena says again.

Iri and Niela exchange a conversation in glances, and Sena closes his eyes. He *can* keep going. Ahead of him, beyond the trees, yellowing grass and a serpentine black road slither up toward the sharp-toothed gate.

Iri speaks first, voice soft but gaze steely. His eyes turn, unerring, to the right, and he rubs the flint rings on his thumbs to create a spark he builds into a sphere, wild flames licking from the circle. "You both go ahead. I'll make sure no one stops you."

"Be careful," he says.

Iri raises an eyebrow. "Surely you know me better than that by now. I will see you when this is finished."

It's probably not appropriate to admit that he doesn't expect to leave these walls once he enters them.

Niela settles in beside him as Iri disappears into the woods, red-lit by his flames.

"Let's go," Sena says.

Anxiety churns in his gut as they walk the wide-open road toward the guard tower. Sena barely dares to breathe. But Iri was as good as his word. No one intercepts them on their way up.

The gate guard behind the window's smoky glass jumps to attention as always, but his posture slackens with shock as he takes both of them in. "Sir! You're . . ."

"I've come with urgent information to report."

"Everyone's saying you were . . ."

Sena forces calm over himself. "I need to enter."

"It's. Um. See, it's complicated, a bit, because your permissions to enter have been revoked with, uh, your presumed death. I'd have to . . . I'd at least need to contact the colonel and—"

"No!" The word tears itself from Sena's throat. "I'll report when I'm inside. Private Jemmes, please. Time is of the essence."

A sigh, a restless tapping on the table. "This is highly unusual. I'll need to see your tab, at least."

Sena's hand dives into the pocket where he keeps it, and he finds nothing. "That's part of the problem," he blurts. "A . . . security breach." Oh, he's awful at this. "Rebels intercepted me near the border" —true— "and took it." Lie? "We need to immediately change security protocols or we'll be vulnerable to attack." Irrelevant, given the situation.

"Oh!" The boy's eyes widen. "If that's the case, surely I should—"

Niela stomps around to the window, and she really is a vision, bathed in Iri's still wet blood and the dried blood from the sheet-covered boy she couldn't save. "Don't you get it? How do you think they found him?" she hisses, and Private Jemmes jolts back, eyes wide. "The higher-ups are *part* of it. Don't you get it? At least one of them is in on it. Are you a gambler, Private?"

"This . . . I can't," Jemmes mumbles. "I mean, I *shouldn't* . . ."

"You should," Niela says, "If you want anyone within these walls to survive the night."

Jemmes blinks rapidly, and the gate whips up into the wall. He stares after them, eyes huge and round, as they approach it.

"Hurry," Niela whispers. "He starts thinking about any of that and he'll find holes big enough to swim through."

Sena resists the urge to apologize until the toothy maw of the gate clamps shut behind them, locking them inside. If the Compound survives, Jemmes will lose his job for this.

At the end of the path, the blacked-out glass of the Compound's entrance casts its interior in subdued charcoal and blue. It opens as they draw near. Sena's feet slowing until he stands, frozen, on the threshold.

"You know, I swore I'd die before I'd come back here." Sharp tines of fear rake down his spine.

Once he enters the Compound, his NOVA will almost certainly be within range. If Kirlov sees Sena, if he visits the Monitor Room to examine his compass—

"Why change your mind? There's no accounting for taste, but Tory seems a bit of a . . . work in progress."

Sena smiles. "Yeah."

Niela's hand settles on his sleeve when he tilts, vision fading. "Be careful. Those injections might help the pain, but they're a stopgap at best. I couldn't heal Randall," she whispers, "and I can't heal you. I'm sorry."

Sena tries on a smile. "Go ahead, find your mom."

"And you go find your idiot."

They enter STAR-7. Niela goes right. Sena goes left.

Not too far in, he runs into a huddled, murmuring group of Seeds. They pin him with a stare as he passes, like they've seen a ghost. Sena's probably looking at them the same way.

"Lieutenant Vantaras, we thought you'd—"

It's easy to fall into the role he's played for so long. "Rumors poison the mind," he snaps. "Why aren't you at training?"

"I—we—"

"Where is Arknett?"

The spokesman of the group opens his mouth, then closes it. He ducks into the group and whispers furiously. Another guy, gangly and tired, speaks up.

"Saw him running down the halls earlier like his ass was on fire."

"Which direction?"

The guy points, and Sena follows.

They sink into whispers as soon as he's put them behind him, but he has no time for them. The hallway blurs past, dizzying and too bright. In the Compound, everything is clear-cut and flooded with cold light. Squinting, Sena scans every room he passes. He doesn't linger, doesn't dare contemplate what the light reveals about him.

He doesn't see Tory. Doesn't see anyone who can tell him where Tory is.

A soldier stops dead as Sena passes, and Sena can't help meeting his shocked eyes. The man hurries away at a near run. Wherever he's going, it can't be good, but Sena has neither the time nor strength to pursue him.

He loses his breath when Tory, pack hanging from one shoulder, stalks across an intersecting hallway ahead of him.

Sena quickens his pace, takes a right down a familiar short corridor: Tory must be heading for the tree.

Sure enough, the click of the door to the central garden spears the silence as it opens.

He grabs it before it can close and freezes there, trying to breathe.

He's here, and Tory's here, and he's not the least bit ready to see him.

He opens the door anyway.

CHAPTER TWENTY-SIX

OF COURSE TORY turns the moment the door opens. Sena should have known he would.

His shock is almost comical, his hair a mess, mouth half-open. The bruises under his red eyes say he's probably been sleeping about as well as Sena has.

Sena opens his mouth and can't speak, frozen with the awful, selfish desire to take more than his hands can hold. It was easier being apart.

Tory's face flits through several expressions—something open and painful: hope, maybe; confusion; determined stillness. It settles on a sharp-edged thing. Not anger, but nothing Sena can put a name to. "I can't—" Tory shakes his head, walks straight at Sena. He's trembling, and an apology sits on Sena's lips, unspoken.

Sena tears himself from his paralysis and snags Tory's arm, holding as tight as his hands will allow. "Please."

Tory flinches and scrubs his free hand over his face. "You're *alive*. I—shit, are you—*Sena*. I . . . I don't have time for this now."

Sena doesn't have time for anything except this. "I need you to listen. I'm not sure how long I have before they—" he peers through the open door into the sterile, too-bright hallway. No clamor of running footsteps yet, but it's only a matter of time. He steps forward to let the door slip closed behind him. "Someone saw me coming in."

Tory pins him with that angry-adjacent look, terrible up close. "Why did you come back? I thought . . ."

Sena shifts his gaze over to the tree, serene in diffuse gray daylight. He blurts, "Riese lied to you." Probably not the best place to start, but his limbs are too heavy, and he doesn't know how much longer he'll be able to stand. He explains the rest haltingly. Riese's power, Iri's survival. Riese's plan. If he talks long enough, he won't have to get to the hardest part.

"Why'd you leave?" Tory asks.

Again, he skims the ugliest truth: he won't be able to stay this time, either. "I didn't want to. My energies made you immune to Riese's influence. Travin came into my tent after Riese took you away. He tried to kill me. Would have succeeded, but—I managed to get a hold of his arm and—" Sickness churns in his stomach. Tory may not even believe him. "I—"

Tory doesn't need him to finish, apparently. "His *hand*. Shit, I should've known those weren't bruises. That *bastard!* I hope it rots off slow."

Relief spreads through Sena, warm like the cloak Tory let him borrow.

Tory continues his tirade. "He was all buddy-buddy with me when he brought me here, too, after—after . . . What about Dr. Helner?"

"I met her on my way out." Which reminds him— "She stabbed me a little. I got blood on your cloak. I'll fix it."

"Whoa, back up. She *stabbed you?* A *little?*"

"Just a scalpel. I doubt it was her choice. My best guess is Riese put both her and Travin up to it."

Tory curses and stomps in a circle, and Sena can't help the smile that tips his lips up, the warmth of having someone on his side.

"Sorry," he volunteers. Surely there are better, more precise words for conversations like these, but he's never had a chance to practice them.

It is, Sena discovers, the worst thing he could have said. Color flees Tory's face. "No," he says, and Sena scrambles to understand how he messed up.

"No," Tory says again, rough and low. "*I'm* sorry. When I found you gone, I—"

The worry clears, and Sena breathes. "It's fine."

"It's not! Damn it, Sena, it's okay to be pissed at me."

"I know. But I'm not, and we are—again—on a timeline."

Tory frowns. "Fine, okay. Later, then."

Did Tory just schedule a time for Sena to be angry with him? Happiness is a fragile flutter in Sena's chest. "Later," he lies.

"Wait, you got *stabbed*. We need to fix it." Tory looks around, like maybe a medical kit will be lying on the ground.

"No need. Someone wrapped it for me. We should get to work."

As if he's just remembering, Tory says, "The Monitor Room! Was that part true? If it's destroyed—"

Sena's stomach sinks. "That part's true."

"I meant to—Sena! If we destroy the compasses, they won't be able to disable your Core! It's not—It's not the perfect solution, but it could work, right?" That *smile*, like an epiphany or a promise, childlike in its uncomplicated joy. "Everyone here, free. Your dad's war effort derailed. And both of us . . ."

Sena wants Tory's words to be true with a fierceness that brings physical pain. He can have *this*, anyway, for a little longer. He dredges up a smile. "We should get to it, then, huh?"

"Yeah. Let's mess some shit up."

Tory thrusts his left hand forward.

It's such a ridiculous thing, that it's his left. Tory isn't left-handed, and the only way Sena can think to explain it is maybe he's either noticed that Sena is having difficulty moving his right at the moment or that Sena is, in fact, left-handed. It's such a small thing, a gesture to meet Sena where he is. He aches with it.

Tory's radiant smile crinkles his eyes, and he looks so young, his stance loose and open, extended hand an invitation to something Sena has barely dared to hope for.

Steady, like taking what he wants could really be so simple.

Star-blessed, Sena's mother called him. To everyone else, he was strange, uniquely dangerous. Sena got the message quickly enough; he was something to be used and feared. No one offered nearness. It was easy enough, after a time, to avoid it entirely.

He'd do anything to keep this. Yet here he stands, frozen like a fool.

Tory's smile flickers, fingers curling and eyes flashing doubt.

Sena wants this and more. He's wanted it since he knew his hands could make things grow. Drawing as deep a deep breath as his chest will allow, Sena peels the glove from his left hand and drops it onto the moss between the tree's roots. He extends his hand. The trembling is faint enough that Tory won't notice, surely.

He regrets it instantly. There are so many reasons why it could be a bad idea, and maybe Tory doesn't even want—

He gasps as a strong grip closes around his hand, warm skin callused and real against his. He loses an embarrassing amount of time looking at the way their hands meet, skin against skin. Tory is so warm.

Tory clears his throat, but he's *beaming*. "It's called a handshake for a reason. You shake it, and then you *let go*."

Sena laughs. He doesn't mean to, and it startles him. Startles Tory, too. Sena withdraws his hand, tingling with the heat of another person's touch for the first time since he was nine. He feels lit up, like he's bumping against the netted dome over the tree and could slip through and float up into the sky. Laughing hurts, but he can't stop.

Tory joins him. "You're so weird," he says. Then, "You know, you owe me."

Sena frowns. "Owe you what?"

"A story. You never finished telling me about that—sky-dog or whatever, and the Seeds."

Sky-dog. Something in Sena shrivels. "*Celestial Beast*," he says. "And you keep saying my stories are terrible. I don't owe you anything. Anyway, my mother tells it best."

Traitorous, his mind spools out images of his mother as he last saw her, and Hina as Sena imagines her, and Tory listening raptly to the tales that gave Sena such hope when he was small. It's nice, like all impossible things are.

Dark haze closes in around his eyes, and he squeezes the bridge of his nose and breathes until it recedes.

Tory opens his mouth like he wants to say something, but Sena shakes his head.

"The compasses. We should get started."

"Yeah. Let's cause some chaos. Oh. Speaking of! They brought those prototypes your dad made with your blood. I ruined them all, just like you asked me to."

He did ask, didn't he? By the fire. "I would have liked to see that. Thank you."

"Any time." Tory claps a hand down on Sena's shoulder—the shoulder with his decaying Core, with the wound, the arm blistered by Helner's injection—and Sena makes a sound he'd be ashamed of if his whole body weren't burning.

He flinches, crumples—barely manages to catch himself with his left hand, splayed bare on the moss, grass, and gravel.

He tries to force his feet to lift him. He can't ruin this fragile peace. "Sorry," he slurs. "I'm . . ."

"Sena." Tory's voice from above him is quiet. "What's that on your neck?"

Sena burns with something hotter than pain. He lifts his shoulders to hide it, but it's too late. The roots of his dying Core must be visible. If he's lucky, Tory won't understand. "Let's just go."

He can't look at Tory's face, at the dawning horror on it.

"Sena, are you—"

Obligingly, the world falls apart to spare him having to answer.

The sound comes first—a rumble, then a deep and hollow *crack*. Another follows it, then another. The world shakes, then there's nothing and everything, and Sena is on the ground, vision fizzing.

His head is screaming. Something's screaming, anyway.

Someone? A high whine. Rock dust and smoke clog his nose, and he doesn't want to cough but he can't stop. Smoke burns his eyes and something wet tracks down his face. Colors swirl above him, white and gray and green, green, green. Muted thuds all around.

Roots beneath him, digging into his back, and—

"Sena, move!"

Hands pull him beneath the branches of the tree. More thuds shake the ground.

The sky falls in great chunks.

He catches his breath, manages, "What . . .?"

Tory's face is wet, too. Red. In his hair and down over his ear. Sena reaches up, gets it on his bare hand. Tory hisses, and Sena snaps back to himself. This, he understands. "You're hurt."

"That doesn't matter!" Tory's eyes dart beyond the tree, and Sena's head is still screaming and all the colors are yelling, flaring bright and sharp enough to stab a man, but he squints and sees what Tory sees.

The wall around the garden lays in ruins, exposing the Compound's innards. No longer is it lit in cold colors. Bursts of flame light the semi-darkness blue and gold. Smoke billows out, and the cracks race up and up and—

The dome over the garden has crumbled on the same side, netting hanging down and beams littering the ground. One, indeed, right where Sena was lying.

"What . . .?" he says again. Perhaps a better question: "Why?"

He can barely hear his own voice over the screaming. His awareness trickles back slowly. *Not* screaming—the wail of alarms and a ringing in his ears.

"I don't—" Tory shakes his head. "Oh." His eyes shift to Sena, his lips bloodless white, and they're all Sena can focus on as he says, "I did this. This is my fault."

*

Tory did this.

He turns to the gaping wound in the wall in front of him, surrounded with spidering lines. "One in Intake." Then to the cracks splitting the wall at the right rear end of the circular, enclosed garden. "One in . . . in residence quarters." Finally, he turns to the third place that shows damage, a hole disgorging chunks of stone and twisted metal into the garden: the room that was numbered, not named. #004.

The damage sits in a neat triangle, and Tory knows it well. He spent the better part of an hour running around the Compound to place those devices. "I did this." Tory swallows. "I didn't mean to. He said—"

Riese said they'd create a *distraction*. He never said what kind. Tory just assumed it would be benign.

"I was so stupid."

"You didn't know." Sena moves Tory with a hand at his back. "Come on. Let's go."

A wrenching snap at the rear makes his point for him. Cracks spread up the wall. Another corner of the dome crumbles, dropping metal beams into the erstwhile flowerbed overrun with vines. More chunks of the wall collapse to fill the hole, and the area sags. Sena drags at the door in its warped frame, pulling it until there's a gap large enough to escape through.

Sena tips his chin toward the gutted remains of the room formerly labeled #004. "Central power. If the blast destroyed the stellite core that powers the facility and centralizes its security, the existing arrays will only have what little energy they currently hold—or whatever's in the much smaller backup core, if it survived." He pales. "We have to hurry. We need to get to the Monitor Room before the switch."

"Why?" Tory pushes through the door and into the hallway. Sena follows, but he, like Tory, caught some shrapnel, and his face is wet with blood.

"Because if it switches to backup, the tabs will no longer work, and we'll be locked out. Faster." He says it as much to himself as to Tory. "My presence won't go unnoticed for long. If the colonel—"

The lights dim to sickly gray as they half-run through the halls. A rumble punctures the tense silence, shuddering up through the soles of their feet. Sena staggers.

Part of the building must have collapsed.

It's not a good time for it—not a good time for anything, but Tory can't get those stark blue-black lines up Sena's neck out of his head. He saw those vein-like roots just yesterday on a platter in front of him, except his were a deep red. Sena's pallor, the way he crumpled when Tory touched his shoulder—it tells a story Tory doesn't want to contemplate. "Your Core."

Sena squeezes his eyes closed. "Tory, please . . ."

"How?"

The halls grow hazy with smoke, and Tory coughs and squints.

"Helner," Sena finally whispers, supporting himself with a hand along the wall. "The 'antibiotics' she gave me."

"I'll *kill her*." Helpless anger careens through him and leaves him shaking.

"It wasn't her choice."

Tory growls. "Riese, then. I'll gag the bastard and gut him slow."

Sena sighs. "Don't worry about it."

"What do you mean, don't—" Tory closes his lips on the flood of words he wants to say, but some escape, anyway. "How did I get stuck doing this?"

"Doing what?"

"Hoping there's a way to fix this. You're so fucking calm, and you're *dying*, and I can't keep—" His conversation with Jeffra comes back and he breathes out an awful laugh, because he has his second chance, his *next time*, but he has no idea how anyone is supposed to do this better. He doesn't know what to do because there's nothing he *can* do but watch Sena leave again.

Sena reaches out, but his fingers close before reaching Tory. "You don't have to," he manages.

"Too fucking bad. I can't help it."

*

The Monitor Room waits for Sena like a sea of wide-open eyes.

The brittle, processed stellite that powers the facility leaks energy like a sieve. The compasses in the Monitor Room, though, each with a hook and a plaque with the locker number of its corresponding Seed, are powered by the energy of the Core-bearing Seeds. The crystals at the center of the tracking compasses for all the still-living Seeds glow brilliant white. For any who are farther away, the glow is dimmer and more orange-tinted, the compass needle fixed in the direction the holder must travel to find them. For the dead, the light is gone. Many lights are gone, after the explosions.

Sena seeks out his own slot at the far end of the room, below the plaque labeled #001. It's empty.

Someone was here, looking for him.

The compass labeled #002 swings on its hook, like whoever took Sena's compass was in a hurry and knocked its neighbor on the way past.

The compass swings like a pendulum, a cruel countdown.

The person who took it to hunt Sena must have left just before they arrived.

Perhaps it was taken for a mundane reason. Sena hasn't had the opportunity to observe what the slow death of a Core inside its bearer does to the light on the compass, but it can't be a pleasant thing. Perhaps they assumed him dead and took the compass to the labs for disassembly so the number could be assigned to the next Seed to come through STAR-7.

But when has he ever been so lucky?

The murmuring Seeds in the hallway and the soldier who hurried away double-time flicker through his mind. But none of them would have access to this room. Sena wouldn't even have been able to get inside if Tory didn't return his tab to him, sheepish, when they arrived at the door.

Sena's knees knock when Tory's hand lands on his shoulder, and he suppresses the childish urge to turn toward Tory and lean against him.

"That's not good."

Only officers have access to this room.

Kirlov, then. Sena's muscles lock in anticipation of pain, and he forces them to slacken. He chose this, and he won't let even Kirlov stop him from seeing it through.

Tory withdraws a crystal core from his pack. It's several times larger than the delicate point hanging from Sena's pendant, but it's only half as pure.

Tory feeds energy into it until the crystal glows as blue as it did back when Tory touched the Legion. It's lovely, Sena thinks. It's a good color for Tory. The one time Sena fed his energy into stellite, before he startled and killed it, turning it a milky gray, the light it emitted was frightening red.

The compasses along the wall brighten, flicker—glowing for just a moment with Tory's colors.

Sweat breaks out on Tory's forehead, and Sena gives himself permission to lean into him. Just for now. If Tory asks, Sena will say it's because he thought Tory might fall over.

The crystal continues to glow, searingly bright. Sena hears little pings. Cracks.

Tory is overloading the stellite, but all the compasses have already shifted pure blue, overwritten. They can never be used to track another Seed again. Everyone here is now free, even if they don't know it.

The crystal continues to ping and pop, even when Tory lets go.

Sena has seen this, too. The first time they tried to make the Compound's Seeds use the stolen Legion units, they tried a method like this one. The results were devastating, though Helner contended they were also *educational*. They did, after all, allow her to coin the term *stellite backlash injury*.

"It's going to explode," he tells Tory. "That's what happens when you feed too much energy into stellite in a short period of time. If you're not far enough away, your energy suitably shielded, it will kill you."

"Riese mentioned that." Tory grabs Sena's elbow and pulls him out the door, into the dim and graying hallway, its sick lighting sinking ever closer to perfect dark.

Sena scowls. And how, exactly, did Riese expect Tory to defend himself against it, with no Sena around to neutralize Tory's energies and prevent the backlash from reaching him? He would have had to put *significant* distance between himself and the crystal to avoid the backlash on his own. *Reckless.*

Sena has not often considered himself capable of harming another person with malicious intent, but the urge swells in him.

"I would like to hurt him," he tells Tory.

Tory laughs when Sena is the one to push *him* to go faster, and he yelps and scurries ahead when the blast in the Monitor Room flings the heavy metal door against the opposite wall and spits smoke and rubble into the corridor. Dust whooshes past Tory and Sena, blurring the air.

The dim, dying energy from the inset lighting fades out, and scarlet light picks up in panels along the floor. It makes a womb of the smoky hallways, the light pulsing like a heartbeat.

"Emergency power," Sena says, and points them toward the nearest exit.

Soon, they come upon a group of Seeds, dragging an injured friend with them. Tory turns to Sena. Sena nods.

"Hey!" Tory gestures at the group. "We're getting out of here! This guy knows the way."

Their eyes shift to him, and Sena shrinks back.

"You know the way, too," he mutters at Tory. But everyone's *looking at him*, so he draws himself up. "We'll aim for the typing and registration labs. If the outer walls have been breached anywhere, it's probably there, and the lab is far enough from the main entrance that we're marginally less likely to encounter resistance."

The group huddles together. As they walk, the fizzy drone of sirens grows closer.

"As soon as we get out, run," Sena says. "As far as you can."

They come upon a group of three, then a staggering crowd of maybe twenty. They fold in together, Tory at the head. Sena takes up the rear, guiding the injured ones along.

The larger the group gets, the more unwieldy it is, clogging the narrow halls. They dodge rubble where the ceiling has crumbled, baring open sky.

The smoke in the enclosed hallways grows thicker as they hurry toward Intake.

A door they pass hangs on its track, inner walls blackened. In another room, obscured by rubble from a fallen wall, is a shock of white hair too much like Lieutenant-Colonel Menden's.

"Don't look," Sena whispers to the Seeds beside him.

It gets worse as they walk on. Flames lick from doorways. Soot blackens the walls.

The young man bringing up the rear, shirt pressed over his mouth and cheeks wet with tears, mutters, "What's going on what's going on—" in a hollow litany; it cuts off in a choked scream.

The boy staggers. Sena can hardly bear his own weight, but he grabs the boy by the arm and looks for injury.

He finds the source of the boy's pain quickly enough. A dart. He rips it out, and the last of the pressurized fluid inside the syringe empties onto the ground. But what went into the boy was more than enough. On the side, printed in neat black letters, the dart reads N001.

Null. And Sena is the only one here who can't be affected by it.

"Tory!" He pushes the screaming boy into the safety of the crowd and spreads his arms to take up as much space at the back of the group as he can. The whole seething, nervous crowd separates Sena from Tory.

By the time Tory calls back, "What?" it's too late.

Kirlov rounds the corner, lit vital red by the lights, the shadows of his face carved deep. He's as put together as he's ever been. With one stone-steady hand, he aims a tranquilizer gun at the crowd. From the other, Sena's compass dangles, its core lit foggy, flickering gray. Kirlov's eyes find Sena, brutal and unerring.

"Lieutenant," he says. "I thought I'd find you here."

PART FOUR:

Free

CHAPTER TWENTY-SEVEN

Even ugly things have a beginning.

This is the dawn of the world according to Sena's mother: *Once, when our Seren was a young planet, fresh and new, the Celestial Beast who fashioned the universe swam in the great river of stars. Traveling by, it fell in love with the planet that had blossomed vibrant green and jewel-blue in its absence, a gem brighter than any star. On the surface of the planet, great hunters toiled, men and women with unbroken spirits. With the children of the land, the Beast was also pleased.*

This is how Sena Vantaras begins: seventeen, accepting a salute and an armful of awards and an assignment as far away from the capital as they can send him. He returns the salute with gloved hands. He does not celebrate with alcohol and loud parties like the others. The noise is sandpaper on his skin. He's led to a room where they lay him on his belly and lock soft restraints around his hands. He burns as they slice a perfect line along his spine. They talk like they're adding something to him. A precaution, they assure him. They don't say a word about what they're taking away.

So the Great Beast descended from the heavens to admire the planet. It watched the people and the land they worked and was exceedingly pleased. At first it only visited, but after a time, it would not leave. The Beast traveled through the skies of Seren even though it belonged in the river of the universe. Solitude can make even the vastest domain into a cage, and starlight is no gentler a prison than any other. To know warmth and let it go was not in the beast's nature—or in ours. As if in answer, the world reached up with fingers vibrant green and strung with flowers and pierced the flesh of the Beast to fill the void within it, slithered between crystalline scales and into its core, vines like veins within the arches of the beast's ribs. And so it was that the heart of our planet beat also within the Beast.

But perhaps Sena begins at nine years old: blood sharp on his tongue, a small hand wrapped around a strong ankle. Flesh drying up, dead on a still-living body. His father looks at him and sees not a boy but a weapon. To no one's surprise except his own, he's sent where all weapons go: to war.

Life eternal can make a soul old, but the sweet blue planet offered peace. The Beast lingered long on Seren and watched its people toil to take sustenance from the land. Its body, though, made from the stuff of stars, with galaxies aglow in every scale, was not meant to be contained in such a way. An age passed thus, and the Beast began to die.

Maybe he begins like this: six years old, with his mother's hands rubbing pungent herbs onto his chest and coaxing him to breathe. *Miokh*, she whispers, hands on his fevered forehead, the endearment like a farewell. She exhales scriptures and legends into his ear, stories that make the world sound ordered and on purpose—the kinds of stories Sena needs to hear. Miokh. My heart. My soul. My *core*, his mother calls him. Sena loves that word until his father orders his skin split open and a different sort of Core planted inside him.

Or this: a young man named Erwin Kirlov, born into poverty, enters officer school on his own merit and single-handedly lifts his family into the lower middle class. Like Sena, he is sharp and quiet and studious, an outsider who graduates with all honors. Like Sena, he should be assigned to the capital, but he has no family name to back him. Like Sena, he is both too much and too little. When Sena Vantaras graduates and the old men at the top are looking for a hole in which to bury Michal Vantaras' little Seedling, Lieutenant Colonel Erwin Kirlov is the perfect victim. They make a fuss about promoting him, about the honor of overseeing the son of the Grand General. They send him away from the capital and his family, away from any hope of advancement. His name becomes a joke, a cautionary tale, Sena the chain around his neck.

But the Beast longed not for life. After some time had passed—short for the Beast but long for the people of Seren, the Beast died. When it did, it shattered and scattered scales like stars upon the land and sea, and they grew bountiful and rich. The people no longer toiled.

Maybe Sena began years before he existed, in a small village where a charming general-to-be entered Arlune for a diplomatic exchange trip and met a young woman who yearned for travel. The stories Sena knows go like this: the young officer laughed with the woman for hours, sharing slices of ham as they swung their legs over the edge of the Arou cliffs and stared into the swirling mist and crashing waves below. His face wrinkled up when she fed him pickled vegetables and she kissed the sourness away. She grew up on the border and spoke his language. He never learned a word of hers. Her name was Yarana Hahka, but he called her darling, called her beautiful, called her Ana. He called her *his*.

Soon after, the first of the Children were born: the first Seeds. And the world rejoiced, for the Beast had given them magic. They revered the Seed of the Void and the Seed of the World, and from them came many more, each one a gift.

Sena should have known the children his mother bore would belong to the general, too. Men like Michal Vantaras can do whatever they wish with the things they own. They can love them (he still calls his Ana *darling*) or use them.

When he swears he can feel his NOVA wrapped around his spine, pincer-like, Sena remembers Kirlov urging him to his feet before the wooziness from the anesthesia wore off and saying, "All Seeds are dangerous, but you're uniquely so. You understand why we had to do this."

The four families go to balls and Sena and his ilk go to battlefields.

So it was in the land of Arlune and the lands all around. And the world was blessed with bounty.

This is how the world began: a god died to water it and allow its Seeds to blossom. Some stories are like that. Someone has to die.

This is how Sena Vantaras dies.

*

Sena steps in front of the weapon Kirlov levels at the huddling group of survivors and aims his own handgun at the chest of the man who once controlled him. A sickening sense of wrongness nearly makes him stagger, but he doesn't move. This—steadiness in the face of fear that might otherwise break him—is something he learned because of Kirlov.

"Tory. Take them and run," he says. And, to Kirlov, "If you move, I'll shoot." He does not say *Colonel*, does not say *sir*. It will take Kirlov longer to switch from the tranquilizer gun to a weapon that can harm Sena than it will take for Sena to pull the trigger, and he knows it.

With his teeth, Sena tugs the blood-stiff glove from his right hand and lets it drop, soundless, to the floor. Kirlov follows it, lips twitching in something Sena has learned the hard way to identify as disgust.

He's spent every moment since he was nine horror-struck and breathless at the idea of losing control and hurting someone. That first time, the eyes of the world turned on him and found him lacking. His mother meant well when she gave him that pair of gloves—his first—but he let them become a barrier between him and the world.

Around him, fires blaze, cratered remains of the Compound's hallways strewn with rubble and blackened by the explosions. Sena prefers it this way. The hallways, closed and clinical, white and gray with the guiding stripe of cold blue, are no more. This place—his prison—is open to the air, burning. There's peace in that.

It's fitting that he should be here, now. It's as good an end as any.

His legs tremble.

Niela warned him not to overdo it. He locks his knees and hopes they'll hold him.

Tory stumbles into the crowd toward him, bloody face soot-streaked. "Sena," he breathes.

"*Go.* Get them to safety. I'll meet you outside."

Tory can probably tell he's bluffing. This feels like a good lie, though.

"I can't just—"

Kirlov moves, a quick twitch of aborted motion. This stalemate won't last long.

"Leave!" Sena barks, all the cool, emotionless authority of his rank behind it. It's the hyper-competent mask Tory hates, the one Sena left behind what seems like ages ago.

Of all the responses he expects from Tory—the foremost being *actually going away*—dry laughter is not among them.

"Fine! But I'll be back as soon as they're safe, and we're going to *talk* about you and your warped sense of self-preservation."

Sena's heart squeezes in his chest. He can't spare more than a glance to Tory—red-lit, grinning and irreverent and warm—and maybe that's the worst part of all of this, that he's not allowed to linger.

"Fine," he says. Then, quiet enough that Tory won't hear, "Hurry."

Tory goes. The survivors shuffle away behind him, and Sena breathes.

His gun must waver, or his attention, or *something*. Kirlov recognizes an opening. His hand goes for the dial on his wrist.

Adrenaline spears Sena, and he responds without thinking, lunging to touch the device before Kirlov can activate it.

In a split second, the metal ages, rusting and flaking away. Before Sena has time to draw a breath, it crumbles, and he jolts backward. Triumph burns through him.

In reaching for the dial, Kirlov exposed the holster at his side. With a quick swipe, Sena frees the weapon and flings it into the rubble and flames behind him. He draws back (too close, he needs more space between them) and levels his own gun, finger twitching on the trigger.

"*Lieutenant Vantaras!*"

It's the voice that promises Kirlov will twist the dial until Sena can't stand, can scarcely breathe. His body conjures an echo of pain and horror, draws back to obey as he's done for years.

It takes maybe three seconds for Sena's will to override his body's reflexive response.

It's three seconds too long.

Kirlov vaults forward, wrests the gun from Sena's left hand, then twists it behind Sena's back, spinning him until he crashes into what remains of the blackened wall. He gasps smoke and coughs helplessly, cheek pressed against the too-warm concrete. Flames blister the paint on the wall to his left. When the shock wears off, he registers the ugly irony of this moment: this is the first time Kirlov has gotten close enough to touch him. It's a dubious victory, forcing the man's hand like this.

The barrel of his own gun presses against his spine.

"Sena," Kirlov says. "I'll kill every one of those creatures in your name."

"I won't let you."

A huff of breath raises the hair on his neck. "You think you have a choice?"

Sena wrenches his body and elbows the arm that holds the gun. Pain bursts in his lower back, hot then cold; the sound of the gun firing registers belatedly.

It's the moment he needs, if only he could force his body to *move*.

With his last shred of strength, he whips around, grabbing for any part of Kirlov he can reach. He finds Kirlov's bare wrist and squeezes.

Kirlov screams. The skin wrinkles and thins and grows spots that spread, then darken, then *blacken*, decay rushing like flames to his upper arm.

Not enough.

He wrenches his ruined arm away before the decay can get to his heart, and Sena falls. The last thing he sees is his superior officer clutching his arm and stumbling off, gun in hand.

I'll kill them in your name.

Kirlov is nothing if not a man of his word.

Rasping and coughing in the smoke from the burning Compound, Sena stares through the ruined ceiling at the sky. Black shapes writhe over the low-hanging gray ceiling of the world, sick and insidious like blots of ink, spreading.

The pain from the bullet wound—through and through, more insult than death sentence—blends into an electric throb that blends into something quiet and slow-spreading and faraway.

He could close his eyes here.

A laugh wrenches its way from his throat. Except he can't. Not yet. He's not done.

He told Tory—

Sena grits his teeth and tries to rise. Fails, legs liquid. Again.

He doesn't want this to be the end, a bare sliver of gunmetal sky between billows of choking smoke. He doesn't want it to end at all.

Again. He bites his lip against the noise that wants to escape him. His own blood smooths the way as he pushes himself up along the soot-smeared wall, vision fading. He doesn't know how he'll get his leaden feet to move, but that's nothing new. Sena has been practicing his whole life to move when his body says no.

He lifts the pendant his mother gave him, and even in the smoky grayness, it glitters like the night sky. The little chunk of stellite takes the world's light and beams it back brighter, turning the cage of his bare fingers to a wash of brilliant starlight.

Sena is neither trinket nor tool, but there's nothing of the Celestial Beast in him, either—star-strewn and crystalline, sacred and so at peace with sacrifice. Sena can't stride into war unarmored and unafraid of death like Arlune's soldiers.

He's so afraid of losing this precious thing he's gained that he can barely breathe.

With a sick lurch, Sena understands why Tory hated that story about kuhlu and the stars so much. Being torn apart, reaching but never having—it's awful. There's no beauty in it. It can't be over so quickly, before he's even had a chance to treasure it.

I'll meet you outside, he said.

Tory must be waiting, ready with hands on his hips and a rant about *self-preservation*, as if there's a single thing Sena wouldn't give up to stay with him.

He takes one step, swallowing a noise of pain, and then another. His vision shutters, and he grips the guide-rail along the wall and lets it carry most of his weight.

He walks because there's someone to walk toward.

CHAPTER TWENTY-EIGHT

As Tory staggers into gray daylight, lending his hand to lead survivors over the rubble of the outer wall of the intake lab, he finds chaos.

Familiar faces flicker into view before he can call a warning: Travin and Spark, the team that dropped him in the woods what feels like years ago. They're just as effective now. Spark closes a hand around the neck of one of the survivors. Her victim convulses and falls—then she's gone.

"Shields up," Tory cries. An instinct from training.

A forcefield flickers to life, but the range is limited—they don't have a full set of Fielders. A woman on the outskirts screams. The few who weren't inside the parameters of the shield when it was raised fall shortly after.

The rear end of the shield flickers and glimmers, and Tory swears under his breath.

The Fielder at the back is on his knees, choking from smoke inhalation. He won't last. As soon as his part of the shield falls, the survivors are sitting ducks.

Sena's still inside. Tory bites his lip. "Come on, come *on* . . ."

He can't abandon them.

"Anyone who's any use at offense, face this way!" Tory says. "You'll need to be ready when—"

The shield breaks down. Spark blinks into view in front of the exhausted Fielder and reaches for his skull. An attack from a frightened Kineticist goes high and wide, and Tory scrambles for Spark's energy, but it's odd and difficult to handle in the split second she activates it.

"Spark, wait."

Her Seed flickers out before she can use it and she pouts at the speaker.

Fury boils in Tory's gut as Riese Larsen strides over the ground toward him, hair tied back and sweater knotted around his waist, short sleeves baring the red tattoo.

Tory promised to gut him slow; it's a promise he intends to keep.

"Glad to see you. You're injured. I was worried!" Riese says, and *oh*, he doesn't know Sena's here. He still thinks Tory is an ally, thinks Tory doesn't know. "Everyone, stand down. Tory—"

"I'm glad to see you, too." Tory paces over, offering Riese his most beatific smile. "I wanted to thank you personally."

Riese's bland expression slackens. "Oh?"

Tory winds up and punches him in the mouth. He goes down like a sack of Thatcher's brick mix.

Travin and Spark gasp, but Riese's last order was to *stand down*, so they're dazed and slow to respond, their own instincts battling his compulsions. Tory takes advantage of that, using his teeth to tear a strip of cloth from his ugly, hateful shirt. He's on Riese from behind, sliding the makeshift gag between his teeth before he can even roll onto his side and knotting it so tight and so many times behind his head that he might've broken some teeth.

Riese makes a startled, gurgling noise, but no words come out. His hands rise to tug at the gag, but Tory yells, "Something to tie him with!" and someone in the group he led here flings a belt over.

Riese's people must have gathered their wits, because he feels the whiz of Seed-enhanced Kinetic energy coming at him, and he flings it back at its source, barely pausing when he hears a terrible choked noise.

He wrenches Riese's hands behind his back and loops the belt around them over and over, uncaring how tight the bonds are. Riese won't be alive long enough for it to matter.

He steps back when it's done, just in time to see someone flicker in behind Spark and Travin. Wide, dark hands settle on their shoulders, and both of them stagger and drop.

Jeffra steps over them in her bright yellow apron, halo of curls still held back with a polka-dot band. "Tory." Her hands fall on her hips, and he feels inexplicably chastised. "Did I or did I not tell you to keep yourself out of trouble?"

Her words—and the wry smile that accompanies them—pull a broken laugh from Tory.

Niela, Iri, and Dr. Helner step out from behind Jeffra, and Prentice waves from the back. "Special Diet Junior!" he calls affectionately, straggly gray-brown hair wrapped in a hasty bun and face soot-streaked. "Remember me?"

Helner kicks Travin, plum-painted lips pursed. "I could've pulled out his kidney, Jeffra."

Jeffra glares. "And make me fix him later? What if we need another Porter?"

Prentice waves his hands. "I'm plenty enough Porter to go around, thank you."

Tory blinks down at Travin, crumpled on the ground, then up at Jeffra, who's supposed to be a *Healer*. "Wait, aren't you gonna . . . ?"

Jeffra peers at him, eyes narrowed. "I know the body inside and out, young man. A little medical coma is nothing to me." She nudges

Travin with a foot. "He'll live. As for that one . . ." she gestures at Riese. "What did *he* do to deserve your ire?"

"He's the one who—" Tory bites his tongue. "Sena. What happened to Sena was his fault."

Jeffra's warm demeanor goes ice-cold so fast Tory shivers. Thoughtfully, she says, "I'll bet he doesn't know a Healer can make a body feel pain so intense it can drive men to madness. Let me take out that gag. I think I might like to hear him scream."

Tory grabs her arm before it reaches the cloth. "Don't. He can make a person believe anything he says."

She stops. "Ah. Do we kill him, then?"

"Of course we kill him." Iri stomps over, sleeves rolled up to bare the scars that lick up his hands and forearms. "He threw me out on a battlefield to die for a cause it turns out I don't believe in, so *you* are all welcome to argue ethics, but I'm going to fry him."

Helner smiles. "I at least deserve to pull out his spine before you do your thing. You're not the only one he used."

"Spine's too quick." Iri makes sparks and rolls a little ball of flame from hand to hand. "Let me sear him on both sides first."

"What I'm asking is, *can we use him?*" Jeffra clarifies. "Is there anything we'll need him to do for us? Because if so, I have my ways to keep him docile until we need him."

The group pauses. "Oh," Helner says. "Well, it *would* be convenient to point him at Michal Vantaras and have him nicely suggest walking off the nearest cliff."

Jeffra rubs her hands together. "It's decided, then. Give me just a moment, and I can—"

"*Stop.*"

Tory's halfway to turning back when the word halts him in his tracks.

Halts everyone in their tracks.

It's only then that he realizes they all took their eyes off Riese. Out of the corner of his eye, he watches Riese lift his head and offer them a placid smile.

A smile.

The significance of it hits Tory a moment too late, because Riese opens his mouth again, every word a cage. "Be still, all of you," he says, slow and warm and terrible.

Impossible. That should be impossible. Tory tied him up *tight*. But Riese stands, free of his ties and gag hanging around his neck. The cloth of it is frayed like he ground it between his teeth and dark with a combination of blood and saliva.

"Bastard!" Iri grits out.

"Shh. No one here is going to hurt me."

Now that he knows to feel for it, he can sense the energy of Riese's Seed. It's hot but not painfully so, like the warmth from a winter stove. Even if Tory had the ability to counter it, he's not sure he'd want to. Still, he tries to make it happen, tries to reach for the energy that's fallen over him and tear it off. No luck.

Riese lopes over to Tory, canines bared in lazy satisfaction.

"Tory." Something warm and wet taps beneath his chin. "You may speak."

"Fuck you." Suddenly, Tory regrets destroying those nullifying vests. One of them would come in quite handy now.

There's something wrong with Riese's hands, the skin bloody-raw. He must have dislocated or broken multiple bones to tear free from the belt. His left hand is barely recognizable as anything other than a stringy collection of exposed flesh. The belt is still buckled around his right wrist, and that hand and wrist are far more intact. He must have chosen to sacrifice his left hand to get free. Tory wouldn't have imagined anyone capable of that sort of self-mutilation, but he *should* have. A trapped animal will chew its own leg off.

"Sufficient desperation," Riese says with a nod, hairline specked with sweat. His blood paints the yellowing grass of the yard. "I knew you'd understand. Look at you, those *eyes*. I told you we'd sharpen you up. I wasn't sure I'd see you again, but I'm glad you made it out."

"I'll *kill* you."

"I don't think you will." Riese walks over to Jeffra and lifts his hands. "Heal these, would you? You may move, but you won't hurt me, and as soon as you're finished, I'll need you to be still again."

Her expression is murder, but the hands that rise to heal his wounds are clinical and gentle. Jeffra's teeth close on her own bottom lip so hard that a bead of blood drips down, and she manages to croak out, "*You—*"

She's using pain to break free.

"None of that." He shakes his head. "Sufficient desperation, indeed. None of you will harm yourselves."

He returns to Tory, flexing healed hands. "Much better. You, too. Oh, look at you. *This* is the boy I met in the back of that caravan, blood-hungry. I knew he was still in there."

"Yeah, but the throat I'm gonna tear out is yours."

"Don't say that. I made you stronger, Tory. I made you a leader. A leader can't be chained to anyone. It hurts now, but I swear it was a kindness."

"What you're doing isn't leading." Tory raises his voice in case any of Riese's people are conscious and listening. "If any of you can hear me, think about this: did any of you know what Riese's power was before this?"

"*Don't* speak to anyone else."

Tory's mouth snaps shut.

"It's rude. We were having a conversation." Riese's hand rings Tory's upper arm, just over the tattoo, and the body Riese has told to be still won't even shudder for him. Nausea makes his knees weak, but Riese just sighs and keeps talking. "I thought you would understand. We could never have made it this far without bloodshed. We're here, having wrested so many weapons from Vantaras' hands and made it nearly *impossible* for him to continue the war against Arlune, against *Seeds*, at the same level, because I wasn't afraid to trample a few flowers on the way. This progress—"

"Maybe you're right, but what's your progress worth if the only ones left to enjoy it are people like you and me? The jaded, messed-up ones?" Tory spits. It takes so much more strength to be kind in an ugly world than it does to be removed from it. Sena is one of the strongest people Tory's ever known, and *this* is the man who made sure he can't survive this. "You talk about *freedom*, but that's not what it's called when you're the only person who decides who's free. It's just a different cage."

"Be *quiet.*"

Tory's voice chokes in his throat, but he still has control of his face, so he puts as much venom into his expression as it will hold.

"It will be a shame to have to kill you. This place truly has ruined you."

This place *tried* to ruin him. Sena saved him, before Tory even knew that's what he was doing. His eyes burn, and he looks away into the quiet yard. He blinks when something flickers in the smoke. A person, dressed in red, picking their way over the rubble of the front gate. A newcomer?

"Look at me."

Tory's eyes swing back to Riese, but he sees the interloper approach slowly from behind.

"I'm sorry I have to do this to you," Riese says. "I wish things could have been different." He withdraws a handgun from his waistband, and the red interloper is closer but is barely a blur in Tory's peripheral vision because Riese said *look at me*, and Tory hates that this asshole will be the last thing he sees.

That, more than anything, lights a fire inside him. Riese asked them not to harm themselves, but there are plenty of other aches for Tory to press on. He imagines something worse than death: he imagines surviving this only to watch Sena fade.

How was it that Iri described it? The more ideological dissonance, the easier Riese's work is to unravel. It couldn't be more dissonant. Riese stilled hands that want nothing more than to wrap around his throat and squeeze, make him feel fear like Sena must be feeling.

Tory imagines a life that would've been his ideal mere weeks ago: a life free and alone and far away. No roots to bind him, no awful, unnameable feelings to knot him up.

No Sena.

He picks at those feelings like pulling off a scab to tear the healing wound wide open again, and Riese's power over him becomes heavier and heavier—more suffocating. More *tangible*. He can't tear his eyes from Riese's because the compulsion still has him, but he feels around the edges of the energy that binds him. He can *move* this.

The handgun rises, blessedly, to block his vision of Riese with the cold eye of a pistol.

"Not even gonna give me any last words?" Tory says.

Riese huffs. "I didn't think it would be wise."

He's right, of course. Tory tugs, experimentally, at the edge of Riese's compulsions. It's so easy after the first pull. Tory peels Riese's energy from his body like shedding a cloak. He twitches his fingers, one by one, heat flooding through his limbs.

"It will be fast," Riese says. "Merciful."

"No thanks." Tory throws up a hand to divert the barrel of Riese's gun. "I don't trust your mercy."

Riese's eyes blow wide, and he swings the gun back to Tory. "You—" He takes only an instant to adapt. Eyes narrow, he says, "*Don't move.*"

But Tory recognizes the energy that tries to fit to him like a glove and flings it back on Riese instead.

Oh, and it's *satisfying* to watch him go so terribly still. "What have you done?" Riese says. He's shaking like he's trying to resist his own words. His gun is still pointed in Tory's direction, finger on the trigger, if only he could pull it. "Tory, you'd better—"

"Another order? I suggest you think about your words before speaking them. How does it feel to be denied control over your own body, your own *mind*? Look me in the eyes and tell me this is freedom."

"I did what I had to. I would have stopped as soon as we were safe."

He probably believes that. He might even truly mean it. Maybe Michal Vantaras meant it, too, when he swore to return the country to the hands of the other families after the war was over. But how long does a war last?

Tory is so *tired*. "Jeffra," he says. "Come do your thing."

"Oh, absolutely fucking *not*," says a voice. A small, delicate handgun rises, and Tory remembers with a sharp burst of fear the red-clad figure striding through the smoke. He was a fool to forget—

But the voice, and the stance, and the aroma of turned earth and pipe smoke relax his muscles before they can tauten. Riese, though, is the farthest thing from relaxed.

He blurts, "Stop—"

But Hasra scoffs. "Should've thought about that before you tried to kill my kid."

An eardrum-rending boom splits the air, and Riese Larsen falls onto the dying grass, eyes empty and one side of his skull blown in.

Tory looks up to find Hasra, gun in hand, pipe in mouth, and smile on face.

"You—that's . . ." Tory blinks down at the body, waiting for it to move. Awkwardly, he says, "You can't . . ."

"I just did," Hasra says. It's strange, nearly impossible to reconcile her presence here.

"I'm not your kid," he mutters, head spinning and ears ringing. His own voice sounds drowned, trapped inside his skull.

"You sure give me enough trouble to be! Lucky I was still smoking. That *asshole*—"

Dumbly, he says, "We'd planned on keeping him alive for a while."

Hasra frowns. "Ah. A bit late for that."

"How are you *here*?"

"Did I or did I not tell you I'd chase you down if you took too long? You took far too long! Seems like I was just in time." She kicks Riese's lax body. "Anyway, how many more of these kinds of people *are* there? Makes my skin crawl. I thought Ari was bad."

Tory scans the yard urgently, but it looks like Hasra and the others have it handled. All of Riese's allies are on the ground.

"Hey," Hasra says. "Are you in shock? Tory, you're bleeding. Is he the one who did this to you? Oh, I should've made it hurt more."

She's kneeling, and her hand is on his shoulder, and he throws himself against her. He's shaking and he has no idea why. "That was . . . quite an entrance," he rasps.

"Well." She holds him bone-crushingly tight. "I like to be seen." She lets go and squeezes his shoulder, helping him to his feet. "Catch me up, then. What did I miss? You look different."

"It's . . . It's a long story."

"My favorite kind. Does anyone here need tying up? I'll have you know my ropework is *excellent.*"

Prentice, who must have been the one 'porting Jeffra around to drop all of Riese's allies, steps up to hand Jeffra something he was holding—a birdcage, covered with a blanket.

Something pangs in Tory. "Sena!" he blurts, and Jeffra's eyes widen and go to him. Hasra turns to him, too, but he doesn't have time to explain. "He's—he's here! I need to get back to him. He's . . ."

Jeffra must see something in his eyes. "Not too late after all, then." She offers a sad smile.

"Clearly I've missed a lot." Hasra's eyebrows go up. "I expect you to catch me up when you're back."

Jeffra waves him away. "We've got things here. Go on. The things that matter . . . when you've got them, hold onto them."

When he has them—as long as he has them. Tory can't force words past the knot in his throat.

He runs.

*

The smoke has grown thick, clogging the halls where the Compound's structure is still sound and coiling out where the walls have crumbled to expose sky. He breathes only where the smoke is thinnest and follows the pulsing blood-red lines along the floor into smoke haze and darkness.

"Sena!"

He has to be somewhere around here. Not too far, surely.

He smiles into the scarlet fog as he catches sight of someone staggering toward him. "Sena!"

A bullet zings into the wall a foot away.

"Sena, it's me!"

The figure walks forward, gun raised and mostly steady in his left hand, strange rifle slung across his chest. The haze clears enough that, as the lights glow their brightest, he catches pale hair and the bearing of a general.

Kirlov.

And if Kirlov is here, alive, alone—

He squeezes off another bullet as the pulse of red light fades, plunging them into blackness. When it floods back again, Tory finds the bullet. Off, this time, by a few inches.

He's lucky Kirlov's not left-handed. His right arm hangs loose at his side.

Another bullet, and another. Tory's ready this time. The theory is the same as it is with balloons and arrows and explosive shells. He takes the velocity off them and throws it at Kirlov's knee, relishing the guttural noise of pain and the wretched, wet crack of bones breaking and flesh splitting.

Kirlov drops hard. This close, Tory can make out dark stains and spatters of blood on the sleeve of his right arm. Sena's blood, probably. Anger boils inside him, and all he can see is Sena on the floor of Kirlov's tent, barely breathing as Kirlov twisted the dial on that awful watch. Tory left him behind to that, again.

"Bastard," he hisses, stepping in close enough to grab the collar of his uniform. "You—"

Too close.

He registers the sound of the pistol hitting the tiled floor too late. It's followed almost immediately by pressure against his abdomen, a hollow *click-thunk*, and a dim pain.

A syringe is buried in his belly, and liquid floods into him, breaking him down. He cries out and staggers back against the wall. The stolen cube in his pack crashes against the wall and jolts with the groan of metal on metal, but it doesn't matter, because Tory's burning from the inside out.

Something coils inside him and mutes him, swirls outside him and *creates* him, something electric-hot and—

—and familiar. He *knows* this energy.

He laughs. Reaches for it, and it jumps to him as easily as it did in the clearing with Iri. The pain vanishes as he pulls the energy off the fluid in the syringe and discharges it harmlessly into the air. He staggers away from the wall and brings an elbow down hard onto Kirlov's left shoulder as he tries to slide up the wall without putting weight on his shattered knee.

Kirlov falls again, and hot satisfaction courses through Tory's blood. He wrenches out the syringe of Null and tosses it away so it shatters against the opposite wall. Glass shards scatter across the floor like falling stars, and Tory can't tear his eyes away. His blood sings, alive with something unnameable. His head swims, mouth dry, every sense razor-sharp.

Shit, the box. It must have opened when he fell.

The *Legion*. He's moving at half-speed as he slips his pack off and reaches in with numb fingers. The lid of the containment box is skewed, the metal at the corner warped. Inside, its crystal pulsing cerulean light against a cradle of vines, sits the Legion, fully awake.

Tory's consciousness pulses and fades with the weapon's light, body slow and clumsy, mesmerized.

Not now, he doesn't need this *now*.

Tory tries to force the lid back on, but the warping along the edge makes for an imperfect seal. The tapered edge of a vine sneaks through and tickles the tip of Tory's finger.

He shudders and drops the box. Its lid skitters free, and the roots rise to reach for Tory.

They widen and contract with each pulse of light—too much like the rise and fall of a living chest. All of this, and he'll die, stabbed to death by a *tree*.

No. Sena said—he said Tory was controlling it before, in the lab, that it protected him.

He can do it again, surely. But *how?*

A voice cries out, wrenching his attention from the blue-lit stellite and the breathing vines that embrace it.

"Tory, his gun!"

Sena's voice. *Sena!*

The distraction holds Tory too long, mind still syrupy-slow.

Kirlov dropped the pistol, and Tory knocked him to the ground right beside it.

Now, Kirlov has it in his hand, and Tory's energies are slow to respond, just like Iri's took time to uncrumple after Sena extinguished them in that clearing.

His eyes dart up to find Sena—and he's *close*, shaking and barely standing, and what's to keep Kirlov from turning the gun on Sena after he kills Tory? Sena darts toward Kirlov, reckless.

Tory thinks *no*, and every part of him blazes with it.

This is not how it ends, in the dark at the hands of the man who's hurt Sena for so long. This prison is not the last place either of them will ever see. He won't stand for it.

The muddled energy slowing his thoughts and his limbs sharpens into something fine and focused. Kirlov stops, stone still, and makes a sick gurgle.

Three braided roots drive all the way through his chest and *shit*, Sena was behind him—

But Sena stands unharmed. The bloody vines curl out of Kirlov and around and behind Sena as if to hold him up. Slowly, they withdraw, and Sena lifts his hand from the back of Kirlov's neck. The man who thought he could control Sena crumples like a puppet, stringless. The back of Kirlov's neck—where Sena bears his scar—is matte-black, dried-up and dead.

"*Nice*," Tory breathes. He grabs the lid for the containment box and drops it back on, trying to stomp it closed as the roots draw back inside, at rest.

One peeks through the tiny gap where the metal is crumpled, and Tory thinks *no* again.

It withdraws as if stung. Tory closes it into his pack and swings it back onto his shoulder.

"Ha! That was—that was . . . What the *fuck*." He's never telling Helner about this. She'll come at him with needles and knives. "Sorry, I mean, you clearly had it covered. I—I didn't even think, it just . . . I think that thing likes me, maybe."

"I don't think it's capable of liking anyone," Sena murmurs. He stares down at Kirlov, stock-still and waiting. "He's—is he . . .?"

Tory kicks the corpse. "Deader than dead. A shame. Would've liked to zap *him* a bit, make him dance."

"He's . . ." Sena exhales a voiceless laugh and shifts his gaze up to Tory. A smile breaks over his face, and he looks *young*, overjoyed and disbelieving, shaking. He shields his expression with a bare hand as the laughs turn to quiet sobs. His right shoulder against the wall bears all his weight. "You came back." It's more breath than sound.

"'Course I did." Tory has never wanted to hold a person more. His hands clench at his sides before he realizes he doesn't have to restrain himself, probably. He pulls Sena in, as gentle as he can manage for all the broken bits, and regrets it almost immediately, because how is anyone supposed to do this?

Sena seems to feel the same. He goes ramrod straight, and Tory moves to withdraw. "Sorry, I wasn't—"

"Don't. It's f—it's just . . . Stay." Only one arm—the left one—goes around Tory's back, careful and light. Almost too quiet to hear, Sena whispers, "Stay with me."

"As long as you'll let me." Tory smiles. It's better, that they're both shit at this.

Sena chokes out another one of those wrenching laugh-sobs and trembles against Tory, hooking his chin over Tory's shoulder.

Sena sighs, warm and slow, but it catches on the exhale. He staggers.

If the world were fair, Tory would be able to keep him from falling, but he's not bearing any of his own weight, and Tory can't bear it for him. They both fall, and Tory's knees crack against stone. He hisses in a breath but doesn't scream.

Sena hits with the same force.

He doesn't breathe at all.

CHAPTER TWENTY-NINE

TORY HOLDS ON. Sena's forehead tips onto his shoulder. His hands hang at his sides, lit awful red with each pulse of the emergency strips.

The wall he leaned on—clinical white and gray and powder blue—is slashed through with a dark stain.

"Sena?"

Quiet, steady, something drips to the floor. A blackish trail marks Sena's passage through the hall behind him. Tory's hands jump to Sena's shoulders, then his back, and come away wet. "*Sena.*"

No answer. No sound. No reassuring breath against his shoulder where Sena's hair tickles at his nape. Tory presses two fingers to the artery at his neck.

This is what a heart feels like before it fades: a thready, shivering pulse.

Another, off-rhythm—

Then nothing.

Sena's weight against him is at once too little and impossibly heavy. Tory wraps his arms all the way around and forces his aching knees to lift them both. Smoke turns the dim hallway to a tunnel of red.

"I've got you," he says, too late. "I've got you. I'm right here."

He tugs one of Sena's arms around his back. Sena supported him like this on the way to the infirmary, back when he feared touch and Tory still mostly loathed him.

"You can't do this. You *told* me—" He told Tory about that stupid tree. The plaque the tree swallowed, the roots that chipped away at solid stone, a story where just *living* was a triumph. Tory says, "We're almost out, okay? Ugly as anything, this place. This is a terrible place to—to . . ."

And, "You really are the worst at self-preservation, I can't keep pulling your ass out of the fire."

And, "Sena, please."

No answer. Sena's blood soaks into his clothes.

He gets three rooms away from the typing and registration lab before he can't navigate the rubble with Sena's dead weight. He lets Sena down on the filthy floor on his back. This can't be right. Sena was talking to him a second ago. Tory presses his fingers against Sena's wrist, against his neck, hard enough to bruise living flesh. No pulse.

"No, no, fuck—" Helplessness crushes the air from his lungs.

His hands press against Sena's still chest. He can't bear this, not again, and he's useless, can't even heal—

He reaches out, instinctively, like he did in Riese's wagon on the way back from the battlefield, ready to run up against that impossible barrier.

He runs up against nothing, and it's so much worse. Helner said traditional Healers can't heal the dead because there's nothing to amplify. It was an easy thing to know in theory. In practice, it's unspeakable. All of Sena's vast, wild energy is gone, nothing Tory can expand over miles or try and fail to collapse. There's no reservoir in him that a Healer could take and mend him with.

Adrenaline sears through Tory, because that's not all Helner said.

Tory, after all, is not a Healer.

He doesn't *need* Sena's energy. He can channel his own.

Restoration, Iri called it. *Time.* The one thing Sena never had enough of. Tory can give it back to him.

He reaches out, the unpleasant shift of time flowing in a direction it wasn't meant to hitting him like a slap, as always. Tory shudders at the assault of information it reveals. Sena's body is broken, bruised, poisoned—everywhere. This is not just fever, nothing as simple as a broken bone. Restoring Kelly enough to allow the possibility of survival left Tory immobile for days.

Doing this will kill him.

In the smoky dimness, Tory laughs. He waits for the clawed clench of fear his mother created in him. For so long, he's tied himself up in knots just to survive. To die here would be meaningless. Tory's not a fool. The fear's there, but on the other side of the chasm it carves in his chest is a solid place, unshakable.

Some things matter more than survival. Sena said it back then, before Tory was ready to understand. This is one of those things.

Sena is one of those things. Sena who told him about kuhlu, who loves the sad stories, who looked like a child, so bright with joy after he made something grow. Tory spent so many years trying to follow his mother's advice, but all this time, he should've followed her example instead. It's not a bad feeling, not really, to love someone to the point of ruin.

Because this feeling *is* love, one of a thousand shades. There's a love that would give itself away on a battlefield, a love that would die to offer a child a chance at freedom. A sharp-edged, clumsy love that would have stolen the Madam's earrings and bled to pick those damn tree berries back in Hulven. A love like in the story Sena told him, habitual and hungry, reaching for the stars.

And *this*, sunshine-bright—deep-rooted and wrenching, woven through him so well it might tear him apart when it goes.

Tory's lungs sit like stones in him. His traitorous heart pounds in his chest.

His healing, since he discovered it, has always been a tool, a way to ensure acceptance and silence. He's never needed so badly for it to work.

He'll die to fix this. He will. And it's fine.

Tory lets himself go. He closes the gunshot wound first, in through Sena's lower back and out through his gut in the front. His blood, when Tory presses his hands to the sodden cloth of his shirt, has grown tacky and lukewarm, but the flesh and viscera respond like an extension of Tory's body, knitting together as he urges them to remember what it was like to be whole.

"You're gonna be fine," he murmurs, and it doesn't matter if it's a promise or a lie. He works because he can't imagine making any other choice.

He's freezing when he finishes with the wound. Tory clenches his teeth to keep them from chattering and reaches out to identify more damage. It washes over him faster than he can process it.

Blood clots. Dying tissue. Failing organs. Overtaxed lungs filling with fluid.

Broken ribs. Sena said there was maybe one. There are three.

Tory experiences the shift in the body after death—the slow fade of every flavor of energy that fuels a mind, body, and soul. In Hulven, he would have given it up for lost.

Tory opens himself up, feeds everything he has into the boy on the ground. His breath comes slow and hitches in his chest. His fingers go cold. His vision fragments and fades.

He works in reverse. Cleans poisoned blood. Restores ruined lungs. Renews dead tissue. Seals broken bones.

Pushes—with the last energy he has to spare—that still heart to beat again.

He isn't finished with Sena. They've barely begun.

Sena's heart stutters, but it's not enough. Tory's numb hands betray him. His vision blinks out. This last damnable wall, the barrier between life and death, refuses him passage.

He sinks, against his will, into something deep.

*

He rises from it in a panic, choking until he tastes smoke.

His eyes flick open to a barred darkness lit ocean-blue, wobbling and unreal. There's noise all around. The ground shakes. The air reeks of fire and blood, and Tory is on his side in the dirt amidst the chaos.

"You're back," says a dry voice next to him. "You're lucky they went back in to find you before you killed yourself."

Helner. Tory grimaces. Reason returns slower than everything else, but an overwhelming sense of wrongness clamors at the back of his mind. Something's wrong. Something—

"This is a *fascinating development*, by the way." Helner gestures up. "It did this as soon as we set you down."

He can't push words out yet, so he makes a rasping growl and trusts her to translate it.

He squints up, and the slats of light through whatever structure he's in illuminate leaves in fresh green and long strings of bell-like flowers in vital blood-red dripping from . . . vines.

A dome of them, braided together by the hundreds and tucked protectively close around Tory and all the other Seeds.

How odd to think this is the same thing that destroyed the lab in response to Tory's fear, that killed so many people on the battlefield. How *beautiful*. It's all around him, but it doesn't feel like a tomb or a prison. The blossoms shed the honeyed fragrance that muted the reek of fuel in Hulven.

Sena will love it.

Tory tips his head to the side, seeking him. "Told you," he murmurs. "Told you they like me."

There's no response.

The horror of the *why* crashes into him with a weight that presses the air from his lungs.

"Sena!" he rasps. "Where . . ."

Vision blurred, he peers through a cacophony of shifting feet and finds him.

Not far away—almost close enough to touch if he could make himself move—he finds Jeffra, eyes wide and wet, on her knees over someone on the ground. "Please," Tory says, levering himself up. He could get to her if there weren't so many *people* in here. "Please."

But she's already leaning over Sena, hands gentle against his still chest. She looks over at Tory, stricken, and doesn't say a word. She doesn't have to. Her hand on Sena's chest goes soft and soothing, motherly. She sucks in a breath and exhales a sob. "Oh, Sena." She shakes her head. The feet part for her as she moves to Tory and kneels. "Tory, he's already . . . There's nothing to—"

Her eyes dart to Sena. "I can't do anything. But maybe I can help you help him."

Tory forces himself upright and his vision shutters. He crawls until he's beside Sena.

Jeffra's hand settles warm and solid against his back, filling his cold body with warmth. Tory breathes, and breathes again. He still has work to do, but he has no idea how to do it.

The Core is still inside Sena, rotten and poisoning him—and it's one thing Tory can't undo.

"His Core," Tory says. "I can't."

"*I* can."

Helner drops to Tory's side, Jeffra shifting to make room for her. She looks entirely unlike herself, the intensity she wears like a second skin gone from her as she examines Sena's still body.

Tory's voice comes out a growl. "*You.*"

"Me," she says. "I—when Riese asked me to 'treat' Sena, he phrased what I was supposed to do to him as a mercy. Maybe it was. But he didn't deserve that. I can't change what I did, but . . . if his Seed is gone, I can at least remove his Core."

Tory's muscles bunch, body charged with the need to push her as far away from Sena as he can get her. But she's right.

"Why should I trust you?"

Her lips quirk up. "Never said you should. But I'm damn good at what I do, and I've never offered a freebie before. I'd suggest taking it."

If nothing else, they can give Sena the peace of dying free from the Core.

The ground shakes. Smoke and light rush into the cocoon of vines.

The feed of warm energy from Jeffra dissipates as a cry rises up in the back. "Mom! We need you over here!"

Jeffra squeezes his shoulder. "Work to do. I'll be back."

"So?" Helner raises both hands. Some wild, vertiginous energy rushes into them.

"Do it."

From everything he's been told, the process of separating a Core from a body is an exercise in frustration. For a living Core in living flesh, that's probably true. Helner reaches into Sena, though, with gentle hands. For all the pain it caused, removing his Core is a matter of a moment. She withdraws her cupped hands, expression complicated.

The Core she pulled from Tory was a visceral red. This one is blackish and shriveled.

"For what it's worth, I *am* sorry." She tosses the Core into the dirt. "He had more guts than all of us. You got it from here? I need to go kill something."

"I've got him."

Her hand brushes his shoulder as she passes. "Good luck."

Tory turns his attention back to Sena. The Core may be out, but the damage it left behind isn't gone. He closes his eyes and sinks down, finding inflamed and infected flesh and returning it to health. He locks his elbows to support him and shakes, body throbbing. Whatever energy Jeffra gave him, it's nearly gone.

He aches, burns, and it hurts because it matters.

He breathes, and that, too, aches, like he's been holding his breath all this time.

He works, and he works, and Sena's body is healed but his heart remains still.

Someone settles in beside him, lays a hand on his shoulder, and Jeffra's warm energy flows through him again. He fists his hands in

Sena's shirt and keeps going. His vision doesn't return. He navigates Sena's veins in the dark, the roar of his own blood filling his ears.

His body is healed, but the line between *here* and *gone* remains impassable. Sena's heart never picks up its tune.

Sometimes it tries. Weak contractions, like shivers. Blood moves through Sena only when Tory makes it.

He keeps going.

"Damn you," he mutters to the tune of his own heart. "You don't get to do this."

Somewhere along the line, freedom stopped being a mere concept and became the people he shared it with. Sena doesn't get to bow out like some motherfucking self-sacrificing idiot. That's not how this works.

"Shh," Jeffra murmurs, "You're doing so well. Now this. Feel what I'm doing." Her warm energies root around in him, and adrenaline floods his body. "Just like that, but give it everything you have."

He does, and it floods through Sena. It's better. The flicker of his heart is a flutter, then an irregular squeeze. Everything Jeffra gives him, he pours into Sena.

There's life at the core of Tory and he can channel that, too. He gives it away, throwing it against that impassable wall, but it's not enough. All his strength, and it's not enough.

"Tory, hon, maybe it's . . ."

Niela settles down beside him and together with Jeffra, she stokes the warmth inside him to life once more. He's a bonfire. A bomb. Tory grabs the growing energy and pushes it into Sena, finally pushes *past* the wall he couldn't break through.

Sena's body jerks with it, and the weak shiver of his heart—stops.

"Shit, no, no—"

And beats again. A strong, deep thrum flushes blood through Sena's body, and then another, and another. The static energy of the Voidseed ignites again and pushes Tory out. He chokes out a laugh and lets himself drop, ear against Sena's chest, savoring the pulse of his living heart. His lungs expand, skin flushed, again, with life.

Tory's vision fades in and out again.

Tory sinks into the steady, strengthening song of Sena's heartbeat and the ocean-blue glow of light through his closed eyelids.

CHAPTER THIRTY

THE LAST THING Sena knew before death was the crush of warm arms and *I've got you, I've got you* guiding him down into the dark.

He's reborn to the distracting unpleasantness of knuckles on his sternum. He doesn't have the strength to push them away, but he makes a passable effort at it.

A familiar laugh. "See? An *exemplary* response to painful stimuli. He'll be fine."

Tory's voice: "He's awake?" Pressure on his shoulder. A hand on his chin. "Hey. Sena?"

He opens his eyes to flowers swinging overhead in arterial blood-red and the eerie, electric blue of Tory's eyes, both like and unlike Kirlov's.

Kirlov is *dead*, and Sena is alive.

He never dared to imagine the moment that followed freedom from control. A breath pushes out of him in an odd hybrid of laugh and sob.

A smile softens Tory's face. "Hey," he says. "You're back."

Sena mumbles something that approximates a reciprocal *hey*. "Wh-what . . . happened?"

Niela leans over him, teeth bared in a grin. "You died a little. Nothing irreparable. Glad to see you've decided to return to us. Sorry about your sternum."

Sena has dealt with worse than a brisk sternal rub. "Don't worry about it." To Tory, he offers, "I thought I wouldn't see you again."

Tory's face warps. "Yeah. I—I've been meaning to tell you something." He steels himself, and Sena readies himself for the gentlest letdown. Maybe something like, *I have to go now*. Or even, *It was easier being beside you when I knew there was an expiration date.*

Sena interrupts before Tory can finish. "You can go," he whispers. It's always been easier to be the first to walk away. Maybe it will hurt less if he does it this time, too. "The things I need to do—they're only going to get harder from here."

"Absolutely fucking not," Tory says, at around the same time a red-clad, dark-haired woman drops into a threatening crouch on Sena's opposite side and says, "I think I'm owed a proper introduction!"

"Not now, Hasra!" Tory yelps, flustered.

"Oh, am I interrupting something?"

But Sena can't focus on her, because suddenly Tory's hands are on his face, work-rough and warm, tipping his chin so all he can see are Tory's steady blue eyes, and Sena can't breathe.

"Just—*listen*," Tory says, and Sena can't do anything else. "Because I'm shit at this stuff and I can't say it twice. Being with you is the scariest thing I've ever done, okay? I can't *think*. I feel sick, and nothing makes sense, and I'm frightened of things that never used to worry me, and I've never gotten so close to dying so many times as I have since I met you."

"Ohhh," says the dark-haired woman. Eyes wide, she stares at Tory. "Oh, damn. Tory, I'm going to need *details*."

"*Hasra*," Tory whines, which is an interesting sound coming from him. Sena doesn't dislike it. "Please. A minute."

"Oh, fine." With a firm nod, she seizes Sena's hand, mutters a quick, "Much more pleased to meet you this time than the last time we met, I think," and retreats.

Sena splits his attention between Tory and the woman across from him with her ever-narrowing eyes. Tory's words bounce around in his skull. No matter how he thinks about them . . . "That all sounds . . . unpleasant."

"It's *horrible!*" Tory agrees. "But I think—I'm pretty sure that means it's important. *You're* important. Because I also haven't ever felt as alive as I do with you. I've never wanted to know someone as well as I want to know you. I've never—never *wanted*—" He sucks in a breath, and Sena's chest aches, and neither of them are looking at each other. "I think the best things are the ones that can ruin you. If that's true, there's no fucking way I'm letting you go again. I'm in this until the end, whatever that looks like."

Sena's mind blanks, an eternal drone of gray silence. "What does that mean?"

"I don't know!"

Sena doesn't miss the way the woman—Hasra, that's the *Hasra* Tory talks about, which is a panic attack for another time—snorts at the way Tory's voice goes shrill on the last syllable. He can't miss the way Tory's eyes are wide, his cheeks flushed, his pulse a frenetic thud in his neck that Sena could almost swear is echoed behind his own ribs. Sena must be smiling. It must be bigger than any he's ever worn before. His face hurts, his chest so full he's surprised his ribs haven't cracked.

"You have to tell me what you're thinking," Tory begs.

"I'm thinking you're terrible at this."

"You don't get it, I really *am!* I'm so bad at feeling things. I've got no practice. It could be the worst thing that's ever happened to you. You could hate me for it."

"Never." Sena sets his hands butterfly-light over the ones that still cup his face and feels the shiver that travels through Tory in response. His mouth is dry, head spinning. He waits for his heart to stop trying to break free of his bones.

It doesn't. It just keeps pounding out an urgent tune that washes like waves against his eardrums. He's *alive*, and Tory is here, and Sena *hates* words. None of them in any language he's ever studied are big enough for the things he wants to say. His hands against Tory's say more than his mouth ever could, if only Tory knew how to translate it.

Awkwardly, Sena manages, "I think the common advice is that practice begets progress."

Tory snorts, but he's smiling, so Sena figures he didn't do too bad.

"I suppose I should stick around, then."

Sena's eyes burn. *Stay*, he begged at the last minute he expected to be alive, and even then he barely dared to hope Tory would. "What if it takes a long time?"

"With the two of us as bad at this as we are? Might take forever."

Before Sena can find words for the warmth that fills him, another voice breaks in.

"Is it finished? Am I allowed to stop pretending I can't hear you?" Hasra turns around to give them very long looks, eyebrows vanishing into her hair. "Tory, this is a story I need to hear immediately."

"Soon," Tory promises. "We have some things to finish up here, first."

He's not wrong. Sena holds out a hand. "Help me up?"

Tory takes it, skin warmer than sunlight, and it really is that easy.

Sena tests his balance and his breath when he's on his feet. He feels good. "What's the plan?"

Tory shrugs. "We have a lot of skill here. I'd rather not kill them, but . . ."

Helner wiggles red-slick fingers. "Ah, good, I was wondering when we'd get back to the topic at hand. If we're taking votes . . ."

Iri, beside her, raises his voice. "I'd rather we waited. I'm in no great hurry to kill Seeds, regardless of their allegiance. Riese is gone, but it will take time for some of them to separate what they want from what he made them want. They should be allowed to do that, as I was."

Helner scowls at him. "That's no fun. Fine. We'll give them time to decide that they themselves want to be assholes, and *then* I'll pull out their internal organs."

Tory paces toward the dome of vines surrounding them. "Still, they brought the fight here. We need to stop them, and I'm not averse to using this guy to do it, if I can just . . ."

When he reaches the wall, it parts in front of him to create a wide opening, a window to the burning Compound.

"It's connected to you." Iri gestures at the shifting vines. "Think about what you want it to do or be, and it should respond."

Tory squints, and the threatening braids of roots tear from the ground and coil back around themselves until the Legion unit, melon-sized, still pulsing blue, walks itself over on spindly legs and rolls up into his palm. "It needs a name," Tory says, apropos of nothing.

Sena sighs. "Please don't name it."

Iri smiles. "They already have a name."

"Legion," Tory says. "I know. It's hardly cozy."

"That's your name for them, because you see them as threats. They're called miokh in Arlune. It means—"

Heart. Soul. "Core," Sena says. A lullaby word. An endearment whispered into his ear at night. The most essential part of a thing. It's appropriate—so unlike the cruel Core Westrice plants in its Seeds.

"Sena," Tory says. "You should touch it."

"I—you *saw*—" He stumbles back a step, vision full of the destruction he's caused. Crystals fractured and blackened, dead vines brittle. If he loses control, it could happen here, too. "I shouldn't."

"You're not just a weapon."

He could be. He *has been*.

He doesn't want to be. Not anymore. He's alive, and he can create things, too. Sena, trembling, reaches for the sphere. The roots, as expected, contort themselves around his hand rather than allow his fingers to touch them. He pulls back.

Tory pokes the ball. "Hey," he says. The roots return to their former shape. "Remember what you told me? It's responding to how *you* feel about it. Try again."

He's healed. He's not dying anymore, not struggling with a Seed gone haywire. His touch will only hurt this thing if he wants it to, and he's spent a lifetime learning control. He's so much more than his father created him to be. Sena hauls in a shaky breath and reaches out.

This time, the roots withdraw, slow, to expose the crystal at the center of the thing, bright with Tory's colors. Sena lays his hand on the crystal, and his vision ripples crisp and clear. The light from the crystal burns blood-red for a moment before settling into a warm, steady purple.

Tory grins, unbearably smug. "It likes you, too," he says.

Like sound through water, a series of explosions echo from inside the Compound, preventing Sena from forming a reply. A section of the building shifts—and with the groan of twisting metal and the crackling of glass and a sound like a sigh, it collapses.

In the center of it all, exposed and regal, stands the tree, damaged but alive, rooted deep and branches high, reaching for something impossible. Sena can't stop smiling.

He turns to the group. "I have a plan."

*

The ground is slick with blood. Bodies litter the grass, and the air hums with energy and violent intent—the kind of conflict that refuses to end as long as there are bodies to fight in it.

It helps that, as if in response to Tory's determination, the Legion unit has made a threatening half-dome over his and Sena's heads, restless vines shifting, ready to rain chaos down on anyone who gets the wrong idea.

Tory shoves Sena's shoulder, grinning. "Told you it likes you! Look, it's trying to protect you."

Iri just stands there, looking smug. "I don't think *it*'s the thing that likes him."

Regardless, the looming, twisting roots shut everyone up quite nicely.

Helner speaks first, addressing the scattered collection of soldiers from the Compound. "This isn't your fight. You can leave, now, or this little guy—" she gestures up at the serpentine roots, "—will help you leave. I suggest being speedy about it. If we ever face you again, you won't know mercy from us."

The soldiers make their decision with little pause, hurrying toward the front gate, which is barely more than rubble. When the first ones pick their way through and disappear beyond the wall, Tory turns back to the remaining group. Riese's people.

He barely has to reach for Sena's energy. It leaps to his fingers and expands in the direction he asks of it. All around, the energy from the rebel Seeds crumples. Tory releases it. If his experiment with Iri was any indicator, it'll take around a minute until their abilities return.

"We're not here to hurt you. We have a proposition."

One of the rebels snaps a gun up and aims it at the departing soldiers.

"None of that."

Jeffra 'ports in behind him with Prentice and squeezes the guy's shoulder. He falls, and Jeffra nudges him with her foot until he's face-down in a slick of gore. She offers the group a dry stare. "This was the carrot, dear ones. He's only sleeping. If you want the stick, I'll swap with Dr. Helner, who's eager to bring some insides outside."

A low murmur passes through the group. The ones remaining on their feet choose to be reasonable.

"Riese is dead," Tory starts. "I'm sure that upset some of you. Maybe it surprises some of you, too. I imagine a few of you have already guessed why, but . . . Iri?"

He steps in front of Tory, and the members of the group mutter and turn to each other.

"I know," Iri says. "I should be dead. I would be, if not for *her*." He waves at Niela, still in her fatigues, and the mutters turn to a cacophony. "She risked her life to keep me alive, stayed awake all night exhausting herself to heal me over and over when I was shot and Null kept the healing from sticking. I couldn't even move for hours, which gave me plenty of time to think. What's Riese's Seed?"

"He's—" someone starts, then breaks off. "He's . . ."

"It's funny, isn't it, that you don't know. That you followed him anyway. Think about that. Then think about what you've been fighting for. Maybe you agree with Riese on a lot of things. Maybe even all of them. Start asking yourselves questions. Find the ones you have a hard time answering, and ask why. Some of the beliefs you hold may not be your own. Mine weren't."

Silence. Every face bears cutting emotions—confusion, betrayal, and determination.

Tory takes advantage of the quiet. "Some of you, like Iri, may find the things you've believed until now are at odds with what you want. If that's the case, you're welcome to join us."

"For what?"

"For what all of you want. To take this fight straight to Maran. What we've done here cut Vantaras' war efforts off at the legs, but right now, he's amassing anti-Seed weaponry to fight us. It won't be easy."

"We didn't do any of this because it was *easy*," Spark spits.

"Good," Tory says. "I agree with Riese that Seeds shouldn't be bound to serve Westrice against their will, but we don't have to kill other Seeds to make some of us safe. If you remain dedicated to his ideals and attack us, we won't hold back. If your head is clear and you have no intention of killing your fellow Seeds, come with us."

One or two shift on their feet in the group but subside when no one else steps forward.

The expressions on a few faces get stormier.

They get stormier still when Sena speaks up. "With everyone here—with your support and Belmin's and Iri's, with Arlune's, with the Seeds who were trapped here—we have a chance."

"*He's* part of this?" one of them hisses.

"If you have complaints, the door's that way." Tory gestures to the ruined gate. As he does, a chunk of stone breaks from the wall and crashes to the ground.

Sena scrubs a hand over his face. "An easier question, perhaps: who refuses to be a part of this and wants to leave?"

There are maybe four. Judge is among them.

"Go now," Helner says. "If we see a weapon turned our way, we'll do worse than kick you into a puddle of guts. I have not torn out *nearly* enough spleens for the shitty day I've had."

They go. When they, too, pass through the rubble of the front gate, Tory returns his attention to the handful who remain.

The first one comes over to stand with Tory. A few others follow. Travin and Spark join last, Spark drawling a, "Disappoint me and I'll fry you."

Blandly, Sena responds, "You can try."

Spark's eyebrows go up, and she folds herself into the group of survivors from the Compound.

Ahead of them is only open air and the crumbling gate. Tory turns to Sena. "You ready for this?"

Sena offers a wan smile. "Not in the least. You?"

"No."

Helner paces ahead of them, sidestepping the unconscious man. "Doesn't matter. The full wrath of the Westrian military will be on its way as soon as someone sees the smoke. We don't want to be here when they arrive. This story doesn't look good for us from any angle, and they'll spin it ugly faster than we can open our mouths to protest."

Tory nods. "We'll aim for Serpentshead to gather and plan; Belmin's people are already there. We'd better get moving."

Behind them, the Compound falls into itself piece by piece, the tree at its core shrouded by black smoke lit with flickers of orange flame. It has survived worse things than these fires.

Tory is here, and Sena is alive, and this is where it starts. Maybe this is where it was always meant to start. One set of walls broken down and cities more to go, until every wall is dust and they stand in the home of a fearful man who turns his terror to violence and makes weapons of children and sons.

With Iri, with Hasra and Ariana Belmin, with any Seeds willing to stand behind them—they'll tear this festering country out by the roots.

The others walk on ahead, until only Tory and Sena remain behind in the yard.

"You don't have to do this," Sena reminds him.

He's right. There's no deal between them to coerce him, no Core to trap him. The future they face could hurt him, break him, end him.

For the first time in a long time—in a lifetime, maybe—Tory doesn't have to, but that's why he chooses it. "Were you listening to a word I said? No way you're getting rid of me that easy."

Sena smiles, lopsided and dry. "I'd hoped not."

Tory walks outside the crumbling walls into open air that smells of blood and ash. He aches all over. Sena, shoulders squared, walks a step ahead, into the darkness under trees that hum with life, and Tory follows close. They'll shake the world, the two of them.

It feels like flying, like falling from a great height.

It feels right.

ACKNOWLEDGEMENTS

IN SUMMER OF 2020, I sat down to fast-draft the back half of a story about hurt, isolated people finding each other and carving out a small pocket of warmth in an ugly place.

I wrote this story I loved, fearing there might be no one who could love it with me, and I don't know how I got lucky enough to find the amazing people who did. Endless appreciation, always, to Maddy Belton and Molly Powell, agent and editor extraordinaire (respectively), for their patience and care when I pulled this book out as a contender for book two, dusted it off, and said, *this one, please. I love this one.*

Once again, I owe a great debt of gratitude to the amazing Hodderscape team. Assistant editor Sophie Judge, thank you for your kindness and insights and for keeping everything flowing smoothly! I was overjoyed to see the wonderful Alyssa Ollivier-Tabukashvili back for copyedits, as well—thanks for following me through two books! Tom Cole blew my expectations out of the water once more with this absolutely beautiful cover, and Daisy Woods killed it on the design front! Many thanks to Laura Bartholomew in marketing, Kate Keehan in publicity, Inayah Sheikh Thomas in production, and Annabel Maunder for proofreading! So thankful as well to

ACKNOWLEDGEMENTS

audio editor Dominic Gribben and narrator Sebastian Humphreys for giving these characters a voice.

To Sunya, who pulled Tory and Sena from the 2020 Pitch Wars slush pile and gave them more attention and care than I could have dreamed of, thank you for your faith and patience! To the 2020 mentee group, especially my chaotic friends in the sprint channel—I owe you all so much. Truckloads of appreciation also go out to Aty, whose enthusiasm for these chaotic boys brought me joy.

To Claire, a bookseller to reached out when I was fumbling with my debut and whose kindness made the process brighter—thank you for giving me hope that my small books might one day do great things.

Libby (fellow connoisseur of sharp teeth and boys who need soup) who named a plant after Sena and shared a picture of *the spine dress*: thank you for being one of Tory and Sena's earliest and most enthusiastic supporters! To Ayida: your love for these characters has never, ever stopped giving me hope that their story might find other readers who love them like that, too. To Leanne, glorious friend and generous, light-bringing reader when we were both in dark places—I can't believe I get to live in a reality where our characters share space in the wide world together. May they meet on a shelf one day! Jessie, with whom I connected based on a CP-matching event and have never stopped blabbering with—so much gratitude for your friendship, and thanks for all the sprints. To Alice, who read this book in great gulps at a time when I started to wonder if maybe it was Nonsense, Actually—you're amazing, and I'm holding my breath for the day I'm allowed to scream about your books! L.M., thank you for reading this in two days when I was on deadline and kindly assuring me it was not the worst thing you'd ever read.

ACKNOWLEDGEMENTS

And to Chy, who read the first half of a long-abandoned book and whose enthusiastic comments and listening ear sparked the desire to make it whole: without you, I would never have finished telling this story in the first place. J.B., reader of sci-fi who read this funky fantasy blend anyway (twice) and loved Sena despite it all, you're a treasure! Nina, London, Tobias, and Stephanie—you are more valuable than all the gold in a dragon's hoard, and I'm so happy to be in a writing group with you!

To Reese's Pieces, which I used to motivate myself to fast-draft the back half of this book in three jittery, stress-filled weeks: I owe you one. It was lean times when I sat three of the aforementioned Pieces beside my laptop to mock me until I finished writing the book, but boy was it good motivation. They were stale by the time I was finally allowed to eat them, but they tasted like sweet, sweet victory.

So much love to my mom, who learned hard lessons from a hard life and found out how to love not by example but by doing it. To my dad, who told me he believed I could: thanks for having faith in me when my own faith flagged. Special thanks to my siblings (especially my sister) who have graciously listened to no end of publishing-related rambling.

And to you, the reader. I still firmly believe that authors are just weird people who commit their strangenesses to paper and throw them out into the world, hoping beyond hope that they might find someone with whom they will resonate. If this was your preferred flavor of weird, welcome, and thank you for giving *Cage of Starlight* a try! It's difficult—sometimes it feels downright impossible—for small authors to find a foothold in the world of publishing, but no matter how this book found you, I'm so glad it did.

WANT MORE?

If you enjoyed this and would like to find out about similar books we publish, we'd love you to join our online Sci-Fi, Fantasy and Horror community, Hodderscape.

Visit hodderscape.co.uk for exclusive content from our authors, news, competitions and general musings, and feel free to comment, contribute or just keep an eye on what we are up to.

See you there!

NEVER AFRAID TO BE OUT OF THIS WORLD

@HODDERSCAPE   HODDERSCAPE.CO.UK